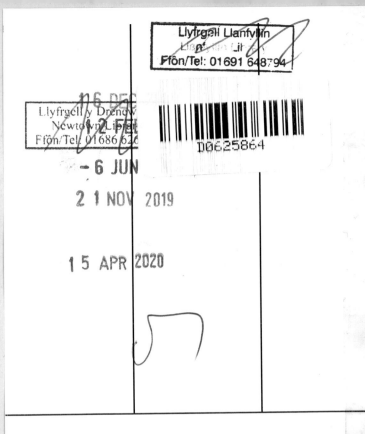

Dychweler erbyn y dyddiad olaf uchod
Please return by the last date shown

LLYFRGELLOEDD POWYS LIBRARIES

www.powys.gov.uk/llyfrgell
www.powys.gov.uk/library

Also by Douglas Jackson

CALIGULA
CLAUDIUS
HERO OF ROME

and published by Corgi Books

DEFENDER OF ROME

Douglas Jackson

CORGI BOOKS

TRANSWORLD PUBLISHERS
61–63 Uxbridge Road, London W5 5SA
A Random House Group Company
www.transworldbooks.co.uk

DEFENDER OF ROME
A CORGI BOOK: 9780552161343
9780552167253

First published in Great Britain
in 2011 by Bantam Press
an imprint of Transworld Publishers
Corgi edition published 2012

Addresses for Random House Group Ltd companies outside the UK
can be found at: www.randomhouse.co.uk
The Random House Group Ltd Reg. No. 954009

Penguin Random House is committed to a sustainable future for
our business, our readers and our planet. This book is made from
Forest Stewardship Council® certified paper.

Printed and bound in Great Britain by Clays Ltd, St Ives plc

Typeset in 11½/14pt Sabon by
Kestrel Data, Exeter, Devon.

4 6 8 10 9 7 5

For Bill Jackson
1929–2010

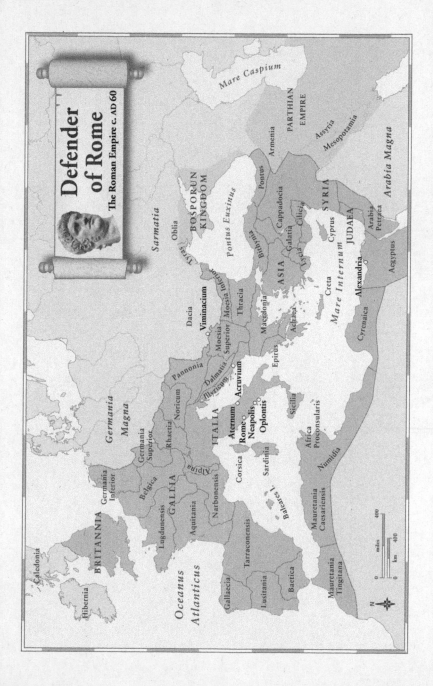

Defender of Rome
The Roman Empire c. AD 60

I

Rome, AD 63

They came at him in waves over the crushed summer grass, tall and lean, bred to war, their spear points glittering in the low morning sunlight and the sound of their coming like thunder. And, as they came, he slew them.

He had been born for this: to bring death. His mind exploded with the savage, atavistic joy of the warrior as the point of the *gladius*, with the power of his strong right arm behind it, took out throats and spilled guts, each stroke confirmed by the haze of scarlet that is the only true signature of battle.

One by one he watched them die and he counted his victims by the names of the Romans he avenged. For Lunaris. For Paulus. For Messor. For Falco.

For Valerius.

The next stroke faltered and the battle froze around

him, the screams of the dying trapped like flies in a web; spears caught at the very moment of the plunge; entangled enemies balanced precariously on the razor edge between life and death. No, not Valerius. Gaius Valerius Verrens lives. *I am Gaius Valerius Verrens.* The words echoed in his head and he wondered if he had joined the gods in their Elysian fastness. That was when he felt her presence. A flare of flame-tipped auburn at the very edge of his vision. Piercing green eyes that drilled into his soul. Boudicca. His enemy. At her unspoken command battle resumed. The spears fell. Men lived or died. But now the tempo had changed. Always, in the past, his had been the speed, his had been the vision. Other men had been too slow or too blind. Other men had died. Now it was different.

Caught in a trap of his own making, Valerius moved with the leaden torpor of a man forcing his way through a chest-deep lake. The sword was a dead weight in his hand and he struggled to keep the big curve-edged shield high. The blades of his enemies flashed and darted, a blizzard of bright iron that sought the weak points in his armour and the soft flesh of his throat, and he was helpless against them. The sting of edged metal made him scream in frustration and pain and for the first time he knew the despair of the vanquished. He called upon his gods, but knew they had already forsaken him.

'Valerius?'

A woman's hand held the sword that killed him.

'Valerius!'

He opened his eyes. 'Fabia?'

'You were dreaming. You cried out.'

It took a moment to resolve the familiar sights and scents of the bedroom with what had gone before. His body trembled with nervous energy and the sheets twisted beneath him were damp with sweat. It had not been like that at all. He had stood back like a coward, aloof from the battle, a new-made cripple. Men had died, in their thousands and their tens of thousands, but he had not killed a single one. Fabia leaned over him, golden and beautiful and safe, and placed a cool hand on his brow. Eyes the colour and complexity of polished sapphire filled with concern, and something more than concern. A pinprick of guilt speared him and he instinctively reached for the pendant at his throat. It was a tiny golden boar, the symbol of the Twentieth legion.

'You must have loved her very much.' It was a statement, not a question.

I killed her. It wasn't true. He had betrayed Maeve, but the sword that had taken her life in Boudicca's last battle had been another man's.

Fabia bent to kiss the mottled stump of his right arm, her breasts brushing lightly against his stomach. The loss of his hand had been the price of life. Each day he awoke surprised it was no longer there. Each day he endured a pain for which there was no cure. It was his burden and he would carry it for ever. Like his guilt.

He lay back and stared at the painted ceiling. Plump, cheerful nymphs hunted deer and antelope across lush grassland as the goddess Diana looked on approvingly. Fabia sighed and settled half across him, her body supple and soft against his angular hardness. He was three weeks from his twenty-sixth birthday and it had been almost two years since he returned from a Britain bled dry by Rome's vengeance to be acclaimed Hero of Rome; the Corona Aurea placed upon his brow by Emperor Nero himself. The honour had brought him fame, which he neither wanted nor deserved, and Nero's favour, which time had taught him was a fickle thing and not to be relied upon.

At first, the young Emperor had delighted in having a man close to his own age – a champion of war – close by his side. Valerius must attend court each day at the gilded palace on the Palatine Hill to decorate Nero's assemblies and delight him with his tales of battle and comradeship and sacrifice. Of course he was flattered: what soldier, even a soldier as damaged as he, would not be? Great men, consuls and generals, bowed to him amongst the marbled pillars and painted statues, beautiful women sought him out and ushered him to shadowy corners where they whispered of unlikely possibilities and even more unlikely certainties. And all the time, he felt the Emperor's hard little over-bright eyes following his every move and growing ever hotter. He wasn't a fool. He had heard the stories. In the legion he had lived with men, good men and bad, and knew that every man's taste did not follow natural lines and that some men knew no boundaries at all. As a boy he had known love, or something he had believed was love, but what was acceptable between boys did not have to be right between men. Before the offer was made he let it be known that it would be refused.

To avoid the storm which would inevitably follow he had spent a year living in Greece, hoping to be forgotten. The self-imposed exile gave him the opportunity to resume his philosophical studies under the great Apollonius, who had halted his wanderings for a time in Athens. But when he returned his name was still on some courtier's list. He continued to be invited to the Palatine. He was watched. But now the watching was different. Dangerous. Previously, when he had praised the tactics of Britain's governor his audience had cried out in agreement. Now his listeners turned away with shakes of the head, muttering words like 'despot' and 'butcher'. Paulinus had gone too far, they said, he had despoiled the province when he should have revitalized it. Paulinus was to be recalled. Now when men stood at his shoulder he understood they were not listening, but memorizing and recording for the time when . . .

A slim finger trailed through the cooling sweat that had pooled in the hollow of his chest. 'We should bathe.'

Valerius dashed the melancholy from his head and smiled at her as she uncoiled herself from his body and led the way to the little bathhouse. When they had enjoyed the mixed pleasures of the *caldarium* and *tepidarium*, Fabia wrapped herself in a sheet and ushered him to a polished stone table where she oiled his body with practised hands, easing each muscle of his shoulders, back and legs, then turning him over to do the same to chest and stomach. As her strong fingers fluttered over him he felt the hot blood of desire rising again. Before he could act on it she dropped the sheet and swung herself up to settle over him in a single movement. The intensity of her heat made him gasp.

'I suppose this means you'll cost me more,' he grumbled, attempting to think of anything but what was happening below his waist.

'Oh no, Valerius.' Fabia's voice was the texture of raw silk drawn across rough wood. 'This is my gift to myself. Stay just the way you are.'

Much later, she saw him to the door and raised her lips to allow a decorous farewell kiss. Fabia Faustina, high class courtesan, friend of the Empress Poppaea Augusta Sabina, and probably the most beautiful woman in Rome. Strange that she should love him when she knew he could never return it.

'And what do the courts promise today? Are you defence or prosecution or both?' she asked lightly.

'Neither.' Valerius allowed himself a sad smile. 'I must be with Olivia.'

Fabia stared at him, but her thoughts remained concealed in the blue-gold depths of her eyes. 'Tell her I send my prayers.'

Where Fabia's beauty glowed like an imperial park in full blossom, Olivia's was more ethereal: an Alpine snowfield touched only by the wind, or a sculpture of virgin marble before the artist applied the first brush of paint. Valerius stared down at his sister as she lay in the house on the Clivus Scauri. Regal and pale as an Egyptian princess, her long, almost raven hair framed her face, each strand placed precisely by her maid, Julia. His sister had the sculpted features so admired in the family, but more delicate than in the male line. A slim aristocratic nose, a long, curving jawline that reflected resolve and strength of purpose, and a mouth that, before her illness, had always seemed ready to smile. In fact, as he studied her, he realized she had changed even in the short time since he had last seen her, and he replaced the word 'delicate' with 'fragile'.

'She is wasting away.' He tried to keep the accusation from his voice.

The fastidiously dressed man at his side stirred uncomfortably. 'We are doing everything we can. The serving girl administers the daily draught as she has been instructed. She bathes her mistress only with warm water and serves thin soup three times a day.'

'More is spilled than eaten,' Valerius pointed out.

Metellus, the physician, frowned, making his pendulous jowls quiver, and the watery eyes narrowed. 'We can only force so much upon her or it will do more harm than good. She is thin but not yet skeletal. With the gods' will there is still hope. You have sacrificed to Asclepius as I advised?'

Valerius's faith in the gods had been sorely tested by the two days he had spent in the Temple of Claudius waiting to be torn limb from limb by vengeful British warriors. The fact that he had survived had done nothing to restore it, but he would do anything that might help Olivia. 'I visited the hospital on the Tiber island this morning and the priest dedicated a white ram to the god.' The doctor nodded, impressed. A white ram was no mere token. He wondered if his fee was quite sufficient. Valerius continued: 'The maid, Julia, has also carried a sacrifice to the Good Goddess.'

Again, this was only sensible. Bona Dea, the goddess of women, healing and fertility, could be counted on to intercede on Olivia's behalf from her temple on the Aventine Hill.

'Then you also are doing everything you can.' He hesitated. 'Perhaps if your father . . . ?'

Valerius shook his head. 'He won't come here.' He didn't have to say more. His father Lucius had staked their family's future on a match between Olivia and an indecently rich but very elderly second cousin of the Emperor. Olivia had taken one look at the balding, wrinkled figure of her betrothed, a man blessed with a single blackened tooth, and vowed to cut her wrists there and then. Lucius's reputation had suffered more from the fact that he had capitulated to her threat than that she'd rejected Calpurnius Ahenobarbus.

Under the law, he would have been entitled to sell Olivia into slavery or even kill her, but for all his stuffy patrician pomposity he had always been a loving father and had chosen disgrace rather than cause more distress to his daughter. Since the scandal he had locked himself away on the family estate at Fidenae and devoted himself to his grapes and his olive trees. Valerius had contacted him three times with the news that she was sick, but on each occasion his messenger had been turned away. The physicians who treated her speculated that the gods were taking their revenge for Olivia's lack of filial devotion, but Valerius dismissed the theory as a desperate attempt to justify their failure. He suspected that Metellus, a well-meaning drunkard who claimed to have studied in Smyrna and Alexandria, had now joined their number.

As he watched, Olivia's eyes opened, shale dark, liquid and slightly bemused. Recognition came slowly, but when she was certain of his identity her pale lips parted in a faint smile and before the eyes closed again her hand fluttered towards his. He sat on the bed and took it; it was cool and almost weightless. Olivia sighed lightly and he felt her fingers tighten. It will be like this when she dies, he thought, this helpless emptiness. I will sit here and her hand will grow cold and the room will grow dark and I will beg her to stay, but her spirit will fly from her as I have seen it fly from so many dying men. He began talking, of hope and love and the future, knowing she heard him but not whether she understood. And as he talked his mind drifted back to a time when a skinny girl with a dirty face and a torn tunic dogged his every footstep, forever asking foolish questions he couldn't answer. *Why?* And *How?* And *What?* Everlasting days by the narrow, tree-lined river that provided water for the estate, hunting little green frogs among the weeds and plastering each other with slimy, speckled spawn. Other days spent chasing elusive brown songbirds among the vines in the certain knowledge that they would flutter to the next row and the chase would be up again. The bitter taste of unripe grapes and the awfulness that inevitably followed. Watching each other grow.

And the day that caused him to wonder what kind of man he truly was. When his patience finally snapped and, encouraged by the slave boys, he had locked her in the cellar below the house and walked away. He would never forget the look in her eyes when he returned an hour later to find her frozen in the darkness. Or the note of accusation in the whispered child's voice. 'Please never leave me alone again, Valerius.'

He squeezed her hand and stood up.

'I will do anything to make her well.' He knew the words alone meant nothing. He might have been talking to himself. He might have been talking to the gods he no longer believed in. Instead, he found he was addressing the fat physician whose presence he had entirely forgotten.

Metellus felt a thrill of panic at the certainty in Valerius's voice; the tall, commanding presence and the hard eyes that pinned him like a legionary javelin. He had done all he could, truly he had. He raced through the remedies in his mind as if he was arguing for his life. The herbs mixed in warm leaded wine to cool the fever. Wolfsbane in minute doses to stimulate the blood. Extract of hemp to calm. The regime? Exemplary. Each step taken with a physician's care and forethought. Was there anything more? No. Twice no. Except . . .

'There may be a man . . .'

'Where can I find him?'

II

Rome was changing. Nero had vowed to turn the city into the kind of modern metropolis befitting the capital of an Empire which ruled over forty million people. If a street fell into terminal disrepair or an urban slum burned, he had dictated that it be rebuilt around an open square, allowing space and freedom and light for the residents, and providing a barrier against the fires that could spread with such lightning rapidity through the city's fourteen districts. In doing so he followed the lead of his uncle, Caligula, but where Caligula had forced the residents to pay for the improvements from their own pockets, the young Emperor increased his popularity by accepting the burden himself. Unfortunately for Valerius, some of the worst areas of the city remained untouched.

He held the torch high as he studied the narrow, fetid street ahead. From an alleyway to his left came the sounds of raucous, humourless laughter and screams that might be ecstasy or terror. I should have hired a bodyguard, he thought, and cursed as he stood in something which could have been animal or vegetable, but was undoubtedly obscenely soft and stank like a week-old corpse. Why must it always be the Subura? Rome's cesspit. Apartment blocks six and seven storeys high towered like cliffs above him, smoky oil lamps glowing in windows that held, at best, the threat of the contents of a night soil pot, if not the pot itself. Twin wagon ruts doubled as an open sewer, the contents reeking in trapped heat that barely cooled from one day to the next. Every step was an invitation to fall into a trap and every darkened entrance a potential ambush.

Still, he'd had no choice but to wait for Julia's return and if he'd tried to recruit some battered ex-gladiator or retired legionary from a tavern, the likelihood was that he'd only be paying for the dagger that tickled his liver or slit his throat. Left or right? He ran the physician's directions through his head as he considered the junction of two identical passageways. It had seemed much simpler in the comfort of the villa's atrium. 'Just follow the old Via Subura until you reach the Via Tiburtina and carry on until you're a hundred paces from the Esquiline Gate. He has rooms in the *insula* on the right. Ground floor.' In daylight Valerius would have had to fight his way through a surging mass of people, at risk from nothing more than carelessly wielded chair poles or bony elbows, jostled and hustled, melting in the heat, but never directly threatened. Now he was trapped in a pitch dark, verminous labyrinth where every street appeared the same and the only consolation was that the hour was so late the few inhabitants he'd come across had been rolling drunk.

He turned sharply at a rustling sound, the hand beneath his cloak reaching instinctively for his sword. The rustling stopped, to be replaced by a low whine, and he laughed at himself. Gaius Valerius Verrens, Hero of Rome, the man who had held the Temple of Claudius to the last man, scared of a scavenging hound.

Left or right?

Right.

He had pleaded to stay in the legions, even though he knew his injury meant he would never again fight in a battle line. No, his father had said, this is our great opportunity: the law, then the Senate; make the name Valerius ring through the marble halls of the Palatine. He'd obeyed, out of duty: the same sense of duty that had made him the soldier he had once been. And he had prospered thanks to the patronage that the Corona Aurea attracted. Every retired veteran, be he general or legionary of the third rank, wanted to be represented by Gaius Valerius Verrens. As with his battles, he won more cases than he lost, because he took a professional care in his preparations and fought hard for his clients, even when he didn't believe a word they told him.

The street widened and he saw a pale light ahead. Some sort of open space.

'He is a medical man just arrived from the east,' Metellus had said. 'Some say he is a worker of wonders and some say he deals in perfumed smoke and polished mirrors. A Judaean, he works among his people, seeking no profit. He does not advertise his services. You will have to be very persuasive. What does he look like? How should I know?'

The light came from a noisome drinking den behind an open yard with a stone fountain carved in the shape of a fish. Valerius hurried by, trying to look like just another drunk. But the eyes that watched him were the eyes of predators, not those of ordinary men.

A man might survive in Subura without being part of a gang, paying a gang or owning a gang, but his hold on life, and his family's, would be precarious. Red-haired Culleo, bastard son of only Jupiter knew whom, had been running with gangs for as long as he could remember. First as a lookout while others stole, then as a thief, learning to steal bread and fruit and meat from the streetside stalls while the younger boys distracted the owners. With growing strength came greater opportunity and he had become an enforcer. He had killed his first man by the time he was fifteen and cut the throat of his predecessor three years later. He favoured the knife, and he carried two: wickedly curved, long-bladed weapons that he fondly kept killing sharp and which were equally good for stabbing or slicing. Culleo was short and wide, but his build disguised his speed, which was usually enough to frighten other men into dying quietly. Unless a lesson had to be taught he preferred to attack from behind because it was quicker and simpler. In Subura, or at least in the streets around the Silver Mullet, he was the wolf and any man who didn't belong was his prey.

The torch Valerius carried attracted Culleo like a moth to the flame. Why would a drunk carry a torch when he could bounce home off the walls he knew as intimately as his mother's left tit? Once they had spotted him he was theirs. A tall man, though he crouched and tried to hide it, dressed in an expensive cloak. A fool then. Any cloak waved about the Subura was asking to be stolen and a man with a cloak would have other things worth stealing, even if it was only his clothes and his shoes. There was something else, too. From a dozen paces away Culleo's sharp eyes had noted the little details another man's might not: the way the fool carried himself, the slight favouring of his right side, and the strong jaw and sharp planes of his face. The description could have fitted twenty other men – apart from one important detail that could easily be hidden beneath the cloak, but Culleo had sensed. Word had been passed down to him from the invisible network that all the gangs knew to obey. Even the wolf must give up a proportion of his kill to the hungry tiger. Culleo knew that if you were to survive in the Subura 'they' were to be answered to above all others. He smiled, revealing a carnage of rotting teeth; someone wanted this man dead and was willing to pay handsomely for it.

He studied his victim's speed and direction, knowing the cloaked man would increase his pace once he was past the open courtyard. Who would walk slowly through the Subura at night? 'Iugolo? Fimus?' He called two of his men from the tavern, one older and massive, with a single eye and a red, weeping socket, and the other wiry, deceptively boyish and, even for the Subura, remarkably dirty. 'Take the back road by the tannery and cut him off before Tiburtina. If we're quick we can catch him at the Alley of the Poxed Tart. Don't move until I get there with the Greek.' Four against one: was it enough? He could gather more men but it would take time to rouse them from their beds and sober them up. By then the target might be gone. It was enough. The mark was a fool. A sheep to be shorn. No, he grinned to himself, a lamb to be slaughtered.

Valerius moved fast after he passed the inn, but his eyes never stopped searching for danger. The street narrowed again and the flickering orange torch-light bounced from filth-spattered walls creating the illusion of constant movement, so his senses continually reacted to non-existent threats. A pair of almond-shaped eyes glowed eerily at him from a doorway. Strange how a rat's eyes reflected red in the torchlight, yet the cat's which hunted it were like luminous emeralds.

He almost didn't see the movement.

It was just the merest glint of light on metal fifty paces ahead in a place and at a height where there should be none. His breathing quickened. He willed himself to be calm, sought the stillness which had always been his before battle. Let it build slowly, a heartbeat at a time; the countdown to violence. His muscles tensed and his senses sharpened. How many of them? It didn't matter. He couldn't run. This was their territory and they would hunt him down in seconds. But they didn't know he'd seen them and that meant, at least for the moment, they and not he were the hunted. He maintained his pace but his fingers tightened on his sword hilt.

When they stepped into the street he could have laughed aloud. Only two? A skinny feral child with a gap-toothed snarl, armed with what appeared to be a leatherworker's awl, and a one-eyed giant wielding a nailed cudgel that was like a toy in his massive hands. Did they really believe he was so easy to kill? One-armed or not, he had fought Boudicca's champions to a standstill on the field before Colonia. Had walked among the numberless dead on the bloody slope where Suetonius Paulinus, governor of Britain, had manufactured her destruction. He did not fear these men.

'Go back to your whores or your sisters, whichever it is you bed.' He spat the challenge, but the boy ignored the threat and capered right and left to block the street while the giant smiled and stroked his cudgel.

The mocking smile gave Valerius his warning. The smile wasn't aimed at him, but at someone behind him. He spun, letting the cloak billow wide to create a more awkward target, knowing the torch in his hand would attract the eyes of whoever was coming for him. Two more, less than five paces away and attacking silently at the run over the cobbles. No point in trying to hold them off. It would only give the giant time to pound him to mincemeat ready for the boy to take his eyes out with the spike. It had to be quick. The attacker on the right, a swarthy dark-browed creature, had slightly outrun his companion. Valerius took advantage of the split second it gave him to dash the blazing torch into the brigand's face and the man fell back screaming and clawing at his burned-out eyes. The momentum of the spin took him into the path of the fourth robber, a confident red-haired bruiser armed with a curving blade that slashed at the Roman's throat. Valerius brought up his right hand to block the sweeping blow and was rewarded by a puzzled glare as the blade bit into something solid with a sharp snap. Culleo still wore the look of disbelief when the *gladius* in Valerius's left hand darted from beneath the cloak. The triangular point punched into the soft flesh below his ribs before Valerius angled the blade upward into the squealing gang leader's heart. He twisted the short sword free, feeling the familiar warm liquid rush as another man's life poured out over his hand, and turned to face his surviving ambushers. But the boy and the one-eyed giant were not prepared to die for a cloak, not with their leader quivering in a widening pool of his own blood and the Greek mewing for his mother with a face like an underdone steak and eyes that would never see again. They backed quickly down the alley and vanished into the darkness.

Valerius studied the remains of the torch smouldering in his right fist. It was smashed beyond use. He sheathed the *gladius* and, with his left hand, pulled the smoking bundle free from the carved walnut replica that had replaced the missing right. The artificial hand had been designed to carry a shield, but did the job of torchbearer just as well. It was a little singed, with a deep score across the knuckles where the red-haired bandit's knife had struck, but it had done its job. He checked the bindings of the cowhide socket to which the hand was attached. If they loosened, the leather chafed against the flesh of his stump, but normally a little olive oil ensured it sat comfortably enough.

He'd thought he would never fight again, but he soon realized that many men were just as capable of defending themselves with their left hand as with their right. He had toured the *ludi*, Rome's gladiator schools, until he found the man he needed: Marcus, a scarred old fighter who had won his freedom by his skills in the arena. Now he trained with the gladiators most mornings and he prided himself on becoming a better swordsman with his left hand than he had ever been with his right. The first thing Marcus had taught Valerius was how the wooden hand could be used to block an opponent's swing and expose him to a counter-thrust.

Which way to the Via Tiburtina? He walked on without looking back. Let them rot; it was what they had planned for him. The blinded man was still pleading for his mother when someone cut his throat an hour later.

Valerius had noticed a subtle change since he returned from Britain where, in the same instant, he had been both betrayed and saved by the woman he loved. For a time death had seemed preferable to the loss of Maeve and his hand, but as the months passed he realized that she had provided him with a precious opportunity. Before he had served with the men of the Twentieth legion, he had been young, naive and selfish. The naivety and the youth had been soldiered out of him, leaving a new Valerius, toughened both physically and mentally, the way the iron core of a sword is hardened by the combination of heat and hammer. But he had still been selfish. Only now could he see how wrong it had been to expect Maeve to leave her home, her family and her culture and follow him to Rome, where she would have been shunned as an exotic, uneducated and uncultured Celt. Gradually he had resolved to live his life differently. That was why he had finally agreed to his father's demand that he return to the law, when he wanted nothing more than to breathe the stink of old sweat and a damp eight-man tent, eat cold oatmeal for breakfast and lead men into battle. And why, if it was offered, he would take up the quaestorship of a province: the next step on the *cursus honorum* and his road to the Senate.

The road widened as he approached the Esquiline Gate. The apartment block Metellus had described could be any one of three dilapidated structures on his right and at first Valerius despaired of finding the Judaean. On closer inspection, he noticed that the ground floor of the centre *insula* contained a shop selling exotic eastern spices and herbs. No goods were on show at this time of the night, but on the wall below the window the trader had marked prices for his wares. Since every physician was a herbalist of some sort, Valerius could think of no better place to begin his search. A chink of light at the edge of the heavy sackcloth covering the shop doorway told him at least someone was awake, and he could make out the subdued murmur of voices.

A natural wariness made him hesitate. The Judaeans were a haughty people, from a province that had been under imperial rule for fifty years but had achieved neither prominence nor importance. Trade with the Empire had brought Judaea prosperity and drawn thousands of its inhabitants to Rome, presumably including the man he sought. They were respected as drivers of hard bargains and despised for the barbarism of their religion, which a dozen years earlier had incited Emperor Claudius to expel every Judaean from the city. Now they were returning, but mostly kept to their own districts. It was unusual to find a Jew carrying out business in the centre of Rome.

He approached the curtain and took a deep breath.

III

What he'd mistaken for murmured voices turned out to be a kind of low, rhythmic chanting from the rear of the building. A single oil lamp spluttered in an alcove by the doorway, casting a dull light and emitting foul-smelling black smoke that clouded the upper part of the room. Sacks and boxes lay stacked against the walls and a table with a set of brass scales stood in the centre of the floor beside a chest covered by a white cloth. This building was one of the older *insulae* in Rome, constructed perhaps fifty years earlier; solid at least, unlike the shoddy thin-walled skeletons of more recent times, but showing its age where the plaster had dropped from the lime-washed walls. In the far corner to his left was another door, and it was from this that the chanting emerged, but not, he thought, directly. Again he hesitated, reluctant to interrupt a family gathering or religious ceremony, however barbarous. But his sister's life was at stake.

'Hello.' The word echoed from the stark walls.

Silence. A sudden, total silence that almost made him wonder if the chanting had only existed in his mind.

'Hello,' he shouted a second time, feeling foolish now and sorely tempted to just turn and go.

After a moment, the silence was replaced by an odd rumbling sound, like muted faraway thunder, and a small head crowned by a shock of jet curls appeared round the corner of the doorway. Two walnut eyes studied him with frank curiosity.

'Greetings to you.' The tawny girl looked about six, and he gave her his most reassuring smile. 'I am looking for the physician who lives in your building.'

Without a word she took his hand and led him through the inner doorway into a narrow corridor. At the end of the corridor they turned into a poorly lit room where a thin, grey-bearded man sat hunched over a wooden bench crushing herbs in a crude mortar, each circle of the heavy stone pestle accompanied by the rumble Valerius had heard earlier. The man looked up and nodded and the girl hurried out.

They studied each other for a long moment, the way men do on meeting for the first time, the older man seeking any sign of threat or danger and Valerius trying to reconcile the shrunken figure at the table with the conflicting stories Metellus had gabbled.

He guessed the Judaean's age at between fifty-five and sixty. The heavy, tight-curled beard would be with him until he died, perhaps a little whiter. Deep lines that might have been carved by a knife point etched hollow cheeks and a high forehead, providing a permanent reminder of a life of toil, trial and, Valerius suspected, physical suffering. The folds of a thick eastern coat engulfed his thin frame, yet beneath the robe lay a suggestion of power conserved for more important days. The eyes, solemn and steady and the colour of damp ashes, had an ageless quality, and their depths contained conflicting messages: wariness, which was only sensible in the circumstances; understanding, but of what? Humour was there, held in reserve for a more appropriate moment, and knowledge for the time it was needed. But a single quality stood out above all. Certainty. This man knew precisely who and what he was.

'*Salve*. You are welcome to my home.' The greeting was formal and the curious lisping accent turned the v into a w.

Valerius bowed. 'Gaius Valerius Verrens, at your service. I apologize for the late hour and the lack of an appointment, but I have come on a matter of urgency.'

The beard twitched, but Valerius couldn't be certain whether it was in irritation or acknowledgement. 'May I offer you wine?'

'Thank you, no,' the Roman said, not impolitely, but aware that he was unlikely to enjoy anything served in this household. He glanced at his surroundings. Small cloth sacks, each with its clear label, were stacked in heaps along the rear wall. Shelves filled with stoppered jars. Odd-shaped objects whose origin he didn't like to speculate. The scent of herbs and spices filled his nostrils, but there was something else too, a heaviness in the atmosphere that told him other people had shared this room only a few moments earlier. He wondered again about the chanting, and noted that the Judaean had made no attempt to introduce himself. The grey eyes studied him and he found himself resenting the frank, penetrating gaze. 'My sister . . .' he blurted.

'Is sick.'

'Yes.'

'And you come to me for help . . . at this hour? Are all your Roman physicians asleep?' The man smiled gently to take the sting from his words.

'As I say, it is urgent. Olivia . . .'

'I am sorry.' The Judaean shook his head. 'I regret I cannot help you. It is forbidden. I may only work within my own community. You understand? With my own people.'

Valerius felt a momentary panic. 'Please,' he said. 'At least listen to what I have to say.'

The physician turned back to his work and the rumble of pestle in mortar was an invitation for Valerius to leave. But he had underestimated the Roman's determination. Valerius's sword came half clear of its scabbard and the unmistakable metallic hiss brought the grinding to a halt. The Judaean raised his head with a look of regretful distaste.

'So, a true Roman warrior. At his best when his

35

opponent is unarmed. You would threaten a harmless old man? Would it salve your conscience? Would it make . . .' he frowned, 'Olivia . . . well again?' He shook his head. 'Spilling blood never solved anything, my young friend.'

Valerius held his gaze, but the grip on the sword loosened. He hadn't even realized he'd drawn it. 'They said things about you. I had hoped they were not true.'

The bearded man gave a humourless laugh. 'They fear me. They say I am a fraud and a murderer. That I poison husbands for their wives and wives for their husbands. They say,' he stretched for a jar behind him, reaching inside to display its contents, a slimy piece of off-white flesh, 'that I use the fruits of our circumcisions in my potions.' Valerius swallowed. The Judaean smiled. 'The poison sac of a sea snake. It has medicinal qualities. As you can see, all that they say is true.'

'They also said you were a magician. I had hoped *that* was true.'

The older man gave a dismissive grunt. 'Do you pray? Then pray to your gods to help your sister.'

Valerius had an image of Divine Claudius, immortalized in bronze, towering over the doomed fugitives huddled in the grandiose temple built in his name. 'I no longer pray. The gods have deserted me.'

For a few moments the only sound in the room was the faint, irregular buzz of the old man's breathing. 'Tell me.'

Valerius closed his eyes and the words came out in a rush. 'She woke up one morning a month ago and had lost the use of her arms and legs.'

'Entirely?'

'No. Not completely. She could move them, but not use them properly. She made a slight improvement, but two weeks ago she could not get out of bed. She has been in it since. Now she cannot raise her head to take food. She weakens by the day.'

The Judaean chewed his lip. 'Has she had convulsions, seizures?'

Valerius shook his head.

A long silence developed from seconds into minutes. Eventually, Valerius could take the tension no longer. 'Can you help us?'

The Judaean turned to him, the grey eyes serious. 'Perhaps. Please fetch Rachel for me. She is in the next room.'

When Valerius returned, the man whispered instructions in the girl's ear and she hurried off, returning a few minutes later with a small twist of cloth, which she handed to the Roman.

'You must dissolve this in boiling water and make her drink every drop. You understand? Every drop, or it is wasted.'

'Then?'

'Then you wait.'

Valerius hesitated. He looked down at his hand. Was this all he'd come for? A tiny twist of grey powder? But what more had he expected? 'Thank you,' he said, reaching for his purse.

The Judaean shook his head. 'When the day comes to repay me, you will know it.' For some reason a chill ran through Valerius at the innocuous words. He waited for further explanation, but the physician continued: 'Do not raise your hopes too high. The elixir will help for a time but the effects will not be permanent.'

He ushered Valerius out, accompanying him through the corridor and into the room which led to the street. The white cloth had slipped from the chest, which told Valerius where the Judaean kept the powder. He noticed a faint symbol carved into the wood. It looked like a large X transfixed by a single vertical stroke with a small half-circle attached to the top.

The old man saw his interest. 'The symbol of my craft,' he said dismissively. 'Interesting, but unfortunately valueless in Rome.'

Valerius turned in the doorway. 'Will you visit her?'

The Judaean sighed. 'My name is Joshua. Yes, I will visit her.'

IV

The performer gazed out over his audience seeking signs of genuine approval. Instead, all he saw were the imbecilic fixed smiles of those too uncultivated to appreciate the finer points of his art and held in thrall by the singer, not the song. The song was the tale of Niobe, which he had performed at the Neronia, the festival he had endowed, and told the story of a woman brought low by her own ambition; a queen who had attempted to supplant Apollo and Diana with her own children, only to lose them all. He heard his voice quiver with emotion as he reached the point where the seven sons and seven daughters were hunted down by the arrows of the gods and their mother turned to stone, a memorial to her own greed. A tear ran down the cheek of the Emperor Nero Claudius Drusus Germanicus. His mother, Agrippina, had likewise died of greed.

Hadn't he given her everything, palaces, gold,

jewels and slaves? Influence even. Perhaps too much influence. Still it wasn't enough; she had to have power. She thought he was still a child. They were staring at him now, mouths open, and he realized he had stopped singing before the end of the song. How strange she still had such an effect on him. He smiled, and bowed, and the slack faces resumed their grinning and the cheering began, washing over him like a warm, oily sea, sensuous and invigorating. How he despised them all.

Yes, she had to have power; he of all people could understand that. When one has tasted ultimate power, the power to decide whether a man – or a woman – lives or dies, no other power will suffice. He had been weak at first, even kind, in the years after he had ascended to the throne of Rome. He had listened to his advisers. But when *he* had spoken those close to him had not listened nor understood. That was before he had proved he was capable of wielding true power. After a few carefully chosen disposals even Seneca had listened, he who had never known when to keep his mouth closed but had still managed to survive the wrath of Uncle Gaius and devious old Claudius. He liked Seneca, had even trusted him once, but now he was nothing but a nuisance. He picked up a flower that had been thrown at his feet. It was long-stemmed with a fringe of small white petals and he began to pluck them one by one, still smiling and acknowledging the cheers; kill him, don't kill him, kill him, don't kill him . . . He continued until he came to the last petal and paused . . . don't kill him. He sighed. Seneca, always the fortunate one.

Not Mother. He had tried to warn her, but, like Niobe, she just wouldn't listen. So she had to be removed. They should have been singing about her death for a thousand years, a death worthy of the gods themselves. Only a true artist could have devised it. A ship that collapsed upon itself, leaving the after part to float off still containing the crushed remains of poor, dear Agrippina. Lost at sea. Plucked by Neptune to sit at his side for all eternity.

They had botched it, of course, the fools of carpenters, and she had lived. He hadn't even known she could swim! Still, the deed was eventually done. And those who had deprived her of her opportunity for immortality would never make another mistake.

He walked down the broad stairway to where his wife Poppaea waited, flanked by slaves holding a golden canopy. She looked truly enchanting today, her flawless features framed by tight curls of lustrous chestnut. Smiling, she took his arm and they marched through the throng as rose petals fell at their feet and perfumed water scented the air around them. He nodded at each shouted compliment – 'A triumph, Caesar'; 'The glory of the world'; 'No bird ever sang sweeter, lord' – and knew it was all lies.

He knew it was lies because he understood he was not the great artist he wished to be. Did they think him a fool to be deceived by such flattery, he who had expended so many millions in the quest to become

41

what he was not? Oh, he improved with every tutor and every hour of practice, but he had come to understand that genius was god-given and not some whim that anyone could command, not even an Emperor. All the hours of practice and the degrading, stomach-churning deceits he had resorted to and he could barely hold a note. Yet when he was on the stage he *felt* like a god, and the sound of the applause lifted him and carried him to Jupiter's right-hand side. He would not give up the applause.

Agrippina would have understood, but she had abandoned him. She came to him in the night, sometimes, lamenting the ordinariness of her end and still admonishing him for the loss of the snakeskin bracelet she had placed on his wrist in his infant bed. Her visits left him shaking in terror, though he would reveal that to no man. He hadn't understood his need for her until she was gone. Whom could he trust if not his own blood? Now there was no one. He gripped Poppaea's arm more tightly, and she turned to him with a puzzled frown, the limpid green eyes full of concern. He smiled at her, but he knew she was not convinced by the mask because the frown deepened. Dear Poppaea, clever and faithful. Octavia, his first wife, had hated her. But Octavia was gone and Poppaea was in her place. Poppaea had wanted Octavia dead. How could he deny her?

But what about the letter?

The letter vexed him.

Thoughts of the letter brought Torquatus, his

trusted and feared prefect of the Praetorian Guard, to mind, and from Torquatus it was but a short step to the one-armed tribune, the hero Verrens. A darkness descended on his mind and the noise of the crowd diminished. He had wished to be the young legionary officer's friend, a true friend, and had given freely of his devotion and his patronage. And what had he received in return? Rejection. Did Verrens truly believe the slight could be ignored? He wasn't even as pretty as the other boys, the charioteers and the lithesome young palace servants who squealed so delightfully and were so . . . flexible. Did this part-man think a common soldier was too good for an Emperor? Did the hero believe he, Nero, could not match his bravery? He felt Poppaea squirm and knew he'd hurt her, but his grip on her arm didn't loosen. Well, in time, the hero would discover the folly of his ways. In time.

But, for the moment, Torquatus believed he could be useful in the matter of the letter.

V

'Is there any improvement?'

Julia, the russet-haired Celtic slave who was Olivia's closest companion, shook her head. 'Nothing.'

He read something in her voice. 'You do not approve?'

'I approve of anything that makes her well again, but these people . . . they are so different. We should trust in our own gods.'

That word trust again. Valerius wanted to believe, but everything he saw with his own eyes made him doubt. They had given Olivia the Judaean's potion an hour earlier, but so far there had been no effect. A thought sent a shudder through him. Perhaps the gods were punishing him for his lack of piety and *he* was the reason Olivia lay there helpless, a pale shadow of the cheerful young woman she had been a few months ago. But if he believed that he would go mad. 'We must do everything we can, whatever it costs.'

She nodded, and as she left she allowed her hand to touch his. He knew it was an invitation, but that had been a long time ago, and his life had enough complications. He slept for a while on a couch beside his sister's bed until some inner sense detected movement. Olivia's eyes opened and she looked up at him. This time recognition was instant and he saw the wonder in her face. But it wasn't only at his presence.

'I feel strange.' Her voice was hoarse from lack of use and he quickly fetched a cup of water from the jug in the corner of the room. He felt a moment of panic. Strange? Had the Judaean poisoned her? When he placed the cup to her lips he was surprised when she raised her head to meet it, something she hadn't been able to do for a week.

She surprised him again by gently raising her arm, wondering at her own ability to achieve the simple task. And again, by smiling at him. The old Olivia.

'Is Father here?' she asked. 'I thought I heard the sound of his voice.'

He shook his head. 'He is busy with the estate. They're getting ready for harvest.'

'I wish I could help with the harvest the way I once did,' she said, the simple statement breaking his heart.

'You will be able to soon. When you are properly well.'

'I feel well now,' she insisted, and attempted to raise herself to a sitting position.

He pushed her gently back. 'One thing at a time, baby sister.' Olivia smiled at the old endearment.

'First we have to build you up. You need to eat.' She looked at him as if food was an entirely new notion. He backed off. 'All right. A little broth then?'

'No. Please. It's just . . .' She shook her head. 'It seems such a long time since I ate proper food. I'm ravenous.'

He called for Julia, who burst into tears when she saw Olivia awake.

Valerius watched his sister eat – a little boiled chicken breast with a ripe peach from the garden – and studied her. The change astonished him. A few hours earlier she had been an invalid; now, she looked almost capable of dancing. His joy was tempered by Joshua's warning: *the effects will not be permanent.* Even so, this was hope and hope was something he hadn't felt for many weeks.

When she had eaten, she insisted Valerius help her sit up. 'I will have a conversation like a human being,' she said. 'I have had enough of being a corpse.' She studied him as he had been studying her. 'You are unhappy, Valerius. I can see it in your eyes.'

He shrugged with a little half-smile, but couldn't find the words to tell her what he felt.

'Me?' she said, reading his mind. 'You must not mind, Brother. I know I am dying.' He opened his mouth to protest, but she put a finger to his lips. 'No, do not deny it. Even though you have worked this magic today, I still feel myself fading. But do not be sad. I suffer no pain, only weakness. The gods are calling me, and when the time comes I will

46

go willingly. All I ask is that you remember me at the *lemuria*. I would like to see Father again, but . . . I understand. But it is not just your little sister. I have seen it since you came back from Britain.' She stroked his wooden hand. 'Something changed you there, and not just this.'

They had never talked of it before, but a hollow feeling inside told him this might be his last opportunity. 'I met a girl, but she is . . . gone. I made a new life as a soldier and I miss it.'

'Then be a soldier again. You are still young. Still strong.' She picked up his left hand and ran her finger over the calluses he'd earned from the long hours of training with the *gladius*. 'You were a good soldier?'

'Yes, I was a good soldier.'

'Then they will find a place for you.'

'There is Father. He wants to see me in the Senate.'

She laughed, and it was like the tinkle of a delicate silver bell. 'You will never be a politician, Valerius. The first time some greasy aedile seeking promotion tries to bribe you, you will throw him in the Tiber.' Her face became serious again. 'You cannot live your life for Father. You must find your own way.'

She lay back and he placed his hand on hers. He remembered her as she had been on the day she turned down their father's marriage candidate, her eyes flashing with fire and filling the air with scorn. No wonder the old man was afraid to see her.

'Tell me about Britain,' she said. The request prompted a moment's hesitation. He had never revealed the truth about his experiences in Britain, not even to Fabia. But, like the good sister she was, Olivia eased the path for him. 'But only speak of the happy times.'

So he told her about the fine land, the forests and the meadows with their endless unnameable shades of green, the bounteous hunting and the pride of the legions; about his beautiful Maeve and her unscrupulous father Lucullus, and Falco and the defenders of the Temple of Claudius, and of Cearan and the fearsome Iceni warriors he had led.

'He sounds very handsome,' she said. 'For a barbarian.'

'He was. And a good man.'

'If you serve in the legions once more, where would it be? Britain again?'

He shook his head. 'Britain has too many memories for me, so not there, at least for now. There is always trouble on the Rhenus frontier and a good officer would be welcomed, even with one arm. Or up beyond Illyricum fighting the barbarians on the Danuvius. But the most likely place would be Armenia, in the east, where General Corbulo is campaigning against the Parthians.'

'So Armenia it is, my hero brother. Tomorrow you must petition Nero for a position on General Corbulo's staff and' – her voice took on a fair imitation of their father's pompous tones – 'do not return unless you add new laurels to the name of the Valerii.'

He would have replied, but she lay back and closed

her eyes. Within a minute she was in a deep sleep. He arranged her as comfortably as he could and kissed her gently on the forehead. Her skin felt fever hot against his lips.

On the way to his room he met Julia in the corridor.

'Is she . . .'

'She's asleep, but I think the medicine is wearing off.'

Tears welled up in the slave girl's eyes. 'Please ask the barbarian doctor to help my mistress. If . . .'

He touched her arm. 'You can ask him yourself. He has promised to visit, but don't call him a barbarian. He might turn us all into frogs.' The old joke made her smile. 'And Julia?'

'Yes, sir?'

'Mistress Olivia said she thought she heard a man's voice today. Have there been visitors you haven't told me about?'

'No, master,' she replied. But she took a long time to say it.

Valerius rose before sunrise the next morning, the twelfth day of June and the third of Vestalia. At this time of the day the streets were cool, and by the time he passed the Temple of Vesta a long line of women were already waiting with their sacrifices to the goddess of the hearth. The festival was the only time the temple was open to any except the virgins who maintained the sacred flame, and then only to women and the Pontifex Maximus, Nero himself. The scent of baking reminded him he hadn't broken his fast, but he smiled at the thought of eating the tasteless salt cakes the priestesses produced as tributes to the goddess.

The gladiator school was on the flat ground known as the Tarentum, outside the city wall on the west side of the Campus Martius. He turned off the Nova Via on to the Clivus Victoriae and then across the open space of the Velabrum until he could follow the river round to the old voting grounds. The stench from the Tiber gagged in his throat, but he knew he would become used to it, just as he would become used to the sight of the bloated corpses of dead dogs and deformed newborns floating in its sulphur-yellow filth. The river flowed sluggishly on his left and to his right the fading grandeur of the Pantheon and Agrippa's baths were highlighted by the early morning sunshine.

By the time he reached the *ludus* a score of men were already sweating as they faced each other on the hard-packed dirt under the critical gaze of the *lanista*, the trainer who would hire out his troop to the *editores* who staged games for the Emperor or for rich patrons who wanted to impress their friends. Mostly they fought for show, but occasionally, if enough money was on offer, these men who shared barrack rooms and meals, and sometimes beds, would fight each other to the death. Valerius had once been a staunch supporter of the games, with his own favourite fighters, but now he stayed away. In Britain he had seen enough blood spilled for a lifetime.

Most of the gladiators were slaves, former warriors swept up by the Empire's wars and spared the living death of the mines and the quarries for the entertainment value they promised. A few were unblooded: troublesome farm slaves sold on by their owners because it was more profitable than killing them and bought by the *lanista* on the strength of their size and fighting potential. Fewer still were the freeborn who fought of their own free will: debtors, gambling their lives to release themselves from some financial millstone, or men addicted to the thrill of combat and seeking the eternal fame that was a gladiator's greatest prize. The odds were against them. Most would never find it, only a painful death squirming in their own blood and guts on the sand.

He saw Marcus, his trainer, working with two fighters in the centre of the practice ground and walked through the gate and into the shade of the barrack building to do the loosening-up exercises the old gladiator insisted upon. Most of the gladiators trained naked, but Valerius preferred to cover his modesty with a short kilt. He removed his tunic and carefully folded it on a bench by the doorway. A few of the men glanced at him, but none acknowledged him. He would never be truly welcome here among the living dead. He felt the tension rising inside him. He was ready. First, short runs to simulate attack and retreat. Then stretches and muscle movements. More runs. More stretches. Only when a man had broken sweat and could feel his breath searing his lungs and his heart ramming against his ribs was he ready for the fight. As he took a drink from the fountain a shadow loomed over him.

'Not too much,' Marcus warned. 'I have a treat for you today.'

Valerius eyed him suspiciously. Every time he'd heard those words they had been followed by pain and humiliation. The trainer grinned, turning the scar that split his right cheek into a crevasse. Stocky and darkly handsome, despite the missing left ear which was a permanent memento of his career, he was the fastest man Valerius had ever met, with hands that could blind you with their speed.

He introduced the figure who walked up to join them. 'Serpentius of Amaya.' Valerius looked into eyes that hated you in an instant and a face that said its owner liked to hurt people. The narrow white seams that marked the shaven skull told of past battles won and lost. The man was thin and dark as a stockman's whip and looked just as tough.

'Serpentius,' Valerius acknowledged, but the other only stared at him.

'We call him Serpentius because he's so fast. The snake, right?' Marcus explained cheerfully. 'A Spaniard. Even faster than me.'

Valerius picked up his wooden practice sword. 'I might as well go home then.' He spun round to bring his blade down on Serpentius's upper arm, only to feel the point of the Spaniard's own sword touching his throat.

Marcus howled with laughter. 'Quick, eh?'

Valerius nodded, his eyes never leaving his opponent's. 'Quick.'

It looked like being a very long two hours.

The men around him practised with sword against net and trident, sword against sword and sword against spear. Valerius only ever used the short legionary *gladius* or the *spatha*, the longer cavalry blade. With the *gladius*, a man killed with the point; quick, brutally effective jabbing strokes and a twisting withdrawal that tore a hole in an opponent's guts the size of a shield boss. With the *spatha* it was a combination of the razor edge and brute strength that could bludgeon a man to death or chop him to pieces. But today wasn't about killing. They would use wooden practice swords and it was about speed and endurance, building strength and discovering weaknesses, his opponent's and his own. Unless, of course, Serpentius decided differently.

They took their places in the centre of the training ground and Valerius shuffled his feet into the dusty earth to get a feel for its grip. His opponent carried only a sword, in his right hand. Valerius always trained with sword and shield; sword in the left, shield attached firmly to the carved wooden fist that served for his right. No point in strengthening his left arm by constant practice if he allowed his right to wither away. He would not be a cripple.

He felt Serpentius's eyes on him. When he looked up the Spaniard was staring at him with the same expression he'd seen on the face of a half-starved leopard in the circus.

'Ready?' Marcus demanded.

Valerius nodded.

'A legionary, eh?' Serpentius spoke so quietly that only his opponent could hear. 'Legionaries killed my family.'

'*Fight.*'

The practice sword was twice the weight of a normal *gladius*, but for all the trouble it gave Serpentius it might have been a goose feather. Somehow, the point was instantly past Valerius's guard and only a desperate lunge with the shield knocked it aside and saved him from a bone-crunching thrust to the heart. Before he could recover, the point was back, jabbing past the shield at his eyes, his belly and his groin. He managed to parry the first thrust and block the second with the shield, but the third caught him a glancing blow on the inner thigh that would have unmanned him if it had landed square. Already the sweat was in his eyes blurring his vision, and he struggled to keep pace with the dancing figure beyond the shield. For the first five minutes it was all he could do to survive. He took hits to the shoulder and a strike that might have cracked a rib. But he fought on, spurred by pain and pride, never touching Serpentius, until gradually his senses came to terms with the speed of his opponent. His brain began to match the thrusts as they were launched, and the sword and the shield anticipated the Spaniard's attacks.

Serpentius felt the change, and altered his tactics. Now he used his speed to wear Valerius down, always keeping him turning to the right so that the Roman's sword could never reach him. Constantly changing the line of attack. Now high, now low. A painful crack on the ankle left Valerius hobbling for a few seconds, but the stroke was only a feint. Serpentius's real target was the eyes. A practice sword might have an edge that wouldn't cut a loaf of bread and a point barely worth the name, but it could still take your eye out, and Valerius saw more of the tip of Serpentius's sword than he cared for. By the time Marcus called the first break he knew every splinter and notch intimately, and it was only good fortune that had saved him from being blinded.

He crouched down, his chest on fire, the breath tearing his throat. Marcus knelt beside him as the Spaniard stood a few yards away drinking from a goatskin and barely sweating.

'You've got your sword in your left hand, but you still think like a right-handed fighter,' the older man said. 'You're allowing him to dictate every move and you're a yard slower than he is. If you keep going like this he's going to kill you.'

'Will you let him?'

Marcus let out a bellow of laughter. 'He's a gladiator. He could die in the ring tomorrow or the next day. He's a slave and you are a fucking overfed, underworked lawyer. He wants to kill you, and what are they going to do to him if he does? It's not a question of will *I* let him. Will *you* let him?'

Valerius nodded. 'You're right.' He started to get up, but Marcus put a hand on his shoulder.

'Don't fight like a one-handed man, or a two-handed man. Fight like a killer.'

Serpentius heard Valerius laugh out loud, and wondered what the joke was. The Roman wouldn't be laughing in another few minutes. He was tired of waiting. It was time to finish it.

Valerius waited for the command. Think like a killer. Don't think like a cripple. Think like the man who stood before the bridge at Colonia and dared Boudicca's hordes to come to him. Think like the man who slaughtered the bastards by the dozen. He remembered the tattooed champions, tall and proud, who'd fallen before his sword. He remembered a man with burning eyes who ran a hundred paces to kill him, but had died under his shield. Think like a killer.

'Ready.'

Before Serpentius could move he smashed the shield towards the Spaniard's body with all his weight behind it and felt the satisfying crunch as the layers of seasoned ash hit solid flesh. If the shield had been equipped with a metal boss he might have disabled his opponent, and as Serpentius retired he kept up the onslaught, always following and never allowing him to set his feet for an attack. He knew he couldn't maintain this pace for long, but it was enough for now to keep him on the run and make an occasional touch with point or edge. Batter forward with the shield to pull in Serpentius's sword, then twist to attack from his undefended side. Always moving. Dictate. Cripple the bastard if you get the chance. No. Kill him if you get the chance.

Serpentius was surprised by his opponent's recovery, but not concerned. His feet would keep him out of serious trouble and he knew he was still going to win. A man carrying a shield had to tire before a man who didn't. All he had to do was bide his time. He'd make the Roman pay for the bruises.

But the Roman was turning out to be tougher than he'd thought. Valerius was still moving when Marcus called the next break, even though he could barely speak when the former gladiator came to stand at his side and he didn't dare crouch in case he couldn't get up again. Instead, he leaned on his shield like a drunkard.

'Better,' Marcus said. 'You're wearing him down.'

Valerius smiled at the joke, but it hurt his eyes. Dried sweat caked them as if he was staring out of a salt mask. Above, the sun beat down from a cloudless sky and his flesh felt as if it was on fire. 'If I don't finish it soon he's going to kill me.'

'Then finish it.'

From the word of command, Valerius attempted the same tactic as he had in the second session, but this time it was obvious to everyone watching that he was too slow. The other fights had come to a halt as the gladiators were drawn to the epic, mismatched contest between the crippled former tribune and the born killer who hated every Roman. They whispered bets to each other and no man put his money on Valerius except old Marcus, who accepted the odds with the distracted air of a gambler who knew he had already lost. You could almost feel sorry for him.

Each time Valerius attempted to use the shield to pin Serpentius back, the Spaniard was able to skip clear and launch an attack from another angle. Time and again it appeared he had made the decisive strike, but somehow Valerius always managed to get sword or shield in the way, just enough to avoid what would have been a broken bone or gouged eye. But it couldn't last. Serpentius was laughing now, mocking his opponent as a coward and a cripple, mimicking the staggering steps as Valerius attempted to stay on his feet. Then he saw his opening. It was the shield. Valerius had held it shoulder-high all the heat-blasted morning, his arm a single bar of agony and the pain in his stump long since transformed into a silent scream. Now the shield wavered and fell to one side and Serpentius swept past it with a snarl of pent-up frustration, the point of the heavy *gladius* aimed not for the eyes but in a killing blow at the throat that would leave Valerius choking on his own blood. At least the Spaniard's mind told him he was past it. The Roman could barely hold the shield, never mind move it. So how could the upper edge be slicing towards Serpentius's jaw, and his head be jolted backwards with a force that made the sky fall in and darkness come several hours early? When he regained consciousness he found he couldn't raise his head and his throat felt as if it had someone's boot on it. He opened his eyes and far above him at the end of the long pale slope of the shield was a red-eyed vision of Hades.

'What is it you do with a snake, Marcus? Cut off its head?'

Serpentius heard Marcus laugh. The pressure on his throat increased and he said a choked prayer to Mars, at the same time cursing the fickle god for deserting him.

Valerius stared down at the pinned man. He only had to shift his weight to break Serpentius's neck. But the killing rage was gone. With a grunt of effort, he lifted the shield from the Spaniard's throat.

'Die in your own time.'

VI

Valerius found two men waiting in the atrium when he returned home after a frustrating day at the courts, and he glared his annoyance at Tiberius, the steward who had invited them in. His body still ached from his bruising encounter with Serpentius and his temper wasn't helped by the fact that the smaller of the two men, a greasy, overweight youth who couldn't have been more than eighteen, addressed him as if he were the owner of the house and Valerius a none too welcome guest.

'You are Gaius Valerius Verrens, former tribune of the Twentieth legion?' he demanded in a high-pitched, petulant voice.

'Gaius Valerius Verrens, holder of the Gold Crown of Valour,' Valerius corrected, winning a smirk from the taller of the two, whose broad shoulders and quiet alertness marked him as a bodyguard, as did his face, which had collided with solid objects more often than was good for it. 'And who might you be?'

The plump youth fumbled beneath his cloak. 'Claudius Helvius Collina,' he announced, brandishing the gold ring bearing his seal of office like a betting ticket. 'Imperial messenger.'

Valerius reached for the ring and noticed the big man tense. He didn't have any doubt it was genuine, but it didn't do to make life easy for pipsqueaks with ideas above their station. The messenger snatched it away, but Valerius insisted and eventually Collina handed it over, although he maintained his grip on the chain.

When he was satisfied, Valerius gave the ring back. 'Very well. What message do you have for me?'

'You are to attend the gatehouse at the Clivus Victoriae tomorrow at the second hour.'

'I don't want to hear it, I want to read it.' He held out his hand.

'The message is to be relayed orally. This man is here to confirm that it has been done and the wording is correct.'

For a moment Valerius felt like someone who hears a rumbling in the distance and knows it is an avalanche, but finds he can't move his feet to get out of the way. A summons was bad enough, but one without written confirmation hinted at trickery, or worse. This was no invitation to a reception or one of the Emperor's recitals. He considered his options and quickly decided he didn't have any.

When the two men had left, a kitchen slave asked when Valerius would want his evening meal, but he discovered he wasn't hungry. He knew he should go to Olivia, but he felt as if he were sitting on a volcano and if the volcano erupted it would consume Olivia just as it would consume him. He needed time to think. Who knew everything that went on in Rome from the Palatine to the prison cells below the Castra Praetoria? A silken voice whispered inside his head and he had a vision of a beautiful face.

Fabia.

How much should she say? Fabia Faustina handed Valerius a gilded cup and lay back on her couch. When the servant had arrived asking for an appointment her heart had lurched like a fourteen-year-old virgin's. What was it about the young soldier that made her feel this way? Yes, he was handsome, with the determined features of a young Caesar. And he had the hardened physique that only military service or manual labour gave a man. But many of her clients were handsome men with fine bodies. The missing arm didn't disgust her, quite the opposite, but neither did it account for this unlikely infatuation. He was brave and honest, but these were not attributes she necessarily found attractive. Not his courage nor his looks, then. It was something *inside*; the melancholy he tried to hide behind his eyes. So many of the men who came to this house sought her love, but had to make do with her body. Of them all, only Valerius would never be able to love her in return, and that was a challenge she could not resist.

But now? How much should she say? What should she tell him? And, more important, what should she not?

'I do not think you need fear for your life, Valerius.'

'Perhaps not yet,' he agreed. 'But I have an old soldier's instinct for survival and I smell an ambush somewhere along the road.'

'Old soldier?' The description amused her. 'How old are you? Not yet twenty-six years. It will be a long time before you are an old soldier, my dear, and you have many more laurels to win before that time comes.'

He smiled with her. 'Experienced, then. Experienced enough to know when to watch my flanks as well as my front.'

'That is always wise in Rome,' she agreed. 'One pair of eyes will never be enough to guard against the potential dangers here.'

'Which is why I came to you. Have you heard word of anything unusual at court? It is still only June but the city feels like a boiling pot with a jammed lid.'

'You think I am an old busybody who is only interested in gathering gossip, Valerius?' she mocked.

'Not old, nor a busybody.' He smiled back. 'I think you are clever and wise, which are very different things, and I think you will always be beautiful and always be desirable.'

She gave a little laugh and bowed her golden head

at the flattery. 'Pretty words from a simple soldier, and words any woman would be happy to hear, but time will ever be the enemy of beauty and age the enemy of desire. All we can hope is to use what we have well.' The last sentence reminded him of Olivia and she saw it in his face. 'The Emperor has many responsibilities and many concerns, Valerius. Since the death of his mother he has turned to his astrologers more often than to his advisers. He would not be Nero if he did not suspect everyone. He studies his predecessors and notes that they were destroyed by those closest to them. Where others revile his late uncle, Gaius Caligula, Nero admires him, for his ambition if not his aptitude for survival. He has the same ambition but understands the need to keep his Praetorians close. He believes his mother poisoned both Claudius and his natural father, which is one of the many reasons he removed her. When he sent Seneca away he thought he had cleansed the nest. Now his augurs speak of an enemy within the gates of Rome. A sinister force akin to a beast with many heads that is burrowing into the rock of the Palatine itself and undermining him. They say the very Empire is threatened. Nero wishes to lash out. Fortunately, he has advisers who preach more prudent counsel and reason stays his hand, for the moment. It is said he is confused and unhappy and it is when he is confused and unhappy, not when he is angry, that he is at his most dangerous.'

'Who says this?'

She shook her head. 'People tell me things, Valerius, but do not ask me who, or how, or why, because you may not like the answer. Accept what you are given; do not question the motives or the validity of the source.'

He nodded. His trust, at least, he could give freely. 'I don't doubt that what you say is true, but I still cannot see how it helps me.'

'Poor Valerius, who does not recognize his own value. You look at tomorrow and see only your fears. Consider the advantages. The opportunity to regain the Emperor's favour.'

'The last time I had the Emperor's favour I did not like the advantages it brought.'

'He tried to seduce you and you refused him? Do not look so shocked, Valerius, of course I could see it. And if he had succeeded? What fools men are to take the act of physical love so seriously. Warmth, comfort perhaps; if you are fortunate, a little passion and a fleeting moment of pleasure. Would it have altered you? I have done things, Valerius, that would perhaps change your opinion of me, but I have not let them change me.' She spoke the last sentence with a ferocity that made him wonder if it was true. It had never occurred to him to feel sorry for her. But Fabia was nothing if not an actress, and she quickly recovered her poise. 'Whatever anger Nero felt against you is long past. If you had been one of those simpering slave boys he surrounds himself with, or one of his lusty charioteers, he might have had you killed or put away, but you are a Hero of Rome. He dare not touch you, because to harm you would risk alienating the legions and he cannot rule without their support. My advice to you is this: whatever he asks, be prepared to at least consider it.'

Despite his doubts, he knew that she was right. He had asked for her advice; how could he refuse it?

'Will you stay with me for an hour?' This was different. Their meetings had always been, for all their pleasure in each other's company, on a purely commercial basis. Her voice had changed, the tone low and husky and filled with desire. He knew he should refuse.

'Of course.'

As she led him through to the bedroom she wondered what he would think if he knew the truth. Would he ever forgive her?

It was late when Valerius returned home, his head full of that half-floating sensation that comes after long hours with a beautiful, sensuous and passionate woman intent on ensuring her own satisfaction and yours. His body gave a pleasurable shudder at the memory of the miracles Fabia had wrought and the feelings that had accompanied them. Perhaps . . .

He heard the sobbing as he entered the atrium and he rushed to Olivia's room to find Julia lying hunched on the bed beside his sister. She looked up. 'It is as if yesterday had never happened,' she sobbed. 'She hasn't woken or moved all day. You must help her. She's dying.'

'I'm sorry, Julia. I shouldn't have left you. I will find someone else tomorrow. A nurse or a companion.'

'It isn't a nurse or a companion she needs. It is her family,' the girl said accusingly.

He stared at her. He would never have taken those words from another slave, but Julia and his sister had been together since they were children. She was Olivia's best friend as well as her servant.

'I'll send a message to the Judaean. He said he would visit Olivia.'

The suggestion calmed the girl, and he waved her from the room.

'I'm sorry,' he whispered, taking his familiar place beside the bed. 'I neglected you today for the wrong reasons and tomorrow I will have to neglect you for the right ones. Do you remember . . .'

Her eyes remained closed, but her face told him that she could hear him.

VII

The Victory Road clung to the side of the Palatine Hill, sloping first from the west, then turning to climb across the northern face. A faint haze hung in the air, but the low sun quickly cleared it and halfway up the hill Valerius, who had dressed in his finest for the occasion, turned to look out over the centuries-old glory of the Forum and the shimmering sea of terracotta roofs that disguised the festering reality of the Subura. He wondered if he would look upon it again. At his back soared the marble splendour of Nero's sprawling palace, home of every Caesar since Tiberius. Many of the men who had followed this path had entered it and never left. In theory, no Roman citizen could be tortured or sentenced to death unless he was guilty of treason. Caligula, and, in his final years, Claudius, had shown that the reality could be very different. Their blood ran in Nero's veins.

But some journeys had to be made, even if each

step was reluctantly taken. He squared his shoulders and approached the gatehouse, where he surprised a pair of black-clad guards lounging sleepily against the wall.

'Gaius Valerius Verrens.'

The senior of the two yawned. 'Early, aren't you? We don't generally have anyone official at this hour.' He studied a list pinned to the gatehouse door and shook his head. 'Doesn't say you're expected. I'll need your pass.' He held out a hand.

Valerius shook his head. 'The invitation was delivered verbally.' The Praetorian noticed the stress on the word 'invitation' and raised his eyes.

'Verrens?' The tone was polite but the way the two Praetorians straightened told Valerius everything he needed to know about the speaker. Stunted but solidly built and in early middle age, he wore his hair cropped short and had features that might have been crafted with a blunt knife. The skin on the left side of his face had the texture of melted candle wax and made Valerius wonder if he'd been caught in a fire at some point. It was a face that would scare children and repel women. On another man it might have inspired pity, but not on this man. You knew instantly that the mind behind the mask was as ugly as the misshapen features he presented to the world.

'At your service.' Valerius kept his voice neutral, but didn't bow, which made the face twist into a parody of a smile.

'Lucius Licinius Rodan.'

Now Valerius understood why the Praetorians were so nervous. Officially a lowly centurion of the Praetorian Guard, Rodan was the one who, if Nero had an enemy, would ensure he was an enemy no more. By assassination if necessary, but the Praetorian was rumoured to prefer more subtle methods. Perhaps the man's younger son would be found with his throat cut; would he risk the elder? His wife might be molested in his house; who was to know when the molesters would return? If his horses burned to death in their stalls, he would understand that his family would be next. Rodan was one of the most dangerous men in Rome and his presence made this meeting all the more unpredictable.

'Has he been searched yet? No? Then what are you waiting for?' Expert hands ran over Valerius's body, missing nothing. The Praetorian delicately held up Valerius's walnut fist for inspection.

'It could make a good bludgeon,' he suggested.

'Fool.' Rodan shook his head. 'I think we can leave him his hand. After all, he did lose it in the service of Rome. Follow me.'

The gateway led directly into the palace gardens where a path wound along an avenue of pear and apple trees, through parkland studded with fountains and flower beds. Valerius walked a pace behind his host, whose bearing made it clear that a missing hand and a military honour did not add up to any form of recognition in Rodan's world. Rodan provided a reminder of his power a few moments later. A group of slaves were working to replace plants near the path when one of them accidentally sprinkled a few grains of soil on the Praetorian's gold court slippers.

Rodan halted as if he'd walked into a wall. 'Overseer!' he shouted. 'This man assaulted me. He is to be taken to the Castra Praetoria for questioning.'

The slave, a thin dark-haired boy of about fourteen, turned death pale. His hands brushed desperately at Rodan's feet until there was no sign of the offending dirt. 'No, sir, please, sir, I beg . . .' Without warning, Rodan kicked the boy full in the face with enough force to break his jaw. Valerius saw three white teeth fly as the young slave somersaulted backwards to lie groaning on the path. Rodan stood over him, casually considering whether to kick him a second time before deciding that the lesson had been absorbed. Two men picked up the slave boy and carried him away. Valerius had come across men in the legions who meted out violence as readily as Rodan, but never quite so coldly. He comforted himself with the thought that they were always the ones carried from the fight with spear wounds in the back.

They walked quickly through a colonnade until they reached a large door guarded by Praetorians matched like a pair of thoroughbred horses. Nero was said to choose his palace guard personally, with all the care he gave to the choice of his chariot teams, for their looks and physique. Clearly, Rodan had been selected only for his talents. Inside, everything was marble and gold. Ahead of them stretched a long

71

corridor lined with gilded busts of the Emperor and his predecessors. At set intervals curtained alcoves framed statues of Apollo, Venus or Jupiter and other lesser members of the godly pantheon. Enormous vases filled to bursting with vibrant yellow flowers continued the colour scheme. A display of neck and arm rings made of twisted strands filled part of one wall and Valerius recognized trophies taken from British kings. Another held plates and ornaments which could only have come from the east, a small part, he guessed, of the plunder Corbulo had gathered as he subdued the Parthians in Armenia. Valerius would have stopped to study them more closely, but his guide glared at him.

'This way,' Rodan said irritably, indicating a doorway to the right.

They entered a large open room dominated by an enormous statue of painted marble. It was incredibly lifelike and portrayed a naked man and two younger male figures being tormented by writhing snakes. The man was reaching upwards with one arm half entwined with a serpent, while his right hand attempted to keep a second snake's gaping jaw from his body. Valerius recognized the group as Laocoön, high priest of Troy, and his two sons. He remembered that Laocoön had warned the Trojans against Greeks bearing gifts and wondered if it was a portent for this meeting. Rodan ignored the sculpture and turned to his left where a set of six wide steps led upwards to a golden throne.

The throne was empty.

'Wait here.' Without another word the Praetorian returned the way he'd come.

Minutes passed while Valerius stood in solitary silence. He knew the wait was designed to make him uneasy, but knowing didn't make it any more bearable. As his eyes adjusted to the light he noticed detail that had not been apparent when he entered. The wall behind the throne was not solid, but a silk screen carefully painted to blend in with the garden scenes behind. It was almost translucent, so that if he looked carefully he could see faint shapes moving behind it. A slight rustling confirmed what he already knew. He was being watched.

He measured time by the shadows creeping arthritically across the floor. By now tension had developed into a slow-burning anger. He willed his feet to stay where they were. Seneca stood here, he thought. Seneca had suffered the same creeping uncertainty; the cramping of the legs and the roaring inside his skull. Lucius Annaeus Seneca was an old friend of Valerius's father, with a country estate in the next valley. At the age of fourteen, Valerius had been sent to study under Seneca while the latter endured exile in Corsica. The philosopher had returned from his banishment to serve as Nero's teacher and guide. He had danced the political tightrope for half a lifetime, but his fall now seemed inevitable. It was said he no longer had the Emperor's confidence. That his judgement was unsound. He was old, tired;

Nero needed a younger man to guide him, someone who understood his needs. Someone like Decimus Torquatus, the man who controlled Rodan and his Praetorian wolves.

Valerius kept his eye fixed on the wall and allowed his mind to drift back to long days on the parade ground with the Twentieth. Nero could not hurt him. The best of him had died on that final day in the Temple of Claudius. He might live and breathe, but this was merely the long prelude to the afterlife. The only people who truly mattered were Olivia and his father. For their sakes he would endure this petty torture.

His thoughts were interrupted by a soft giggle from behind the screen and an apparition dressed in startling emerald green appeared, its golden hair styled in long ringlets. A weak chin with a sparse fair beard, bad skin disguised by white powder and heavy sensuous lips painted a rich, ruby red. This hermaphrodite creature was served by four naked satyrs; plump, pre-pubescent children who still managed to exude a nauseating sexuality as they danced around their charge. Valerius found himself caught between horrified bewilderment and an urge to laugh out loud. Nero. In a woman's dress and made up like a common harlot.

The Emperor studied him seriously, eyelashes fluttering. 'What do you think?'

There could only be one answer. 'Astonishing, Caesar.'

'You recognized me as Pandora? The others didn't, but what do they know about art? At the close of the gymnastics I will give a performance then hand out gifts from Pandora's box.' The voice was as Valerius remembered it: high, but not shrill, more boy than man. It still managed to carry a ruler's power and for some reason it sought his approval.

'I am sure they will be gratefully received, Caesar. What more could a man ask than a gift from your own hand?'

The shining eyes narrowed and Valerius wondered if he'd gone too far in his flattery. He found himself holding his breath.

'So, a courtier as well as a soldier.' Nero waved a hand and the four satyrs disappeared behind the screen. He came closer. 'Of course, you were trained by Seneca, as I was. We have much in common, you and I. We have both suffered in Rome's name. We should be friends.' He raised his hand to Valerius's cheek and the young Roman couldn't prevent himself flinching from the manicured fingers. Nero's eyes darkened and the room seemed to freeze; the unnatural stillness was broken only by the sound of the Emperor's hoarse breathing. The scent of a strong perfume trickled into Valerius's nostrils and made him need to sneeze. He wanted to turn away, but the unblinking stare held him like a vole in the grip of a kestrel's claws. Very slowly, Nero brought his face close. Valerius tried not to smell the sour breath or see the outlines of the small pus-filled spots that dotted the skin beneath the powder. He felt his gorge rise as the painted lips touched his. A thick tongue probed his closed mouth and the urge to vomit became almost irresistible. He knew that if he gave in to the sensation he would surely die. He stood, still as the marble statue on the other side of the room, and endured.

After a few moments without a response, Nero took a step back. His tone mirrored the astonishment on his face. 'You will not return your Emperor's love? Is this what a soldier calls loyalty, or devotion, or duty?'

Valerius could feel the fear rising in him. Against any other form of attack he could have defended himself, even if it meant his death, but this? 'Not will not, Caesar.' From somewhere he found the right words. 'Cannot. It is not within my gift or my power.'

Nero's head swayed on its long neck, the cold eyes never leaving their prey. 'But it is within mine.' His voice quivered with righteous anger. 'I could have you held down and use you as I willed.'

'Then it would not be love, and you would have lost my loyalty and devotion.'

'And *you* would have lost your life.'

'My life is my Emperor's to take, though I had hoped to give it willingly on the battlefield.'

For a dozen long moments Nero studied him. Without warning he gave a girlish laugh and flounced away. 'Am I not the greatest actor in the world? With nothing more than a kiss I have a Hero of Rome disarmed and trembling in fear.'

Valerius bowed his head, not in acknowledgement, but to ensure that the other man could not see murder reflected in his eyes. He had never felt such fury. He wanted to reach out and take the scrawny neck in his hand and squeeze until the breath rattled in Nero's throat like a dying chicken's. To flail with the walnut fist until the pasty, overfed face was smashed into a bloody pulp. Slowly, he willed the rage to subside and when he looked up the Emperor had taken his place on the golden throne, with the emerald dress ruffed up around his thighs and his thin, pale legs hanging ludicrously below.

Now the voice took on a new authority. 'I brought you here for another reason, Gaius Valerius Verrens, Hero of Rome. Will you serve your Emperor – unto death?'

There could be no hesitation, though the words choked him. 'I will, Caesar.'

Nero waved a hand theatrically towards the balcony. 'Look out and tell me what you see?'

Valerius hesitated. There were so many answers. 'I see Rome and its people.'

The Emperor shook his head, flinging the ringlets left and right. 'No,' he snapped. 'You see a nest of traitors. Rome's laws are flouted. Rome's gods are mocked. A disease is already within our midst. It is spreading with every hour. You will discover the source of the disease so that we may eradicate it. You have heard of a man called Christus?'

Valerius shook his head at the unfamiliar name. 'No, Caesar.'

'A Judaean troublemaker, from the province of Galilee and put to death almost thirty years ago, but he makes trouble still. Before he died he promised the Jews eternal life. A small number accepted the lie. A carpenter came close to setting the province afire. Those who survived continue to plot in his name. They travel the Empire holding secret meetings and preaching that he is a god. It is said they drink the blood of children, and if that is true I will not leave one of them alive. But Seneca taught me to be just and I will not believe it without proof. You will supply that proof. We have evidence that they are already in the city. You will find the followers of Christus and pass their names to my servant Torquatus. You are our Hero of Rome. Now I name you Rome's defender against this evil and appoint you honorary tribune of the guard. If you succeed, you will be for ever in our favour. Here.' He reached inside the folds of the dress and retrieved a ring on a gold chain, similar to the one the courier had shown Valerius, who walked up the stairs and took it, brushing his lips against the back of Nero's hand. 'The imperial seal. Use it well, and when you are done return it to us and receive your reward. Torquatus!' A tall, handsome man appeared from the far side of the screen, his unlined face set in a mocking smile. Valerius wondered how long he had been listening. 'Torquatus will furnish you with the details.'

The two men bowed and backed away, but the Emperor wasn't finished.

'And Verrens?' Valerius looked back at the greatest actor in the world on his lonely stage. 'Fail us at your peril.'

'You are very fortunate,' Torquatus said as they left the room.

'What do you mean?'

'It's not every man who receives a personal performance from the Emperor. You played your part quite well.'

Valerius bit back his anger. 'I would rather not have had a part.'

'You are a man who finds it difficult to hide his emotions. You wanted to kill him, and he knew it. But it only made him desire you more.'

'If I had wanted to kill him he would be dead.' The sentence was out before his brain had the chance to consider how potentially lethal the words were.

Torquatus stared at him. Coming from another man that declaration would have warranted imprisonment and execution, but perhaps not this man; not for the moment. He pointed back towards the balcony. 'You have never been closer to death than you were in that room. Four of the finest archers in the Empire stood behind those windows with their arrows aimed at your back. He would have required only to raise a single finger.'

A chill settled on the centre of Valerius's spine. 'Why me? Surely there are others better qualified to carry out this task.'

Torquatus stopped at the junction of two corridors. 'Because you are available. Because you have proved yourself brave and resourceful.' Somehow the words 'brave' and 'resourceful' emerged as deliberate insults. 'The Emperor commissioned a private report from Julius Classicanus, our new procurator, on the causes and conduct of the British war. Governor Paulinus naturally attempted to blame everyone but himself, but he was forced to admit that if he had acted upon the information you provided about the Iceni the conflict might have been avoided.' He smiled coldly. 'Of course, a more politically astute general would have had you killed when he had the opportunity. As it was, only yourself and young Agricola came away from that contemptible little island with any laurels. You had the opportunity to rise high in the Emperor's service if only you had humoured him a few moments ago. A small price to pay. You might have had a legion – he has rewarded other men with more for less – and, for a resourceful man with a legion, no prize is beyond reach.' Valerius found himself staring. What was Torquatus suggesting: that one day he might supplant Nero? The lazy eyes stared back, touched by the shadow of a smile. No, he was telling him that he would have had him killed. This man had spent years plotting the destruction of Seneca; he would not stand by and watch another rise to take *his* place at Nero's side. Torquatus nodded, his pale eyes glittering. 'Good, we understand each other.'

They entered a room with a large desk at its centre. Torquatus took his place behind it, but didn't offer Valerius a seat. An opened scroll lay on the desk, pinned at the corners.

'Twenty thousand Judaeans in Rome, most of them in the district around the Capena Gate, but a few living in scattered pockets in the north of the city. Twenty thousand suspects, but only a few will be followers of this Christus. The Jews despised the man as much as we did, probably more. However, the Emperor is minded to go a step further than his stepfather Claudius and remove them permanently from the city. He has his own reasons for this. I have my reasons for advising against it.'

Valerius waited for him to expand on this unlikely humanity, but Torquatus continued to study the document. Eventually he looked up.

'Twenty thousand Judaeans and only one of them matters. He is the leader of the cult in Rome, a man known as the Rock of Christus. A melodramatic title for the leader of a few fanatics, but he is also a resourceful man because he has thus far managed to elude us. You will identify him to me.' He paused. 'But the seizure of this Rock is not your primary purpose. The Judaeans who follow Christus are of little consequence, but the Roman citizens they have seduced with their lies and their promises are. Caesar is right to compare this sect with a disease. Like a disease, they spread their poison silently through the population. And like a disease they target the vulnerable. In this case the vulnerable are not the poor, for whom the prospect of everlasting life is not immediately appealing, but those who have the means to enjoy it. Knights, aediles, quaestors, generals and tribunes. It is possible this evil has reached the Senate. Here is the greatest danger, perhaps even to Rome itself. Hunt them down. If you find one, he – or she – will lead you to the next.'

'Do you have names?'

Torquatus sniffed dismissively. 'If I had names I would not need you.'

'My resources? How many men will I have?'

'You have the Emperor's seal. You are his agent in this matter. If you need to recruit anyone else you have his full authority. They will be paid through the Treasury and should be accounted for to Centurion Rodan, whom you have already met. This is not a job for squads of soldiers, or I would have flooded the city with Praetorians. It requires subtlety and stealth. Low cunning, if you like, which I sense you have in abundance.'

Valerius ignored the insult. 'I need all the information you have on this Christus and his followers.'

Torquatus shrugged. 'There is very little, but I will have everything sent to your home.'

When the younger man had left, Torquatus returned to the paper on his desk. It was a letter, which contained certain allegations against an unnamed someone in Nero's inner circle. His face had the look of a fisherman who has just felt the first tug on his line.

VIII

Valerius arrived at the *ludus* to find the gladiators lounging in the shade of the barracks, sipping at goatskins of tepid water and gossiping. They'd rest for another two hours until the heat went out of the sun and they returned to their relentless training. He approached one group and asked where Marcus could be found. A heavily built fighter jerked his head towards the doorway and Valerius entered to find the scarred veteran muttering over a piece of scroll filled with figures.

'Things are a little slow,' the old gladiator said without looking up. 'Too many recitals by the songbird on the hill and not enough blood and guts. Someone should remind him that he's allowed a bet.'

Valerius smiled at the veiled reference to the Emperor, whose dedication to the finer arts was not always appreciated in a city coarsened by three hundred years of more down to earth entertainment.

Nero had famously banned gladiators from fighting in the arena at Pompeii over the small matter of a few deaths in a riot involving rival supporters. There had even been a rumour that he planned to stop opponents fighting to the death altogether. Valerius shook his head at the thought. He might as well try to ban the chariot races that were his obsession. 'I always thought you appreciated music, what with all the practice you get in the Green Horse.'

Marcus grunted. 'That's only for the ladies. And to what do we owe this honour, lord Valerius? Come for another sparring match with Serpentius, or have you finally decided to take up an honourable profession?'

'I'm looking for some hired help.' Valerius pulled the chain with the golden ring from his cloak and placed it on the table. 'Two or three men who know how to look after themselves and can keep their mouths shut.'

Marcus gave a low whistle when he recognized the ring. 'Interesting. And dangerous?'

'Worth good money to whoever signs on, though.' Valerius had already decided to fund the men from his own purse. He suspected it would be more secure if Torquatus remained unaware of the type of help he was hiring.

'Do you have anybody in mind?'

'I wondered if you might be interested in a change of scenery.' Valerius shrugged. 'We'll need someone to carry the rations.'

'Someone to hold your hand, you mean,' Marcus growled. 'Anybody else?'

'I thought I'd leave it up to you. You'll be their leader.'

'How many?'

'Four, for a start. If we need more we know where to come. I'll compensate the *lanista* and fund clothes and weapons. Good quality, no auxiliary rubbish. Three meals a day and a roof over their heads. In return I'll expect military discipline and no chasing women until I say they can.' He mentioned a sum of money for Marcus and a third of that for his men.

The gladiator chuckled. 'For that much, who do you want us to kill?'

'Nobody, I hope,' but even as he said it Valerius had a suspicion it wasn't going to be true. 'Call it legal research. Just a little snooping around.'

On the short walk from the *ludus* to the Basilica Julia he took time in the shade by Pompey's theatre, stopping off as always to read the inscription on the great marble-faced arch dedicated to Germanicus Caesar. Germanicus was the father of Caligula and the man who, but for his untimely death, would have been Emperor in his stead. In his heart lay the true glory of Rome, unsullied by corruption or dishonour. Germanicus, whom men hailed as the noblest of Romans, had been Valerius's hero since boyhood, and Valerius made a habit of saying a prayer to his shade whenever he passed beneath the monument with its golden chariot.

Duty done, he doubled back towards the Forum. His pulse always beat a little faster when he entered the hallowed ground between the imperial palaces on the Palatine and the great Temple of Jupiter on the Capitoline summit. Here was Rome's beating heart. Here he was at the centre of the world. All around him were tributes to the men who had made Rome great: emperors and generals, consuls and senators, some whose deeds were long forgotten, but whose names would live on for ever in this sacred place. A pair of giant triumphal arches commemorated the victories of Augustus and Tiberius. On the Rostra Julia the great orators still made their pronouncements above the beaks of ships captured a century before at Actium, beside the frozen stone figures of Scipio and Sulla and Caesar and Pompey. Here was the little shrine to Venus Cloacina, goddess of the sewers, and, along the Via Sacra, fluted pillars topped by the golden figures of Mars and Jupiter, Venus and Minerva. And, in simple contrast to the man-worked grandeur all around, the little group of olive and fig and grapevine which marked nature's most precious gifts to Rome.

Other men would say that the heart of the heart was the Curia, where the Senate sat, but for Valerius it would always be the Basilica Julia. Already, though it was only early afternoon, slaves and servants were making their way to the shops and stalls on the margins of its pillared aisles. He knew the lawyers would be slower to return from the midday meal with their families and took his time. He had three cases outstanding which needed dealing with before he could begin Nero's mission. They couldn't be more different: an inheritance dispute he was defending before the Court of the Hundred; a complicated civil case involving the demolition of a semi-derelict apartment block on the other side of the Pons Aemilius that would take some delicate negotiation; and, by far the most pressing, an accusation of water theft which he was due to prosecute for the water commissioner. Fortune favoured him when he noticed Quintus Fuscus, a lawyer he knew, a dozen yards ahead on the Vicus Jugarius. Valerius explained his dilemma, but not the reason for it. 'I can put off the building case and I owe the water commissioner some kind of explanation, but I need someone to take the inheritance suit off my hands.'

The case was the most lucrative of the three and Fuscus's face lit up. 'I'd be delighted to oversee it; I haven't tried a case before the *centumviri* for years. It will be a pleasure.'

Valerius thanked him and walked on to his next meeting.

'This is most unusual,' Commissioner Honorius complained. 'The case is ready to present and all parties are available.'

'If you wish to find another prosecutor I will be happy to withdraw,' Valerius assured him.

'No, no. It's just that I believe you underestimate the importance of this case. The theft of water from Rome's aqueducts has always been a most serious offence and is on the increase. The time is right for an example to be made.'

Valerius made his apologies and agreed to speak to the representative of the accused, a builder with interests all over the city who was alleged to have tapped into one of the main aqueducts feeding the capital to supply his brickworks.

By now the Forum hummed with activity. The avenues were thronged with senators, each with his guard of bullies and drifting cloud of clients; with lawyers and their clerks and the crowds of gawpers who had come to see them win or lose; with money changers, soothsayers, shoppers and worshippers, men offering themselves for work, and the beggars, blinded and maimed, who reminded Valerius of the ache in his missing arm. It was as he fought his way east along the Via Nova past the House of the Vestals that he felt someone brush against him. His first thought was that he was being robbed, but then he realized that something had been placed in his left hand.

He looked down and discovered he was holding a torn piece of scroll.

IX

Poppaea Augusta Sabina lay back on the padded couch and took a sip of well-watered wine. From the other side of the wide table in the shaded gardens on the Palatine, Fabia smiled at her old friend; two of Rome's most striking women comfortable in the knowledge that they would never need to rival each other. The tone of their relationship had been set by the manner in which they had been introduced, a manner which tolerated no shyness or embarrassment on either side. They were of a similar age, when giggling girlhood was long past, but the first true challenges of the passing years still lay in the future. As they studied each other they knew they would never appear more beautiful. Had circumstances been different it might have been Fabia who shared an Emperor's bed and Poppaea who endured any rich man's company, but circumstances were not and neither of them would ever mention it.

'It is such a pleasure to be able to speak freely and enjoy another's companionship just for the sake of it,' Poppaea sighed. 'I think palace servants were born with flapping ears. Even when they are not spies they are gossips for whom no secret is sacred.'

'Even your ladies in waiting?'

'*Particularly* my ladies in waiting.'

'Then your husband will be told of my visit. I hope it won't cause you any difficulty.'

Poppaea laughed at her friend's naivety. 'Has it ever before? The very thought of our friendship has my husband panting like a little bull at the sight of a tethered cow. He understands that he profits in the bedroom from each little secret you impart.' She lowered her voice to a whisper. 'I even give you the credit for some of the more interesting ideas I introduce myself, because it arouses him to imagine us discussing them together and rehearsing them for his pleasure.'

'I thought . . .'

'Because you are no longer summoned to join us?'

Fabia nodded. It had been months now. At first she had been relieved, but relief had turned to concern and then to outright fear. She had known it could not last, but the rewards of the relationship had been beyond her imagination and it could be dangerous to be discarded by the Emperor. And the truth was that Poppaea created physical desires in her that were just as intense as any inspired by a man. She was certain she aroused the same feelings in the dark-haired woman. She studied her now, long slim legs peeping from the crimson shift as she lay languidly on her side, and imagined her naked and wide-eyed on a bed. The thought produced a liquid sensation and she shifted slightly. She saw a look of understanding in Poppaea's eyes, resignation too, for without Nero's sanction there would be no more such encounters. The Emperor's jealousy extended to anyone, male or female, who took their pleasures where he did not and his retribution would be swift and final.

Poppaea's tone changed and she lowered her voice. 'Let this be entirely between us, Fabia. You should regard yourself as fortunate that you do not share his bed. His appetites grow ever more dangerous. Even with your experience and inventiveness I think you would be hard put to it to keep him interested for long. Sometimes, more often than I would like, his passions do not satisfy my needs and I must watch as he plays with his squealing boys and lisping geldings.'

Fabia risked a glance around to ensure no one was within hearing distance. This was dangerous territory. Nero had agents everywhere and she had experience enough of spyholes and listening tubes to know that they were not confined to brothels.

Poppaea saw the look. 'Do not think me such a fool, Fabia. We are so far away that not even the trees can hear us and I have checked every inch of the grass. Unless the dandelions have ears we may say what we like and that man will never get to hear it.'

That man. Poppaea had harboured an almost irrational fear of Torquatus since Octavia, Nero's first wife, had been first banished then killed. The conspiracy had cemented the Praetorian prefect's power on the Palatine. Now he saw Poppaea as his rival for Nero's affections and trust, and any rival of Torquatus must necessarily check beneath the bed for vipers. Outwardly, Poppaea was like any other rich, spoiled Roman matron – only interested in the latest fashions, hairstyles and palace gossip – but as their friendship developed Fabia had seen a different Poppaea, one torn by doubt and capable of clutching at any passing fancy and making it her life's passion. Parthian mystics, astrologers from Aegyptus and a smelly, bearded Gaulish ancient who called himself the last Druid had all found refuge in her household at one time or another.

Experience told Fabia her friend was for ever destined to be disappointed. Her fate would always lie in the hands of her husband.

That night Nero stared from his palace window over the city of a million people he ruled, centre of an Empire of forty million and more. The thought, as always, sent a thrill of panic through his breast and he had to hold on to the balcony. So many people. So much wealth. So much power. All his to command.

So why did they taunt him, all these millions? He could hear them inside his head, a tumult of voices that never left him alone. *Nero does nothing. Nero has achieved nothing. Nero gives us songs but what has he given us to ensure he is remembered? Nero sits in a palace built by other men, looking out on a city built by other men. Caesar, Augustus, Tiberius, Caligula, Claudius. Who is this Nero who dares to stand alongside them and call himself their equal?* They taunted him and he had no answer.

The thought began a chain reaction in his stomach and he vomited over the balcony, a choked, retching spew that dribbled in strands from his mouth. Tears filled his eyes. He knew the taunts meant his mother would visit him tonight and that made the panic return. At first, in the dreams, she had been beautiful, as she had been in life, but lately that had changed. She had begun to disintegrate before his eyes: hair falling in hanks from her skull, parchment skin breaking open to reveal rotting flesh, eye sockets filled with wriggling, milk-white tadpoles. Still, he could have endured it if only the whispers would stop. He had explained why he had to have her killed. It had been his time, not hers. Didn't she understand that he could not live in her shadow? Why not take out her anger on those who had been as complicit as he, or Seneca, who had stood silent as the decision was made? They were to blame, not him.

The moonlight fell on the giant table he had commissioned, the scale model of Rome with the moveable buildings; a single beam of white light fell directly on the Forum. A sign. A sign from his mother? A sign from the gods? He studied the wooden city and decided it was a deceit. This glory of Rome was nothing but a sham. Poverty and filth and degradation hidden beneath a veneer they liked to call civilization. With one hand he swept buildings from the table, sending the wooden blocks clattering across the mosaic floor and leaving a vast empty space in the centre of the city. The breath caught in his throat. It was perfect.

He would build a new Rome.

'Caesar?'

The fury rose in him like a flame. *Not now. Not when I have just begun to understand.* He turned, ready to bring his hand across her face, and was only prevented by the concern in the round, frightened eyes. He touched her silken hair instead, running the strands through his fingers. She stood as tall as he, lithe and slim as a dancer, with the face of an Assyrian queen.

'Poppaea? You startled me.'

'I was concerned for you, lord,' she said with the little girl's pout she knew made him burn. A gossamer robe of the palest blue did nothing to hide her heavy, pink-tipped breasts or the shadowy secret of her sex. He felt his desire stir. So different from Octavia, who did her *duty*. She tried to hide it from him, but he knew Poppaea revelled in what other men would call his depravity, but he was moved to call his *pleasure*. When she offered herself to him the offer was unconditional. Everything she had was his to be taken as and when he desired. He dropped his hand to caress her breast through the thin material and watched the nipple harden, then took the ripening bud between his fingers and squeezed it so she gasped.

'I wanted a boy today, but I could not have him. It vexed me.'

'Then punish him, lord.' Her voice was a husky whisper.

'I cannot punish him.' He slipped his hand to her other breast and felt her breathing quicken. 'For he is a Hero of Rome.'

'You are the only Hero of Rome, lord.' Her body moved against his now, soft and urgent.

'Will you reward your Hero of Rome, Poppaea?' His voice could have belonged to a ten-year-old. He dropped his head to her breast and she gave a low moan.

'Yes, lord.'

'How will you reward him, Poppaea?' The desire was thick enough to clog his throat. 'Will you be his boy?'

She turned away hiding her face and dropping the robe so the silken flesh of her body turned silver in the moon-shadow. Slowly she bent forward over the table so he could take her in the way he chose. 'Yes, lord,' she whispered. 'I will be your boy.'

When he moved over her he wasn't sure whether she cried out in pain or pleasure.

Later, when she was gone but he could still smell the raw scent of her on himself, he stood at the window again.

Was she betraying him?

X

The message contained a time, a place, and a name. Valerius drew breath when he recognized the name. Why should he be surprised? They hadn't set eyes on each other for at least ten years, but this was a man who had spent more than a decade at the very heart of the Empire, close enough to hear every beat.

Should he go? What did he have to gain? Or lose? The meeting place was convenient enough for his purposes, but they had never been friends. Their short relationship had been closer to master and servant. He remembered feeling used at yet another demand to fetch water from the well or recite from memory a complex argument by Apollodorus of Seleucia, or one of a dozen other wordy, overblown Stoic texts. But he had learned. His mind had quickened and his grasp and understanding of the subjects had grown with each passing day he spent in the great man's presence. Great? Seneca hadn't been great then. A few slaves, most of them spying for the Emperor. A trusted servant who no doubt betrayed him to his enemies. His 'villa' had been a run-down Corsican chicken farm and the fine court clothes he affected were worn and patched by the time Valerius had been sent to him. Exile had cracked him like one of the eggs his hens laid among the vines, but it had never broken him. Seneca consoled himself with his studies and his teachings and the letters he wrote to his mother, and ignored the heat and the filth.

Strange that a life devoted to logic and forbearance should have been almost destroyed by such an enormous capacity for human recklessness. The irresponsibility which had brought him into conflict with Caligula was bordering on suicidal. A woman had been the cause of it. That folly might have been forgiven, but to argue semantics with an Emperor who thought himself the new Aristotle was perhaps pushing Stoicism beyond its acceptable limits. Caligula's acerbic dismissal of Seneca's writings as 'lime without sand' had been more painful even than the threat of execution. And how could a man who had fought so hard to resuscitate his career throw everything away for a second time by conducting a flagrant, pointless affair with his new Emperor's niece? Even benign old Claudius couldn't allow that to go unpunished. Seneca had been fortunate to escape with nine years' misery in exile. It had been Agrippina who finally recalled him and saved him from madness, and had entrusted him with her son's education. His genius had made him first indispensable and then a liability. He was finished, but he didn't seem to know it. And that made him doubly dangerous.

Of course, there was another possibility. It could be a trap. Valerius smiled at the thought. Proximity to the Emperor was making him paranoid. The writing was in the same firm, controlled hand he remembered.

But why now? This was no invitation to a pleasant afternoon of philosophical debate and discussion. The whole tenor of the note and the way it had been delivered was designed to intrigue him. It was the bait thrown to a hungry carp in a stew pond. Yet the bait was so blatantly presented that there was no disguising it could also be an invitation to put his neck on the executioner's block.

So he should be suspicious, and he was suspicious, but that didn't mean he wouldn't take the bait.

He went through the arrangements in his mind, aware that the dangers ahead could be as great as anything he had faced in Britain. When he answered Nero's commission he had laid aside the cosy trappings of civilian life to become a soldier again. He just wasn't sure yet what he was fighting for.

Valerius rode out early next day through the valley between the Quirinal and Viminal hills and then up on to the Via Salaria, with the winding course of the Tiber away to his left. In the relative cool of the morning even the streets of the Subura proved

100

bearable and once he was in sight of the massive red brick Praetorian barracks he was able to enjoy the prospect of the open road ahead.

Fidenae lay only six miles beyond the city walls, but his father's estate was tucked in a valley a further three miles to the west of the town, a sprawling untidy mix of vine and olives around a villa that had once been fine but, like the estate, suffered from lack of investment. Still, it would take him only two hours at most and it would be good to see the old man again. Perhaps this time he could persuade him to visit Olivia. The road was one of the oldest in the Empire, the route the Sabines had once used to fetch salt from the Tiber marshes, and later in the day it would be busy with people travelling to and from the city. As he rode past the first of the tombs lining the highway the air grew warmer and he allowed his senses to be lulled by the low buzz of insects, the bittersweet scent of horse sweat and the murmur of the wind in the roadside trees.

It must have been close to the third hour when he reached the gateway to the estate. He experienced a strange sense of wellbeing as he rode beneath the stone arch. This was truly home, though he hadn't called it that for years; the place where he had spent his childhood, carefree and safe among the hills and the streams. Twelve years earlier he'd been sent away to study, first under Seneca and then in Rome. Apart from a single short visit before he joined the Twentieth, and his mother's funeral, he hadn't been back since. He spotted a slave boy in a ragged tunic sprinting through the vines on the ridge above the dirt road and smiled: once *he* would have been on watch up there.

By the time he turned the corner and saw the familiar low outline of the villa, an elderly man with lined, careworn features and straggling grey hair was waiting to welcome him with a jug of water and part of a loaf. Despite his years, the old servant's limpid eyes were still sharp and they lit up when they recognized Valerius.

'Granta,' the young Roman shouted. 'You haven't aged a day.' He slid from the horse and ran to his father's long-suffering freedman, stopping short when he remembered he was no longer a child and couldn't greet him with a hug. They studied each other for a few moments.

'You have grown into a fine young man, master Valerius.' Granta's voice, which could tear a hole in a barn wall if he found a slave shirking, shook with emotion. 'We were so proud when we heard about your great honour.' The old man was smiling, but Valerius noticed the familiar shadow that never seemed to be far away whenever he met an old friend. Britain had marked him as surely as if the Iceni had pressed a slave brand against his skin. He saw Granta eyeing his wooden hand.

'Even better than the old one.' He grinned and pulled back his sleeve to show the carved fist attached to the leather socket that sheathed his arm. 'It can hold a shield or a cup, as long as it's not one of your best, but it can't get up to mischief.' Granta laughed, grateful to have the delicate subject out of the way. Valerius took a drink from the cup and a bite from the bread. 'Is my father home?'

The smile stayed in place, but Granta shifted uneasily. 'He has been out tending the olive trees on the north slope since dawn. I was about to send a slave to him with bread and oil when you arrived.'

'Then I'll take it, and surprise him.' He saw a shadow cross the old man's face and laughed. 'Don't worry, it will be a gentle surprise. I'll make sure he doesn't have a seizure.'

Granta wondered politely whether he wouldn't prefer a bath to wash off the dust, but Valerius insisted and a young slave brought him a leather waterskin and a parcel made up with vine leaves. Before he set off, he removed his sandals to enjoy the warm earth between his toes, but he hadn't gone far before the memory of the big black scorpions he once trapped here made him tread more warily. And, if he was honest with himself, that wasn't the only recollection that invoked a prickle of fear. Life on the estate hadn't always been idyllic. His father had brought him up by an aristocratic code which dictated that any deviation must be punished with the rod. He had sometimes hated the old man for it but, as an adult, he wondered just what it had cost Lucius to make him suffer.

The walk from the villa to the north slope took twenty minutes and he was sweating lightly by the time he reached there. He knew he was getting close when the neat rows of vines were replaced by gnarled olive trees his family had cultivated for generations. The warm, scented air tasted fresh and pure and for the first time he felt able to banish thoughts of Nero's vile kiss. At least here, among the shades of his ancestors, he could feel clean. But he couldn't forget everything. Seneca's estate lay on the other side of this hill and once more he pondered the philosopher's motives. Seneca had always been a leader, not a follower, and had developed his own, flexible theory of self-determination. Virtue might be sufficient for happiness, as he had preached, but survival was another critical factor. How happy could a dead man be? The same logic told Valerius that Seneca had seen a way out of his predicament and the only reason for the meeting was because he, Valerius, had something Seneca needed or wanted.

A flash of blue against the dusty green of the close-ranked trees drew his attention and he smiled. He doubted whether his father had ever worn anything so vivid even in the days when he was close to Emperor Tiberius. Lucius must have brought someone to help him with his inspection. In a way, it was a surprise to find him out here at all. His father had never been a man of the soil. Running the family estate was an obligation, but the task of working it could safely be left to his freedmen and his slaves. Yet here he was, rising at cockcrow and getting his hands dirty.

As he approached, the blue turned out to be turquoise and belonged to a skirt whose owner was part hidden behind a tree. Valerius saw no sign of his father, but he could make out the low drone of a man's voice. The twisted olive trunks and low branches disguised his approach until he was a few paces away. He saw the girl in the instant she saw him. Long black hair, a pair of frightened brown eyes and a sharp gasp as her hand flew to her mouth. She sat at the base of a tree with her legs half tucked beneath her and the skirt draped decorously around. His eyes were drawn to the high breasts that quivered beneath her shift and he smiled to show she had nothing to fear. He turned to face his father.

Lucius stood directly across from the girl. Valerius had intended to surprise the old man, so a little shock might have been expected, but not the anguish that was written plain across his face, nor the ferocity of a man ready to kill to protect whatever terrible secret he'd been discovered in. A pruning knife lay at the old man's feet and Valerius realized he was fortunate it hadn't been in his father's hand.

'Father?' He grinned uncertainly. 'I brought you food.'

After a moment's hesitation the old man's face slowly crumpled and the fire vanished from his eyes. Lucius stumbled forward to take Valerius in his arms, then stepped back to stare in a kind of wonder at the wooden hand.

'I am responsible for that. I sent you there.' Valerius shook his head, but Lucius smiled sadly. 'No, do not deny it, we both know it is true. But I swear here and now that I will repay this debt before the end.'

The girl had taken herself out of earshot and now sat a few yards away, her head bowed and her face concealed behind the dark veil of her hair. She was younger than Valerius had thought, probably no more than seventeen.

'Ruth,' his father called. 'You should go back and help in the kitchen.'

She rose with a dancer's grace, and, still without looking at Valerius, walked off down the slope.

Lucius's eyes followed her swaying back and his face radiated a kind of awkward, bemused contentment. With a shock Valerius understood the reason for his father's reaction. Surely it wasn't possible? He was ancient: in his sixties. The girl could be his daughter. His *granddaughter.* And she was a slave. Lucius, the defender of all things moral, who would have damned another man for even thinking such a thing? Yet what else could explain his earlier defensiveness? And he *had* changed. Already Valerius had seen that Lucius was more at ease with himself than he had ever been.

'She is very pretty,' he said.

'She is just a slave,' Lucius replied in a tone that invited no further conversation.

Valerius leaned back against a tree. If his father wanted to believe no one knew, he was happy to

106

go along with it. But it was just as well he'd found out. Ruth *was* pretty. And desirable in a wholesome, vulnerable way. If he hadn't been aware of his father's feelings he might have invited her into his bed. He pushed the thought aside and returned to the reason for his visit. 'You should see Olivia.'

Lucius frowned. In the past he would have rejected the suggestion outright. Now, Valerius was heartened to see, he was prepared to consider it. But the old man would not give in easily.

'She shamed me,' he grumbled. 'She should have accepted my choice of husband. A woman's duty is to obey her father.'

'You made the wrong choice.' Valerius's words had no force behind them; this was a subject they had argued to the bones.

'Perhaps, but still . . .'

'You are always welcome. She has been asking for you.'

'I will think on it.'

Valerius turned the subject back to the estate and they walked together through the olive trees, commenting on this one or that. Did it need pruning? Was it too old to provide the best quality oil? Lucius complained about dwindling profits, but hinted that a solution was in hand. Twice on the way back to the villa Valerius had the feeling that his father had something important to say to him. Twice the moment passed.

'Will you stay the night?' the old man asked.

'Granta and Cronus would enjoy your company – as I would.'

'I cannot. I have an appointment . . . with Seneca.'

A shadow fell over Lucius's eyes. 'Be very careful, Valerius.'

XI

The villa of Lucius Annaeus Seneca filled the mouth of the valley: a great stucco palace bordering three sides of a landscaped garden that would comfortably have held the tents and horse lines of a legion. And the main part of the complex, the building that faced Valerius as he approached, was as deep as it was wide, extending back to the hills two hundred paces beyond. In the foreground peacocks and tiny antelopes the size of terriers grazed the irrigated lawns and nipped the heads from flowers beginning to wilt in the heat.

His host waited for him in the shade of the colonnaded portico. Seneca looked relaxed, overweight and successful, his fingers weighed down by gold rings and his puffy, heavily jowled face saved from being ugly by a strong nose and shining grey eyes that radiated benevolent intelligence. The only sign of anxiety was in the hand he ran across the mottled skin of his bald head as he beamed a welcome.

'Valerius, my boy, it has been much too long. Let me see you now. By the gods, you have become a man, and what a man. Those shoulders, that chest. You exercise every day? Of course you do. And the hand?' Valerius lifted the walnut fist so Seneca could see it clearly. 'A masterpiece. You have been through the fire, and it is the fire that makes us who we are.' Valerius had witnessed a law court hushed by the sound of Seneca's voice addressing a crowd from the rostra sixty paces away, but in conversation the philosopher was softly spoken, almost mellow in tone.

'I'm glad to see you well, master Seneca.'

Seneca laughed, but for the first time Valerius detected a hint of bitterness. 'I am no longer your master, Valerius. I am no man's master, perhaps not even my own.' He brightened again. 'You have been to visit your father? Of course. A son's first duty is to his family and you were always a dutiful son.'

Valerius felt as if he was swimming against a tidal wave of flattery and fought back with a little of his own. 'You have a fine house, sir, and a wonderful estate.'

'And I am forgetting my manners. Please come inside.' Seneca led him through a large vestibule and across a broad inner courtyard, striding out like a man ten years younger and talking as he went. '*They* say I am too rich.' He didn't identify who *they* were, but Valerius knew Torquatus would be among them. '*They* say I could not afford this if I had not been stealing from the Emperor's purse. What do *they*

110

know of Lucius Annaeus Seneca? For the first time in Rome's history is a man to be condemned for being successful? I have lived each minute of my life in the pursuit of profit or contentment, and sometimes the two are not exclusive, though both, I grant you, can be difficult to come by.'

They reached a room with large windows and walls painted in imitation of the gardens outside. Seneca lay on one couch and Valerius sat opposite him. The philosopher studied him seriously.

'There is a sickness in the air, a political sickness that could very well be fatal. I do not intend you to catch it, Valerius, though you may feel I have exposed you to its vapours by bringing you here. In this room we may speak freely; the acoustics are poor and, as you see, the nearest doorway far enough away to keep the slaves honest. You have been clever, as I intended you to be. A young man visits his father's estate and makes a neighbourly call upon his former tutor. Is it not natural? Your presence will be reported, certainly – they have six spies in my household that I know of and who knows how many that I do not – but I doubt it will arouse suspicions, and if it does, I believe you are agile enough to allay them.'

Valerius found himself caught between admiration of Seneca's cunning in trapping him in the quicksand of whatever plot he was hatching, and alarm at the knowledge that he was already up to his neck and sinking fast. Clearly, if he refused the proposition about to be made it would take only a single word in the right ear to condemn him. Yet he had always known it would be this way. Implicit in his decision to come was trust in the philosopher's judgement and faith in his integrity. He would give Seneca the truth.

'The Emperor has charged me with investigating a group of Judaean agitators he believes are plotting against Rome who he fears have infiltrated the highest levels of government.'

Seneca nodded gravely. 'I am aware of your assignment. Indeed, it was I who instigated it.' He saw Valerius's confusion. 'Oh yes, Valerius, I am not yet without influence. Torquatus thinks the suggestion was his, but it was I who sowed the seed. It has placed you in a position to do both your Emperor and your friends a great service.'

For a moment the words lay between them like pieces on a gaming board, but Valerius was still reluctant to make the decisive move. 'I don't understand. Why me?' The question echoed the one he had asked Torquatus a day earlier. To his surprise, so did the answer.

His host gave a sigh that would have been more at home on a stage. 'I could tell you that you are brave, that you are wise and that you have a mind that is never satisfied with the first solution it finds, and all that would be true. But the real answer is simpler: I trust you.' Seneca rose and his voice changed as he began to pace the room. Now again Valerius saw Lucius Annaeus Seneca, the statesman. 'Do you love Rome, Valerius? More important, do you *believe* in

Rome? Of course you do. The blood of men who lived and died for Rome runs in your veins. You are the son of a man who once risked everything for Rome.' Valerius struggled to justify this vision of his father, but Seneca was no longer speaking to him, he was speaking to the Empire. 'Rome is an invalid tottering on the brink of the abyss, and evil men are gathering to push her over the edge into chaos, depravity and, ultimately, a carnage that will consume her. Rome's Emperor is not strong enough to stand in their way. He must have help. Nero cannot rule alone, Valerius; he is no Caesar or Augustus. He was fated to rule, but he needs a guiding hand; a firm, honest hand to steer him in the direction that is best for his people. Without that hand he will always be the servant of his urges and the servant of those who provide the means to satisfy those urges. He will shift with each changing wind and with each shift he will become less of an Emperor. With every passing hour it becomes more difficult to return him to the true path and the path that could lead him to true greatness. The followers of Christus are a danger to Rome, but Torquatus and the band of degenerates he cultivates are a greater danger still. As long as I breathe I will never plot against the Emperor, but I *will* fight to return to his side, and you, Valerius, can place me there. I will help you find the man known as the Rock of Christus and you will deliver him to me and help me discredit Torquatus and his gang. Together, Valerius, we will save Rome.'

Valerius stared at him. He knew the speech was

calculated to appeal to Gaius Valerius Verrens, tribune of the Twentieth: a call to arms designed to stir a soldier's blood on the eve of battle. He wasn't blind. He saw through Seneca the statesman to Seneca the actor. But somehow that didn't matter. His blood *was* stirred and he *was* ready for battle. Now, at least, he knew what he was fighting for.

He didn't need to speak. Seneca saw the impact of his words. He nodded. 'In every life there comes a moment to choose, Valerius. You will never regret the choice you have just made.'

'Tell me about Christus's Rock.'

Seneca made him wait. He called for servants to bring food and it was only after they had completed their meal that they resumed their discussion.

'It is impossible to tell the story of the Rock without telling the story of Christus. When did it begin? Was it the moment he was born, or the moment he died, or somewhere in between? You will hear that Christus was a mystic, an insurrectionist, a teacher or a criminal, but I think the truth is that he was a mixture of them all. He came, without education or wealth, from an obscure Galilean village, but within two years he had gathered men who had both to his side. Oh, they will tell you that he had made a vow of poverty, but no man could have achieved what Christus did without substantial resources. How else could he have retained what became a small army of followers? He claimed he was the son of God and to each man he gave a reason to believe.

114

He is said to have carried out miracles, all of which can be disputed, but none of which can be entirely disproved. So why did they follow him? Why did they believe him? Because he offered them the chance to live for ever. Eternal life was in his gift and that of his father.' Seneca shook his head at the absurdity of it. 'The Judaeans hated and feared him because he cast doubt upon their own religion. Eventually they persuaded the governor that he was as much a danger to Rome as he was to Jerusalem and Pilatus ordered him crucified. Pilatus was foolish. Left alive, Christus would have become a figure of ridicule, a simpleton who promised everything but delivered nothing.'

Valerius nodded, but one question intrigued him. 'And how was a person to be guaranteed eternal life?'

Seneca smiled. 'That was the genius of Christus. First, a man had to earn the right to immortality by his deeds during his own life, deeds determined by the teachings of Christus. Second, he would come to eternal life only after he died. You see the wonderful paradox? One had to die to live for ever, and only after death would one know one had achieved it.'

'And this Rock is a believer in such foolishness?'

'The Rock, Simon Petrus, was the first of Christus's followers, another Galilean, though Torquatus chooses to band him with Rome's Judaeans; a simple fisherman hypnotized by the words of a cleverer man. He followed him to Jerusalem, saw him die there and' – Seneca snorted his disbelief – 'claims he saw him rise again.'

Valerius wasn't so certain. 'It's not impossible,' he

pointed out. 'I've seen men lying on the battlefield who looked as if they were dead and thought they were dead, who rose up to have supper with their comrades. Most of them died later from their wounds, but still, a man can be difficult to kill. Simon Petrus?'

'Simon is his given name. Petrus, the Rock, is the title Christus awarded him for his loyalty. Many lost their enthusiasm for the teachings of Christus after he was tried and crucified, but Petrus continues to spread his message. When the authorities in Jerusalem made life difficult for him he moved on to Antioch, and now to Rome, where he calls himself bishop, but wields no power and has little influence except among his closest followers.'

'Then why is he so dangerous?'

'Because he is a master of deception and because of the message he preaches, which denies the authority of the Emperor. Because those he now targets are Roman citizens with the power to influence other Roman citizens, even those in the Senate. Petrus is a dangerous man who gathers other dangerous men to him. If Petrus has his way the only god in Rome will be the God of Christus. He would wipe away the very foundations of our society. I am not a religious man, Valerius, but I fear this Petrus.'

Valerius studied the figure across from him. Why did he feel this prickle of unease? 'So Petrus is the most dangerous man in Rome. A shadow who has denied the Praetorians for months, it seems. Yet Lucius Annaeus Seneca, confined to his humble home in the hills, appears to know everything about him. You have his name. Perhaps you can tell me where he lives and who he meets, or even give me his description?'

Seneca's ringed fingers stroked his head. 'You are suspicious, and so you should be. We are swimming in dangerous waters, you and I, and it is right that we should understand each other fully. It is well known that I have maintained contacts in the east since my days in Aegyptus. While I had Nero's confidence I wielded a power you would not imagine, and that power allowed me to expand those contacts still further. You will admit I am a man of some little talent?' The false modesty made Valerius laugh, as it was intended to. 'Then put your trust in me, Valerius, as I put my trust in you.

'Petrus is in his sixty-third year, of medium height with the strong features typical of the easterner. He wears a full beard, not to mask them, but because it is his custom. He walks with a slight limp, and he has a reputation as a healer. You will know him when you look into his eyes.' He raised a hand. 'No, I can explain no further. You will understand when the time comes.'

Valerius somehow kept his face emotionless. 'If I have news, how can I get word to you?'

'I will have a man watch your house. Place a lamp in the window above your door at dusk. That will be a signal for a meeting at noon the following day at the north corner of the Castra Peregrina.'

Now it was Valerius's turn to frown.

'Where better for two conspirators to meet than on the doorstep of a nest of spies?' Seneca chuckled at his own genius. The Castra Peregrina, as its name implied, was the base for foreign soldiers posted to duties in Rome, but also the headquarters of the Emperor's *frumentarii*, messengers who often acted as the Emperor's spies, occasionally as his assassins. Seneca saw that Valerius wasn't convinced. 'If you wish we can appoint another meeting place?'

Valerius shook his head. 'No. One place is as good as another and the busier the better.'

'The Emperor will demand a swift resolution, but despite what I have told you Petrus will not be an easy man to find,' Seneca warned. 'In six months Torquatus and Rodan have not even come close. Your investigation must be taken one step at a time. This will be your first step.' He gave Valerius a name which surprised him. 'You will wish to begin as soon as possible.'

Valerius knew when he was being dismissed. He had a dozen questions he would have liked to ask, but he doubted Seneca would answer any of them. They embraced as if they were father and son and as Valerius rode off towards the Via Salaria he pondered the astonishing name Seneca had given him.

And the biggest surprise of all: the description of Christus's Rock, the man called Petrus, who sounded exactly like Joshua, the doctor in whom he had placed his faith.

*　　　*　　　*

Seneca was still standing in the doorway when Valerius passed out of sight.

'Do you think he suspects?' The quiet voice came from the shadow behind him.

'No. He is an honest, straightforward young man. He will complete his task or die in the attempt.'

'Then may he live long enough to complete it.'

Seneca turned to face the man who could have been a younger version of Petrus. 'You realize what this could cost? Nero will have no mercy.'

'We must all make sacrifices. Those who die will have died for Our Lord. Petrus is a good man but he is too soft to lead us to the Promised Land.'

'And he favours a different path?'

'Just so.'

'You are a hard man.'

'Just so,' Saul of Tarsus said again.

XII

Poppaea fought the familiar animal squirm of panic. Everywhere she went she felt Nero's eyes on her. But he couldn't know, because if he truly knew she would be dead. Or worse. Yet even that was of no consequence, because soon she would be free and nothing they could do to her would matter. Just one more step. One more simple act, and it was done.

Loneliness and fear had been her lot ever since her father had married her off at the age of seventeen. She had been young and naive, a pretty plaything who knew nothing of the natural bounds of marriage or the power a wife might hold if she only understood her strength. Instead, she had submitted because her husband said she should, even when she knew it was wrong. Each night she would endure the pain and self-loathing that went hand in hand with the acts she was forced to perform for him. Each night she would cry herself to sleep. That should have been enough, even for him, but of course it was not. She thought she had married a strong man, but events had proved that what she had taken for strength was mere bravado, and what she had thought was courage only a disguise for bluster. A coward and a braggart who had bragged once too often.

What a fool she had been the night they were invited to the palace. She had been excited, proud that the man who ruled their Empire should seek the company of her husband, even a husband she had grown to hate. That was the first night she'd felt the little eyes roving over her skin, and later the hands, cold and clammy, the way a snake should feel, but does not, slithering across her breasts and her belly and . . . And later? Later he had watched again, those same eyes glittering as her husband used her. Yes, used. Not slept with, or made love to. Used. And when her husband was finished with her, he was ready. She knew that to refuse him was death, but she almost did. Almost. When that barrier was broken the rest was just more of the same. The servants and the slaves and the soldiers who shared the wide bed. And Otho, her husband, had *rejoiced* because he had the Emperor's favour and the Emperor's favour meant power and riches. And, though he was too foolish to understand it, danger.

Three months later, Torquatus had sent for Otho and ordered him to divorce her. She remembered the day he returned from the palace, his face the colour of dead flesh, hands shaking and eyes glazed with terror.

Not out of concern for her. Not because he was going to lose her. But because he feared for his position and his life. She had despised him then and she despised him now, cowering in his Lusitanian exile praying for a speedy return to the inner circle, which would never be forthcoming as long as she had influence. She had been glad to be rid of him. Oh, what a fool she was.

Now she lived behind a mask, as much an actor as the man whose bed she shared. A better actor, she hoped, because her life depended upon it. She gave him everything he wanted, because it meant nothing to her now, these physical acrobatics and pointless, almost laughable penetrations, but it was never enough. It had been her initiative to introduce Fabia, though Fabia wasn't aware of it. Fabia who had taught her to live with Otho's demands, and eventually how to satisfy them. With Fabia, she could find comfort as well as pleasure, a hand to hold when it all became too much and a shoulder to cry on when it was over. Yet even to Fabia she could not speak of the true depths of her despair.

It had been a mistake to make an enemy of Torquatus. She had underestimated his ability to slither, serpent-like, through the long grass of palace politics. He had supported Octavia against her while Nero's first wife still retained some of her power and it had only seemed right that she should undermine him. A few quiet words in the sultry aftermath of passion should have been enough. A suggestion of eyes lingering too long, perhaps a touch that could not be disproved, and she believed he would be gone. But that was not Nero's way. Her husband's greatest pleasure was to pitch those around him against each other in a never-ending dogfight that ensured the master was always in control. Now, with Octavia dead, Torquatus had made it his goal to either remove Poppaea or possess her. She didn't know which she feared most.

She had sacrificed to the gods for her salvation, and when it became clear they had failed her she had considered – planned – her own death. Cornelius, who had been as much a prisoner as she, had shown her the path she must take. Why had she confided in Cornelius? Not because of the puppy eyes or the pretty smiles and prettier compliments. No, there had to be something more. She had recognized it on the night Nero's degeneracy had reached its shameful low and he had placed her at the disposal of a pair of enormous Nubians for the entertainment of the narrow-eyed perverts who clung to him like leeches on a swollen leg. The memory of it made her gorge rise, but it had been then that she had seen the pain in Cornelius Sulla's eyes and behind it discovered the tenderness and compassion of a *good* man. Here, at her lowest, most degraded point, she had found the only person on the Palatine she could trust.

Cornelius had opened her eyes to a world beyond her own world and a god who would not forsake her. It had been he who engineered her meeting with the Judaean who had spoken to her of Christus, the Messiah who had sacrificed himself for the good of all mankind, and of the god, the true god, who would protect her and keep her safe even as her body was being abused and her mind driven to the edge of madness. Despite her initial doubts about a religion which at first seemed exotic, if not outlandish, she had found herself persuaded by the old man's luminous integrity. She had feigned illness to create a pretext for the meeting, convincing her ladies that if the Emperor discovered the true reason for her visit to the Greek physician, his reaction might endanger them all. Once inside the treatment room, the Greek had been replaced by the man Petrus. She had listened and she had believed. The truth was that she *needed* to believe. He had placed his hand upon her and she had felt energized in a way that astonished her. She had *seen* the light. She *understood* the truth. Now she had only one more step before she would be welcomed into God's company. But how would it be achieved?

Petrus had said he would make the arrangements and she had placed her faith in him. That had been weeks ago. Lately, she had sensed that the surveillance within the palace had become more intensive. Was it her imagination, or were the slaves hovering a little more closely and her ladies more attentive? Cornelius would barely meet her eyes, and when he did she had seen the fear and the puzzlement in his. Her saviour was as trapped as she was.

A tear ran down her cheek as her eyes lighted on the painting that covered the wall of her room. It was her escape from everything that happened here in this palace that had become her prison. A country scene, a sunlit villa on a hill overlooking the sea. Her villa. The villa where she had grown up. The place where she had last been happy. She closed her eyes and she was back in the long pool in front of the house with the sound of the waterfall soft and comforting in her ears. But she couldn't stay there for ever, not now. She must plan and scheme as if her life depended upon it, because it did.

The shop was deserted, the wares removed. The only thing that remained was the tantalizing, sweetly pungent scent of spice. Valerius stood in the doorway and pondered his next move. What else had he expected? The man had survived as a fugitive for thirty years; of course he must have developed a sense for the changing patterns around him.

'Want us to talk to the neighbours?' Marcus asked.

Valerius nodded. 'It's probably a waste of time, but it can't do any harm.'

Marcus called Serpentius and the other men he had hired. At first Valerius couldn't believe the former gladiator had engaged the man who had made such a determined effort to kill him. But Marcus made a convincing argument. 'He's the best fighter I've got, you saw yourself how fast he is, but he's too good a hater to be a successful gladiator. He was going to get himself killed. Now you've saved his life. It won't make him hate you any the less, but he owes you and

Spaniards pay their debts.' Three more of the scarred veteran's pupils completed the group. Heracles, an ox-like Sarmatian with the face of a twelve-year-old child, who Marcus insisted was cleverer than he looked and whose additional talents included the ability to crush a man's skull with one giant paw; Felix, the Brindisian, a habitual thief whose skills would no doubt be useful; and little Sextus, who could be trusted to wait, watch and keep his mouth shut.

Marcus studied the crumbling plaster beside the door. 'What do you make of that?'

It was similar to *graffito* you could find on any Roman street corner, but the crude carving resembled a slim bag closed at the neck. The bag lay horizontally with the letters MCVII beneath it. The design had been recently cut, which might make it significant.

'Some kind of sign, but it could mean anything. The number might be eleven hundred and seven, or MC might be a street in the seventh district.' Valerius looked at the carving again and something stirred in his memory. Seneca had said Petrus had been a fisherman. 'Could it be a fish?'

'Funny-looking kind of fish, but maybe they're different where he comes from.'

'I think it's a message from Petrus to his followers. Leave Serpentius here and tell him to watch for anyone who comes along to take a look, then follow them.'

Marcus nodded. 'And us?'

'Lucina Graecina.'

The gladiator looked as if he'd just bitten into a lemon. 'Is that who I think it is?'

'That's right.'

'I knew this was going to be trouble.'

Lucina Graecina: Rome's empress without a throne. The woman rumoured to have been Claudius's lover before he had been seduced by Agrippina. The woman who despised Nero more than anyone in the Empire.

'Is it true Nero only keeps her alive because he's worried she'll be waiting for him on the other side?'

Valerius nodded. 'That and the fact that her husband is the man who conquered Britain. Aulus Plautius and Lucina have ample reason to hate Nero. Lucina blames the Emperor for killing their son.'

Lucina seldom showed her face in the city, preferring to travel in a closed litter carried by six British slaves. The original bearers had been members of King Caratacus's personal bodyguard captured by her husband in the great battle which had won Britain for Rome twenty years earlier. Lucina was said to have worked them to death in three years. Since then she'd replaced them several times, always from the same tribe, the warlike Catuvellauni. Naturally, Rome being Rome, the gossips whispered that it wasn't only carrying her that had worn the muscular Britons out.

Valerius had seen her only once, when she had been forced from the litter at a Praetorian checkpoint. He remembered a narrow, glaring face masked by the white powder of mourning; a tall, bony woman of late middle age with a back as straight as a cavalry spear. They couldn't have been more different in appearance, but her bearing had reminded him of the Iceni queen, Boudicca. He told Marcus: 'I want a watch on her house day and night and a report of all her movements.'

For the next two days Valerius barely left Olivia's side, listening to the sound of her shallow breathing as she fought whatever demons were consuming her from within. Since Lucius had abdicated responsibility for her, it had fallen to Valerius to take over his sister's guardianship. In theory, according to the Twelve Tables, the rules that were the very foundation of Roman law, he had the power of life and death over her, even though she was a respectable widow who had run a married household for five years. The thought made him shake his head. If he truly had power he would use it to save her from this insidious living death: which brought him to his dilemma.

Whether as Petrus, the Rock, or Joshua, the physician, the Judaean's skills were Olivia's best, perhaps only, chance of salvation. Yet Valerius was under orders from Nero to deliver him for torture and execution, and under obligation to Seneca to do the same. When he found him he would have a decision to make. But first he had to find him. What made a man like the Judaean leave everyone dear to him to follow a charlatan like this Christus? He remembered the intelligent eyes and the ageless, worn-out smile; taut self-control and a well of inborn compassion. A *good* man, by anyone's definition of good. No hint of insanity or covetousness or ambition. Valerius had heard of men who could control the minds of other men through drugs or by weakening them with deprivation. Could that be Christus's magic? Yet the mystic had died thirty years ago on a cross; how did it explain Petrus's continuing to risk his life to spread the man's words? It seemed absurd. And yet Petrus had believed. Valerius shivered. The room seemed to have gone cold. If a man like Petrus could be convinced, then perhaps dead Christus and the men who followed him truly *were* the great danger Nero imagined.

XIII

It would be the glory of Rome. Nero stood over the table and the familiar seven-hilled landscape filled with intricately carved wooden houses and temples. Today there was a difference. In the area between the Palatine and Esquiline hills now stood a structure so magnificent it gave him a feeling of almost sexual pleasure. A single, monumental building on a scale with the hills that flanked it, which dwarfed every other surrounding construction. Three hundred rooms, miles of lakes and parklands. He would fill it with the wonders of the world and cover it with gold and men would come to marvel at it from the ends of the earth. Aegyptus, Babylon, Troy and Sumeria had nothing to compare with it. This would be his legacy. This would be his triumph. His and his alone. Within it would be a great artistic and cultural centre where he would entertain and mesmerize those worthy of his talent. Music would soothe the blood of his enemies.

Fine words would seduce those who opposed him. In this house there would only be harmony.

Of course, he thought, remembering the hundreds, perhaps thousands of wooden dwellings scattered across the mosaic floor, there would be obstacles. But a good workman could clear away any obstacle if he had the tools. He would allow nothing to obstruct his dream. They would thank him in the end, all those small people who would have to make way for it; the people who lived in the cramped dunghills beneath the terracotta tiles amid the oppressive, swirling miasma of corruption. Seneca had taken him there once, disguised in the clothing of the common man, to let him see his people. People? Animals fighting and rutting and squatting in the mud and the straw and the filth. The stink had almost made him faint. He had as little in common with his *people* as he had with cows in a field or the monkeys in the Palatine menagerie. Let ugliness make way for beauty, ordinariness for elegance, mediocrity for magnificence. He ran the last thought over his tongue, testing it for quality and rhythm. Yes, with a little polishing he could include it in a song or a poem.

He picked up his harp and strummed through the scales, smiling as the hundreds of songbirds in the cages by the window reacted to his notes. Here at least he could always find an audience who truly appreciated his music. The cage was not their natural element, just as the barless cage of duty he inhabited was not his. Sometimes he longed to fly free and when that melancholy took hold he would open the cages and watch the birds stand nervously on the threshold before taking to the skies; trilling blackbirds and song thrushes, pink-cheeked goldfinches and drab, honey-voiced skylarks, the robins and wrens and redstarts. Sometimes they would die in their cages and he would mourn them.

Lately, he had been pondering his own mortality. Torquatus had tried to explain to him the tenets of the Christus religion, but he did not fully understand it. In fact, he was fairly certain Torquatus didn't understand it either. He frowned. This was when he needed Seneca's genius. Seneca could take a subject and peel back the layers until a child could understand its meaning. But Seneca was old and defeated and had taken to disagreeing with him at the end. He could not even outwit a man as dull as Torquatus, so how could he guide his Emperor? As he saw it, in simple terms, a man could achieve immortality only after submitting to the indignity and inconvenience of death. To do so, he needed to have believed, in life, that Christus truly was the son of the Judaean god Yahweh. But, and this was what made it all seem so unlikely, how could someone of even average intelligence be convinced of the authenticity of a man who had been dead for almost three decades? He had considered having the body of the Galilean exhumed. Surely it would show some signs of his god-like capacity; a lack of mortification of the flesh or an ability to speak from beyond the grave? He fully expected to become a god himself.

After all, if old Claudius could be declared divine, surely he, of all his line, could take his place beside Augustus and Caligula. But *he* had the blood of gods running through his veins. To believe some foreigner born by a muddy puddle in the desert could stand at his side was an insult. It was like suggesting a beggar from the slums should have a temple dedicated in his honour. The Judaeans believed in the same god, and he was one of the reasons they despised this Christus, but they accepted the authority of the Emperor, which was why, for the moment, he tolerated their barbarities. Surely the more gods a man worshipped the better? Jupiter, Mars, Mercury and Minerva had all come to Rome's aid in times of drought and famine and war. What could a single god do that many could not do better? If one god failed a man he was within his rights to sacrifice to another and another, until he found the god who could help him.

The more he turned it over in his mind, the more unlikely the Christus claims appeared. Still, he would put the man's followers to the question. If they had stayed and worshipped their God and their son of God in some desert cave he would have ignored them, but they had not. They had come to his city, Rome, the heart of his Empire, and they had refused to acknowledge his authority. Worse, they had attempted to weaken Rome from within, suborning its citizens even at the highest level. He would test their faith upon the rack and the roasting plate and through glowing iron and blazing fire until they cried

133

out their falsehood or revealed the true secret of their immortality. Unless the handsome hero failed him.

He remembered the kiss and Valerius shrinking from the touch of his lips and remembered another succulent mouth that had done the same. He had found that a reluctant boy could be moulded into a lover through a combination of pain and affection. Remove the reason for reluctance and he became pliable and cooperative, especially if he knew that the next step was to remove his head. Sporus had been like that, uncooperative until he'd been visited by the gelding knife, when he'd quite entered into the spirit of it all. Nero had been much younger then and it had seemed such fun to set up house, but the old men had spoiled it all with their righteous outrage, tattling to his mother when they were all just jealous. In the end Sporus had become tiresome, nagging him almost as badly as Octavia, so he'd had to go.

If the hero failed, he would have Valerius, willing or not.

XIV

Valerius couldn't disguise his frustration. An entire week and the watch on Lucina Graecina has produced no new information.

'There's nothing we can do about it,' he admitted to Marcus as they discussed their plans in the house on the Clivus Scauri. 'We have to be patient.'

The former gladiator pursed his lips. Patience didn't come easily to him. 'I've sent Serpentius and Felix out into the streets beyond Subura to try to get a feel for the way the wind's blowing. If you're right, these people are fanatics, and fanatics find it even more difficult to sit still and wait than we do. Your man Petrus might be lying low, but I'm betting that one of his friends just can't wait to stand up on a street corner and let everybody know why he's in Rome.'

Valerius was impressed and said so. 'But why beyond the Subura? Why not around the Porta Capena where most of the Judaeans live?'

Marcus frowned and tried to articulate what had been an entirely instinctive decision. 'Because the followers of Christus are more likely to be known among the Judaeans, their own people, than they are among Romans. They dare not live among their countrymen for fear of betrayal. More sensible to stay in family groups in the main population. And beyond the Subura because I think your physician won't have moved far. In the shadow of the Praetorian barracks will be as good a place to look as any.'

'Serpentius will like that.'

'I've told him to stay out of trouble, and he knows he'll go straight back to the arena if he doesn't. I doubt it will do any good, but it increases our chances from nought to a little more than nought.'

Valerius smiled and raised his wooden hand. 'I've faced chances like that before, my friend, and I'm still mostly here, so I'll accept the odds.'

Marcus grinned back, the deep shadows of his scars creating unearthly patterns on his skin. 'A jar of wine on it then.'

They were interrupted by a shout from the door. Marcus stood and his hand strayed to his sword, but Valerius waved him down. A slave entered and announced that the 'old master' had arrived.

'I'll check with Serpentius and report back.' The gladiator made his exit towards the kitchens, but Valerius was already on his way to greet his father in the vestibule.

'It is too long since you graced this house, sir.'

Valerius bowed. 'Come through to the atrium and I will have Julia bring us some wine.'

His father gave an embarrassed smile. 'I am afraid I cannot stay long. I am in the city on business and I have a meeting at the seventh hour. I . . . I would like, if you permit it, to visit Olivia.'

Valerius didn't attempt to hide his pleasure. 'Of course, please come. You remember the way to her room?'

Olivia was as he'd left her. She'd hardly moved for a week. Valerius felt the pleasure at his father's visit wash away to be replaced by a new hopelessness. If he couldn't find Petrus, she would die. If he did find him, the Judaean's fate would be inevitable and terrible. He looked up to find his father watching him from the other side of the bed.

'Her illness is taking its toll on you also, I see,' the old man said. 'I am sorry. I should have offered my support much earlier. You are doing everything you can?'

'Everything.'

'Then all I can do is pray for her.' The grey head bent over the dark hair and Lucius kissed his daughter tenderly on the forehead. His father's unconscious affection made Valerius feel as if a fist had gripped his heart. For a moment all he wanted to do was carry them off, far away from the political cesspit Rome had become. He reached out for the old man's shoulder, but withdrew his hand at the last moment. Lucius straightened. 'I must go now.'

'Do not stay away so long again.'

The old man gave a bittersweet smile. 'If the Fates allow it.'

Valerius had barely seen his father to the street when Marcus, red-faced and breathing hard, rushed in through the kitchens. 'You have to see this,' he gasped.

They walked briskly through the streets and Marcus explained that he'd intercepted a message from Serpentius ten minutes after he'd left the house. He indicated a thin, ragged child jogging at their side. Valerius tossed the boy a silver coin, which the urchin caught skilfully. His face broke into an enormous grin when he realized what he had.

'It was your fish,' Marcus continued. 'Serpentius has good eyes. He noticed another that had been freshly scraped on a brick where the Vicus Patricius meets the Via Subura. At the bottom of the Viminal Hill? It had the number seven scratched beneath it and he guessed it must mean the seventh hour. He took a chance on this being the day and it paid off. He's there now.'

Valerius felt his heart quicken. 'Petrus?'

'No, a young man, not a lot older than the messenger. Hopefully, we'll get to him before the Praetorians do.'

By the time they reached the road junction a crowd had gathered where an orator shouted to be heard above the clamour of insults and jeers. Marcus had been right: he was little more than a boy, perhaps seventeen, with arms and legs too long for his body and dark hair slicked greasily against his forehead and flecked with eggshell. His accent marked him as Judaean and provoked sneers from his audience, but he spoke with a calm determination that belied his age.

'He's a tough little runt,' Serpentius said admiringly as he sidled up beside them. 'They've been throwing rotting fruit and old eggs at him for twenty minutes. It'll be rocks soon.'

Even as he spoke, the boy staggered and a line of blood ran down his cheek where he had been struck.

'Bastards,' the Spaniard muttered, but the boy's eyes lit up as if he had just been offered a gift.

'Jesus said: "Let him who is without sin among you cast the first stone" and no man among them would throw. I am not Jesus, but I repeat his words: Let him who is without sin among you cast the first stone.'

'Have one of these then,' called a rough voice from the far side of the crowd. A stone the size of a hen's egg smashed the boy in the mouth, drawing more blood and making it difficult for him to speak.

'Jesus came to offer you everlasting life.' The words were thick with pain and as mangled as his lips. 'He died for you. Will you not live for him?'

'Jesus?' Valerius looked to Serpentius.

'Must be his pet name for this Christus.'

'If he died for me why haven't I had anything from his will?' The voice of the rock thrower was accompanied by cackling laughter from his friends.

'He—'

'The Guard!' A cry from the direction of the Vicus Patricius interrupted the speaker. The street led directly towards the Castra Praetoria and the Praetorians were never gentle when breaking up an illegal gathering. The crowd quickly dispersed into the surrounding streets. Valerius saw the bleeding boy dart up a nearby alleyway and ran after him. After a few minutes his quarry slowed to a walk and Valerius took step beside him.

'You spoke well,' he said.

The boy looked up suspiciously, the blood still dripping from his mouth. 'You are following me. I saw you with the watcher at the back of the crowd.'

'Yes,' Valerius admitted. 'But I mean you no harm. I am not like them.'

The young Judaean managed a semblance of a smile. 'Do not judge them too harshly. They know not what they do.'

'You would forgive those who hurt you?'

The boy looked surprised. 'Of course. It is our Lord's teaching.'

Valerius took him by the shoulder. 'I am looking for a man called Petrus. He is known as the Rock of Christus. Do you know where I can find him?'

The boy glanced down at the wooden hand resting on his arm. 'If you seek the Rock of Christus for the right reasons, you do not have to look for him; he will find you.' With a twist of his body he wriggled from Valerius's grasp and ran off down the alley.

Valerius saw Serpentius slip after him and merge

into the crowd. He turned to look for Marcus and found himself staring into the eyes of Ruth, his father's slave girl. She quickly averted her gaze and walked in the opposite direction. But not before he recognized a look of pure hatred.

XV

'It has happened again!' Valerius turned, ready to defend himself, but it was only old Honorius, the water commissioner, bearing down on him from the direction of the Circus Maximus, rheumy eyes bulging in a face the colour of a ripe plum. 'It can't go on!'

'No,' Valerius said reassuringly, not quite certain what couldn't go on.

'Thousands of gallons a day from the water castle up on the Cespian Height. A veritable river siphoned off somewhere between there and the Subura. Stolen from the state. Larceny on a grand scale. It must be stopped.'

'It will be.'

Honorius glared at him. 'But when? When will you prosecute our case?'

'I need a little more time.' He lowered his voice. 'Imperial business.'

Honorius's outraged expression softened. 'Ah,' he said knowingly. 'State business.'

'Two weeks? Perhaps a month?'

The water commissioner sniffed. 'Two weeks then.'

Valerius watched him go. The man was like a hunting dog; he would never lose the scent. All he thought about were his aqueducts and his pipes, his water castles and his springs. But without the aqueducts and men like Honorius to ensure they were maintained Rome would be a desert, and a stinking one at that. Not only did water from the Aqua Claudia and the New Anio and their like slake the thirst of a million people through private supplies and public fountains, it also served to flush out the sewers into the Tiber, taking the threat of disease and plague with it. During the preparations for the case, Honorius had hammered into him the history of Rome's waters. How the city had been supplied by the Tiber and local springs until three hundred and fifty years earlier, when the censor Appius Claudius Crassus had brought to Rome the waters of a spring on the Lucullan estate eight miles outside the city. Aqua Appia was the first of the nine, and was followed forty years later by Old Anio, which took its supply from above the falls of Tivoli. Then, more than a century later, came Aqua Marcia, the first to be carried above ground and her waters travelling an astonishing fifty-four miles to reach Rome; Emperor Augustus had given Rome the Julia, the Tepula, the Virgo and the Augusta, used mainly for irrigation; Gaius Caligula had begun the Claudia, which was completed by the uncle whose name it bore, and Claudius had also ordered the construction of the New Anio, the most modern and technically advanced. If the water castle the commissioner spoke of was on the Cespian Height between the Viminal and Esquiline hills, it must be on a spur of Old Anio which entered the city close to the Porta Viminalis.

But Valerius had more pressing concerns. He was certain he was being followed.

During Suetonius's campaign of retribution in the wake of Boudicca's rebellion, Valerius had lived with the constant threat of ambush from defeated British tribesmen with nothing more to lose. He had developed an instinct for survival akin to a third eye. The alarm signal was a prickle at the back of his neck and it had been prickling for days now. He'd tried all the usual methods to detect his watchers: backtracking when it would be least expected, stopping suddenly as if he'd changed his mind about something, turning off into some narrow alleyway where a follower would be easier to identify. Nothing. Today he'd been more subtle.

When he reached the house he walked straight through the atrium and the kitchens to the garden. Marcus waited with his backside perched on a stone cabinet where the winter vegetables were stored, crunching a pear from one of the trees that lined the walls. The old gladiator grunted a welcome.

'You weren't seen?' Valerius had installed the five

men in a rented house about a quarter of a mile away, beyond the city wall.

Marcus shook his head. 'I came by the servants' entrance. Anyone spying on you would watch the front door. They're not interested in the slaves, but I was careful in any case. We stayed well back. Knowing your route and the timings helped a lot, although the old boy with a beetroot for a nose almost caught us out.'

'Honorius, the water commissioner.' Valerius smiled. 'I couldn't get rid of him.'

'Well, he did us a turn. They were good. They kept their distance and switched places often enough to make sure you wouldn't mark them.' He described three men, and Valerius hadn't noticed any of them. 'I thought there were only the three of them, but with you stopped for so long they got a little confused, eyeing each other up as if they didn't know what to do. Next thing they're having a conference in a doorway with this fourth fellow. Stocky lad, looked as if he knew how to handle himself. He had that *aware* look, if you know what I mean?'

'Anything to distinguish him in a crowd?'

Marcus pondered for a few seconds. 'At first I thought he was just another hired thug. But there was something about him that didn't fit. Maybe the way he walked? Then I got a proper look at him. You can tell when a man's been knocked about, even if it was a while ago. The left side of his face looked as if someone had shoved it in a furnace.'

Valerius smiled at the perfect description of Rodan. So, he'd been right, but what to do about it? 'If I need to, can I lose them?'

Marcus considered the question. 'There's nobody better at starting a fight than Serpentius.' He nodded towards the far corner of the garden and Valerius noticed with a chill the slim figure standing motionless in the shadow of one of the trees. 'He'll start on one of them. Their friends will come running. You slip off up the nearest alleyway and I'll cover your back. We can meet up later if you need us again. Where are they now, Snake?'

The Spaniard didn't hesitate. 'One watching the house from across the street, the other two in the bar on the corner. The ugly one left as soon as he saw you home.'

Valerius turned to Marcus. 'Is there anything else I should know?'

The gladiator grinned. 'Your old nag came first in the race of the day.'

'Nag?'

'That horse-faced old bitch Lucina. She thought she was being slippery, but I had Heracles on her and he's a handy lad for such a big lump. She likes her gardens does Lucina, and there's one she's taken to visiting regularly up on the hill by the Temple of Diana. Very private, high wall, but as I say he's a handy lad and he slips over it so's he can keep an eye on her while she's smelling the pretty flowers. Lucina does the rounds, but she's not taking that much interest. Heracles thinks

146

— maybe she's only there to get away from the old man, except she's too watchful and he has to hide in a bush a couple of times in case she spots him. After about fifteen minutes it happens. Out of the trees on the far side a man appears. Oh ho, thinks Heracles, now the fun starts. He's young, good-looking if you like them skinny, rich clothes, and shoes that won't fall apart in the rain. Just what a dry old sow like Lucina needs to get the juices running again. Next thing they'll be at it like rabbits on the grass. Only they aren't. He's respectful. He stands just the right distance away. He listens to what she says, he bows and he leaves.'

'Just like that?' Valerius knew from the glint in Marcus's eye there was more to come.

'Just like that. Only now Heracles has a problem. Does he stay with Lucina, who we know is up to something, or does he try to follow the boyfriend?'

'He's a bright lad.'

'That's right. He's a bright lad. He skips up the nearest tree and over the wall, sprints round to the far side of the garden just in time to see the boyfriend disappearing down towards the meat market. Now your young man is a proper aristocrat, begging your lordship's pardon, who knows how to stay busy doing nothing for hours on end. Heracles sticks with him as he wanders from shop to shop, only looking, never buying, stops in a tavern and spends an hour over a cup of warm wine and a sausage. You're biding your time, thinks Heracles. You're waiting to meet somebody. But if he does, Heracles misses it, because all of a sudden it's up and we're off, to a big house across the other side of the Via Flaminia from the Septa Julia and so fast we struggle to keep up. He owns the house, or thinks he does – you can tell by the way he treats the doorman – and it's only a few minutes before he's out, in a new tunic and cloak, and we're off again. To the Palatine.'

Valerius went over the details, trying to follow the young man's reasoning. 'He knew he was being followed, or suspected he was.'

'Or he was just making sure he wasn't. Heracles doesn't think he was seen.'

'Yes, that would fit just as well. Where did he go on the Palatine?'

'Heracles stayed with him until he walked up the Clivus Palatinus, then he left him. Did he do wrong?'

'No. Someone would have questioned him and he might have ended up in trouble. He did well. Make sure he's rewarded.'

Marcus nodded. 'Before he came to report to me he went back to the Via Flaminia and asked at a stall across the street who the big house belonged to.' Valerius sensed that, in his roundabout way, the gladiator had just come to the point. 'The name was Cornelius Sulla.'

Valerius remembered languid eyes and a mocking smile across the great receiving room in the Domus Transitoria. Cornelius Sulla was one of Nero's favourites who had taken particular delight in seeing him fall from grace. An arrogantly handsome boy-man with soft golden curls that fell in waves to his neck and a bloodline that went back to the great dictator Lucius Cornelius Sulla. Yet if the blood held iron, Cornelius was careful not to display it. Nero treated him like a pet, forever absent-mindedly stroking and caressing his flesh, while Cornelius purred with pleasure and asked for more. Some of Fabia's more scurrilous gossip hinted that the young aristocrat was the plaything of the Emperor and his wife, with Torquatus acting as ringmaster, and Valerius could believe it. The question was why a man whose future seemed so bound to Nero would risk everything by consorting with the woman who had declared herself the Emperor's greatest foe?

'I want Heracles to stay with Cornelius, and he can have Serpentius's help if he needs it. We need to know everywhere he goes when he's not at the palace, and everyone he talks to. I want Sextus and Felix watching my back. We'll leave Lucina for the moment. It's plain she knows she's being watched by Torquatus. She has taken one gamble this week; she's unlikely to take another.'

Marcus disagreed. 'By meeting Cornelius in secret she has proved she's prepared to risk everything. That makes it more likely she'll act, not less.'

'You may be right,' Valerius admitted. 'But there's nothing we can do about it.'

He spent the evening at Olivia's side, just listening to the sound of her breathing. He remembered the

149

morning of her eleventh birthday, when he understood she would one day be beautiful, and the irrational conflict that had raged between pride and jealousy. Soon she would leave and become someone else's friend. It seemed unfair that he would lose her just when she was becoming interesting. He had watched her grow from girl to woman and was surprised that the battle inside became all the more intense, and that it was accompanied by sensations he would never begin to understand. She was intelligent, perhaps wiser than he was; elegant, cultured and refined. He resented it. For a short time, when teenage arrogance overwhelmed good judgement, they had hated each other, but it didn't last. When she was betrothed he had punched a wall with such impotent fury that he'd almost broken his knuckles, and when she married he went off to sulk among the olive trees the moment the traditional rites had been observed. She was part of him, and he of her.

Two deaths had brought them back together. First, when the thing in their mother's breast had eaten the life out of her. Mama's decline had been long, undignified and accompanied by a pain that no amount of courage could conquer, or tincture of poppy dull. As the ashes were placed in the family sarcophagus, Valerius and Olivia had stood side by side, united in their desire to replace the lifetime of love that had been torn from their father. On the day of her husband's funeral it had been Valerius Olivia had turned to for support rather than Lucius.

He wondered now if that reversal of roles after the death of one husband had been part of the reason for his poor choice of her next. In the aftermath of the storm that had followed Valerius had found himself responsible for her. Now he had failed her.

Amidst all the uncertainties he knew only one thing. He had to find Petrus.

XVI

'Are you certain you possess the zeal your Emperor requires of you?'

The summons had come as a surprise and the atmosphere in the room was relentlessly hostile. Torquatus sat behind his desk, with Rodan, conspicuously armed and in the dark tunic of the Praetorian Guard, smirking over his shoulder.

Valerius stared at the two men. On the face of it he'd been called to the Palatine to explain his lack of progress, but he suspected there was another motive. 'In an inquiry of this nature lack of zeal cannot be equated with lack of progress,' he pointed out. 'As I'm sure you are aware, prefect, it is a question of ensuring all the pieces are in place before you make your decisive move.'

Torquatus was unimpressed. 'The future of the Empire is no game, Verrens,' he snapped. 'Perhaps the Emperor did not impress upon you enough the seriousness of your commission. It would take but a stroke of the stylus and you would be no more Hero of Rome.'

Valerius allowed himself a laugh. If Nero had wanted to get rid of him he wouldn't be standing in front of Torquatus's desk, he would be having a much more painful conversation in the torture chambers which existed somewhere beneath the hill. That thought reinforced his decision to keep what he'd discovered about Lucina Graecina and Cornelius Sulla to himself. There were things he needed to know before he handed them over to Torquatus's tender mercies. He stared directly at Rodan.

'I'm told you've been searching for Petrus for six months without any success. Is that why the Emperor asked for me? I'm sure your zeal cannot be questioned, prefect, but perhaps the competence of your investigators . . .'

Rodan let out a low growl, an attack dog confronted by a rival. Torquatus's lips compressed into a thin smile. 'So that is what you and Seneca talked of. I was curious. My spies in his household had grown careless. They have now been replaced. A word of warning. Do not put your faith in a man whose time has passed, Gaius Valerius Verrens. Seneca will be too busy saving himself to worry about you. However . . .' His voice changed and it was like hearing a snake speak, sibilant and seductive, but with the fangs barely concealed. 'If you were to give your undivided loyalty to a man whose time has come, you would not find him ungrateful. Do not look so surprised, young man. I am not blind. I have recognized your talents just as the Emperor has, but, like him, I require proof of your devotion.'

'What proof?'

'The followers of Christus are not the only threat to the Emperor. You are popular in the courts. People tell you things. Perhaps they are occasionally indiscreet?'

'You want me to spy on my friends?' Valerius struggled to keep a dangerous edge from his voice. 'And what would be the reward for this service, apart, of course, from your gratitude?'

Torquatus smiled. 'We talked of a legion, did we not? A single word from me to your Emperor would win Gaius Valerius Verrens the scarlet cloak of a legate. A year, perhaps eighteen months; a successful command in some profitable but not too arduous theatre of war. Then a place in the Senate. Why not? It is your birthright. You would have your seat before you were thirty and, with good fortune and the right friends, your consulship when you come of age for it.'

Valerius relaxed and returned the smile. Torquatus offered him everything his father had ever dreamed of, and more. The consulship? It was almost laughable. The only thing he hadn't placed on the table was a promise to restore his right arm. How like this man to overplay his hand. If the offer had been genuine, a legionary command would have been bribe enough.

'You are too generous,' he said, hoping Torquatus

154

was as immune to irony as he was to subtlety. 'I will do what I can, but finding the Judaean is my first priority. I hope you won't have cause to question my zeal again.' He turned to leave.

A word from Torquatus stopped him. 'Valerius?'

'Yes.'

'You are right not to be distracted from your investigation. The others can wait – for now. The Emperor is becoming impatient and my offer means nothing without progress in this matter of Petrus. I urge you not to take too much upon yourself. You may call on Rodan for what support you require. He has already begun to bring together evidence that may assist you.'

'Evidence? What kind of evidence?'

Torquatus's tone was almost kindly, but it sent a knife point running down Valerius's spine. 'Perhaps you should ask your father.'

Ask your father. Valerius left the palace with the words still ringing in his ears. Torquatus was trying to keep him off balance, he understood that, but was there anything more? Politically, Lucius, despite painful experience, was still a babe in arms. His friendship and position as client to Seneca also made him vulnerable. The message was a threat, but how great a threat? Olivia, Petrus and now his father. How many more burdens must he carry?

He almost missed Felix among the crowd loitering on the steps of the Temple of Jupiter Stator. The Spaniard nodded to indicate that he was still being followed. As Valerius walked back towards the Clivus Scauri he struggled to work out his priorities. He had to find a way to reach Petrus. The boy had predicted that if Valerius sought the Judaean, Petrus would eventually come to him, but he couldn't depend on that. He had two sources of leverage. Lucina and Cornelius Sulla. It was a question of who was most likely to provide the information he needed. And that was really no question at all.

The brothel stood at a crossroads in the valley between the Caelian and Esquiline hills. It was one of Rome's more superior establishments, with a pair of muscular watchmen at the door to ensure that the social status of the customers matched the aspirations of its owner. The three men stood on the opposite side of the street. 'He's been in there for more than an hour. I don't know where these young fellows get the strength,' Marcus grumbled. Serpentius muttered something from the darkness that made the old gladiator laugh. 'Oh, there's always money for a good shag, Snake. And this Cornelius is obviously prepared to pay for the best.'

Valerius laughed with them, but he wondered why Cornelius Sulla, who had free access in Nero's palace to the greatest and most degenerate brothel in Rome, had need to visit somewhere like this. True, it was of the better class, but with a word in the Emperor's ear Cornelius could have any handsome boy, beautiful slave girl or even senator's wife who took his fancy.

The doorkeepers studied the three men suspiciously and Valerius could hardly blame them. Streets around brothels tended to be haunted by robbers and he still wore the cloak and hood he'd used to evade Torquatus's followers. It had been deceptively simple. Serpentius had accused one of the watchers of attempting to steal his purse and as the others were drawn into the brawl, Valerius had slipped away to join Marcus.

When he wasn't busy fawning over the Emperor, Cornelius spent a puzzling amount of time at the brothel, and it had been no surprise when he turned up this evening. Valerius sweated copiously beneath the heavy wool of his cloak, but he dared not remove it for fear of alerting his quarry. For once the rich smell of cooking overwhelmed the usual rancid street scents and his stomach warned him he hadn't eaten since dawn. The smell came from a nearby bar where a few regulars had gathered to drink the sour wine and complain about their wives. The shouted conversations reminded him that he had only one more year of respectable bachelorhood left. But who would want a one-armed cripple? Strange that Fabia's face should enter his mind. She would have begun her career in a place like this, and only a potent mix of beauty, intelligence and charm had won her way out. She was now more mistress than courtesan, although mistress to a dozen men who paid for the privilege. Most of these women would end their career on the streets, used up, ill-treated and available for the price of a cup of wine.

Could he marry Fabia? He smiled at the absurdity of the thought. In any case, a man didn't marry for love, he married for wealth or patronage. He wondered what she would say if she knew he had linked her name with the word love. Would it draw some saw-toothed jibe, or . . .

'He's here,' Marcus hissed.

Valerius looked from under the hood to where Cornelius Sulla loitered by the door of the brothel, his golden hair shining in the lamplight. The aristocrat held a girl in his arms. Dark-haired, she was blessed with heavy-lipped, sensuous features and breasts that spilled from the front of her dress. Valerius watched as Cornelius attempted to cover her up in a way that was almost brotherly. The girl playfully knocked his hands away and bared herself all the more, dusky nipples peeping from the folds of material. There was nothing brotherly in the way they kissed, long and passionate, their hands searching each other, until they parted breathless, Cornelius grinning inanely.

'Silly bastard's in love with a tart,' Marcus muttered. 'Who would have believed it?'

Eventually, someone called the girl inside and Cornelius was joined by two men who had been hidden in the shadows. One, burly and muscle-bound, with a rolling walk that hinted at more time spent on a horse than on foot, glared towards Valerius and whispered something to the young knight. Cornelius threw them a dismissive glance and shook his head. Valerius gave the three men time to move off before he followed, keeping pace a few yards behind. He knew they were aware of his presence, but that was how he wanted it. After about a hundred paces they stopped and the two bodyguards drew a pair of lethal-looking cudgels and moved protectively in front of the younger man. Valerius allowed his hood to fall back and Cornelius stiffened as he recognized his follower in the flickering torchlight.

'What do you want?' he demanded.

Valerius lifted the seal on its gold chain so all three could see it. 'This is imperial business.' He directed the words at the senior of the two guards. 'Your master will be safe with me. Walk on for twenty paces and he will join you in a few moments.'

The men looked at each other, then to Cornelius, who stared at the seal as if hypnotized.

'Twenty paces,' Valerius repeated. 'In the Emperor's name.'

Cornelius nodded. One guard's jaw came up as if he was about to argue, but the second man pulled his sleeve and they walked reluctantly away. When they were alone, Valerius directed Cornelius towards the shadows at the side of the street, but the younger man shrugged off his hand and glared furiously at him. Valerius decided he'd seen friendlier cobras.

'What do you want?' Cornelius demanded again. His eyes betrayed no concern because he was Nero's favourite and he intended to make Valerius pay for this insult. For his part, Valerius stared into the

159

handsome face and knew the boy's arrogance made any attempt at compromise pointless.

'Two days ago, you met in secret with the lady Lucina Graecina . . .'

'You lie,' Cornelius hissed, but Valerius ignored him.

'. . . in the Horti Sallustiani. The lady was unaccompanied. You were unaccompanied. The lady reached the gardens first and waited fifteen minutes for your arrival. You spoke with the lady for approximately two minutes before leaving by the same concealed door by which you entered.' Cornelius's face shone like a pale orb in the torchlight. His flesh took on the look of aged parchment and fear replaced the anger in his eyes. 'I want to know the reason for the meeting and what was said.' Valerius raised his left hand with the imperial seal. 'In the Emperor's name.'

'I . . . It's not true.'

'The mother of a man the Emperor ordered killed meets in secret with a member of the Emperor's court?'

'She . . .'

'She may survive, because she is Lucina Graecina, but what will happen to the Emperor's favourite, Cornelius Sulla? Nero is not known for his mercy, or his forgiveness. A single word from me, Cornelius, and you will be a dead man. Why did you meet her?'

'I cannot tell. Do what you must.' The boy's voice shook, but his tone betrayed a defiance that made Valerius almost like him. He wished there could be another way.

160

'Whether it is true or not, he will believe you betrayed him. Have you seen a traitor die, Cornelius? Citizenship will not save you. No merciful opening of the veins for you. It will be the cross or the fire. A slow death and a painful one. Could you bear it?'

'I cannot tell . . . please!' A tear ran across the fine down of his cheek.

'What was said?' Valerius kept his voice hard.

Cornelius bit his lips as if it was the only way he could stay silent.

'You may be willing to die, Cornelius, but is she?' The boy's eyes flashed white as he realized 'she' didn't mean Lucina. 'They will make you watch her die. They will remove her beauty a little at a time for your pain and Nero's pleasure. Do not make me do it, Cornelius. Tell me and you will both live. On my honour.'

XVII

Lucina Graecina waited alone in the cent
garden. Where was he?

She hated unpunctuality. Bad enough that
wait until he was certain they were alone,
kept here for . . . She took a deep breath a
herself to be calm. What was it Petrus had s
patience is like anger. Any negative emotio
our ability to do God's work.'

She smiled, and the narrow, pinched
transformed. They were doing God's work. SI
towards the trees growing a few feet from th
walls and the flowers in their beds beside th
earth of the path. Every colour and every shap
All God's work.

Another ten minutes passed and she reta
inner harmony apart from a single glance at
ner from where she knew he would come.
been dying until they found her – or had s

162

'Whether it is true or not, he will believe you betrayed him. Have you seen a traitor die, Cornelius? Citizenship will not save you. No merciful opening of the veins for you. It will be the cross or the fire. A slow death and a painful one. Could you bear it?'

'I cannot tell . . . please!' A tear ran across the fine down of his cheek.

'What was said?' Valerius kept his voice hard.

Cornelius bit his lips as if it was the only way he could stay silent.

'You may be willing to die, Cornelius, but is she?' The boy's eyes flashed white as he realized 'she' didn't mean Lucina. 'They will make you watch her die. They will remove her beauty a little at a time for your pain and Nero's pleasure. Do not make me do it, Cornelius. Tell me and you will both live. On my honour.'

XVII

Lucina Graecina waited alone in the centre of the garden. Where was he?

She hated unpunctuality. Bad enough that she must wait until he was certain they were alone, but to be kept here for . . . She took a deep breath and willed herself to be calm. What was it Petrus had said? 'Impatience is like anger. Any negative emotion impairs our ability to do God's work.'

She smiled, and the narrow, pinched face was transformed. They were doing God's work. She looked towards the trees growing a few feet from the garden walls and the flowers in their beds beside the beaten earth of the path. Every colour and every shape unique. All God's work.

Another ten minutes passed and she retained her inner harmony apart from a single glance at the corner from where she knew he would come. She had been dying until they found her – or had she found them? – shrivelling inside like the desiccated occupant of a hundred-year-old tomb, her mind devoured by rage and thoughts and images of revenge against that man: the man who had defiled and then destroyed her son. Five years locked away in the self-sought oblivion of mourning and never a moment's joy. Then she had met *him*, and he had reopened her eyes to life.

'Lady?'

The wrong voice. She whirled, and speared the intruder with needle-tipped darts of contempt. 'This is a private garden. Please leave at once.' She turned away, her back reinforcing the message of her eyes, but her heart thundered so she wondered it did not break free from her breast. What could have happened? The secret way was known only to a few, not to this well-set young man with the stern features.

'Cornelius is not coming. He was to bring me, but he has disappeared, along with the girl.'

She felt her heart flutter. Girl? What girl? She must not faint. She put all her strength into her voice. 'I know of no Cornelius. I will not ask you to leave again.'

'Perhaps you would like to call your servants. I'm sure they would be interested in what I have to say.'

'More interested than I,' she huffed, and turned for the gate.

'I don't want you. I wish to talk to Petrus,' Valerius persisted.

Almost without realizing it she halted. 'More names. More mysteries.'

'You are familiar with mysteries, I understand, my lady Lucina.'

'But not with riddles, young man. You waste my time and yours.'

He shook his head. 'You are a follower of the Judaean mystic called Christus. You have taken part in rituals conducted by the man I seek. You keep certain religious objects in your home, which I will find if I use this authority to enter it.' He held up the seal and she caught the glint of gold in the corner of her eye, enough to make a guess at its identity. 'All this I had from Cornelius, along with the fact that he had lost contact with Petrus and today you were to reveal where he could reach him.'

She turned and her eyes narrowed dangerously, a she-cat cornered by hounds. 'If you have harmed him you will be damned for all eternity, as will your master.'

Valerius allowed himself a smile. 'So, you admit your complicity, if not your guilt. You mistake me, lady. I will keep Cornelius from harm if I can find him, and I admit to no master but myself.'

'You have his seal and you carry his stink. I freely admit both my complicity and my guilt. Death holds no fears for me, young man, whatever horrors the act of dying comprises. I will go to the afterlife willingly in the knowledge that I shall be content for all eternity in the company of those I love. Do what you will.'

She walked away and he couldn't help admiring

her. She had fought him to a standstill and when he had placed the point of his sword at her breast she had disarmed him as easily as if he had been a child. But he had one more question. 'What does MCVII mean?'

She stopped abruptly and turned to face him. Her eyes settled on the artificial wooden hand. 'What is your name, young man?'

'I am Gaius Valerius Verrens.'

'Then you must ask your father.'

Valerius spent the night tormented by irrational fears and tortured by dreams of wild beasts closing in from the darkness. He woke dry-mouthed and with an unaccustomed feeling of helplessness. When he set off for Fidenae, he left Marcus with instructions to concentrate on the hunt for Cornelius Sulla. Cornelius had taken the girl from the brothel and vanished the morning after Valerius had questioned him. They'd searched his usual haunts without success and unless he had hidden away on the Palatine, where Marcus and his men could not go, it seemed that he had either taken refuge among the alleys of the Subura or left Rome altogether.

But Valerius had concerns of his own. He rode out of the city before dawn taking what precautions he could, though he knew there was no guarantee that he'd lost Rodan's watchers. His mind was bowstring tight. *Ask your father.* The same loaded suggestion from two entirely different and equally dangerous sources. What did his father know about the Christus cult and plots against Caesar? Lucius had never been politically astute, but he was no fool either. Apart from two or three letters which had probably never reached the Emperor, there was little likelihood that Nero even knew his name. But Torquatus did and it seemed Torquatus would use any lever to increase his hold on Valerius. *Ask your father.* He felt dread hovering over him like a thundercloud.

He left the road a mile short of the gate, ensuring no hidden watcher would announce his arrival today. His horse plotted its own way through the familiar hills until they met the track leading from the gateway to the house. Everything seemed normal, but his mind sharpened with every clatter of the animal's hooves.

When the villa came into view he reined in beside a clump of black poplars and sat for more than a minute, watching and listening. Nothing out of the ordinary. Then why did he have this overwhelming sense of danger? Dismounting, he led his horse into the nearest barn and tied it next to a pair of matched roans superior to anything his father had ever owned. Beside them stood an elaborately painted four-wheeled coach. His suspicions growing, he walked out into the sunshine and across the courtyard. The door was closed, but not barred, and he entered silently, immediately experiencing the intimacy of surroundings he'd known since childhood. Each tessera of the mosaic floor was as familiar as when he'd crawled across it as a child. He was approaching the interior garden with its open roof and white-washed columns when he heard the raised voices.

Three men lay on couches around a stone table beside the central pool, with his father furthest away facing the doorway. Despite his relaxed pose, Lucius gave the impression of being a reluctant member of the group. He lay with his body pushed back as far as the couch would allow and with his cup clutched defensively to his chest. His eyes darted between his two guests like a dog wondering which was going to hit him first. The man to his right could have been the villa's owner as he casually picked at grapes from the table. He had dark hair that curled back from a wide brow and a neatly trimmed spade beard. Deep-set, obsidian eyes seemed to focus upon something interesting in the middle distance. The third man had his back to Valerius, but his bulk and his posture made him unmistakable. Seneca.

The dark man turned to Lucius with a tight smile. 'It seems we have a new guest.'

Lucius looked up and his face froze when he recognized Valerius.

Seneca didn't even turn his head. 'Welcome, my boy. Two visits within two weeks? Your filial devotion surprises even me. Come, we are just going.' He raised himself from the couch with surprising ease for such a big man and turned with a smile, as if he found the unwanted intrusion amusing. 'A social call to discuss matters of mutual interest among neighbours,' he explained. 'May I introduce my business acquaintance, Saul of Tarsus.'

The bearded man's eyes flicked a warning to Seneca, but the philosopher waved a languid hand.

'We are among friends here.' He looked to Valerius for confirmation. 'Discreet friends. Your work goes well?' The question was heavy with emphasis, but the young Roman decided to treat it as a social enquiry.

'Life in Rome is always interesting, as you know, master Seneca.'

Seneca laughed. 'A good answer. I taught you well, Valerius.' He turned to Lucius. 'I bid you good day. You will bear in mind what we discussed?' Lucius bowed.

Saul of Tarsus approached Valerius. He was an inch or two shorter than the Roman and older than he first appeared. Something about him stirred a memory. 'Your father speaks well of you, young man. I wish you success in your every endeavour.'

Valerius nodded his thanks, but, when the two guests had left, the impression he had of Saul was of a prison pallor and an unmistakable prison scent. In the silence that followed he realized that the traditional father-son roles had become reversed. Lucius stared from the window refusing to meet his eyes, and Valerius felt a growing certainty that the older man had somehow placed them all at risk. What games was he playing that had come to Torquatus's notice? Where was the link between these men and Lucina? He tried to keep his voice steady but the words emerged rough-edged as a saw blade. 'You warned me only a few days ago that I should be wary of Seneca. Why should I take your advice when you clearly cannot?'

On another day his father would have snapped a rebuke, but now he only waved a weary hand. 'If a neighbour visits me am I to turn him from my door?'

'Seneca does not make social visits. Who was the man with him?'

'Saul of Tarsus is a friend of Seneca's brother. A good man, and a Roman citizen despite his birth.'

'A good man does not carry the stink of the jail on him.'

Lucius looked up sharply. 'Yes, he has been in prison for his beliefs, but he was spared to carry on his work.'

Valerius's heart sank at the way Lucius pronounced the word 'beliefs'. 'What are you doing to us?' he demanded. 'Don't you understand that you are putting Olivia in danger? Is it not enough that you refuse to help her, but you must drag her with you to the executioner?'

'I have done nothing. I—'

'Nothing? Two days ago the Emperor's Praetorian prefect advised me to ask my father if I wanted to know how to get close to a man Nero wants to see dead. Yesterday, a woman who condemned herself by her own words said the same thing. Since then I have been asking myself what it could mean. Now I understand.' Lucius shook his head soundlessly. Valerius made no attempt to keep the frustration

169

from his voice. 'I have been ordered by the Emperor to seek out the leader of a religious sect accused of spreading sedition in Rome. They worship a criminal named Christus, who died on a cross thirty years ago. A madman who believed he was the son of a god and could work miracles. But you are already aware of that, because you worship him too.'

'You know nothing of what you speak.' Lucius's tone recovered some of its authority. 'I am still the head of this family. Leave my house now.'

'What does MCVII mean?'

'Go!'

Valerius shook his head. 'Tell me where to find Petrus, Father. Tell me where they meet.'

'Get out, please.'

'For Olivia, if not for me.'

'Please, Valerius, leave me.' Lucius slumped on the furthest couch. 'I can tell you nothing.'

Valerius was suddenly overwhelmed by the same helplessness he felt when he sat by Olivia's bed. He would learn nothing more here. He made for the door. 'You are a good man, Father, but you do not understand the danger you are in. Take your own advice. Beware Seneca – and this man Saul.'

It wasn't until he reached the barn that he realized they were both caught in the same net.

He struggled to marshal his thoughts. How had the world become this blur of contradictions? It seemed impossible, yet deep in his heart he had known it since Lucina spoke those three fateful words in the garden.

Lucius, an intelligent man and a good Roman, had become a Christus-follower. *He believed*. Believed in a man who claimed to have walked upon water. A crazed Judaean rebel who thought he was the son of a god; a god who must be worshipped exclusively and all other gods abandoned. Valerius remembered the comforting family routine of daily libations to the kitchen god, the coin for the god of the crossroads when Olivia married, sacrifices to Jupiter and Minerva, Bacchus and Mars, on the appropriate days for the appropriate purposes. Good harvests, good health, sweet wine and sweet victory. A Roman should be surrounded by gods. How could his father have changed so much?

'You must not judge him too harshly.' The soft voice came from above and behind him. Ruth sat like a serious-faced meadow sprite on a hillock of grass overlooking the road. To his surprise, he found he was glad to see her, but he wondered how she had known to be there.

'You have not had time to water your horse.' She rose to her feet and skipped down to a path that led through the trees. 'Come, I will show you a place.'

He hesitated, puzzled at the change from their previous encounter, but she smiled and he followed her, out of curiosity and for other reasons he would have found difficult to explain. The path was one he had used many times as a boy and he knew where it led. She slowed to allow him to walk at her side.

'He was lost, but now he is found,' she said cryptically.

'I don't understand,' he replied, knowing as he said it that it wasn't quite true. He found her presence disturbing; it provoked a kind of asthmatic breathlessness he hadn't experienced for a long time. She wore the same blue dress as the day in the olive grove. It was loose and unflattering, but the generous curves that lay beneath made themselves known in various subtle ways. She really was quite beautiful. Smaller than Valerius by a head, but lithe and athletic, her dark hair hanging long to her waist. Ruth's skin glowed the colour of golden cinnamon and when she smiled her nose wrinkled like a little girl's. The next words she spoke were an admission of treason, but she spoke them without fear in a way that made her very naive, very trusting or very brave.

'There is but one God, and Jesus is his son,' she said with simple faith. 'When I came here Lucius had nothing. No family. No friends. No love. He was empty. We talked of our fears and I told him about my God, who is a loving God, and how I was never alone, because I believed.'

The talk of love reminded Valerius that she belonged to his father. 'He had me. He has Olivia.'

'You were lost to him.' She said it quietly, making no accusation.

They came to the pool, as he had known they would. He tethered the horse to a tree with enough play on the reins to allow it to drink. For a time there was nothing but silence and the song of the river. They stood a little apart. Ruth was entirely at ease, but Valerius found himself trying to untangle the knot of conflicting feelings she awoke in him. Desire was one, mixed up with the beginnings of a deep, almost brotherly affection, but it was not the strongest. No, the most powerful feeling she inspired in him was a sense of his own inadequacy. She had an almost mystical quality; a disturbing ability to reach deep into his soul. When he was with her he felt ashamed of what he was and what he had done. He wanted to tell her everything: about Nero, Torquatus and Petrus, Maeve and Cearan and the bloody field of Colonia; but somehow the words wouldn't come.

Ruth saw his confusion, but affected not to notice. Instead, she continued her story. 'One day we went to the city and he heard a man speak of goodness and love and of another man who sacrificed himself so that all men could be blessed with them. The man came to us and spoke to your father. I do not know what he said but your father wept and asked the man to pray for him.'

'The man was Petrus?'

'Yes, Petrus the healer. He who was chosen by Christus and made holy by him.'

'And was my father healed?'

'Later, he asked me to take him to meetings and after a time he took the blood and the body of Christus. Then he was healed.' Valerius felt his gorge rise as he remembered Nero's chilling warning about drinking the blood of children. She saw his look and her face turned serious. 'It is not what you think. We only take watered wine and thin bread. But God is pleased to consider it the blood and body of Christus.'

'Why are you telling me this? You do not know me at all. I may be your enemy and I am certainly a danger to you. I need to find Petrus and I must save my father from the enemies who will hurt him if they can.'

'Your father has already been saved; that is why I am telling you. When you meet Petrus you will be faced with a choice and only by understanding will you make the correct decision. You think of us as the enemies of Rome and your first instinct is to strike out against us. But what are you defending Rome against? We seek only to spread the word of God and bring peace and harmony to all men, Jew and Gentile. Is that so terrible? Rome can be a hard mistress for a man with a conscience, and many a true Roman has listened to the word of the true God and been converted.'

He listened to her voice and imagined he heard the sound of another speaking. Was this some trick of Petrus to win him over to the cause of Christus? Yet there was an obvious transparency and honesty to Ruth, an inner quality he thought must be what men called goodness, that convinced him she was sincere. He still couldn't afford to trust her, but surely he could afford to listen to her?

'It seems I do not know my own father.'

'Your father is a fine man. When I came, he was stern, but now he knows peace.'

'You have been good to him,' Valerius said.

'I have been as a daughter to him,' she replied, answering his unspoken question.

'I don't understand. I thought you hated me. In the street after the boy spoke—'

'We are taught not to feel hatred,' she interrupted gently. 'Only love, but I feared you would betray your father. I was confused. Then I saw that you, too, were a good man beneath the armour you wear to protect yourself along the path God has chosen for you.'

He opened his mouth to deny it, but before he could speak she glanced across to where the fast water entered the pool. 'I was baptized in a place like this. But I was young and I have only a slight memory of it.'

Valerius frowned. 'Baptized? It is not a word I know.'

'It is one of our rituals. Your father has not yet experienced it. I do not truly understand its purpose, only that to enter the kingdom of God one must have been first immersed in water, and that to be baptized is to be saved. Jesus was baptized by John beneath a waterfall. Some say it is enough to pour water over the supplicant's head, but Petrus believes that only by covering the entire body is the ceremony complete. Wherever he goes, he seeks out a waterfall.'

'Can you help me reach Petrus?'

She hesitated, studying his face intently before coming to a decision. 'I will do what I can, but the final choice must be his,' she said. 'When I receive

175

word of our next meeting I will contact you.' She touched his hand and then she was gone, the blue dress disappearing among the trees by the river. Valerius stood for the time it took to recognize the sensation that threatened to overwhelm him. Loneliness.

Later, on the road back to Rome, he was conscious of a curious mixture of elation and confusion. *He was lost, but now he is found.* He understood now what she had meant by it, but not in the *way* she meant it. A miracle had happened. He'd found something he believed he had lost for ever.

But would he be allowed to keep it?

XVIII

Nero's invitation couldn't have been more inconvenient. At best, it would be an evening of excruciating performances by the Emperor and his latest artist friends, the braying actors and falsetto-voiced singers who jostled each other to inform him how talented he was. At worst? Well, Valerius would find out. The memory of their last meeting was still fresh and the thought of the questing tongue and rank breath turned his stomach. He had spent the last hour with Fabia, in a vain attempt to unravel the mystery of Cornelius Sulla's disappearance, and had looked forward to an evening at home. The venue, the circus Caligula had built on the Vatican meadows on the far side of the city, could hardly be worse placed. It made a theatrical or musical performance less likely, but with Nero it was impossible to tell. The arena was mainly used for the horse and chariot races the Emperor loved. Perhaps he was planning to hold a chariot race in the dark.

'Still no sign of Cornelius or the girl,' Marcus reported as Valerius readied himself to leave.

'Don't worry, they'll turn up. Cornelius will probably make an appearance at the entertainment tonight.'

'Do you want us to watch your back?'

He shook his head. 'No. I doubt Rodan will get up to any mischief. Take the others to a tavern for the evening. We'll meet tomorrow to decide what to do next.' He saw the scarred gladiator hesitate. 'What is it?'

Marcus shrugged. 'Serpentius has offered to stay in the house to make sure your sister is safe.'

'That's good of him. He can find a bed in the slave quarters.'

'That's what he's planning. Only I think he's become a bit sweet on that girl of yours. A pretty little piece.'

Valerius smiled. 'He'll find Julia is a little piece with sharp claws if he tries anything on with her. She knows her own mind. The Snake might have his tail chopped off. But I still think it will do no harm to have a man like Serpentius about the house.'

He sent a servant to check if his chair had arrived and walked through to Olivia's room. Julia sat by the bed where his sister lay as pale as any ghost. The girl gasped when she saw the tall figure silhouetted in the doorway.

'I'm sorry I scared you,' he said reassuringly. 'I came to tell you that Serpentius will be staying tonight to guard you both. He may look an intimidating character, but he has a good heart.'

She nodded. 'I like him. He makes me giggle. But I sense a darkness in him; he is almost as frightening as you.'

Frightening? He almost laughed at the thought, before he realized how true it was. In many ways he'd become as stern as his father, all the lightness driven from him by his experiences in Britain and the strains of Olivia's illness. 'You have no reason to be afraid of me, Julia.'

'I wanted to tell you.'

'I'm glad you have. I promise to change.'

'No, I don't mean that. I mean about your father.'

The room seemed to go very still. Outside, beyond the shuttered windows, he could hear the sound of voices and knew the chair had arrived, but he ignored it.

'What about my father?'

'He made me promise not to say anything. When you asked me if we had visitors, I lied. He has been coming to sit with Olivia once or twice each week since she became ill. I wanted to tell you, but . . .'

Valerius placed his hand on her shoulder and turned her face to him. He brushed the tears from her cheek with his fingers. 'Poor Julia, caught between two horrible, frightening men. No wonder you've been so sad lately.' And poor Father, so determined not to appear weak that he couldn't allow the people he loved to know how much he cared for them. 'I have to go now. Look after Olivia for me.' He bent down and kissed her on the forehead.

Four slaves carried the chair and made good time through the centre of the city and across the Pons Vaticanus to the west bank of the Tiber. Trees lined the pathway from the bridge to the circus and, among them, men stacked wood for the bonfires that would light the guests home at the end of the night. To his right, he passed the curious Meta Romuli, the narrow pyramid that marked where Romulus was said to be buried. Ahead loomed the walls of the circus, which was grander, but not greater, than the mighty Maximus on the other side of Rome.

The chair men set him down and he arranged to be picked up by the bridge at the second hour after dark, when Nero's invitation stipulated the evening would end. An imperial aide conducted him along a narrow, tiled corridor to the far end of the circus. Other guests were arriving, but not as many as he would have expected for an event like this. It was obviously to be a select gathering, and he wondered again why he'd been invited. He noted three former consuls and any number of senators and their wives, most of whom were pleased to look down their noses at him. But a few recognized him as a Hero of Rome and he exchanged bows with the elegant patrician Laecanius Bassus, who had just taken over the consulship from his deadly rival Regulus.

Eventually, a crowd of close to a hundred gathered in the grand hall which opened out on to the imperial and senatorial boxes. Valerius accepted a cup of wine and retired to a corner where he wouldn't need to make polite conversation with people he didn't know. He'd been standing there for a few minutes when he detected a sweet scent in the air and felt a malevolent presence at his side.

'I'm surprised you are not showing off your trophy, my hero. Surely this would be just the occasion to impress people with the Gold Crown of Valour?' Rodan wore a broad smile and made no attempt to disguise the mockery in his voice. His ego, never buried too deep, was as inflated as a startled puffer fish. Rodan was pleased with himself and that didn't bode well for someone.

Valerius ignored him and Rodan nodded absently. 'The Emperor and lord Torquatus are grateful for your efforts.'

A simple statement which contained no overt threat. So why did it carry the chill of a dagger point rattling across a skeleton's ribs?

Before Valerius could react a fanfare sounded, and Nero, in a toga of imperial purple and with a gold laurel wreath clinging to his sparse hair, descended the broad staircase with Poppaea Augusta at his side. He smiled benevolently at all around him, but his wife's face displayed nothing but coldness and indifference. She might have been walking through an empty corridor for all the attention she paid to her surroundings. Valerius knew Fabia enjoyed Poppaea's company, but he felt an instinctive dislike for the

Emperor's wife. She created a barrier around herself that was as impenetrable as a legionary *testudo* and her eyes hinted at a capacity for petty cruelty. She glanced towards him and he noted a flash of recognition before the emotionless mask returned. Suddenly the room felt a much more dangerous place. Servants appeared with golden platters of food and the aristocrats fell like carrion birds on dishes of roasted song thrush, delicately fried tongue of lark and flamingo, and white-fleshed moray eel. As the wine flowed, the atmosphere became more intense and expectant, and the chamber filled with heat and noise. Valerius slipped away from Rodan and found his senses swamped by a sea of scarlet faces, bulging, intense eyes and ceaseless, self-important conversation. He allowed his mind to return to the pool with Ruth and it was a few moments before he realized the room had gone quiet and Nero was speaking. He was talking about Christus.

'. . . the weak and the gullible follow a charlatan cast out by his own people; the so-called Son of God brought to earth. A common criminal tried and found guilty under Roman law at the instigation of a Judaean council too timid to bring him to justice themselves.

'And now they are among us, yes, perhaps even among us here, burrowing into the very foundations of the Empire like rock-worms eating away at the stones upon which Rome is built. These followers of the man Christus would tear down our temples and cast out our gods, but I . . . will . . . not . . . allow . . .

it. They believe they are hidden from us, but our eyes are upon them. The man they revere claimed he could perform miracles, and they believed him. He promised them eternal life, but to achieve this eternal life they must first be willing to experience death. *I* rule Rome and *I*, not this Christus, will grant them their wish.'

At his final words the great doors at the far end of the room were thrown open and Nero and Poppaea led the way out to the viewing platform which looked along the length of the circus. Valerius held back, but Rodan appeared beside him and took his arm. 'Oh no, my hero,' he said cheerfully. 'The Emperor has ordered a special place set aside for you. Think of this as a lesson as much as an entertainment.'

Reluctantly, Valerius allowed himself to be led to the front of the great curved balcony that dominated the western end of the arena. The soft, ethereal haze that heralded dusk was settling over the city, but it would not be dark for another hour. Ahead of him the circus stretched away for five hundred paces, a narrow oval of hard-packed sand split by a central spine with a turning post at each end and an enormous carved stone obelisk in the centre. To his right was the lavish imperial box where Nero whispered into Poppaea's ear. Away to his left were the seven bronzed dolphins of the lap counter. Tiered stands overlooked every yard of the circuit and the track on either side of the spine appeared so narrow it was difficult to imagine four- and six-horse chariot teams overtaking each other, but Valerius had seen the Reds and the Greens matched wheel to wheel at the corner. Today the spectators were to be treated to a different spectacle.

The near end of the circus, between the closest turning post and the curved platform, had been turned into a separate arena by a twelve-foot fence of metal bars. As he watched, Praetorian guards herded a huddle of terrified prisoners into the centre of the open space. There must have been close to twenty of them, more men than women.

'Only six or seven of them are followers of the Judaean,' Rodan whispered. 'The rest are condemned criminals, but it is the example that matters, don't you think? Do you see anyone you recognize?'

Valerius froze. What did he mean? He frantically studied the men and women, but they were massed so close together it was difficult to identify individuals. Then he caught sight of a hank of silver hair and a slim, familiar figure. He half rose, but a sharp prick at his ribs stopped him. He looked down to find Rodan holding a small dagger he'd taken from the folds of his tunic.

'No heroics today. We have more work to do, you and I.'

Valerius knew Rodan wouldn't dare kill him without Nero's sanction and he was ready to leap on to the sand to his father's rescue. But, when he looked again, he had a clearer view of the silver-haired man. It wasn't Lucius, but a much older person. Rodan grinned at him and he reluctantly resumed his place beside the Praetorian, his heart numb with dread.

Nero stood to address the captives, his querulous tones ringing around the empty circus.

'You worship one god to the exclusion of all others. Where is your god today? Let him show me a single sign that he loves you and I will spare every one of you.' He paused, studying the sky like a bad actor in a Greek tragedy. 'You see, there is no sign, and there will be none because your god only exists in your own minds, which have been warped by those who lead you. The man you follow claimed to be the son of that false god, but he was a mere deceiver who dazzled simple country dwellers with crude conjuring tricks. He rebelled against Rome and was a traitor to his own people. He promised to save you, yet he could not even save himself. He offered you eternal life and you believed him.' He waved his hand with a flourish and a door swung open in the opposite side of the arena. His plump, perspiring face hardened and Valerius had never seen anything so pitiless. 'I grant you your wish.'

A lion roared, a thundering growl that seemed to shake the very stones of the circus and was quickly joined by the throat-tearing cough of a leopard. The beasts, five lions and two of the spotted cats, must have been starved for days because they didn't hesitate as they burst into the light towards the little group huddled in the centre. A collective cry that tore Valerius's heart rose from the captives and now the herd instinct that had held them together was broken by sheer terror. They splintered in every direction,

185

a few sinking to the ground and raising their arms in supplication, but most fleeing in mindless panic, pleading for mercy they knew would not be forthcoming.

The old man Valerius had mistaken for his father died on his knees as a lioness tore his screaming head from his shoulders with a single twist of her enormous jaws. Blood sprayed bright across the sand. A muscular giant with a red face and heat-scarred arms faced up to a charging leopard, his features set in a determined scowl, but even a blacksmith's strength counted for nothing against a big cat's power. He went down under her weight and her rear legs stripped out his guts in a dozen frenzied sweeps as he howled in disbelief at the outrage done to his body. The wild beasts killed and killed again and the surviving prisoners clawed at the walls and the bars. All except one.

Cornelius's girl.

The dark-haired figure hadn't been visible among the huddle of prisoners, but now Valerius saw her running for her life, crying out for the laughing guards to take the cloth-wrapped bundle she held in her arms. A few paces away a lioness tracked her progress, the glowing yellow eyes never leaving her prey. The girl knew she was doomed, but she refused to give up. She ran on round the inner wall until some instinct brought her to the point where Valerius now stood hard against the balcony. Helplessly, she looked up at him, much too young, the face he recognized from the brothel turned ugly by fear. Among the cries of ecstasy and gasps of horror around him, he heard her shouted plea. 'Please, sir, take my baby. If not me, at least save my child.' Terror made her voice brittle and the words came out in a rush. With shaking hands she held the tiny bundle high, so Valerius could see the small dark eyes and pink, grizzling features. 'Please!'

The big cat covered the ground in three enormous bounds, but the girl was driven by the speed of despair. In the very moment the lioness struck, she launched the baby upwards with every ounce of her remaining strength. Valerius saw it come, a featureless mass, the swaddling wrap fluttering loosely around it. The girl's dying screams filled his ears as he stretched as far as he could reach with his left hand. He felt his fingers close on the coarse brown cloth and for a single heartbeat the baby's weight was in his control. Relief washed through him as he drew the bundle towards the wall. But he had reckoned without the blood-hungry gods of the arena and they would not be denied. Slowly, the blanket began to unravel, uncoiling one relentless fold at a time from the doll-like figure it protected. Frantically he reached out with his other hand, but the lifeless wooden fist could find no grip on the child's arm. A voice screamed inside his head as the soft thud of the child's body on the sand was instantly followed by the snarls of two cats fighting over a morsel of prey.

For a few seconds his world went dark, but soon something nameless and terrible swelled inside him. He had never known such anger or such despair; a killing rage that was born in his lower body and rose up ready to erupt into suicidal violence. Still holding the blanket, he turned back towards Rodan. The Praetorian held the knife protectively in front of him, but fear marked his ruined face.

'Harm me and your father dies,' the centurion cried. 'He dies.'

Valerius knew he could kill Rodan with a single blow, but what was the point when the man truly responsible was sitting a few paces away. 'Your time will come, Rodan, and when it does, I hope it is my sword that sends you across the Styx.'

He turned towards where Nero sat, his jewelled fingers hooked on to the balcony as he leaned forward to savour every moment of the agony below. A dozen black guards separated Valerius from his target and every eye was on him. He knew that to take a single step in the Emperor's direction was to commit suicide. The killing urge subsided, the fleeting moment gone. As he walked to the stairs his gaze met Poppaea's. He expected to see contempt, even triumph, but instead she stared hard into his eyes and there seemed no mistaking the message she passed.

He hesitated, unsure whether he understood, before walking out of the circus into the clean air and the silence.

They stopped him in the long passageway to the entrance and took him to a room with bare walls which might have been a cell but for the scent of the hay that had been stored there. Valerius sat with his back to the cold stone and worked the coarse wool of the child's blanket through his hands. He had promised Cornelius Sulla he would protect them, but the girl and her baby had died because of him. Nothing on earth would persuade him to deliver Cornelius or Lucina to Torquatus now, even if they killed him for it. The thought steadied him. He felt no fear, but the awfulness of what he had just witnessed had numbed his mind, so he had no control over the visions that flew through it. Savagery in war he could understand. Terror and self-preservation made soldiers kill without mercy and constant proximity to death often led to mindless cruelty. Two men fighting for their lives in the arena had a certain dignity, even honour, but to feed helpless men and women to wild animals and relish the spectacle seemed to him the lowest kind of barbarism, worse even than the druids who threw Roman prisoners into the blazing heart of the Wicker Man. They, at least, had the mitigation of hatred, the excuse of religion, however perverted. He saw again the frown of concentration on the girl's face as she ignored her own fate in that last futile attempt to save her infant. Felt the cloth unwrap one fold at a time as the child fell away from him towards the sand.

'It is not easy to be a defender of Rome.' The softly spoken words came from the darkness. 'You think us cruel? You are mistaken. It is not a matter of cruelty, but of duty. We would betray the Empire if we did not do what was necessary to counter this threat to our

189

people. A cruel man might have exterminated every Judaean in Rome, man, woman and child. But we did not. Instead, we tasked our loyal Hero of Rome, Gaius Valerius Verrens, to seek out the leaders and the followers. The job is part done and, for that, we are grateful to him.'

Valerius shook his head. Was he dreaming? 'The child . . . ?'

'It was not our intention to harm the child. The person who failed in his duty has been dealt with. Your work is not finished. Come.' Nero emerged into the light, accompanied by his guards. Valerius raised himself to his feet and automatically fell in by his side. As they walked, he marvelled at the change in the man. The Nero of a few minutes earlier might never have existed. Which was the actor, the Nero of the arena or the Nero of now? Or were there many Neros hidden behind that single mask? Here was no capricious despot, but a ruler reacting to a threat against his people. Reasoned words spoken in honeyed tones. Crime must be punished. Disobedience must be deterred. The greater the danger, the more extreme the example that must be made. Rome would accept the worship of alien gods, but not to the exclusion of Rome's gods. When he spoke of the paradox of power, Valerius might have been speaking to Seneca. When he spoke of his hopes for Rome, he might have been speaking to himself.

It made what was to come all the more shocking.

They had just reached the path back to the bridge

when the first fire was lit and the screaming began. The victim had been tethered to a wooden stake and coated with gleaming black pitch from head to foot. In seconds all that was visible was a writhing column of flame with a tortured spectre at its centre emitting a sound no human had been born to make. Valerius steeled himself against the horror, knowing this was merely another part of the Emperor's sadistic game, but he could not prevent himself from flinching as the first pyre was joined by another, then another, until ten of the ghastly pillars lit the way. The flames burned red, then gold, then red again as the fire consumed the final remnants of the human form. Then they came to Cornelius.

Nero's executioners had left Cornelius Sulla's face and head clear of the pitch, so Valerius instantly recognized the handsome features and golden hair. Bruises marked his flesh and blood flowed scarlet on to the shining black tar on his chest where he had bitten through his lip in his terror. The slight, youthful body shook uncontrollably in its bonds and he kept his eyes tight shut. Valerius thought he saw the aristocrat's lips move and he asked the gods he didn't believe in to grant a merciful end to the young man he, and he only, had placed on this stake.

Nero moved closer so he could study the bound figure. 'He was braver than he seemed. He uttered only a single name when put to the question and he must have understood that name was already known to us.' He nodded to an unseen presence in the darkness and a torch flared close to Cornelius's feet. For a moment nothing appeared to happen before, with a soft, sputtering roar, an inferno engulfed the tethered body. Valerius saw Cornelius's face twist and contort in the heat and the long golden hair was transformed instantly into a halo of golden flame. At last, the clenched teeth parted and his dying screams tortured the night.

'He makes a better candle than a friend, don't you think?' Nero said almost absently. He turned so Valerius could see the flames reflected in his eyes. 'Cornelius Sulla has a brother, Publius. Torquatus will give you instructions where to find him. You will bring him to us.'

He nodded and was gone, leaving Valerius to stare at a blackened skull with startling white teeth and burning eyes that were still alive.

XIX

'Forget Cornelius Sulla. He's no longer our affair.'

Marcus looked up, startled, but the raw edge to Valerius's voice barred any further questions.

'Can Serpentius and Heracles ride?'

The old gladiator eyed him suspiciously. 'Of course. We're all trained to fight on horseback as well as we do on foot.'

'I want you to use the Emperor's seal to purchase three horses, preferably cavalry trained, and two pack mules. We'll need them in three days.'

'Are we going to fight a war?'

'I hope not, but we are going to join a legion.'

Marcus laughed in disbelief. 'Which legion?'

'The Seventh.'

A week later they stood on the dock at Aternum as the horses were loaded on to the merchant ship on which Valerius had arranged passage to Dalmatia. Sextus and Felix remained in Rome to watch Lucina Graecina. Cornelius Sulla's death made it less likely she would provide them with a link to Petrus, but with so few leads Valerius couldn't afford to ignore the possibility. The four-day ride over Italia's mountainous spine had saved them at least another week's sailing and had the added bonus of accustoming them to the saddle, which would be vital for what awaited them on the other side of the Mare Adriaticum.

'Why is Publius Sulla so important?' The question was from Marcus and Valerius's reply had been simple: 'Because he is the next link in the chain.' But nothing in the clandestine world he now inhabited was so straightforward. The truth was that Cornelius had revealed under torture that his brother was an even more important figure in Petrus's organization than Cornelius himself.

'Publius Sulla is building a network of Christus followers in the legions,' Torquatus had grudgingly revealed. 'If he succeeds it will provide them with a platform to combine a military attack on Rome with a rising in the city itself. Their numbers may be small, but the one thing we have learned is that this cancer spreads quickly. It is possible that he has already involved the general of a legion. If so, we need to discover who this traitor is and destroy him. That is why it is so important to reach Publius Sulla and return him to Rome.'

'Why not get the commander of the Seventh to arrest him? It would be much easier.'

Torquatus had tried to avoid the question, but Valerius persisted. 'Very well. General Vitellius has the Emperor's confidence, but we must be certain. A legion's loyalty and its control lie in the hands of a few senior officers. If we are wrong, it could bring the traitors out into the open before we are ready to act. That would weaken the frontier, and, worse, open up the possibility that other disaffected or ambitious commanders might join the rebels. You have Rome's future in your hands, and your own. Do not mistake me, Verrens, this is a test of your allegiance as well as your ability.'

Marcus and the men accepted their new role without complaint, but Valerius kept his next surprise until just before they boarded the ship.

'You are now honorary members of the Praetorian Guard.' He made the announcement in the dockside tavern where they were waiting. Serpentius looked horrified when Valerius produced the black tunics, silver-plated chest armour and helmets he had requisitioned from the Praetorian barracks, but Heracles, the muscle-bound youngster who had tracked Lucina, grinned with anticipation. 'The tunics and helmets should do well enough and if the breastplates don't fit we'll get the armourer of the Seventh to alter them.'

As they waited to board, Serpentius fiddled with his helmet strap. Valerius doubted the Spaniard would ever look comfortable in a Roman uniform. He explained again why it was so important to wear the armour.

'You have to understand what it is to be part of a legion. The Seventh, *Claudia Pia Fidelis*, is one of the elite units of the Roman army. It fought with Julius Caesar in the Gallic wars a century ago and won its title putting down the Scribonianus rebellion to keep Claudius in power. Its men are fighting soldiers who've just moved from their base on the Rhenus to Viminacium, right up on the Dacian border. They won't welcome anyone who looks like a ration thief, and a nosy civilian investigating one of their officers could end up having an unhappy accident. But if he's a Praetorian tribune with an escort of tough-looking veterans he's at least going to have their respect.'

The voyage took them three days and nights and if any sea journey, with all its attendant threat of shipwreck, mishap or monster, could be described as pleasant, this one was. Balmy winds lightly ruffled the wave tops and the only sounds were the occasional barked command, the gentle rush of the waters beneath the bow and the rhythmic creak of ropes and timbers that is the heartbeat of a ship.

On the morning of the fourth day the captain shook Valerius awake and he rose to find a grey-green strip on the far horizon.

'Land,' the seaman explained. 'We're a little north of where we ought to be, but with these winds we should make port at Acruvium before noon.'

Two hours later they were sailing directly towards what looked like a continuous stretch of unwelcoming, mountainous coastline. Just as Valerius was doubting the captain's sanity they turned into the hidden entrance to a broad inlet which narrowed, widened, then narrowed again before opening into a curiously shaped bay with a small harbour at the southern end. A circle of rugged peaks loomed over them like the walls of a gigantic prison cell and Valerius noticed his companions warily eyeing the mountains. Serpentius, whose tribe inhabited the inhospitable hills of northern Hispania, met his eye.

'Hard. Just like home. Takes hard people to live in a place like this; hard as the rocks. They know how to survive and they know how to kill and they know how to hate. Why would you Romans want a place where they sleep in the snow and learn to chew stones before they learn to speak?'

'Because of what lies beyond it,' Valerius explained patiently. 'Since Caesar's time the barbarian tribes have been moving westwards, increasing the pressure on those who already hold the lands along the Danuvius and the Rhenus. The Empire doesn't have enough legions to contain such a huge migration of peoples, so she uses what she has. Rivers and mountains. To hold the Danuvius, Rome must first hold Dalmatia, Pannonia and Moesia. That's why we want a place like this.'

Serpentius spat. What did he care for Rome's ambitions?

Acruvium turned out to be a small anchorage which was one of the few sheltered landing points on a hundred miles of coast. Valerius presented his travel warrant to the port prefect and requested an escort. The officer laughed when he read their destination. He was one of the young men Rome always sent to her far frontiers: polite, educated, capable and expendable. If he lived, a fine career awaited him when he returned home. If he didn't, only his family would mourn him. 'I have two clerks, and a dozen Thracian auxiliaries who are good for stopping bar fights. I can give you one of them to guide you as far as Doclea, but my advice would be to wait here for the next ship back to Italia and get on it. Viminacium is six days east of here if you happen to be a bird, but you're not birds and that means at least twelve days along the river valleys through the mountains, which is the only way to get anywhere in Dalmatia; first south, then east. Baked by the sun during the day, chilled to the bone at night. And that's if Fortuna smiles on you.'

'And if she doesn't?'

'If she doesn't you'll end up dead – or, worse, not dead – among the cruellest people on this earth. See those two over there.' Valerius followed his glance to a pair of squat, hawk-faced villains seated on boulders near the landing place. The men had the watchful intensity of hungry vultures and wore their dark, oily hair in braids. Their outer clothing was fashioned from part-cured goatskin that Valerius could smell from twenty paces away. 'Illyrian bandits,' the young man explained. 'But then everyone around here is a bandit when he's not trying to scrape a living from soil that's an inch deep and only grows rocks. They've seen your armour and your horses and they reckon they could barter them to their chief for enough provisions to feed their families for a year. That makes you worth a risk. But then again they would probably have a slap at you just for fun. Their favourite method of passing the time with a prisoner is to flay him alive an inch at a time and then impale him on the branch of a thorn tree.'

Valerius shrugged. He'd heard such tales before. 'Why don't you kill them?'

'We do.' The port prefect smiled wearily. 'We've been killing them for a hundred years. The only problem is you can't kill them all.'

They left before sunrise after a night in the prefect's quarters with their swords never far from their sides. The narrow mountain tracks confirmed their host's information and they moved cautiously. At one point their guide stopped and studied a narrow gully ahead, his eyes scanning the rocks and scrubby bushes. Without a word he turned and they rode two miles back to where another poor road branched off, re-joining the main track an hour later.

They reached Doclea just before nightfall, a substantial and surprisingly sophisticated city laid out on Roman lines, cupped in a broad bowl in the mountains near an enormous lake which provided the local people with their main diet of fish. This time the administrator was a harassed older man who answered to the legate at Burnum, a hundred and eighty long miles to the north, and Valerius was forced to show the seal before he agreed to provide an escort. 'But only as far as Naissus. That's where the traders gather to carry their goods up to the market at Viminacium. You'll be able to join a convoy there. They believe in strength in numbers.'

They crossed the border into Moesia Superior the next day, but no one noticed the difference. The mountains still crushed down on them with all their dangerous, intimidating beauty; a cursed grandeur that could kill you even as you admired it. Occasionally they would hear the sound of muted thunder and see the dust cloud over some distant valley that marked an avalanche, or the ground beneath their feet would tremble, and Valerius would make the sign against evil in the knowledge that in this gods-forsaken place Hades could not be far below.

When they joined the convoy at Naissus and took the river road east, he relaxed for the first time. Here they were surrounded by men who knew their business as well as any legionary: mercenaries, former auxiliaries contracted by the rich merchants who had organized the caravan. He'd seen men like these before: Scythians with long curved swords, Thracian mounted archers who lived in the saddle and could put an arrow through your eye at fifty paces, tough little Raetian spearmen with constitutions like camels and legs that would march forty miles in a day. More exotic still was a group of strange gold-haired, bearded men from some chilly northern land, carrying lethal double-headed axes. They wore a motley collection of uniforms or part-uniforms that appeared to represent half a dozen countries and fifteen or twenty different units. Plumed and spiked helmets, exotic fish-scale shirts or armour made of padded cloth. They looked tough and uncompromising. The merchants kept their goods covered, partly to avoid attracting the bandits who watched with greedy eyes from the hills, and partly to avoid tempting the escort, who had been known to cut a few throats and run off with some particularly rich cargo.

At first, merchants and escort alike suspiciously eyed the black tunics and silver breastplates that marked them as members of the Emperor's elite. But gradually the barriers fell as they mixed around the campfires as honest travellers do, and tested their languages against each other. Of them all, Serpentius was most at home among the escort, exercising with them in the cool of the morning and testing the legionary *gladius* against the curved swords of the Scythians or hefting the heavy axes of the northern giants.

'You would have done well as an auxiliary, Serpentius,' Valerius advised him, as they rode side by side at the head of the convoy in the dusty heat of the afternoon. 'You could still; you are young enough. Twenty-five years and a pension and Roman citizenship at the end of it.'

The Spaniard's look darkened. 'I am an honoured member of my tribe, even now, though I am a slave.

201

The Romans killed my family. Why would I wish to fight for Rome and become a Roman?'

'Sometimes it is more sensible to put the past behind you than to allow it to control you. As long as I have the Emperor's seal I can arrange it. There is no need to die in the arena.'

Serpentius solemnly lifted his bald head and the dark eyes glittered. 'Serpentius alone chooses where he lives and where he dies.' His face broke into a grin. 'Wasn't it you who told me I could die in my own time?' He whipped up his horse and rode on to range ahead of the column, but almost in the same instant whirled and screamed at Valerius.

'Ambush!'

Valerius used his knees to turn his horse towards the column about two hundred paces back down the rough dirt track. The reins were wrapped around the wooden fist of his right hand and with his left he drew his sword. Arrows zipped past his head and he ducked low in the saddle as he frantically scanned the roadside for threats. A running figure armed with a long wooden spear came at him from his right and he swerved to avoid the point as it sought out his mount's undefended flank. The manoeuvre brought him close to a raised bank on the opposite side of the track and he heard Serpentius shout a warning. Too late. A second ambusher launched himself from the top of the mound and smashed him from the saddle. Valerius landed with a sickening crash that knocked the wind from him and rattled the helmet from his head. He was stunned by the impact, but his years of training took over. For most military tribunes, service in the legions was merely a step towards a career in politics. They stayed six months, making themselves useful or not, and if they didn't die in some Brigantean forest or German swamp they went home. But not Valerius. He had discovered, to his own surprise as much as anyone's, that he was a true warrior; a natural soldier who enjoyed the challenges of campaigning and could kill without hesitation or conscience. Two years in Britain, and the Boudiccan rebellion, had taught him to survive.

He rolled away from the threat and came to his feet in a single movement, crouching to meet his attacker with his sword held low ready to stab at guts or groin. This wasn't the battle line, it was gutter fighting, but Valerius knew all about gutter fighting. It was about doing whatever it took to win. He noticed with only mild surprise that his opponent was one of the Illyrians who had been waiting at the dock in Acruvium. Dark and feral, the bandit held a long curved knife. He'd be fast and he'd be confident. A scuffling from behind alerted Valerius to a new danger and he half turned to find the spearman fifteen paces away and running towards him. The spear held no fears for the Roman, but the man with the long knife was an added complication. By now Valerius's horse had struggled to its feet and he backed away, placing the frightened animal between himself and the enemy who had knocked him from the saddle.

The move won him vital seconds and he advanced on the spearman to provoke an attack. The Illyrian's face broke into savage grin and he thrust the point at Valerius's throat, which was what the Roman had counted upon. He stepped towards the point, angling to his left, and used the walnut fist of his right hand to parry the blow. The spearman had been forced to aim high because of the breastplate protecting Valerius's chest and stomach and it allowed the Roman to knock the point clear of his right shoulder. At the same time he spun down the length of the spear shaft, slicing the *gladius* edge into his enemy's skull. The shock surged up his arm as the iron blade met solid bone and a smear of crimson stained the air. His opponent dropped like a stone, but he had no time to celebrate victory. The spin brought him face to face with his other foe, who by now had worked his way round the horse and was preparing to plunge the knife into his back. The sight of the bloody *gladius* made him pause, but he jabbed the blue-green blade at Valerius's eyes as he sought the weakness that would give him an advantage. He had to get close, but the Roman's skill with the short sword kept him just out of range for a decisive thrust. The Illyrian danced right and left, seeking an opening, and Valerius was reminded of his bout with Serpentius. *Don't fight like a one-handed man, or a two-handed man. Fight like a killer.* Marcus's words made him smile. The assassin saw the grin and for the first time he felt doubt. He'd seen what had happened to his companion, but that

204

only meant the spoils would be all the greater. All he had to do was kill as he had killed many times before. The smile made it different. The smile meant he faced a man who wasn't cowed by his speed and who would meet his aggression with aggression. The smile meant he needed a way out. But Valerius wasn't going to give him a way out. *Fight like a killer.* He used his own speed and the left-handed sword to keep his opponent off balance, always looking for the opening. He saw the wild eyes flick to the left as a scream told him Serpentius too was keeping his attackers busy. The Illyrian was ready to run when Valerius gave him his opportunity. A slight stumble left his right side open to the knife. The blade flicked out like a viper's strike, but the Roman met it with his wooden hand. Designed to hold a shield, it was shaped like a partially closed fist, and now the fist caught the knife blade and twisted in the same movement. A normal hand would have been cut to the bone, but this was no normal hand. The seasoned walnut bent the inferior iron of the knife and trapped it in its grip. The Illyrian frantically tried to tug the blade free even as Valerius drove the *gladius* deep into his body. The point entered below the breast bone and the force of it drove a grunt of agony from the assassin's throat. Still he kept his grip on the dagger. Only when Valerius twisted the short sword free and the blood spurted from the terrible wound in his abdomen did the dying man collapse to his knees.

Valerius turned to find Serpentius calmly leading

his horse towards him, his sword bloody to the hilt. A dozen men came running from the direction of the convoy. The Illyrian spearman's heels still twitched in the dust and someone cut his throat as Valerius's horse snickered nervously over his body. The other man rocked back and forth on his knees, his dark head bowed over his chest and his hands attempting vainly to hold in his insides. As Valerius watched he vomited a fountain of dark heart blood and rolled slowly forward on to his face.

Two riders appeared from beyond the bank where the ambushers had struck and threw a filthy, ragged bundle at Valerius's feet; a boy of about ten, who immediately began pleading in a language the Roman couldn't understand.

The Scythian veteran commanding the escort spat on the sprawled youth. He snarled an order to the two men, and followed them as they dragged the boy away. Valerius tried not to hear the screams.

A few minutes later the Scythian returned. 'He was holding the ponies back there and would have had his share of this.' He tossed a leather bag to Valerius, who caught it in his good hand. 'Silver. Enough to make them lords of these hills.'

'Who paid them, and why?'

'He said he did not know who. These people learn to lie with their first breath, but I doubt this one lied. He claimed it was a Roman who gave them the order and the silver, and they all look the same to him. As to why, it is simple. They were to kill the officer with the missing hand. They have followed us for a week to ensure they had the right man. The cargo was of no interest to them, my Roman friend. Only you.'

XX

Strabo, the Greek geographer, wrote that the inhabitants of upper Illyricum – now Moesia – 'created caves beneath their dung heaps and lived in them', but Valerius saw without surprise that the Seventh legion *Claudia Pia Fidelis* had made itself much more comfortable at Viminacium in a short space of time. On a rise above the meeting place of the Danuvius and one of its larger tributaries the soldiers had demolished a town of mud huts and replaced it with a fortress that made him feel almost as if he was coming home. He could have been approaching Colonia, Glevum or Londinium, or any of the great military encampments in the Empire. Inside the deep triple ditches and the palisade lay the *principia*, the administrative heart of the legion, surrounded by the long lines of wooden barrack blocks, and beyond it the workshops, marked by the smoke from their glowing braziers, the stables and the supply area. Legionaries patrolled the walls and a cavalry wing exercised in a separate annex on the east side. On a flat piece of ground to the north of the fort, merchants from the surrounding area had created a great market, and below was the reason for it. In the mouth of the smaller river the Seventh had built a new harbour, and from here trim, oared galleys of the Roman navy patrolled to north and south, guarding convoys of supplies for the legions and trade goods from the east and south on their way to Noricum, Raetia and, eventually, Italia. But the most astonishing thing at Viminacium was not the fort or the naval base, but the bridge. Downstream from the fortress, legionary engineers had built a slender wooden crossing over the Danuvius that must have stretched half a mile across the river's narrowest point. Each end of the bridge was guarded by a section of brick-tunicked soldiers and Valerius noticed that on the far side a crowd had gathered waiting for permission to cross.

Marcus, Serpentius and Heracles rode up from the rear of the convoy with the pack mules. Dust had stained their tunics grey and dulled their armour and Valerius insisted they stop for a few minutes to beat the worst of the dirt from their clothing and polish breastplates and helmets. No amount of cleaning could wipe away the weariness that etched their faces. Four days earlier, the perpetual, dangerous mountains had given way to endless plains with barely a landmark to break the horizon. Since then, the monotony had worn down man and beast alike, inducing a hypnotic, heavy-eyed exhaustion that even sleep could not conquer. It was as if the very land was fighting them and Valerius had never been more relieved to complete a journey.

As he said his farewells to the leader of the caravan, Marcus nodded towards the fort, where a group of riders had just emerged from the gateway. 'The natives don't look too friendly.'

They trotted up the slope to meet them.

'Your name?'

Valerius inspected the unsmiling young auxiliary prefect and suppressed an urge to tip him from his saddle into the dust. Not only was a Praetorian entitled to the respect his position demanded, he out-ranked the man and it was customary for officers to exchange names and pleasantries. He looked over the cavalry officer's shoulder towards the fort, where he had no doubt keen eyes were watching the outcome of the confrontation. Someone was sending him a message.

'I asked you your name?' This time the question was more brusque, almost an order.

'My name is not your concern, but your legate's.' Valerius's tone might have been reprimanding a recruit on his first patrol and he saw the first seeds of doubt in the prefect's eyes. 'It is enough for you to know that I am a tribune of the Praetorian Guard and that I am on imperial business. My men and I have travelled from Acruvium and I will require accommodation and rations for at least one week. See to it that this is done.'

The young officer frowned. His horse caught his uncertainty and jerked beneath him, so he had to haul back on the reins to control it. 'I—'

'Are you questioning my orders, prefect?' Valerius snapped impatiently. 'Perhaps it is you who should give *me* your name? I doubt the legate will be pleased to discover that the Emperor's personal representative has been obstructed from doing his duty.'

The officer swallowed hard and saluted. 'I apologize, sir. Flavius Genialis, prefect of the Second Tungrian wing, at your service. We have had trouble with spies and Dacian infiltrators.'

Valerius heard Serpentius snort at the lame excuse and suppressed a smile of his own. 'I doubt many of them were wearing Praetorian uniforms, prefect.' He urged his horse up the shallow slope and his grinning companions followed.

Inside the fort, a servant ushered them to the officers' *mansio*, the temporary accommodation for senior guests. Flavius had wanted to billet Marcus and his companions with the legion's other ranks, but Valerius insisted they stay together.

'You think there'll be trouble?' Marcus asked when the prefect had left them alone. 'We're as welcome as a turd in a punch bowl, but I doubt they'd try anything here, not with us being the Emperor's personal representatives an' all.'

Valerius grinned. 'Let's just say that after all the

time we've spent together I'd miss your company.'

He washed and donned a clean tunic. This was an encounter he'd anticipated, but he'd heard so many differing views of the man he was about to meet that he was uncertain of the outcome. Serpentius gave Valerius's sword a final polish and handed it to him. He replaced it in the scabbard on his right hip.

'Let's hope I don't need it.'

'Gaius Valerius Verrens, tribune of the Guard.' The aide announced his presence to the commander of the Seventh legion.

Valerius saluted the man standing at the far side of the room. By rights, Aulus Vitellius should have been leading an army, not a single legion. He had no record as a military commander, but that had never been an impediment to a military career. A decade and a half ago he had been consul and a favourite of Emperor Claudius. Under Nero his fortunes had first thrived, then waned, and now, it was said, were about to thrive again. In his mid-forties his handsome features had a florid, slightly pasty look, as if they had been modelled from damp clay, and he wore his hair brushed forward over a wide forehead to cover the growing expanse of bare scalp. His enemies said he was a drunkard who never held a thought long enough to make a rational decision. His friends said he was a misunderstood genius who would one day sit at the Emperor's right hand.

As Valerius stood to attention, the general studied

him with a hint of amusement in the light blue eyes.

'I had expected you to be older.' The voice was deep, the accent cultured, perhaps exaggerated to counter the detractors who said his family came from rough plebeian origins. 'A year ago, Seneca talked of you as the next Scipio: a general in the making. I see a young man with little experience but a surfeit of conceit. Enough, in any case, to force his way into my command and embarrass one of my officers.'

The general paused, but Valerius didn't respond to the implied rebuke.

'And yet the young man is a Hero of Rome.' Vitellius's eyes took in the wooden hand. 'And he has made great sacrifices for the Empire. They tell me you fight as well with the sword in your left hand as you once did with your right.' Now how did he know that, Valerius wondered? 'Perhaps we should put on an entertainment. A Hero of Rome against my best swordsman. What do you think?'

For answer, Valerius pulled the imperial seal from his tunic and held it out so that Vitellius could see exactly what it was. 'I think I am not some two-headed snake to be paraded for your garrison's entertainment, general. I am here on a mission from the Emperor and I will carry it out with your support . . . or without it.'

'You have it, of course,' Vitellius nodded, untroubled by the lack of deference from the younger man. 'But first I must know the substance of this mysterious assignment. Perhaps you wish to march out at dawn with my legion at your back? I am sure the Emperor would be most pleased if you were to add Dacia to the list of Rome's provinces.'

Valerius smiled politely. They both knew the last thing the Emperor wanted was more barbarians to worry about. 'You have a tribune on your staff, Publius Sulla?'

'A fine young officer, diligent and ambitious.'

'I would like to talk to him; he may have information of value to my investigation. It is possible that he will have to return with us to Rome . . . with your permission, of course.'

The lines on Vitellius's broad forehead deepened.

'I am afraid that may be difficult.' He walked to a cloth map pinned to the far wall and pointed to a position beyond the winding blue ribbon of the river. 'The boy has been pining for an independent command, as you young men do. You know our situation?' Valerius shook his head. 'The Seventh, soon to be followed by the Fourth, has been sent here to curb the ambitions of Coson, the Dacian king across the river there, who seeks to annex land for his tribe on the west bank. Coson knows Rome will not countenance it, but for reasons of internal politics he must be seen to make the attempt. A number of small parties have crossed by boat to the east – here, here and here – some of them made up of warriors, others entire families of dispossessed farmers. We have sent them all back, peacefully where possible, by force if not. Your barbarian, young Verrens, appreciates force. At present, however, we are in a period of negotiation.

Coson has withdrawn his warriors ten miles from the line of the river in return for a substantial subsidy. To ensure this bargain is adhered to I have set up an outpost, here.' The position he marked was well into Dacian territory. 'Publius Sulla commands there.' He smiled apologetically. 'Some wine?'

'Why can't he just send a messenger and bring Publius back?' Serpentius wondered suspiciously.

Valerius adjusted his bedroll. 'It's a matter of face. His and mine. He's testing us to see how far we're prepared to go to complete Nero's task. Maybe he doesn't want to lose a promising officer, maybe he can't afford to lose *any* officers. It happens. A legion is never at full complement and this is a complicated command.'

'I don't like it.'

'I don't like it either, but the only power we have is the power of this seal and these uniforms. If we sit and wait for Publius to come back – and the chances are he's been warned not to – that power diminishes every day. First we'll be sneered at, then we'll be laughed at, and after that . . . well, we'll never get Publius Sulla out of here.'

'So we cross the river?' Marcus sounded thoughtful.

'We cross at dawn. We ride to the outpost and we bring Publius back.'

'What if he doesn't want to come?'

'He'll come.'

'But if he doesn't . . . ?'

'That's why you're here, and we'll have an escort of twenty auxiliary cavalry from the fort. But that won't be necessary. He'll come, for his family's honour, and because if he doesn't he knows his career is finished. Vitellius will eventually be forced to send him back in chains.'

Marcus looked at the two others. They hadn't signed up to go beyond the Empire's boundaries. Heracles nodded immediately. Serpentius hesitated, then followed suit.

'Dawn then,' Marcus said, and wrapped himself in his blanket.

Valerius sat for a few moments before dousing the oil lamp. He pulled his own blanket over his body and closed his eyes. But he didn't sleep.

Because tomorrow they were going into the unknown.

XXI

Poppaea was alone now, and she had never felt more frightened. Cornelius Sulla had been her only link to Petrus and now he was gone. She shuddered as she remembered how Nero had delighted in showing her the avenue of obscene lumps of charcoal that were all that remained of the blazing pyres. He had taken particular pleasure in pointing out Cornelius's grinning skull and recalling details of his agonies that had brought her close to fainting away. At first she had feared he was singling her out and that at any moment a squad of Praetorians would arrive to arrest her. But this was Nero. He took a perverse pride in the unmasking of the Christian at the heart of his court and the way the one-handed tribune, Valerius, had been duped into achieving it. Another triumph for Torquatus, the master spy. The more her husband revealed, the clearer it became that someone close to Valerius must be a traitor. Nero laughed as he told how the Praetorian commander's 'useless louts' had lost all trace of Valerius and his men as they tracked Lucina Graecina. Yet within a few hours of Valerius's confronting Cornelius Sulla, the young aristocrat was locked away. The only explanation was that Fabia's friend was being betrayed by one of his own men.

Her heart quickened as she recalled the glance she had shared with Valerius. She had been aware of him from the moment she and Nero had walked down the stairway into the crowded room, his youth and stern features marking him among the inebriated laughter and pink, grinning faces. She had sensed a power in him that, in its own way, rivalled the power of Petrus. The artificial hand fascinated her, although she would not have noticed it without Fabia's prompting because he carried it so naturally. She had never witnessed such a magnificent combination of anger and torment as Valerius had shown when the beasts were unleashed on their helpless victims. Here was a man to be taken seriously. A man to be feared. A champion. And she had never needed the services of a champion more.

She had convinced herself that Valerius was the only man who could help her. She told herself he had responded to her mute appeal. But what could he do? Caesar had commissioned him to hunt down the very man who had given her hope. It was impossible.

With that thought came despair. She felt her world crumble; a fracturing of the mind that walked hand in hand with panic-stricken terror. What did a single glance mean? She was deluding herself. No man alive could help her now. Slowly, she walked out to the balcony and leaned across the parapet. Far below she could see the temples and the columns and the basilicas and the figures scurrying between them. She raised her arms and pushed her upper body forward until her toes barely touched the floor and the worked stone of the balustrade cut into her waist. One more inch and it would be finished. One more inch and there would be no turning back. The weight of her head and shoulders would carry her over the edge and she would plunge on to those stones so far below. Her head spun. One more inch. She must have the courage. Just one more inch.

She took a breath.

'Poppaea?'

The moment was gone.

'Poppaea?'

She turned and the mask resumed its customary position.

'I am here, Caesar.' She allowed a smile to touch her voice as she walked back into the room where Nero awaited her. He was breathing heavily and the shining pink face made her think of a freshly washed pig.

'I was concerned for you, my love.'

'And I am grateful for your concern, Caesar, but as you can see it is not necessary.'

'I'm so pleased,' he said. His tone told her what was

coming next. 'Because I have a special treat for you tonight.'

He took her gently by the hand and led her towards the room she thought of as his torture chamber.

XXII

Valerius noticed that the Tungrian escort commander was nervous and that surprised him. Vitellius had insisted that such patrols beyond the river were routine. Still, he doubted that the legionary commander had ever ventured into Dacia with an escort of fewer than a thousand men. This was different. Perhaps the man had reason to be concerned. Valerius's hand automatically reached up to stroke the golden boar amulet. It had become his talisman since the day he had taken it from Maeve's neck as she lay amongst the countless thousands of dead on the field of Boudicca's last battle. He had convinced himself the glittering metal was invested with the indomitable spirit and fierce pride she had carried to her grave. It had never failed him and he had a feeling he had never needed it more than he did now. They were gathered in front of the fortress gates, twenty auxiliary cavalry wearing chain link vests over tunics that had once been red, and four in the black and silver of the Praetorian Guard. They waited in uneasy silence, for this was the hour that forced each man to face his thoughts and fears alone. In the chill darkness just before dawn a ghostly blanket of silver drifted around them in the torchlight. The mist hid everything beyond ten paces, but the ever-present rush of vast waters pinpointed the river's position away to their left.

The auxiliary leader, Festus, had briefed his men the previous night, but now he repeated the orders for the benefit of Valerius and the others. 'It should be simple. We will cross the bridge and ride south to the base of the hills, then on to the fort. Eight miles. Two hours at most. Stay alert. Listen for orders. With Fortuna's favour we won't even smell a Dacian. When we get there, we do what we have to do and then we ride home. Any questions?'

Valerius shook his head. Curious that there was no mention of Publius Sulla, but he supposed the decurion was being sensible. No point in inflaming an already awkward situation.

They walked the horses across the bridge, their hooves rapping on the thick wooden planks and echoing eerily in the fog. In the darkness, the slim structure seemed to go on for ever, and the Danuvius, oily, black and swirling, ran worryingly close below. The awesome power of that huge volume of water made Valerius feel a little unsteady.

A minute later they stepped from the end of the

bridge on to Dacian soil. They were beyond the edge of the Empire.

At first, the country on the east bank of the river mirrored that which they had just left. A great flat plain stretched into the distance, with only a thin line on the far horizon to give the impression of rising ground. The cavalrymen rode in pairs, at the trot, the points of their seven-foot ash spears glinting in the first rays of sunlight and the coats of the big horses steaming in the cool air. Festus positioned Valerius and his men at the rear of the little column, which surprised the Roman. Normally the less experienced men would ride in the centre where they couldn't get into trouble. The Tungrian dismissed his concerns. 'If they hit us in the open, we'll see them in plenty of time to run, and I want you at the back where you'll have a head start. If we have to run my lads won't slow up to hold your hands, so put your heels to your horses and your heads down and ride.'

'The Dacians. What kind of fighters are they?' Valerius asked.

'Animals,' the decurion spat. 'If they aren't fighting us, they're fighting the Sarmatians or the Thracians, or each other. You kill all you can find and still there are more, like ants, and each one who dies thinks he goes to sit at the right hand of their heathen god Zalmoxis, who'll give him twenty big-titted wives, so he doesn't give a fuck. They fight with long curved knives. Not killing knives, gutting knives. And they like to decorate their spears with Roman balls. You understand?' Valerius felt an involuntary tightening in his stomach. 'The only good thing about them is that their horses are no match for ours and their warriors have no discipline.'

Valerius attempted to draw him on Publius Sulla, but with no success.

'Cavalry and infantry don't mix. I saw him about the fort. Just another beardless Roman boy. The kind the Dacians eat for dinner.' He gave a sour smile. 'Just like you.'

As they travelled further south the terrain changed and the country became dotted with bushes, then stunted thorn trees. The ground began to rise, the trees closed in on them and the feeling of being vulnerable pieces on a flat gaming board was replaced by the nerve-jangling tension of never knowing what might be round the next bend in the track. Valerius noticed the knuckles gripping the spear shafts go a little whiter and carefully tested the draw of his sword.

After less than two hours, the column halted at the head of a small tree-lined defile and Festus rode back to them.

'One of the scouts thinks he saw something ahead. I'm going to take the patrol to investigate. Wait here and I'll send a man back for you once we're clear.'

Valerius felt Marcus bridle at his side, but he put a hand on his arm. This was Festus's command. He knew the enemy and he knew the ground. Only a fool would question his orders. He nodded agreement and they watched uncertainly as the spear points disappeared into the trees ahead.

Minutes passed and the only sound was the irritating whine of insects and the heavy snort of horses' breathing. Valerius waited for the clink of brass that would herald the patrol's return, but gradually it became clear they were alone and likely to stay that way. He felt the hairs on the back of his neck bristle and exchanged glances with Marcus.

'Anyone else feel like the lamb that's separated out and made to feel very special just before Saturnalia?' Serpentius asked conversationally. The tumble of trees and bushes around them was suddenly much more sinister. Even the birds which had been singing a few moments earlier were silent now.

'We can go on, or we can go back,' Marcus said. 'But we can't stay here.'

Valerius had already made his decision. 'We go on. We have a job to finish, with or without them.'

'Without. They've fucked us.'

Valerius nodded. No point in discussing it. For whatever reason, Festus had abandoned them. The only question was: to what? He saw Serpentius fumbling in the large cloth bag tied to the pommel of his saddle. The Spaniard extracted a short, curved bow and a sheath filled with arrows. Valerius raised an eyebrow.

Serpentius shrugged. 'A gift from the Thracians in the caravan escort. I've never used it from the back of a horse, but it might put one of the bastards off their stroke.'

Valerius took the lead, and they moved ahead cautiously, Marcus covering the right flank, Heracles the left and Serpentius continually glancing over his shoulder to check the rear. The heat of the morning had become oppressive, thickening the air around them. Every tree and every hummock concealed a potential threat and Valerius felt the tension growing in his arms and neck. He adjusted the strap of his helmet and wiped the sweat from his eyes.

'What if the outpost has been abandoned?' Marcus asked, keeping his voice low.

'We'll give it another half an hour and then turn back.'

Serpentius sniffed the air. 'They're out there. I can smell them.'

Valerius searched the treeline, which opened out on the left before converging again into a narrow funnel. The immediate threat seemed to come from the opposite side, the right, and that made the funnel a natural escape route, a welcoming refuge from the storm. To his front was an area of boulder-strewn slope that might have been designed as a trap for their horses. He sensed a dark shadow spreading through the trees.

'Ready,' he called.

They came with a howl, a mass of bare-chested, bearded warriors carrying painted oval shields and the wicked curved knives Festus had described. Swords, too, of similar design but heavier and wielded two-handed.

'Now! Ride on!' The three men reacted instantly to Valerius's roared command. The opening to the left was where the Dacians wanted him to go, which meant that beyond the gap would be a carefully set ambush. Better to take their chances in the open. He kicked his mount to the gallop, aiming for an almost imperceptible break in the line of boulders ahead, and heard a welcome roar of frustration from behind.

But his enemy hadn't entirely neglected the hillside and a line of warriors rose from the scrub in front of Valerius. He heard the zip of an arrow and felt the wind of something past his right ear. At first he thought it was a near miss, but the arrow took one of the Dacians in the centre of the chest and he realized Serpentius was shooting from behind his shoulder. Another horse might have checked at the howling barrier ahead, but this was a trained cavalry mount. Time and again on the practice ground he had been forced to ride through alarming, screaming men like these until he had become certain of his own invulnerability. Without any urging from Valerius the horse surged ahead, teeth bared and screaming his own battle cry. Valerius kept his head down and his sword ready and concentrated on staying in the saddle. A sickening crunch followed by a momentary check. A snarling face appeared below and to his left and he felt hands scrambling for his foot. The sword sliced down and the face disappeared in an explosion of bright blood. More faces among the rocks, mouths gaping in surprise. Then he was through and into the trees beyond the boulder line. He glanced over his shoulder and felt a surge of relief. Marcus galloped a few paces behind, a broad grin on his leathered face. Behind him Serpentius roared with laughter. Heracles rode at his side wearing a grimace of concentration and holding a severed Dacian head between his teeth by its long hair.

'You've never seen anything like it,' Serpentius called. 'A single cut and it spins up into the air, then the crazy bugger catches it with one hand. I told him to get rid of it, but he seems attached to the bloody thing.'

Marcus shouted something at the young Sarmatian, and with a grin Heracles allowed the head to drop free.

Valerius's heart still hammered from the mad charge, but his mind was frantically attempting to work out where they were. He recalled some details of the map in Vitellius's quarters, but the tracks Festus had followed had twisted so much it was difficult to know just what direction they had taken. He looked up at the sun, which was over his right shoulder. Late morning, perhaps approaching noon, which meant it was now in the south. If they turned back and travelled due west, they would eventually reach the river, but that would take them straight to the Dacians. The safest way back was to ride north-west, take a wide arc to avoid the ambush and work their way through the hills until they reached the plain. After that they should be home free.

But he hadn't ridden all this way to give up now.

'Publius Sulla's outpost can't be more than a couple of miles ahead,' he said. 'We go on.'

Marcus wiped blood from his sword with a piece of saddle cloth. 'Do you think he'll still be there?'

'I think there's only one way we're going to find out,' Valerius said grimly. He had no doubt that the patrol's vanishing act and the Dacian ambush were linked to the man he sought, but he would worry about that later. His first priority was to survive. He ordered the three men to conserve the contents of their water skins and Marcus handed out the food he'd brought. The rest of the rations had been with the patrol.

After about ten minutes they came across a path. Serpentius studied the ground. 'Old tracks, but too big for native horses. Roman cavalry mounts, probably a few mules.'

They followed the trail for a mile and a half before they came to a broad, man-made clearing. At its centre stood a small temporary fort surrounded by three wide ditches and a six-foot turf rampart mounted with sharpened wooden stakes. The only entrance was across an earth causeway and the wooden gate was protected from direct attack by a raised bank that restricted the approach. The defences looked pathetically inadequate against the primeval forces they'd met earlier. As Valerius studied the fort, the blast of a horn was followed by shouting and a line of polished helmets appeared above the palisade.

Valerius drew to a halt short of the triple ditch. 'Couriers from General Vitellius,' he shouted. 'With orders for the fort commander.'

From behind the earth barrier came the sound of a gate creaking open.

XXIII

A powerful voice called from the rampart. 'Approach, friend, but do it slowly and keep your hands where we can see them.' Valerius heard Marcus laugh. It was a typically cautious frontier welcome. Better to be nervous than dead. He took a deep breath and kicked his horse forward.

To meet Publius Sulla.

At first sight, the interior of the camp was as unimpressive as the exterior. He doubted whether familiarity would improve the experience. Lines of worn leather tents, sufficient to house a full century, filled the centre, beside a larger tent which would be the commander's quarters. Horse lines and latrines had been set up beside the turf banks of the parapet, all contained within a dusty space sixty paces square. A painfully small squad of men went about the daily business of the fort while the rest manned the ramparts. Two weeks in this place would wear down any soldier's morale. Two months would drive him mad.

Publius Sulla, tribune of the Seventh and brother of the traitor Cornelius, waited alone in the centre of the dirt square that passed for the parade ground. A terrible melancholy overcame Valerius as he recognized the man he had come to take back to Rome. When last he'd looked into those pale eyes they'd been staring at him from a blackened skull. He'd expected a likeness, but no one had warned him that Publius Sulla was Cornelius's identical twin. Different characters, certainly – Publius was leaner, harder and more earnest than his brother – yet in looks they were indistinguishable. A vision of a writhing column of flame engulfed Valerius's mind and whatever he had meant to say died stillborn in his mouth.

'Is this all?' The young commander broke the silence. 'I was expecting a column with a month's rations. What I see is four more mouths to feed.'

Valerius handed his reins to Marcus and the veteran gladiator led their mounts to the horse lines. 'Gaius Valerius Verrens, at your service. I apologize, tribune, but we were parted from our escort and ambushed a few miles south of here.'

'Ambushed?' Publius instantly forgot the missing rations. 'That's impossible. We have a truce with the Dacian king and I spoke with his representatives not five days ago. If the situation had changed my spies in Coson's camp would have informed me before now. Clodius!' A veteran legionary appeared from his place at the parapet. 'Increase the alert and send out a patrol. I want to know if there's any movement within a mile of the fort. It's possible we have a renegade band trying to stir up trouble. But tell them to act defensively. I need information, not heads.'

Valerius was impressed by the young man's professionalism. He issued his orders without any sense of panic or confusion. The ambush was just a new dimension of this complicated command to be dealt with. 'An interesting posting to volunteer for, tribune,' he ventured.

'Volunteer?' Publius's laugh betrayed his bitterness. He led Valerius up a set of wooden steps to the top of the rampart. 'No one would be foolish enough to volunteer for this. You've seen our position. This should be an auxiliary command. Instead, those men lining the walls are the dregs of the legion; the moaners and the shirkers and the brawlers. I have eighty of them, plus twenty horse, to cover fifty miles of frontier, and they stay alert because I've managed to convince them that if they do not they will die here. Not that they should need much convincing. We're ten miles beyond the Danuvius and any chance of reinforcement, and we've been down to half rations for five days. The moment Coson decides to break the truce, which he will, the Dacians will gobble us up like a wolf pouncing on a newborn lamb. This post is meant to be a show of Rome's strength. The reality is that it is a sacrifice to my general's vanity.' He looked directly into Valerius's eyes. 'Now, to your business,

233

Praetorian. Even a lowly junior tribune knows that it does not take four men and an auxiliary escort to deliver orders.'

Valerius nodded distractedly. He had been wondering why Vitellius had lied to him about Publius Sulla's posting. If he'd lied about that, what else had he lied about? He had planned a quick, dispassionate arrest the moment he arrived at the post. Any hope of that had disappeared when he saw Cornelius's eyes in his brother's boyish face. The longer he was with Publius, the more he found himself liking this young man he was about to destroy. 'Perhaps we may discuss it in private,' he suggested quietly.

Publius caught something in the other man's voice and produced a bleak smile. 'As you see, privacy is in short supply in our little home from home. Join me in my tent. My orderly will see that your men are fed what little we can offer.'

He pulled back the flap and they entered a dusty, humid interior lit by vents in the ceiling which allowed in the sun. The tent was perhaps five paces wide by ten long with a floor of beaten earth. The only luxuries were a portable desk and stool to one side, which were faced by a second chair, and a campaign bed set against the rear wall. The tribune removed his helmet and *gladius* and invited Valerius to do the same. Valerius realized he should have insisted that Marcus and Serpentius accompany him, but he could hardly refuse now. He placed his sword belt on the bed beside the other man's.

Publius took his seat at the desk and Valerius sat facing him. 'Please.' The tribune nodded for Valerius to begin.

'I am here to escort you back to Rome.'

Valerius saw the colour drain from Publius Sulla's face, but otherwise there was no reaction to what they both knew could be a death sentence.

'And may I know the reason?' Somehow the young tribune kept his voice steady.

'Only that it is by the direct order of the Emperor.'

The younger man breathed out a long sigh. 'So. That means Cornelius is taken and . . . ?' He looked to Valerius for confirmation of his unspoken question. Valerius nodded. For a moment Publius's face twisted in pain and he shook his head like a man fighting the iron of a sword buried deep in his vitals. He struggled to regain his composure but when he spoke again his voice held only defiance. The earnest blue eyes drilled into Valerius. 'Our work will continue, you know. All through the Empire men like Cornelius are spreading the message of Jesus Christus. Every day, more and more are willing to do God's work, and I doubt that even Nero can kill us all. He seeks to destroy us because he fears us, and he is right to fear us, because no matter what he does to us we will only become stronger. You might think that the legions are stony ground in which to plant the seeds of change, Praetorian, but you would be wrong. Who needs his god by his side more than a soldier about to march out and die? Tell him they are out there, waiting for

235

the day. When the day comes it is God's will that must prevail. But then I doubt you understand what I am talking about.'

'I understand.'

Publius looked up in surprise and something flickered in his eyes. Hope? 'You know about the great forces at work here, yet you still do his bidding?'

Valerius straightened. 'Like you, tribune, I am a soldier, and soldiers follow orders.'

Publius rose to his feet and walked in three strides to the bed. Too late Valerius remembered where he had left his sword. He heard the familiar, almost musical hiss of a *gladius* being drawn from its scabbard. Publius kept his face to the tent wall so that Valerius couldn't read his expression. 'Cornelius was strong, but he lacked physical courage. It was something he was always ashamed of,' he said softly.

'He did not lack courage at the end.' Valerius remembered the crimson streak running down the tar from the young aristocrat's torn lip. 'I have never seen a braver man.'

Publius nodded to himself. 'Yet he would not have fought them. He would have gone with them like a lamb. A lamb to the slaughter. Well, know this, Gaius Valerius Verrens.' He turned at last, the naked blade bright in his hand. 'Publius Sulla is a soldier and will die like a soldier. I will not go gently like a lamb to Nero's slaughter.'

Valerius tensed, ready to meet the tribune's attack. He knew he had little chance of surviving if Publius was as comfortable with the sword as he appeared but he vowed to die trying. When he was dead, Publius would have Marcus, Serpentius and Heracles arrested on some trumped-up charge, perhaps even for Valerius's murder, and there would be an unhappy accident on the way back to Viminacium. Maybe this was the way General Vitellius had planned it all along.

But Publius hadn't finished. 'Senators, soldiers and slaves, men and women of all ranks, aye, to the very highest, even in the heart of the monster's lair at the very centre of Nero's court, are already waiting to replace me. I have only one last request, Praetorian, and I make it because I sense a decency in you that belies your words and your mission. Do what you can for my family.'

With his final words Publius Sulla placed the point of the *gladius* against his sternum and used all his strength to drive its length up into his heart.

'No!' Valerius dived across the room, but it was already too late. With a sharp cry, Publius fell back on the bed, his whole body shuddering, hands still locked on the sword hilt and eyes bulging as his boyish face turned old in a heartbeat. Valerius knelt at the young man's side and cradled his head. 'Publius,' he whispered urgently. 'I will help your family if I can. I will help them all. But you have to tell me how to find Petrus. I must find Petrus.'

Publius opened his mouth, but Valerius would never hear his answer. Dark blood welled up in the tribune's throat and spilled like wine from his lips. He gave one last convulsion and was still. With a sigh Valerius looked down on the dead boy.

Gradually it dawned on him that with his emotional final words Publius might have revealed more than he had intended. 'Senators, soldiers and slaves, men and women of all ranks . . . *even at the very centre of Nero's court*.' Cornelius had been a member of Nero's court, but a peripheral figure, never *at the very centre*. It meant that someone at the highest level had a powerful incentive for thwarting the investigation, and, more important, the power to ensure that happened.

He pulled the tent flap aside and looked across the parade ground. Marcus, Serpentius and Heracles were talking together by a rampart where the cook's fire had been set into the dirt mound. Valerius called them across. Inside the tent Serpentius produced a low whistle and Marcus gave the sign against evil. Heracles just stared with his mouth open.

'We don't have much time,' Valerius warned them. 'I suspect Publius was a popular officer and the likelihood is that the men will take their officer's death badly. We are going to call the senior legionary. When he gets here, flank me, and for the gods' sake try to look like Praetorians.'

He went to the door and asked a passing legionary to send Clodius to the tent. The man shot him a puzzled look, but saluted and ran off in search of the *duplicarius*. When Clodius appeared, Valerius drew him inside. Seeing the dead man, the veteran gave a low growl and his hand went to his sword. Before he

238

could draw it he froze with the needle tip of Marcus's *gladius* against his throat.

'Soldier.' Valerius kept his voice steady. 'Do you recognize what this is?' He held up the chain with the imperial seal. Clodius had to look twice, but eventually he nodded.

'Publius Sulla was an enemy of Rome and has paid for his crime with his life. My name is Gaius Valerius Verrens, tribune of the Praetorian Guard, and I am taking temporary command of this outpost.' Valerius paused and Clodius clearly expected the next order to be for his execution. 'But when I leave, the fort will be your responsibility. Do you understand?'

Clodius frowned, but he risked another nod. Valerius's next words surprised him.

'I can't order you to abandon your position, but with your officer dead and rations running out you would be justified in returning with us. If you choose to leave, the men have an hour to demolish the fort and pack up their gear. My report will state that the decision was made with my full support.'

Clodius hesitated. This wasn't the kind of judgement he expected to have to make. He shot a frightened glance towards Publius's body.

'Whatever you decide nothing will happen to you,' Valerius assured him.

The *duplicarius* shook his head. 'No. I'll stay, and if I stay the men stay. I was accused of cowardice after I discovered my officer had been selling horse feed to the merchants at the river market for his own profit.

That's why I am here. If I stay I have a chance to win back my honour. General Vitellius is not a bad man, just badly advised. Ask him to send a month's rations and a new commander.'

'Can you control your men when they hear that the tribune is dead?'

'I think . . . yes. He wasn't their regular officer. They liked him well enough, but most of them had only really known him for a few weeks. If I can assure them that help and food is on its way, they'll behave. Will you stay the night, sir?'

Valerius shook his head. There was still enough light left to reach the river. 'No, we'll leave as soon as we're ready. Put together what rations you can for us. I'll speak to the men before we go.'

They felt like deserters as they rode from the fort with the demoralized garrison watching from the walls. For all his fine words about honour and courage and his pledge to send reinforcements, Valerius doubted any of the legionaries he left behind would ever return to Viminacium.

He kept his eyes to the front. Behind him came Marcus and Serpentius, and at the rear Heracles led Publius Sulla's horse, with its master's body across its back wrapped in a bedding sheet. Eight of the fort's cavalry troopers escorted them for the first mile and when they left Valerius felt as vulnerable as when they'd been abandoned by the patrol. The others sensed it too.

'If I ever see that bastard Festus again, I'll cut his throat,' Serpentius spat.

Valerius shook his head. 'Vitellius will make sure he's tucked away somewhere safe. I doubt if you'll ever see him again.'

He couldn't have been more wrong.

They rode for close to an hour before they found the first body. The Dacians had hung it by the heels from a tree with a leather strap cut through the tendons of both ankles. He had been stripped naked, but the pale torso and walnut brown arms tied behind his back marked him as a Roman soldier. His captors had suspended him head down a few inches above a large fire, and Valerius didn't like to think about the agonies he had experienced before his skull had exploded.

'Do we bury him?' Marcus asked.

Valerius shook his head. 'It would only tell them where we are and we don't have the time.' And where there was one, there would be more.

'Could have been us. Serves the bastard right,' Serpentius muttered without conviction.

Festus was recognizable when they found him, if you looked carefully, and alive, if you could call it alive. Strange that the young port prefect in Acruvium had described the Tungrian's fate so accurately. The words had been chilling enough: *Their favourite method of passing the time with a prisoner is to flay him alive and then impale him on the branch of a thorn tree.* The reality was fit to drive a man to madness.

241

Festus's eyeballs danced in his skull like white beads in a jar. As well as his skin, his Dacian torturers had removed his lips, his eyelids, his nose and any other useful protrusions. He was no longer a human being, but a mess of blood and tissue wriggling obscenely on a four-foot stake. Valerius wondered why he hadn't mercifully bled to death until he noticed that the gaping wound where his genitals had hung had been stuffed with earth to stop the bleeding and prolong his agony.

'I'll do it,' the Spaniard said. Serpentius dismounted and approached the shivering horror that had once been a man. With a short prayer and a single, almost tender stroke of his sword, he sliced through the vertebrae at the base of Festus's neck. The Tungrian's head flopped forward and his body went still. After that they rode on in silence, each man alert for the first sign of danger and at the same time alone with his thoughts and fears.

It was Marcus who heard the shouts, away to their left. The survivors of the cavalry patrol must have believed they'd reached the relative safety of the plain when they were caught. From a nearby ridge Valerius saw immediately that their surviving leader had chosen to go to ground rather than fight his way out. It had been a mistake. Now the patrol was surrounded on three sides of a bare hilltop by a jeering horde of Dacians who danced among the trees and darted out to hurl spears, scream insults and no doubt threaten them with the same fate as Festus. The only thing keeping them at bay was the wall of cavalry spears the Tungrians had set up on the approaches to the hill, which backed on to a sheer cliff face. The Dacians seemed in no hurry, but how long that would last only the gods knew. At least the auxiliaries still had their horses, hobbled together in a shallow dish at the base of the cliff.

He slithered back to where the others waited. 'What now?' Marcus whispered.

Valerius looked at each of them in turn. He had brought them to this. They owed him nothing. They owed Rome nothing. 'Take Publius Sulla's body. Once you're out of the hills, keep riding west and you'll arrive at the river. Just follow it upstream until you reach the bridge.'

'What about you?' Serpentius asked.

The question had only one answer. 'I'm a Roman soldier. I can't leave other Roman soldiers to die, not even these bastards.'

Serpentius and Marcus exchanged a glance of agreement. 'This uniform says I'm a Roman soldier too,' the Spaniard said. 'Even if I'm not happy about it. Besides, if you get killed who's going to pay us?'

'And you, Heracles?'

'If it wasn't for you I would probably already be dead.'

'Then this is what we will do.'

XXIV

Valerius looked out from the cliff top into the black void below. A ring of Dacian fires blazed around the hill where the Tungrians were trapped, but they shed no light on the perilous descent he was about to attempt. He'd studied the cliff face while there was still daylight and thought he'd chosen the safest route, but now, seventy feet above the sheer drop, he was almost unnerved by niggling uncertainty. What if he reached a point where there were no holds? What if he became trapped until the power in his fingers faded and he plunged on to the rocks below? But there was no point in delaying. He allowed himself to slip backwards over the cliff edge, his feet searching for the first toehold. He was barefoot, the better to find the tiny cracks and hollows that would support him on the descent. The face of the cliff was composed of curious honeycombed rock which provided plenty in the way of hand- and footholds, but the stone was soft so he had to test each one to ensure it would take his weight. There would be no second chances. Just one mistake and he'd end up smeared over the valley floor and that wouldn't do the auxiliaries any good at all.

When he'd explained his plan Marcus had stared at him as if he had lost his mind. 'A one-handed man climbing down a sheer cliff in pitch darkness? It is beyond foolishness. You are committing suicide. Let me try.'

Valerius shook his head and continued unbuckling his armour with Serpentius's help. 'How many cliffs did you climb in all your years in Rome, old man?' He saw Marcus flinch at the reference to his age and smiled to take the edge off the jibe. 'You could do it, Marcus, so could Serpentius, but only I can do what needs to be done when I reach the bottom. They are soldiers, and they will only be led by another soldier.'

'But your hand . . .'

'When I searched the cliffs on my father's estate for pigeon eggs, I often had to climb down single-handed. If anything this is simpler.'

Which was easy to say, but, now that he put it into practice, not so easy to do. It was true that he'd climbed one-handed, but he'd always carried the eggs in his left hand and he'd had the option of dropping them if he got into trouble. Now, he edged his way downwards in the certain knowledge that if the fingers of his left hand lost their grip nothing would save him. He was sweating heavily, and not because of the warmth of the night. Yet the further he descended, the more confident he became. He might only have a single hand, but it had gripped a sword every day for the past six years. The skin had the texture of part-cured leather and the fingers the strength of an iron claw. The walnut fist of his right hand could be used to jam into cracks in the rock, and, even where there were none, to steady and balance himself. At first he clung close to the surface, but gradually he became more confident as his bare feet unerringly found one toehold after another.

He was a third of the way down when his boldness betrayed him.

Valerius knew he'd made a mistake the moment he allowed his weight to settle on the outcrop beneath his left foot. The soft rock crumbled just as his left hand loosed the grip that anchored him to the face. He felt himself falling away and flailed desperately at the rock for some kind of hold. The cliff flashed past his face and he knew he was dead.

He would never understand how he did it. As he fell, his momentum took him in a half-turn away from the wall of rock, which was now out of reach of his left hand. Yet, somehow, he managed to lunge forward with his right. A jagged slash of pain tore at him as the walnut fist jammed into a narrow cleft and the leather strings binding the socket sliced into his flesh, driven by the entire weight of his body. A heartbeat later even that agony was overwhelmed by a sickening jerk that threatened to pull his arm from its socket.

He bit his lip to stop himself from crying out and for a few awful moments hung suspended, praying the cowhide would hold him. Gradually, panic receded and he was able to reach out with his sound hand and pull himself back to the rock face. Once there, he drew himself upwards to take the weight off his arm and managed to unjam the wooden hand from the fissure. He spent the next minute clinging to the face, frozen by a combination of shock and pain, but eventually he willed himself to resume the descent.

When he reached the base of the cliff he crouched for a few moments in the darkness, attempting to get a sense of his surroundings. Ahead, he could see the hilltop silhouetted in the glow of the Dacian fires. The soft snicker of a cavalry mount confirmed that the horses were picketed somewhere to his right. But had the Tungrians set a guard? That was the next hurdle. To make himself known without getting a spear in the throat. He ghosted his way past the tethered horses. If they were watched, the sentry must be asleep because he saw no sign of him. On the brow of the hill prone figures lay scattered like odd-shaped rocks, the only sign of life the almost imperceptible movement of their breathing and the occasional animal whimper. He chose a shape on the outer edge of the group and drew the dagger he'd carried at his belt.

'Careful, soldier,' he whispered as he placed the point beneath the sleeping auxiliary's chin. A pair of dark eyes flicked open and the man's mouth gaped, before immediately closing as Valerius increased the pressure. Valerius nodded slowly and allowed himself a smile. 'I want you to call whoever is in command. Do it in a normal voice and ask him to come over. Nod if you understand.' Valerius lifted the knife point and the Tungrian complied. By now puzzlement had replaced the fear in his eyes. 'Good. Now say it.'

'Lucca?' The call was hesitant, but loud enough to elicit an ill-tempered response.

'What the fuck do you want, Fabius? If you haven't thought of a way to get us out of here go back to sleep.'

'Please, I need to talk to you.'

'I hope it's not what I think it is,' the auxiliary grumbled. 'Bad enough we're all going to die tomorrow without you suddenly deciding you're in fucking love with me.' A dark figure rose from the ground a dozen paces away and scratched energetically before walking stiff-legged to where Valerius crouched beside Fabius.

Valerius stood as Lucca approached. He heard a sharp hiss of indrawn breath and the sound of a sword being drawn. 'I'd have thought you'd lost too many men to go around killing your only reinforcement, friend.'

The man's face was lost in the darkness but Valerius sensed him relax. 'You're supposed to be dead. Festus said—'

'Festus is the one who's dead,' Valerius said brutally. 'But we can discuss that later. For the moment let's talk about our position. How many men do you have left?'

Lucca hesitated, but only for a moment. 'Fifteen . . . no, fourteen . . . Brigio died after we got here. Three of the others are too badly injured to fight, but they can still ride.'

'Horses?'

'Enough for everyone and two spares, but we only have fodder for another day and the water won't last till noon.'

Valerius accompanied the auxiliary while he outlined the position. As they walked in the darkness, Lucca's manner transformed from belligerent suspicion to a subordinate's wary respect.

'I'd have ridden for it, but we'd lost two men among the trees and Festus ordered us to hole up while he went back for them. An idiot, but a brave idiot. He never came back, but we heard him screaming. At least I think it was him. By then we were already in the shit. Hundreds of vermin crawling among the trees and no way out.'

'And now?'

'We were due back before dark. I thought maybe they'd send someone out after us.' Valerius laughed and Lucca joined him. 'I know, but . . . ah, shit!' His shoulders slumped, an admission of defeat. 'How did you get here? We all thought you'd been killed. Festus said . . .'

'What did Festus say?'

'He said you were here to arrest the legate and return him to Rome and we couldn't let that happen. We were to take you out in the woods and lose you.

The Dacians would do the rest. There'd been some kind of arrangement, and we were to ride away, free and clear. Only it looks like nobody told the Gets.'

'The Gets?'

'Getae. The Dacians. Anyway, the bastards ambushed us about half an hour after we left you.'

Valerius considered the story. It made sense, in a perverse, soldierly sort of way. If someone had convinced the Tungrians their respected general was under threat they wouldn't take much persuading to mislay four of the despised Praetorian Guard and hope nobody back in Rome noticed. An unfortunate accident on the frontier. By the time any investigation was launched, the evidence would be a pile of wolf-gnawed bones, if the Dacians left any evidence. It also reinforced his suspicions: someone had known in advance where they were coming and why. They'd tried to stop him on the way east, and now they'd tried again. But Gaius Valerius Verrens was not going to be stopped. Publius had unwittingly given him another piece of the puzzle but he needed to get back to Rome if he was going to use it.

'What happens now?' the cavalryman asked.

Valerius's eyes glinted in the darkness. 'I suppose I could arrest you and your men and when we get back to the fort I can have you roasted over an open fire . . .'

'Only there are fifteen of us and one of you, and we're all going to be dead in the morning anyway.'

'Exactly. Or I can get us out of here and we can forget this ever happened.'

The auxiliary's teeth shone in the darkness. 'I don't know how you're going to do it, but I like the second option a lot better.'

Valerius looked out beyond the fires and tried to imagine the Dacian positions as he'd seen them from the top of the ridge. They surrounded the approaches to the hill, but the keys to this trap were two slight gaps in the trees that potentially provided an escape route for the horsemen. An organized force would have barricaded the openings, but from what he'd seen the Dacians were happy to fill them with warriors and invite the Tungrians to try their luck. What he needed was to draw the Dacian warriors away from one of those gaps.

He'd outlined his plan to Marcus before he'd set out on the treacherous climb. 'The signal will be a burning brand waved three times from the top of the hill. Count slowly to one hundred then create the diversion.'

To Lucca he said, 'Get your men ready, in the saddle and prepared to fight in five minutes. Assign one trooper to each of the wounded. Fabius!'

'Sir!'

'I want a small fire on the rear of the hill where the enemy can't see it, and prepare a torch.'

As he waited for the flames to take hold, a young trooper approached with a saddled horse and Valerius ordered him to hold it until he was ready. He ran to the fire, picked up the torch Fabius had laid beside it and thrust it deep into the flames. The dried grass and twigs caught immediately and he carried the flaming brand to the top of the hill and arced it three times above his head in a blazing rainbow.

'All mounted,' Lucca called. 'Now?' he asked as Valerius leapt into the saddle.

Valerius shook his head. 'Wait.'

It seemed to take an eternity, but it must have been less than two minutes.

'There,' one of the troopers behind him hissed.

'Quiet. Do nothing that might alert them.'

A tree exploded into flame two hundred paces away on the far side of the Dacian ring. Marcus and Serpentius had done their job well. The blaze began in the lower branches, but quickly spread to the dry leaves in the canopy and jumped to its neighbour, which instantly added to the fiery spectacle.

'Wait!' Valerius ordered. The burning trees were close to the further gap and he was gambling that the diversion would draw the Dacian blockaders to it. But he had to give them time to react. He could hear the tension in his own voice. 'Wait. Remember, follow me straight to the trees and once we're through turn along the line of the hills. We stop for nothing or nobody. Slaughter anything that gets in your way. Now!'

The horses had been sawing at the bit for minutes and the moment their riders gave them their heads they lumbered into motion across the upper slope, picking up speed with every stride. The Tungrians plucked their long spears from the makeshift palisade as they crossed the bank and ditch, instantly bringing them to the ready. Valerius felt the ground falling away beneath him. No question of worrying about fox or rabbit holes. Just pray. The trot swiftly developed into a headlong gallop. He could hear the thunder of hooves all around him, but he focused every ounce of his concentration on finding the gap. It was out there somewhere in the darkness beyond the Dacian fires. If he had his directions wrong by even a few yards his men would ride straight into the trees where they'd be swept from the saddle and butchered. But the fires would be his guide. From the top of the hill he'd noted that the near gap lined up with a large boulder at the base of the hill and the midpoint between the second and third pyres. The pale blur of the boulder swept by on his right and he set his horse for the narrow opening between the fires. With unnerving timing the wind came up, flames and sparks shooting high in the air before they swept across the space he was aiming for. But Valerius dared not check. His life and those of the Tungrians depended on this mad dash through the fires. Like his own mount, the animal beneath him had been bred for battle and trained for war; flame, smoke and noise held no fears for her. Shouts of alarm came from his left front and in the fiery light he saw a small army of Dacians racing to cut the riders off. It would be very close but there could be no stopping now. He dug in his heels and pushed the mare to her limit, feeling her surge beneath him. All around him the Tungrians did the same. By now the space between the fires was filled by a wall of flame and it passed in an explosion of yellow and red, a blast of heat and the stink of smoke and singed horse hair. They were through and if he'd calculated correctly the gap in the trees and the relative safety of the forest should be fifty paces ahead. The Dacian warriors had lost the race and they howled in frustration as the riders galloped past. But they had bows and spears and the air swiftly filled with flying missiles. A spear hurtled across Valerius's front a foot from his nose. He heard a sharp cry accompanied by a sickening thud as a body hit the earth at high speed, but he had no time to think of reining in. The dark line of the forest was only half a dozen strides away.

He almost shouted in relief as he realized he'd struck the treeline exactly where he'd planned. In the same instant he saw shadowy figures moving hurriedly among the trees and as he charged through into the deeper darkness his horse smashed into one, hurtling a Dacian warrior aside with the sickening crunch of broken bone and a shrill scream of pain. The impact knocked the mare off her stride, allowing the surviving cavalrymen to pass them. An agile, clawing savage with a knife between his teeth scrambled at Valerius's legs and hauled himself half into the saddle behind him. Valerius knew he was dead the instant the warrior retrieved the knife, and using all his strength he smashed back with elbows and skull in an attempt to knock the Dacian clear, at the same time knowing that to lose control of the horse would be just as fatal. But nothing would shift his assailant. Valerius heard a cry of triumph as the man hooked an arm around his throat, and screamed in impotent fury as he anticipated the deadly sting of the knife point in his exposed back.

With a crack like a branch snapping, the grip on his neck weakened. He darted a glance back just as the Dacian tumbled clear with the shaft of an arrow buried deep in his skull. At the same time a welcome presence loomed out of the darkness and Serpentius appeared grinning at his side, the Thracian bow in his right hand, his horse matching stride with Valerius's own.

They were clear.

XXV

'This is an unexpected honour.'

Aulus Vitellius might have been greeting a guest at his townhouse on the Esquiline Hill instead of in the heart of a rough frontier fortress. Valerius had to remind himself that this man had just tried to have him killed. When he burst into the legate's headquarters still dressed in a tunic stained with Dacian blood he had fully intended to kill him if it became necessary, but Vitellius met him with a disarming smile and graciously proffered a cup of wine. It was difficult to stay angry in the face of such charm.

'I came here on the Emperor's authority to question Publius Sulla,' Valerius said. 'You deliberately put him out of the way.'

Vitellius shook his head regretfully. 'He was a good officer, but I had my doubts about the boy. It seemed safer to isolate him.'

'And you sold us to the Dacians.'

'Of course.' The smile never faltered. 'It's not what I would have chosen, but one does what one must.'

'Why? Five of your soldiers are dead. Festus the decurion.'

'Auxiliaries.' Vitellius tutted dismissively, as if the butchered men were chickens from the quartermaster's store. 'If they had done their job properly they would still be alive and we would not be having this inconvenient conversation.'

'Why?' Valerius persisted. 'You could have kept us in the fort for a week and sent us away without meeting Publius.'

Vitellius took a deep draught of wine, but Valerius knew the legate was only taking time to think. When the answer came it was a surprise for both its frankness and its tone. 'I could tell you that I feared you would be persistent – they said: "Give him a challenge and he is like a hound with a bone; he won't stop chewing until he reaches the marrow" – but that would not be entirely true. You have powerful enemies, young man, and the orders from those enemies were quite specific. They wanted you dead.'

Valerius felt cold fingers settle on his neck. 'I am on a personal mission for the Emperor. Any man who raises a hand against me does so at his peril.' Even as he said the words, he realized how impotent they sounded five hundred miles from Rome, at the mercy of a man who could have him killed with a single word.

The legate laughed at his innocence. 'But which

Emperor? There is the Emperor who sits upon his gilded throne, but, as I am sure you have noticed, my good friend Nero can be many Emperors. Perhaps the Emperor who sent you and the person who wished you to have an unhappy accident are one and the same? And there are those around him who wield an Emperor's influence, and who wish, rightly or wrongly, to protect him from what the irritatingly persistent Gaius Valerius Verrens may find. Then there is the additional possibility that someone with access to the Emperor's power is protecting not Nero, but himself.'

Valerius straightened. Was Vitellius confirming what Publius had said? 'You must know who issued the order.'

Vitellius reached to his desk and picked up a document with a wax imprint in its bottom right corner. 'The imperial seal, very similar to the one you carry. One does not question the instructions which accompany it. You will note that I was also instructed to have Publius Sulla killed the moment he returned to Viminacium.' Valerius looked down at the dark liquid swirling in his cup. The legate smiled at his edginess. 'Don't worry, it is not poisoned. That would be a terrible waste of a remarkably good wine.'

'But you are still under orders to kill us.' Valerius's voice had a hard edge to it and his hand hovered beside the dagger he had smuggled past the guards.

Vitellius gave a delighted shiver. 'Why, you almost frighten me. Young and hard and dangerous. If I had been the type of man you are, Valerius Verrens, I would not be ruling this dusty outpost, I would be ruling the Empire.'

Valerius stared at him. Those were dangerous words. Words that could very easily get a man killed. 'And now?'

'And now, I am afraid, indolence is ingrained too deep. If it was offered to me upon a silver platter I would refuse it. I find work of any kind tires me and it is such a large Empire these days.'

'I meant what now for us?'

He saw Vitellius frown, genuinely disconcerted. 'What now? Gaius Valerius Verrens, Hero of Rome, has lived up to his warlike reputation and defeated two attempts on the lives of himself and his associates. It would be remiss of me to allow a third attempt. Whoever ordered this can only expect so much cooperation. With Publius Sulla's death your mission is completed and you should return to Rome to make your report. You may leave at your leisure or you may return with me, as part of my bodyguard.' He noticed Valerius's confusion. 'I too am to return to Rome, but for a rather more pleasant interview. Nero has awarded me governorship of Africa, where the opportunities for a man of talent are suitably wide-ranging.' The smile grew broader and Valerius understood he was imagining the huge profits to be made from manipulating Africa's vast grain exports. But his next words came as a surprise. 'I will be allowed to appoint a military aide of my choosing. It would not be surprising if I were to select a holder of the Corona Aurea; the gold crown would add lustre to any proconsular retinue. The truth is that I value your soldierly talents, and, as a student of Seneca, your conversation. Of course, this cannot happen until the Emperor dispenses with your services, but, as I'm sure you understand, Africa, for all its rustic provinciality, might be more conducive to your long-term health than Rome. In a way, it is a pity. I have had my legion for less than a year and my enemies will say I have not served because I never fought a battle. But still . . .'

Valerius studied him, searching for the lie, but he suspected that even if it existed he'd be unable to detect it. If the offer wasn't a trap, it was remarkably generous. As the governor's military adviser, he would share his power – and his profits – and, when his term was complete, return to Rome a wealthy man. In addition, and despite his double-dealing and readiness to see him killed, Valerius found he liked Vitellius; someone to be wary of certainly, but likeable none the less. He doubted he would ever be bored.

'I appreciate your kindness,' he said non-committally. 'And it would be an honour to serve as your escort, but I would be neglecting my duty if I didn't return to Rome at the first opportunity.'

'Well spoken!' Vitellius rapped his fist on his desk. 'And you will return by the quickest route, I promise you. We leave by fast galley in three days, and reach Vindobona six days later. At Vindobona, I will release you from your duties and you can ride to the Emperor immediately. In the meantime, you will be able to update me on what is happening in Rome.'

Valerius bowed his agreement. It seemed there was no escape from Vitellius's relentless pursuit.

Marcus, Serpentius and Heracles were waiting for him outside the headquarters. He could tell from their faces that they expected the news to be bad, but they brightened when he explained the general's plans. Marcus nodded approval. 'Better to be rowed halfway home than to be tied to a horse for two weeks.'

'True,' Valerius agreed. 'But we leave Vitellius at the first opportunity. He might be entertaining, but he's also dangerous to know, even when he isn't trying to kill you.'

That feeling was reinforced on the long trip upriver, a journey punctuated by the occasional shout of command, the measured swish of the oars and mesmeric rush of the waters beneath the hull. Vitellius had been a member of the Emperor's inner circle during the early years of his reign and he had an inexhaustible supply of scandalous, and almost certainly treasonable, gossip about Nero.

'He was a fine young man,' the general mused one warm afternoon as the oarsmen powered them towards Aquincum on the river's broad bend. 'With all the usual young man's enthusiasms: drink, Syrian strumpets and vicious amusement. It was unfortunate that he came to the throne before he was fully formed.

Power changed him, as it does any man. At first, he was happy to be advised by Seneca and Burrus and he surprised us all by his grasp of the complexities of Empire, but not even Seneca could compete with Agrippina's meddling. She whipped up a whirlwind when she tried to play the palace aides and the senators off against each other. Eventually, it consumed her.' He shook his head at the woman's folly. 'In the meantime, the Emperor's passion had moved on from chariots to the overpaid, muscle-bound youths who drive them.'

Valerius learned more than he wanted about Nero's carnal appetites. The boys, girls and women – of course, he had heard whispers, but Vitellius's attention to detail when he was in his cups could be stomach-churning. 'Three Sumerian giants, two virgins and his own aunt . . . you have never heard such a caterwauling. The rape of Rubria, of course; the debauch of a Vestal virgin was beyond even Caligula's excesses. We tried to keep it quiet, but at the next inspection . . .'

When he wasn't captivated by the sound of his own voice, the general had a voracious appetite for tales of the British rebellion and Suetonius's reaction; the tactics he had used and why he'd used them, the deployment of auxiliaries and cavalry. Valerius, who was no storyteller, found it increasingly hard to satisfy. In the end he had to repeat the epic of the last stand of the Colonia militia and the final hours of the Temple of Claudius five or six times.

'By the gods, what an end to make. You may think differently now, but you will learn in time that a hand is a small price to pay for having been present. Suetonius was wrong, though, to take such a terrible retribution. I am not too old to learn from his dispositions, but I know that a general, or a politician for that matter, cannot be motivated by anger or hatred. He should have made an example of the woman and her chieftains, enslaved a few hundred noblemen and kept the rest happy by parcelling out the confiscated lands among them. Now, tell me again about the last battle. The slope was where . . .'

By the time they reached Vindobona, Valerius had fought the last battle until he was ready to jump overboard and take his chances in the river. It was a hasty farewell, delayed only by the legate's obvious reluctance to be abandoned.

'Do not forget my offer, Valerius,' he reminded him, offering his hand. 'We would do very well together, you and I, and they tell me that Africa is not such a bad place. Rich, but quiet, and the women are willing and beautiful. By the end you might well have a legion. An African legion, but still a legion. Think on it.'

Valerius said he would, reflecting that a great many people seemed to be tempting him with a legionary command. They agreed to meet in Rome before Vitellius left for his province.

As they rode out of the city he felt Serpentius studying him. 'What is it?'

The Spaniard shrugged. 'I was just thinking you

got on very well with the general considering he tried to get us killed.'

Valerius laughed. 'Isn't that what every general does? You can't fight them all.'

Serpentius grinned and they kicked their horses on, towards the great wall of white-tipped peaks to the south. To Rome, and Nero – and a stark choice.

XXVI

It was strange, this sensation of being one of the walking dead. He could almost feel the executioner's breath on the back of his neck. Of course, nothing was certain in Nero's world, but there was no denying he had failed, and in Nero's world death would always be a potential consequence of failure.

On his return to Rome, Valerius had spent a few minutes with his sister before dropping into his bed, exhausted after four days in the saddle. Julia was nowhere to be seen, but he sensed an unease among his household staff that might have been prompted by Olivia's condition. She had made little progress and it was clear that if he didn't track down the Judaean healer soon it might be too late. When he woke next day he decided against going directly to the palace, but rather to test the political temperature with Fabia first. The beautiful courtesan welcomed him with an embrace that almost crushed his ribs and a kiss that didn't seem respectable at that hour of the morning.

'You must never leave me for so long again,' she scolded, making him feel guilty the way only a woman can. Vitellius's suggestion intrigued her. 'He has powerful friends and it is a good offer. You could be a combination of general, administrator and politician, thus satisfying your own ambitions and your father's.'

Valerius nodded. 'But before I give him his answer I have to survive, and that seems less likely with every passing day.' She turned pale as he told her about the mountain ambush in Moesia and the trap the legate had set for him.

'You must be careful, Valerius. If you have truly made an enemy of Nero you will never be safe.'

'If it is Nero then I am already dead, and there is little point in worrying about it. I will put my affairs in order and act as if every day is my last. But if it is not, then I need to find out who it is and why. I don't trust Torquatus, but I can't see why he would want me killed. If Cornelius Sulla had still been alive I might have suspected him, but . . .'

'Rome still whispers of Cornelius's execution,' Fabia said. 'The Emperor went too far. The rest were slaves and criminals but Cornelius was born a Roman citizen and a patrician. To put him to death without trial, and in such a fashion, went against everything the Empire stands for. If it can happen to Cornelius then no one can feel safe.'

'Publius Sulla hinted that Nero had a Christus follower at the very heart of his court. These people operate in the shadows, but they are not solitary. Their worship is a communal affair. Whoever it is must have the freedom to come and go from the palace – unless they used Cornelius as a channel to Petrus. It's possible that is why he took the risk of meeting Lucina. I need to find out who of the inner circle was most friendly with Cornelius.'

'And you want me to help you? Of course I will try, but it sounds so unlikely. You have experience of palace occasions, but you cannot imagine how suffocating it is to be part of Nero's inner circle.'

'You were part of it,' he pointed out.

A shadow fell over the sapphire eyes. 'Oh, Valerius, you can be so naive. The reality is that I was nothing more than an object to be used and discarded. I neither listened nor spoke, because to do so would have put my life at risk. I played my part in their little games and left.'

'But you know who they are?'

Fabia nodded. 'Too many to make your task simple. Cornelius made himself accommodating to many. Torquatus for one. Epaphradotus, the Emperor's secretary, for another. Poppaea's ladies in waiting. Menecrates, the harper, and Spicillus, who is the new darling of the arena, are the latest targets of Nero's affections. Cornelius was close to both. Any one of them could be a candidate for your Christus follower, but after what happened to Cornelius they are even less likely to stand on the rostrum and shout about it. If you are right and it was one of them who tried to engineer your death they would have to feel very secure.'

'Someone like Torquatus?'

Fabia laughed bitterly. 'I cannot think of anyone less likely to be seduced by the rantings of some obscure Judaean mystic than Decimus Torquatus.'

'I would never have suspected Cornelius,' he said.

She shook her head. 'Not Torquatus.'

He studied her. She seemed very certain and he wondered why. Fabia had always been well informed about what happened on the Palatine. When he'd occasionally asked where she'd heard some of the things she told him she'd passed it off as malicious pillow talk, but, when he thought back, there had been times when he'd wondered how she could know quite so much. Still, every detail could help him understand the nature of the threat against him. 'I can't delay reporting to the Emperor any longer. Tell me what has been happening at the palace while I've been gone.'

When she sulked she looked like a little girl. 'Always business these days, Valerius. You must come for a little relaxation soon. Galba is still out of favour . . .'

He left twenty minutes later and made his way through the Forum to the Palatine. The day had started bright, but while he was with Fabia grey thunderclouds had gathered low above the city, piled up like untidy pyramids over the rumpled expanse of ochre, white and gold that was Rome. The gloom cast by the clouds suited his mood. Here in the monster's shadow his Stoic acceptance of his fate was exposed for the sham it was.

Six stony-faced palace guards who collected him at the summit of the Clivus Palatinus appeared to confirm his intuition. The soldiers escorted him down a set of steep steps to a marble-lined tunnel that cut beneath the palaces and the gardens. It was long and curved and floored with beautiful mosaics, with curtained alcoves set at intervals along its length. The alcoves contained the usual gilded collection of emperors, generals and gods, and it wasn't until he noticed the long neck and soft, boyish features of one of these figures that he realized this must be the passageway where Caligula had been assassinated by men just like his escort. The thought sent a shiver through him. It seemed an unlikely place for such an act of savagery, but it would take only a single word of command and he would follow the former Emperor to the otherworld in a blizzard of swords. He was sweating by the time a second set of steps took them back into the open at the southern edge of the hill. Once, ordinary men had lived here, if you could call men whose names rang down through the ages, like Cicero and Catulus, Marcus Antonius and Quintus Hortensius, ordinary. Their mansions had originally lined the hilltop, but they had been driven out by money and power and by death. Every man had to die, but of all the men he had named only one had died in his bed.

A lone figure in white stood silhouetted against

a sky which grew darker by the minute. Valerius flinched as a bolt of lightning ripped the far horizon and its flash lit the sky. A few seconds later a crash of thunder shook the air and the Emperor turned to him with a smile that was belied by the unnatural light in his eyes.

'Even an Emperor cannot command the elements,' he said regretfully. 'The augurs say it means the gods are angry. Do you believe that?'

Valerius hesitated before deciding it would do no harm to tell the truth. 'No, Caesar, I think wars are the way the gods show their anger.'

Nero nodded. 'It seems to me that we blame the gods for the things we fear. You are a warrior; do you fear war?'

'I do not fear war, but no sane man welcomes it . . . just as no man welcomes death.'

The Emperor frowned, as if the thought had never occurred to him. 'Yes, death . . . you allowed Publius Sulla to kill himself before you could question him?'

Valerius heard the Praetorians moving in behind him and he saw Nero's eyes flick towards them. It seemed someone was a step ahead of him again. He had rehearsed this moment in his mind a dozen times, determined to show no weakness. But reality was different. The words stuck in his throat and he felt shame at the fear he could hear in his voice. 'Yes, Caesar.'

'Then you have failed me. Failure requires punishment. Do you agree?' The last three words were snapped out like nails hammered into a cross.

Valerius raised his head and looked directly into the pale eyes. He would not plead.

A faint rattle of metal told him the men behind him were preparing to strike and he knew – *knew* – that the other man was imagining the swords rising and falling, the haze of scarlet as the blades hacked into his body. He closed his eyes and waited for the first blow.

An eternity passed before the Emperor finally spoke. Valerius winced as another clap of thunder shattered the silence. When he looked up he found Nero studying him.

'I said you have ten days to hunt down this Petrus.' Valerius opened his mouth to protest. But there was worse to come. 'At noon on the tenth day I will have every Judaean subject in Rome driven to the circus,' Nero waved a hand at the great arena a hundred and fifty feet below, 'and put to the sword. And you with them.'

He walked away, leaving Valerius to stare down at the oval of sand that would be stained with the blood of twenty thousand innocents if he failed.

Valerius's feet took him back through the Forum, but the real world only existed inside his head, where his mind wrestled with the terrible implications of what he had just been told. Surely not even Nero . . . ? But yes, he could. Valerius saw again Cornelius's screaming, flame-filled mouth. The girl's pleading face. The merciless glow in a leopard's eyes. It was the same glow he had seen when Nero turned to greet him. But twenty thousand people? Somewhere to his left were the Gemonian stairs where executed criminals were left to rot. Soon his body could be lying among them.

He stumbled blindly through the crowds, bumping into hurrying figures who cursed him or thrust him aside.

'Valerius!'

He blinked and the scene about him came into sharp focus, including the concerned features of Marcus. What now?

'Lucina Graecina is taken.'

He closed his eyes. How many more obstacles could the gods place before him? 'When?' he demanded. 'Where is she?'

'Two weeks ago. In the prison.' Marcus pointed across the Forum towards the base of the Capitoline Hill. 'In the Carcer.'

May the gods help her. People who went into the Carcer seldom came out. But he had no choice, he had to find a way to free Lucina. Standing in the shadow of the great men who dominated the Forum – Caesar, Pompey and Augustus – he suddenly felt very small and wearied to the bone. He was a soldier. He was not equipped for plotting and conspiracy. But what else could he do? Too many lives depended on him to give up now.

It was unlikely any acquaintance would have recognized Valerius when he returned to the Forum the next morning. Now he wore the sculpted silver breastplate of a tribune of the Guard, with the black cloak covering his shoulders and his helmet low over his brow to hide a face which wore an expression of grim resolve. Behind him, equally stern, marched his escort; one tall and swarthy, his face set in a sneer as if everything and everyone around him stank, and an older guardsman, patently nearing the end of his sixteen-year commission, with the scars of his campaigns etched deep on his face.

'Keep your backs straight and try to look like soldiers,' Valerius warned them.

Serpentius set his shoulders and glared defiance at anyone who looked like getting in his way. Marcus muttered something about strutting peacocks and did his level best to stay in step. They were approaching the doorway of the imperial prison on the east side of the Capitoline Hill. Valerius, like all his countrymen, had heard the tales of what happened inside those walls. Now he was going to bluff his way into the most feared building in Rome.

He walked up the steps and hammered on the door of the prison. 'Open in the name of the Emperor! Tribune Verrens to question the prisoner Lucina Graecina.'

With a clatter, a small shutter opened in the door-way to reveal a pinched, suspicious face with the features of a cornered rat.

'Tribune Verrens to question the prisoner Lucina Graecina,' Valerius repeated.

The rat yawned. 'I'll need to see your orders.'

Valerius leaned close to the opening and almost gagged on the stink of the jailer's breath. 'Nothing written down for this one,' he said confidentially. 'The orders came direct from prefect Torquatus himself. That's right, soldier?' He nodded to Marcus.

'Nothing on paper. Tribune Verrens to question the prisoner about crimes against the Roman people,' Marcus confirmed. 'Results to be communicated direct to the Praetorian prefect without delay.'

'Without delay,' Valerius echoed.

The jailer sniffed noisily and sighed. Suspicion was replaced by a look of pained confusion. His job wasn't supposed to be like this. It was meant to be simple. No one got in without orders, unless they made him a decent offer, and even then he wouldn't take a bribe if he smelled trouble. But the tribune's obvious authority and the Praetorian uniforms made it complicated. What made it more complicated were the special instructions he'd been given for the care of the prisoner.

'A moment, sir,' he whined. He disappeared, only to return a minute later with an expression of resigned failure. The shutter slammed shut and they heard the rattle of bolts before the door swung open, bringing with it a waft of stale sweat, dried urine and sour wine.

'Stay here,' Valerius ordered the two men.

'Our pleasure.' Marcus grinned.

Valerius removed his helmet and stooped to enter the doorway. Inside, the heat was stifling and the stagnant air thick enough to chew. His stomach rebelled at a combination of filth and suffering and despair that reminded him of the last day in the Temple of Claudius. The jailer proved to be taller than he had appeared, but he walked with a permanent crouch as a result of his long service in the low-ceilinged chamber. For a place with such a terrible reputation, the Carcer was surprisingly small, and made more so by the wooden partition which hid the rear of the chamber. In the centre of the floor a dark, noxious hole had been sunk, and for a moment Valerius's spirits quailed at the thought that Lucina was being held in the notorious *tullianum*. Below him was the pit of horrors where the Catiline conspirators had met their end, the African king Jugurtha had been starved to death and the executioners had strangled Vercingetorix, the rebel Gaul who had defied Caesar.

The jailer saw his look and his face twisted into an unpleasant grin. 'Nah, we don't keep Mother Rome down there. Not yet anyway. She's marked for special attention she is.'

'Mother Rome?' Valerius was mystified.

'You'll see. Tullius!'

A curtain opened in the partition and a second man appeared, unshaven and as filthy as the first. 'Gentleman wants to see the pretty lady. I'll have your sword, sir, if you don't mind. Rules are rules.' Valerius reluctantly complied. 'Not that you'd hurt her, I'm sure. I was a bit surprised you being sent to question her, though, what with all them others being here day after day.'

The stench from the rear of the chamber was even more noxious than that emanating from the *tullianum*, and at first Valerius found it difficult to see in the gloom. A figure stepped out of the darkness and he cursed.

The ruined face grinned mockingly. Rodan was dressed in a stained white tunic and stank of old wine, but his hand held a sword, a *gladius* like the one Valerius had surrendered a moment earlier.

'I thought you'd be here sooner,' the Praetorian said conversationally. 'Torquatus was very keen you should get a chance to talk to the lady.'

He ushered Valerius forward, but the young Roman wasn't fooled by the show of manners. Rodan's wild eyes, and the way he held the sword, were utterly at odds with the softness of his voice. He took two cautious steps into the chamber. When he saw what waited in the darkness he felt the blood drain from his face. 'Who did this?'

He had seen war in all its awfulness, and cruelty and death that had reached its height on the night he'd watched Cornelius Sulla burn. But the humiliation Nero had devised for Lucina Graecina somehow overshadowed them all.

'She's been in there for more than two weeks,' Rodan reflected. 'She's a tough old bitch.'

They had placed Lucina Graecina in a low, barred cage of the type used to transport wild animals from Africa for the arena. Gone was the haughty noblewoman he had met in the garden. She had been replaced by this naked, filth-streaked crone, her stringy body patterned with burns and bruises and her face hidden behind the matted curtain of her hair. The pen was too short to allow her to lie down in any comfort and too low for her to sit up. Instead, she was forced to crouch on all fours, with the bars cutting agonizingly into her knees.

'Mother Rome.' Rodan laughed. 'With her dry tits hanging down like that, she looks just like the old she-wolf who suckled Romulus and Remus.'

Valerius remembered the pride and defiance of the woman he had met in the garden and restrained the urge to smash his wooden fist into the grinning face. 'You did this?'

The Praetorian spat on the soiled straw at his feet. 'On the orders of the Emperor. *Lucina Graecina is a traitor to Rome and is to be questioned to reveal her associates and anyone connected with the sect of Christus, the Galilean. You are to take any steps necessary to ensure her full co-operation.*' He laughed. 'Any steps.'

'I should kill you here and now, and the jailers. It would be a month before anyone noticed the stink from that hole. If they ever did.'

'You could try,' Rodan said, weighing his sword and moving between Valerius and the doorway. 'Maybe that's what the Emperor had in mind all along.'

'I want to talk to her.'

277

The Praetorian shrugged, amusement in his eyes. 'You don't want to kill me?'

'Let me talk to her. Alone.'

Rodan disappeared through the partition. Valerius could hear the man's laughter ringing in his ears.

When they were alone, he crouched over the cage where Lucina knelt, her body shaking with terror and pain. She felt his presence and cringed away like a beaten animal.

'My lady,' he whispered. 'I will do what I can for you, but first you must help me. I need to know who betrayed you and I need you to tell me the significance of the numbers MCVII. The time for saying nothing is past. Please.'

The bowed head turned towards him and the tangled mass of hair parted. He looked into a face made unrecognizable by her suffering and recoiled from two red-rimmed eyes that mirrored the deepest pits of Hades. Lucina Graecina, noblewoman of Rome, threw back her head and howled like the she-wolf she resembled.

She was quite mad.

XXVII

'Find Sextus and Felix. I want to know the names or descriptions of everyone Lucina has met since they started following her. Between them they shouldn't have missed anyone.'

Marcus nodded. 'She's not talking?'

'I doubt if she'll ever talk again,' Valerius said wearily. He described Lucina's ordeal at the hands of Rodan. 'Watch out for him. I have a feeling they're much closer to us than we think.'

Like a conjuror, Serpentius produced a long dagger from his belt. 'I hope he comes close enough just the once.'

Valerius shook his head. 'There may come a time for that, but this is not it. If we can discover how he knows so much about us, we can use it against him now. Killing him won't solve anything. Torquatus will just find some other executioner.'

'What good is a list of the people she's met?' Marcus

said. 'We can't follow them all and the chances of any of them being involved with the Christus sect are slim. Look at the trouble she took to hide her association with Cornelius – much good it did the poor bastards. Do you get the feeling that every time we get close to anyone they suddenly die on us?'

Privately, Valerius agreed. Too often he had felt he was one step ahead of his enemies only to discover that he was actually one step behind. Was it possible that someone in his household was a spy? Or even one of these men he had come to trust with his life? He met Serpentius's fierce wolf's eyes and dismissed the thought as quickly as it had appeared.

'All I know is that whatever information Lucina had is now in Torquatus's hands and we have to do something. I don't understand why, but this has turned into a race and he doesn't want us to get to Petrus first. We'll meet later at the house.'

That evening, before he looked in on Olivia, Valerius placed an oil lamp in the window above the front door. The change in his sister astonished him. Julia held her hand as she sat up in bed. The young slave lowered her eyes. 'I wanted to surprise you, master. I hope I was right. She has been like this since your father left this morning.'

'Father?'

'He had business in town, he said. But he spent more than an hour with Olivia.'

'I knew he was here, because I could hear his words and they comforted me.' Olivia's voice sounded weary, but she held out her other hand to Valerius. 'When he had gone, I opened my eyes and everything was so much brighter than I remembered. Julia brought me a cushion and I was able to sit up. I have eaten some fruit, Valerius. You should be proud of me.'

'I am,' he said. But he was prouder still that she had somehow found the strength to fight the thing that threatened to destroy her.

'Now, tell me about your latest case!' she said brightly.

He thought about the water theft for the first time in a month. Old Honorius would be foaming at the mouth. 'It would bore you back to sleep,' he said. 'But fortunately I have put it aside for a while. Lately, I have been working for the State.'

'Is that why you are so tired?' she asked as Julia crept from the room.

He smiled. 'No, it is running after my baby sister that makes me tired.'

'Then I must make sure you do not have to for much longer.' They both knew the sentence had a dual meaning, but Valerius chose to ignore it. Olivia continued. 'Julia tells me you have a new companion. She says he is "dark, saturnine and dangerous" but her voice makes him seem kind. I think she likes him.'

Valerius nodded. 'I think she does.'

'She said you have been travelling. If you cannot tell me of your work, you must tell me of your adventures.' She lay back on the cushion and closed her eyes.

He took Olivia on the journey through Moesia: the

harsh, jagged mountains, wind-whipped gorges and unfordable rivers and the proud, savage people who struggled to survive there. He didn't mention ambush or betrayal, but made her smile with his tales of the trip north on the legate's trireme and Vitellius's host of earthy stories and irrepressible optimism. Still with her eyes closed, she said quietly: 'How fortunate you are to be a man, Valerius.'

It was something he'd never considered. Of course he was a man, and she was a woman. How else would it be?

She must have felt his confusion, because she smiled. 'A man is free to travel where he wishes, to buy what he likes and to drink when he wants to. A woman must ask permission to do all these things. Do you understand?'

He laughed. 'I think a woman, at least this woman, has had too much time to think.'

'So,' she said, and a catch in her voice told him he had offended her. 'A woman must even ask permission to think?'

'I meant—'

'I know what you meant, Brother, and that you meant well. Many of my sisters would agree with you, but . . .' she hesitated, for so long he thought she had gone back to sleep, 'but I *have* been thinking. Thinking of my life. And of death. Death seems so eternal, my life so short, and so . . .' she struggled to find the word, 'valueless. If I had a child, it might have been different.' Valerius squeezed her hand and she opened her eyes. He knew that one of the reasons she had turned down Lucius's choice of husband had been the unlikelihood that he could father a child.

'There is still time,' he assured her, knowing that there was not.

'No. It will not happen,' she said, her voice grave. 'I visited the Good Goddess before I became ill and it is not my fate. You see, Valerius? I am only part woman. Part Roman woman. A Roman woman belongs to her father, then her husband, whom she cannot choose herself. Father could have put me away or had me killed, because I would not do his bidding. She is worth less than a slave, because a Roman woman cannot work as a slave works. She must sew and entertain, but she must never labour. I have never cooked a meal or cleaned a room.'

Valerius shook his head. 'You are not a Roman woman, you are a Roman lady. You have slaves to cook and clean, and that is the way it is meant to be. You do entertain and you do manage our household. If it had not been for you, half of my clients would—'

She puffed out her cheeks and let out an exasperated explosion of breath. 'Julia manages the household, as she has always done. I am as much an ornament as that vulgar Crown of Gold you are so proud of.' She smiled to take away any offence. 'I only wish I had been given the opportunity to win it.'

'Win your battle and you will have it,' he said, and meant it. 'My little sister is as brave as Boudicca and as hardy as any legionary centurion, and she makes me proud. Get well again and it will mean more to me than any honour.'

She lay back and he could see she was fading again, but she had the strength for one last whisper that he wasn't sure he'd heard properly. 'I almost forgot. Who was the terrible man who was here while you were away?'

When he was certain she was asleep he unhooked the boar amulet from his neck and fastened it gently round hers. If his own gods could not help her, perhaps Maeve's could.

It was only as he left that he realized what had been nagging at him. Olivia's recovery had been so rapid, so unexpected and so brief that it was almost as if she had been given another measure of the healer's wondrous draught.

The gladiators arrived as the plum-tinged sky of dusk gave way to the inky blue darkness of the Roman summer night. Valerius had stationed a servant by the garden door to let them into the house and another in an alley at the end of the street to check for any followers. They waited until the man reported everything clear before they went indoors.

Valerius had debated whether to tell his companions about Nero's threat, but he had decided it was a burden he must carry alone. It would make no difference to their efforts or to the outcome. Six couches were set out around the central pool of the atrium and he allowed the others to awkwardly take their places before he lay down himself. He ordered a slave to send wine and Serpentius's eyes lit up. 'But not until we have completed our business.' The Spaniard's face fell, but came alive again when it was Julia who set the flagon and six cups on a table by the doorway.

It was almost an hour before Valerius was satisfied with the list produced by Felix and Sextus. Several names were duplicated, or at least it seemed so because the spelling was similar, a number were only vague descriptions of people who could also have been on the other man's list, and Sextus seemed confused as to what constituted a chance meeting.

'How many seconds would I have to count for it to be an encounter? Would they have to exchange words? Sometimes her chair would stop next to someone, but it was impossible to tell if anything was said because I had to keep my distance.'

In the end they came up with a list of twenty. It included one consul, two, possibly three former legionary officers who had served with her husband, and a number of merchants, including one who owned most of the bakeries in the north of the city.

'The consul might be promising?' Marcus ventured.

Valerius shook his head. 'Petronius Lurco has just been elected a pontifex of the Temple of Neptune. Christus only allows his followers to worship one god. You said she singled him out, Felix?'

'That's right. Hailed him in the middle of the Clivus Argentarius. He looked proper put out.'

'She knew she was being followed. For years she

lived like a recluse, avoiding contact with anyone, only ever leaving her house in a covered chair. Suddenly she is approaching people she barely knows and scaring them half to death in the street. She was trying to lay a false scent. We need to look for someone she didn't want us to know she was talking to.'

Serpentius shrugged. 'That could be anyone she passed on the street close enough to exchange two words with. Hundreds, maybe thousands of people.'

'True,' Valerius agreed. 'But this list is all we've got. We have to start somewhere.'

'What about the soldiers?' Heracles suggested. 'Publius was a soldier.'

'I think we're wasting our time,' the Spaniard grunted. 'Use the Emperor's money to hire people to search every street for more fish signs.'

'And tell the whole of Rome what we're looking for? Petrus would burrow so deep we'd never find him.'

Marcus frowned and took the list from Valerius's hand.

'What is it?'

'I just remembered something. You said she avoided contact with everyone? The merchants on this list are all suppliers to the household or her husband's estates. She got her servants to pay them, but then insisted that each of them approach her chair to thank her personally. Why would she do that if she didn't want to meet people?'

Intrigued, Valerius retrieved the list from him. 'Wine sellers, butchers, bakers and builders. Mere plebeians. The old Lucina would have despised them all, even the rich ones. Yet she went out of her way to exchange words with them. That is interesting, but there are how many – ten – and any or all of them could be involved. We need something else.'

They broke up another hour later without making further progress. Valerius acknowledged that Serpentius's suggestion had some merit, but it was without much hope that he dispatched the Spaniard and Heracles to search the surrounding streets next day for any signs related to Christus. Marcus, Felix and Sextus would check out the premises of each of the merchants on the list. It was like trying to pin down smoke, but at least they were taking action.

He went to sleep that night with the nagging feeling that he had missed something.

XXVIII

Valerius spent the next morning working on the household accounts he had neglected for the past month, and after an early meal he slipped out by the garden door and took the short walk across the lower slope of the Caelian Hill to the Castra Peregrina. The barracks overlooked the old Porta Capena and were hidden behind a sturdy wall, and it was by the north corner that Valerius waited for his contact from Seneca. Just when he was beginning to think he'd wasted his time a lumbering figure approached from the direction of the city gate.

Valerius had to look twice. Had the man lost his mind?

Seneca saw the expression on his face and laughed. 'Allow an old gentleman a little indulgence, and give him some credit, my boy. I have played these games before and I believe I can still outfox a fool like Torquatus.'

'You are mad to come here.'

The philosopher's brow creased. 'Not mad, I think, but in a man in my position the senses can be aroused beyond the normal and that heightened arousal may have an effect on judgement. Yet precisely because of that effect the subject himself could well be unaware of his predicament. An interesting proposition,' he smiled. 'But I believe you have a question for me?'

First, Valerius reported his progress, or lack of it.

Seneca sniffed his distaste. 'Yes, I wasn't aware of the peril in which I was placing Lucina when I gave you her name. Though she did lead you to Cornelius who, in time, I'm sure would have led you to Petrus. The question I believe we must ask is whether they betrayed themselves or whether some outside influence brought them to their fate. You have not, for instance, told anyone of our arrangement?'

Valerius stared at him. 'You think someone in my household is a spy?'

'Oh, I am certain of it. But I'm also certain you would not trumpet this business to your slaves and your servants, but . . .'

'I trust Marcus and his men with my life.'

'Indeed you do,' Seneca said significantly. 'I merely urge caution in all things. Cornelius's death was a warning not only to his fellow Christians.' He saw Valerius's look of puzzlement. 'Christians, my boy, is what Petrus and the other members of his sect call themselves.'

'These . . . Christians . . . use some sort of code among themselves to indicate the place and time of their next meeting. I thought, with your contacts in the east, it might be possible to discover its nature.'

Seneca stared out over the valley towards the great tiered palace complex on the Palatine and his nose wrinkled with distaste. 'You may be asking too much, but I will make enquiries. What form does the code take? Do you have an example?'

Reluctantly, Valerius told him about the inscription scratched on the doorpost of the physician's *insula*. The philosopher frowned. 'These people are weaned on secrecy. I can make nothing of it, but I will see what I can do. I will send a courier to your house tonight at dusk with the answer, if there is one.'

'Not to the house.' Valerius gave him the address of the block where Marcus, Serpentius and the others were billeted.

Seneca was wandering off in the direction of the Capena gate when Valerius remembered what else he had wanted to ask. He hurried to intercept the older man.

'You spent ten years as part of Nero's inner circle. Who among them is the most likely to be attracted to this Christian god?'

The philosopher's brows furrowed as he dissected the question, evaluating and discarding. Eventually he burst into laughter. 'Open to new ideas. Impressionable. Unstable and prone to instantaneous and ill-considered enthusiasms. Why, the man most likely to become a Christian is Nero himself.' He was still laughing when he vanished towards the road.

Valerius spent a frustrating evening waiting for word. He called for wine and by the time he was ready to sleep he knew he'd had more than was good for him. Still, even his mood couldn't account for the way Tiberius, the steward, and his other slaves worked so hard to avoid being in his presence. Even Julia disappeared the moment he entered Olivia's room. Something was wrong and it nagged at him like a woodpecker inside his skull. He remembered the feeling that he was missing something. Whatever it was, it had happened since he'd returned from Dacia.

He went over everything in his mind, even though reliving the horror of Nero's ultimatum and Lucina's torment sickened him. Not that. Something else. Something to do with the household. He must remember every whisper. He was almost asleep when it came to him. Every whisper, that was the answer. What had Olivia said? *Who was the terrible man who was here while you were away?*

'Tiberius,' he roared.

It took a few minutes for the old man to answer the call and when he did the fear that showed in his eyes was enough to convince Valerius that his suspicions were well-founded. 'Master?'

'Someone was here while I was gone. Someone I am not to know about. Who was it?'

Tiberius shook his head. 'I cannot—'

'Do you think I am a fool, Tiberius?' Valerius kept his voice low, but the menace in his words was clear. 'This is my household, and you are part of it. Whatever is making you stay quiet is nothing compared to the power of my anger if you do not tell me. I have never whipped a slave, but I am prepared to start. You have always been loyal to me and my family; do not betray me now.'

'He said they would kill—' The old man's voice shook and tears ran down his face.

'Who said?'

'We could not stop them. They had an imperial warrant.'

'Who, Tiberius? I have to know.'

'Praetorians,' Tiberius sobbed. 'A centurion and six men. He said they were here to make an inventory of all your possessions. Everything. A man with a scarred face, master. I could not stop them.'

Rodan. Of course.

'He said we would die if we told. He went to Olivia's room. He . . .'

In an instant, Valerius felt the blood boiling inside his head and his vision went red. He reached out blindly and his hand caught the front of the slave's tunic. Tiberius let out a cry of terror.

'He did what, Tiberius?'

The old man darted a scared glance towards the doorway and Valerius followed the look to where Julia stood, her eyes wide with terror, and something else . . . shame.

Rodan made his way from the Castra Praetoria to the palace at dawn the next day, accompanied by six of the Guard. It was a fine morning and he took pleasure in the fact that everything was going so well. His retirement from the Guard was only a few years away and, apart from his centurion's pension, which wasn't paltry, he'd amassed a small fortune in bribes from people he had led to believe they were on the Emperor's little list. He was still a relatively young man, with a bright future, and, if things went to plan, his finances were about to improve even further.

When the tall figure stepped out into the street ahead, he was surprised, but not concerned. Why should a man with six armed guards fear one with no sword, not even a belt? Valerius wore a long-sleeved tunic against the morning chill, but he was clearly unarmed.

'You're out early today, my hero. What's wrong? The ghosts keeping you awake?'

The words were accompanied by a sneer, but the mocking grin vanished as the young Roman marched silently towards him. Valerius's face might have been carved from stone and his eyes glowed red in the morning sun. Before Rodan was aware of it he was only feet away and for the first time the centurion felt a thrill of fear. 'Wait,' he cried. Two of the Praetorians drew swords, but Valerius brought his left hand up to Rodan's neck above his wolf breastplate, and by some piece of trickery a blade twinkled in the morning sunlight.

'It's only a very small knife.' Valerius's voice was soft, but it held the pitiless chill of the grave. 'But it will make a very large hole in your throat. You've seen a man's throat cut, Rodan? Of course you have. They might kill me, but I'll still have the satisfaction of watching you bleed out. Tell them to put the swords away.'

Rodan hesitated, but only for a moment. He nodded and the two Praetorians stepped back.

'If I hear you've been anywhere near my house again, centurion, I will rip out your guts and hang you with them from the nearest tree. Do you understand? Stay away from my family, or I promise I'll kill you, and you know me well enough to believe that I keep my promises.'

The Praetorian looked into the dark eyes and saw only certainty there. A shiver ran through him as he remembered the day in Caligula's circus when he had looked into those same eyes and seen his death. Rodan had fought on the German frontier; he was no coward. In his mind, he drew his sword and rammed it deep into the other man's belly, but he remembered the stories he had heard and his hands stayed by his side.

Valerius studied his enemy's face and knew he'd won, but it was a small victory and he had no doubt it would come at a price. He turned his back and walked away. He'd only gone ten paces when Rodan found his voice.

'Did I hear a donkey breaking wind?' The centurion's harsh shout broke the silence. 'No, I'm mistaken. It was the last gasp of a dying man. Do you hear that, my Hero of Rome? You're a dead man.' Valerius turned to face him, but Rodan was back with his guards and every one had his sword clear of its scabbard. Hatred made the ruined face uglier still. 'You don't understand, do you? It doesn't matter whether you succeed or fail, you're going to die. It's all arranged. You and your father and sister are all going to die.'

XXIX

It wasn't until early afternoon that Valerius received word from Marcus. When he arrived at the apartment he was surprised to find their visitor was Saul of Tarsus, the dark-visaged easterner who had been with Seneca at his father's house.

'My apologies for the delay. My lord Seneca did not wish to entrust a servant with such an important message, nor did he feel it should be carried in written form. My profession requires me to memorize quite complex pieces of information, therefore he decided it would be prudent to await my return.' He asked for a wax writing block and on it drew the letters MCVII, and a narrow outline that Valerius recognized. 'The Christians use it as a symbol of recognition,' Saul explained. 'You were correct in your assumption that it represents a fish. The men Christus chose as his original followers were fishermen, so the symbol seemed appropriate. See how easy it is to draw?' He ran over the outline again. 'Merely a single straight line, then a curve back to cross the initial line and create the tail. Think of two men talking in the street. The one believes his companion is also a Christian, but he cannot be certain. He scuffs his feet in the dust. Two simple movements and we have a fish. If the other man does not recognize it he is not a member of the sect. In this instance it is the orientation of the fish that is important. Was the head pointing up, down, right or left, indicating north, south, east or west?'

'The head was to the left. West.'

'Then the meeting place you are looking for is west of the inscription's position.'

Valerius shook his head in frustration. 'That still leaves a quarter of the city, part of the sixth, seventh and ninth districts at least.'

Saul nodded gravely. 'Ah, but there is more to learn.'

'The seventh district,' Heracles cried. 'See, M C VII.'

'Not necessarily,' Saul cautioned. 'Yes, the numerals are significant, but not in such an unsubtle way. The initials M and C indicate a person or a place, but to identify this person they must be transposed. So CM. To those who know CM, the name will provide a location.'

'So, we find this CM and go to his house?' Marcus suggested.

The bearded man allowed himself a slight smile. 'VII. Seven. The ceremony will be held within seven blocks of the house of the man or woman CM.'

A bitter laugh emerged from the gloom at the back of the room where Serpentius had been listening. 'You talk in circles and make as little sense as a temple priest. Seven blocks in any direction? You're telling us to search four hundred houses. This is just foolishness.'

Saul turned to Valerius. 'You must understand that Petrus lives in constant danger of discovery or betrayal, and has done so for thirty years and more. Deceit and subterfuge are second nature to him. On the one hand, he cannot pass on his message without placing himself at the mercy of those he is forced to trust. On the other, he protects himself by concealing his true identity from all but a few of his followers, and those few will be unknown to each other. I doubt there are four men in all Rome who know who and where he is.'

'Then he is impossible to find.'

'Not impossible, not for a man of resource. The fish pointed west, so the meeting place will be to the west of the house. You will recognize it by another fish inscription. Petrus is at his most vulnerable when he is spreading the word of Christus. This he does once each calendar month, on the Sabbath day closest to the nones, beginning at the seventh hour.'

'Sabbath?' Valerius didn't recognize the word.

'Holy day,' Saul explained. 'These Christians have trouble agreeing many things. Those who wish to distance themselves from the Judaeans favour a Sunday. Petrus, who is a traditionalist, prefers Saturday.'

'But that means . . . ?'

'Yes, my young friend. It means that you have less than three hours to locate CM and the building where the meeting will be held. Three hours to find Petrus . . . and deliver him to lord Seneca.'

Valerius recognized the subtle threat in the final five words, but he barely registered it. His mind raced. Lucina Graecina knew what the sign meant, if not Petrus's true identity. And if Lucina Graecina knew, Torquatus now had the information. He had three hours to get to Petrus before the Emperor's secret police did.

They waited until Saul had left the building.

'The list?' Valerius demanded. Serpentius placed it on the table beside Saul's drawing of the fish. They crowded over it, but Valerius had already noted the significance of one name.

'Cerialis. What do we know of him?'

'Cerialis Marcellus, the baker. One of the merchants who had regular contact with Lucina Graecina,' Marcus said decisively. 'He has a house in the seventh district, beyond the Campus Agrippae on the Via Pinciana. I was out there yesterday. He owns four bakeries in and around the city.'

'How long will it take to reach there?'

'An hour at most.'

'Then we need to find the meeting place.'

'It's a busy area,' Marcus admitted. 'A warren of shops, houses and workshops, but I have an idea. One of the bakeries he owns is also in the seventh district, quite close to his home. People come and go from a shop like that all the time. Plenty of room there for a meeting and the place will be empty because bakers tend to work in the early morning. I doubt it will take us more than half an hour to find it.'

'Cloaks and swords,' Valerius said decisively, making for the door. 'We'll meet at the house when you're ready. Serpentius? Find your way to the bakery and wait for us there. I want to know who goes in, who comes out, and if the place is already being watched.'

He rushed back to the Clivus Scauri, his mind calculating the possibilities. If they could reach the meeting place before Torquatus and his thugs. If they could get Petrus away. What then? He would be gambling with the lives of twenty thousand innocents. Did he have the right to do that? Did he have the stomach? He would only find out when he got there.

When he reached his door he almost collided with a hurrying figure coming the other way. 'Father!'

The old man smiled distractedly. 'You mustn't shout, Valerius. You will disturb your sister. And now I must bid you good day. I am late for an engagement.'

It took a heartbeat for Valerius to realize what Lucius was saying. He heard the shake in his voice. 'You're going to a meeting of these Christians?'

The benign mask fractured and the possibilities flew across his father's face like a flock of disturbed partridge. Truth? Lie? Bluster? Each second of delay making an answer less necessary.

'You can't go, Father. I won't allow it.' Valerius

placed his arm across the doorway to add a physical edge to the appeal.

'Cannot? Will not allow it?' The words emerged as a whisper of disbelief.

'Must not. For all our sakes.'

'You, my own son, think to *forbid* me? Are you mad?'

'Not mad, Father.' Valerius kept his voice low. 'I am trying to save your life.'

Lucius hissed with suppressed anger. 'My life is mine to spend where and when I wish, and I will not be dictated to in my own . . . in this house.'

'Your life, perhaps, but not Olivia's and not mine. *Torquatus knows*. They will take you and they will hurt you, Father, and you will tell them everything they want to know. Everything. I have seen it. You will give them your friends and your family to stop the pain. You will give them Petrus, and Seneca and the man Saul. I can't let you go.'

The older man stared at him, and for the first time in his life Valerius saw contempt in his father's eyes. 'If you believe that, young man, then you do not know me. Perhaps you are not my son after all.' He shrugged his cloak around him, raised his head and tried to push past Valerius. 'Will you physically restrain your father? I think not.'

Valerius closed his eyes. What could he do? Short of wrestling Lucius to the ground he had no option but to let him go. Then he heard the sound of running feet behind him. Marcus!

He pushed his father back to clear the doorway. 'Marcus,' he called. 'I need you in here. Send the others after Serpentius.'

'I can't stop you, Father, but Marcus can and will. He will keep you safe here. Please do as he says.' He reached out a hand to touch Lucius on the shoulder, but the old man flinched away from him like a child avoiding a blow.

'Master?' Tiberius, the steward, appeared from the kitchens and his frightened eyes flicked from Valerius to his father.

'Do not concern yourself, Tiberius,' Valerius reassured the elderly retainer. 'It is only a minor disagreement.' He nodded and turned to walk out into the sunshine.

'But master,' Tiberius insisted. 'The dark-haired slave girl who was here earlier. She insisted I give you a message.'

Valerius froze. 'Yes?'

'She said "today, at the seventh hour".' Tiberius added the address of a street in the Seventh district and Valerius felt the world stop. He turned to his father. 'Will Ruth be there?' Lucius didn't reply, but his ashen face answered for him. Valerius ran for the door.

By now it was past noon and he found his progress impeded by citizens returning to their families for the midday meal. His way took him beneath the palaces of the eastern Palatine, past the Temple of Divine Claudius, and towards the Forum, where he turned left through the familiar temples and pillars. When he reached the beginning of the Via Flaminia the road became more open and he was able to pick up his pace, but by the time he reached the gardens of the Campus Agrippae and turned up the hill, the streets had closed in on him again and he was forced to push through the crowds.

As he ran, his mind was filled with Ruth's serene face and he prayed he would be in time. He tried to understand what would make his father take such a risk. Of course, one man would be more dedicated in his worship than another, and some gods demanded more dedication from those who worshipped them. But for most Romans the strength of devotion was in direct proportion to the magnitude of their need. If a trader was desperate for a big grain contract, naturally he would sacrifice a fine ram to Mercury to encourage his support. Each day, Julia poured a libation to the kitchen god to insure against culinary disaster. And Valerius would gladly go on his knees before any god he believed could help cure Olivia, even though he knew, deep in his heart, that such help was unlikely to be forthcoming. But why would a man who had spent his life in the service of Rome defy Roman law, betray his Roman friends and risk his life, and that of his family, for a condemned criminal and a band of ragged Judaean fishermen? It defied logic. He acknowledged that the offer of eternal life, qualified and flawed though it was, would attract those who despaired of their current circumstances, or were naive enough to enter into a pact that effectively sacrificed their free will for a place in some unlikely Elysian paradise. Ruth had been raised to believe, but his father? Perhaps Petrus was a magician who kept his supporters in thrall by spells or potions. Yet he had seen the Judaean in his guise as Joshua, the healer, and nothing would have led him to that conclusion. Lucina Graecina, a Roman to the tip of her exquisitely manicured fingernails, had been prepared to sacrifice everything in the cause of Christus, and Cornelius Sulla had stayed silent under the most excruciating torture. Lucina had been no fool, and neither, though he had acted one, was Cornelius. Eventually, Valerius was forced to give up on a puzzle to which his brain could find no answer.

'Valerius, here!' He turned to see Serpentius emerging from a side street, his narrow face flushed with concern. 'We're too late. The Praetorians have the place surrounded.'

The Spaniard's words stopped Valerius like a hammer blow, and he fought the paralysis that threatened to overwhelm him. 'How far to the bakery?' he demanded. However bad the situation, there was always the possibility of salvaging something. If he had learned nothing else from the disaster in Britain he had learned that.

'Just up here, but we will have to be quick.'

Valerius followed the Spaniard's tall figure through the throng as Serpentius's long strides carried him swiftly ahead. They were approaching an open market place when they heard the commotion. To one side, a crowd had gathered to watch a young black bear dance at the end of a chain. Serpentius quickly slipped into the anonymous fold, but Valerius stood transfixed. Dashing down the roadway was a slim figure holding her blue dress up around her knees to allow her to run more freely. It seemed she must be stopped by the wall of people ahead of her, but the power of her fear gave her passage. Now she ran directly towards Valerius, her long black hair flying, and he could see the panic in her eyes and feel the pounding of her heart.

Ruth.

Thirty paces behind and gaining with every step followed four Praetorians, their iron-shod sandals clattering on the cobbled surface and the swords rattling in their scabbards.

'Stop her!'

Valerius's heart stopped as he recognized Rodan's voice. With anyone else he would have taken his chances and tried to talk her out of trouble, but he knew there would be no mercy from the Praetorian. Rodan would kill Ruth just to spite him. He lowered his head, but not before his despairing eyes had locked on hers for a fleeting second.

It was enough for the Judaean girl to recognize him, and through her wild panic Ruth felt an impossible surge of hope. The Christians had been waiting for Petrus to make his entrance when Rodan's soldiers burst in. By good fortune, she had been standing in shadow on the stairs and the explosion of violence had frozen her in position. As the Praetorians lashed out with clubs at the small band of worshippers, she had recovered enough to slip quietly away to the upper room where Cerialis kept his grain. It was from there, through a narrow window, that she made her escape. She had been a few feet from safety when one of the Praetorian guards noticed and made a grab at her arm. Somehow, she'd managed to slip from his grasp, tearing her dress in the process, but his shouts alerted the others. She bit back the impulse to scream out Valerius's name, knowing that it could condemn them both. The terror that threatened to explode her brain eased. Somehow she knew he would save her.

'Stop that bitch!'

Valerius took in the scene in a heartbeat. Ruth's long legs flying as she closed the gap between them. The Praetorians just twenty paces behind, Rodan at their head, impossible to outrun, and, even with Serpentius at his side, impossible to outfight. Behind him, he heard more shouts. They were trapped. The day by the river flashed through his head. In the same instant he saw the flames climbing Cornelius Sulla's body. Lucina naked in the cage. A girl and her baby torn to pieces by wild beasts. There was no time for panic. No time for indecision. The despair that was tearing him apart had to be pushed to the darkest recesses of his mind. He had only seconds. He reached below the cloak.

Ruth's body collided with his, her arms searching for him. He caught her and held her; felt her softness and her warmth and the agitated fluttering of her terror. She looked into his eyes and behind the tears he saw a mixture of fear and love and hope. He wanted to tell her how he could have returned her love. He wanted to tell her . . . instead, he thrust the dagger in his left hand up below her breastbone and felt the moment it entered the pulsing life force of her heart.

The hazel eyes opened wide as she felt the cold iron and a numbing blow to the chest that froze her rigid. Valerius watched the light within first brighten, then fade.

'I'm sorry.' The whispered words were the last thing she would ever hear. Valerius twisted away and melted into the crowd in front of the still dancing bear.

For a few seconds Ruth stood swaying, kept upright only by will, before her body collapsed just as Rodan arrived at the head of his men. Valerius would have stayed, tortured by the need to be close to her, but Serpentius dragged him cursing towards the main road. Before they were out of sight, he turned to take one last look at the pathetic bundle lying in the street like a heap of blue rags. He heard Rodan raging at the dead girl, before the Praetorian pulled back an iron-shod foot and kicked her unprotected face. 'Christian whore!'

Somehow the assault on her lifeless body seemed more of an outrage than the thrust that killed her. Valerius's heart turned to stone and his mind cried out for revenge. Beneath the cloak he drew his sword from its scabbard and moved towards the Praetorians.

'No!' Serpentius caught his shoulder. 'No point in throwing away your life as well as hers.' He dragged Valerius towards safety.

Behind them Rodan belatedly realized the girl couldn't have killed herself. 'Close off the street,' he shouted. 'No one is to leave the area.'

But it was already too late.

XXX

I had no choice.

He remembered an earlier Valerius, a whole Valerius, who had told himself those very same words and done what was right. In the end, the result had been the same.

They would have taken her and burned her, or fed her to the wild beasts. I had no choice.

But he did have a choice. He could have fought and he could have died saving her.

And when they had killed me they would have put her to the torture.

Still, he could have chosen to kill Ruth and die avenging her; that, at least, would have been an honourable end.

But it would have meant abandoning Olivia and my father and condemning twenty thousand innocent people.

Coward! The word rang through his brain like a

clash of swords. Maeve, the British girl he had loved and betrayed, had called him a coward. Was it true?

No!

Coward!

'Valerius?' The voice came from a different world and ended with a choked gasp as his left hand found the speaker's throat. He opened his eyes to see his father's face darkening above him, the rheumy eyes bulging. Just for a second, he blamed Lucius for Ruth's death and might have squeezed harder, but the moment passed and he loosened his grip. The old man retreated from the bed massaging his throat. He stared at Valerius as if he didn't recognize him. Six years earlier he had sent a boy to become a man with the legions. The boy had returned a warrior. Now he realized just what the warrior was capable of and it frightened him. But it wasn't the hand on his throat that had frightened him most. It was the look in his eyes. Valerius had become a killer.

'I'm sorry, Father. You startled me.'

Lucius forced a smile. 'Not so much as you startled me, I think.'

The closed shutters kept the room in darkness, but the temperature and the light squeezing through the gaps indicated some hour around mid-morning.

'You must not blame yourself.'

Valerius shook his head. *I killed her. How could I not blame myself?*

'She went of her own free will and knew the risk she took.'

He felt the anger rising within him again. 'Did they also take Petrus?'

'I do not believe so.' Lucius hesitated. 'Someone would have sent me word. It was his way to let the faithful gather before he arrived. It was more secure.'

Valerius didn't hide his bitterness. 'So he used them as bait in a trap. He used *Ruth* as bait in a trap? What would your compassionate Christus have made of that?'

Lucius turned his face away. 'Petrus is more important than any of us. Than all of us. Without Petrus the faith would wither and die. He is the keeper of the truth.'

'Tell me about him.'

The old man hesitated. Keeping the secret had become a habit.

'When your mother died at least I still had my ambition and my son, who would make that ambition a reality. Olivia married well, you went to Britain with your legion and I was content.' He saw the look in Valerius's eyes. 'I know what you think of me, Valerius. I know that you laughed at my hopes and only accepted your part in them out of duty. This family once figured among Rome's great, and I was determined that we should do so again. Seneca, who is my friend, said he would help me.'

Seneca, Valerius thought, like a spider at the centre of a web, manipulating all around him. And at what price?

'Then Olivia's husband died, and you returned

from Britain, a hero, but a part-man. I looked at you and I saw a candle starved of air, a life flickering on the brink of extinction. You have recovered your health, but when I look into your eyes I know that they have seen too much and you have suffered too much. You will never be the same again, my son, and for that I blame myself. You were changed, but you were not quite lost to me; not yet.' Valerius opened his mouth, knowing what was coming, but Lucius raised his hand. 'No, let me speak. I will come to Petrus in my own time. I searched Rome, and the provinces too, to find a suitable husband for your sister, but I did not have enough to offer them. Who would want an alliance with an old man who last had influence in Tiberius's time? Without mortgaging the estate, the dowry I could offer was not attractive. Olivia is beautiful, but that means nothing to the powerful families I courted. It was Seneca who found Calpurnius Ahenobarbus.'

Valerius sighed. 'A man as old as you are,' he pointed out. 'With a face like a starved warthog and a reputation for degeneracy that would not have shamed Caligula.'

'A rich man,' Lucius countered. 'A man with connections to the Emperor. She should have obeyed me – I am her father. Instead, she shamed me. And you supported her.'

Valerius nodded. 'And support her still.'

'Finally, I had lost everything. A razor and a warm bath seemed more welcome than another day of life.

Next morning Granta brought the girl to the estate. A gift from a friend.'

'Ruth.' Valerius struggled to keep his voice steady.

'She was different from the other slaves. Something inside her shone.' Lucius sniffed. 'How does one define goodness? She sensed my emptiness and she came to me when I was alone amongst my olive trees. At first I sent her away; I did not want whatever it was she had to offer. But she persisted. She too had lost everything, she said, but her God for ever walked by her side and she would never be alone. He protected her from the evils without and within. The temptations of the earthly world and the weakness of her own body. I too could receive her God's protection. She spoke of a man called Petrus.'

'And she took you to him?'

Lucius shook his head. 'Not at first. Petrus must be protected. She had to be certain of me and I had to be certain of myself. I had never heard of Christus, but I knew enough of Rome and Nero to understand the danger. There was a moment when I considered handing her over to the authorities and I think she knew it. She believed the risk was worth taking to save me. That was when I was at my lowest. She told me she forgave me and I wept on her shoulder. Two days later she took me to meet Petrus.'

Valerius remembered Ruth's instinctive compassion and her fearless certainty and knew that nothing would have stopped her. She had recognized something broken in his father just as she had seen it in

313

him. The path she walked would eventually have ended in her death whatever happened that day in the street. Was it blindness or foolishness that made her ignore the danger? No. It was much simpler than that. She was too good for the world. Too brave and too honest. The purveyors of pain and depravity like Torquatus could not afford to have their deeds questioned by the bringers of peace and love. Eventually, only one voice would prevail. He saw again Cornelius Sulla tied to his stake, his eyes squeezed shut and his lips moving in prayer, and he knew it was not death the young man had feared, but only the method of his dying.

Lucius and Ruth had travelled to Rome together. The city was dark and she had led him through streets he didn't know, but Ruth walked without fear and Lucius had taken strength from her strength. Eventually they had reached a house marked in some way that she recognized.

'She whispered the name of Christus and we were shown into a small room where ten others stood, cloaked and hooded as we were.' He shook his head. 'How can I describe the atmosphere in that room? At first I believed it was fear, because that was what I felt, but now I think it was anticipation; a desperate need for what was to come. Then he was there. He drew back his hood and looked upon us; an ordinary man but with extraordinary presence. His eyes sought mine and in that moment I felt as if I was filled with light. My fear vanished and I was lifted up and was able to look down upon my own poor, corrupt body, and those of my fellows, before he placed me back among them.'

When Petrus had spoken, his words had reached out to each person in the room, as if he had taken them aside individually. But, when his father recalled what had been said, Valerius was transported back to the Vicus Patricius and the young man with the smashed lips. *God, who created all things, sent Jesus to die for you and bring you everlasting life. Follow the teachings of Jesus and you will become closer to God.* Petrus had created a network of preachers to carry his message, each trained in the precise wording. Valerius remembered Publius Sulla's words before he died and saw the genius of the plan. Truly, it was like a disease, for each messenger was capable of infecting tens or hundreds more with the teachings of Petrus's God, and from these he would select yet more messengers who would in turn carry the message to a new audience. Worse, according to the teachings of Christus, each slave was of as much value as any knight or senator. Unless Rome could stamp out the new religion, it would eventually overwhelm everything Romans now believed in. If they could no longer worship Jupiter and Mercury and Minerva, why should they worship an Emperor who was of no more individual merit than the savage who tended their dogs?

He heard his father's voice change and take on an almost awed reverence.

'Petrus told how his life changed when he was approached by the Messiah while he was fishing with his brothers.'

'The Messiah?'

'God's messenger. Jesus Christus. When he spoke, he spoke the word of God. Petrus was first amazed, then transformed. From that day onward he followed the Messiah and he has never turned back. He witnessed the miracles.' Valerius noted a slight hesitation and realized that some parts of the Jesus legend still taxed his father's credulity. 'He saw the Messiah walk upon water.'

The idea was so absurd that Valerius laughed, and immediately regretted it.

His father huffed. 'Do not make fun of me. Do you wish to hear the story of Petrus or not?' He didn't wait for answer. 'Of all Christus's followers, Petrus was the foremost, and, when Christus died upon the cross, he became the leader in his stead. He was forced to flee Judaea and preached in Antioch and Caesarea before he understood where the greatest need and the greatest glory was to be found. Rome. Since he arrived here, he has been tested many times, as all our faith must be tested so that it may retain its strength.'

Valerius thought again of Ruth and asked the question he wasn't sure he wanted answered. 'And has your faith been tested, Father?'

Lucius swivelled his head so he wouldn't have to look in his son's eyes. 'I have been tested, yes.'

'Did your faith survive?'

Now the old man turned back so Valerius could see the damp sheen on his cheeks. 'God will be the final judge of that.'

XXXI

The next morning, Valerius went downstairs to discover a package had been delivered for him. It was of a type only rich men sent to each other, wrapped in waxed calfskin and stitched to ensure the contents wouldn't be damaged in a rainstorm. He studied it suspiciously. In the current circumstances it was as likely to contain an angry cobra as anything more welcome.

A bright red seal fixed to the leather confirmed his suspicions. The imprint was a mirror image of the golden bauble he kept on the chain beneath his tunic. It meant the package was from Nero.

He reached for it . . . but drew his hand clear. Why? Five days had passed since the Emperor pronounced his suspended sentence of death. Each minute without progress represented another step towards the execution block. At first he had been energized by the challenge, but with every setback the road became steeper and the weight he carried heavier.

First Lucina Graecina, then Ruth. Two channels to Petrus sealed for ever. Without Petrus he could not save Olivia. His father, brave fool that he was, now appeared to provide his only hope, but he sensed that Lucius had revealed as much as he was ever going to. He had never felt so tired, or so defeated.

A voice he hadn't heard for almost four years whispered inside his head. *Can't take it, pretty boy? I always said you were too soft. Just a rich boy playing at soldiers.*

Valerius laughed, short and bitter. Seneca had once said that the greatest battles are fought within oneself, but Seneca had never seen a real battle. Valerius had been in more fights than he could count and he knew that there came a point when it was easier to give up than to stay alive and make the next sword cut. That was when true heroes were made. He was a Hero of Rome, though he had never wanted or deserved it. Now was the time to prove he was worthy of the honour. He picked up a fruit knife and began working on the stitching.

It wasn't until he had the package open in front of him that he remembered Torquatus's promise more than a month earlier to send him what he knew about the Christus sect.

On his desk lay four scrolls, cracked and ragged with age and use, and twice as many scraps of parchment.

The first scroll he picked up was a Greek transcript

of the trial and conviction of Jesus Christus by the governor of Judaea, Pontius Pilatus. He scanned through it and found that it contained little of interest. The charges of sedition against the Roman Empire were far from conclusive, but it was clear the man had caused unrest among the Judaean community and in the end the priests of the temple had competed to condemn him. Even so, Pilatus had been reluctant to convict, but the defendant's outrageous claims and conduct in court had given him little choice.

Valerius unrolled another of the scrolls and found himself reading an earnest and rather dull treatise on the Jewish religion and its offshoots, of which the Christus sect was only one of a remarkable number. It outlined the history and practices of Judaism in substantial detail, but, disappointingly, gave little space to the new and rather obscure Christians. The writer's conclusions were given in a dismissive tone, as if he had no doubt the sect would fade away in its own good time now that its leader had been disposed of. On the face of it, there seemed few differences and many similarities between the Jewish and the Christian religions. When the document was written, Christus worship had been practised exclusively by Jews, who clung to many of the old religion's rites. It was said that the coming of a Messiah had been foretold by Jewish prophets, although the man Jesus was only one of three or four possible candidates. The main distinction between the two religions appeared to be the question of sacrifice, which played a central role in Judaism but was abhorred by the Christians, who carried it out only symbolically through the substitution of wine and bread for the blood and body of Christus.

He discovered more of interest among the fragments of parchment, which had plainly been cut or torn from scrolls of much greater length. They contained intriguing insights into the early life of Christus and highlighted a number of contradictions which Valerius found fascinating. There was little doubt that he had been born in Galilee, probably in the village of Nazareth, although another account had Bethlehem, an unlikely seventy-five miles away, laying claim to him.

The only reference to his childhood was a torn and crumpled scrap of poor quality parchment which had evidently been cast aside and picked up by someone's spy or passed through many hands until it reached the Emperor's intelligence services. It had apparently been written in good faith as evidence of the child Jesus's power, but Valerius doubted it would ever find its way into any Christian account of their hero's life. Petrus would hardly want to claim that the Messiah had either killed another boy or been responsible for his death when he was just five years old.

Little more was recorded until his mid-twenties when some transformation had taken place in his life. Now he was a healer and a teacher – a man who believed he was the son of a god – travelling across Judaea and preaching against the temple authorities, railing against sacrifice and the worship of idols. According to the source you chose, Christus could be a man torn by his desires and overcoming them, or one untouched by earthly temptation. Confusingly, his supporters seemed to be unsure whether he was man, god, or some mixture of both. In fact, this Jesus Christus appeared to be a remarkably convenient shape-changer who could dazzle and bewitch at will. A man – or a god, if he so chose – capable of being all things to all men. Unless your name was Simon Petrus.

Petrus and the brothers John and James had been the constants in Christus's early life, and though they were later joined by other acolytes it was they, as far as Valerius could ascertain, who had been responsible for creating the Jesus legend. First-hand accounts of miracles came from either one or all of the trio. They and they alone had witnessed the anointment of Christus by his father, God – the only discernible evidence that he fulfilled the Messiah prophecy. From what Valerius read, without Petrus, Jesus Christus would have remained an obscure mystic wandering through the desert in search of his next meal.

It was Petrus who had built up and organized a following of thousands who believed in Christus and his God, and had so terrified the Judaean authorities that they had convinced Pilatus to kill him. And it was Petrus, his organization disintegrating around him, who conveniently witnessed the unlikely resurrection of Christus and restored the nerve of his few remaining followers. And Petrus who, with most Jews unwilling to continue their support for a dead Messiah, received a message from God that the time had come to bring Gentiles into the Christian fold.

Valerius could barely believe what he was reading. True, much of it was the work of government agents with a talent for dissembling and an interest in exaggerating the organization they had been sent to infiltrate, but even so Petrus's accomplishments were astonishing. Jesus Christus might be the figurehead, but the sect which worshipped him was the creation of one man. Simon Petrus.

He shook his head, half admiring and half in frustration. It was all very interesting, but it wasn't bringing him any closer to his man. He turned over the last piece of parchment, another learned discourse on the Christian rituals, and he was about to cast it aside when one passage caught his eye:

The Christian rite of baptism involves full immersion in running water, whereas the Judaic is merely a washing or cleansing. The Christian Messiah is said to have been baptized beneath a waterfall in the upper reaches of the River Jordan and each of his followers must undergo a similar ritual before they can gain entry to the Kingdom of Heaven. Since the Christian faith has been proscribed, baptismal rites have generally been carried out in larger groups and in great secrecy.

For a moment he was back by the pool on his father's estate. Ruth had been baptized in her homeland and he hoped she had been welcomed into the Christian heaven. But where were Petrus's Roman converts baptized? Not in the filth of the Tiber, that was certain. And not in any public place; it would attract instant arrest. Ruth had said that where possible Petrus would seek out a waterfall, and Petrus hadn't struck him as someone who would be diverted by a minor difficulty such as the fact that none was available. So what would he do? Gradually an idea formed in his mind. He remembered the ornamental waterfall in Nero's reception hall. Not there, certainly. But for a man of enterprise like Petrus an artificial waterfall would not be too difficult to find . . . or perhaps even create. The problem was, in a city that accounted for each and every drop of its water, where would he source the volume needed to supply it?

The answer came from a harsh, braying voice that echoed through his head. *Thousands of gallons a day from the water castle up on the Cespian Height. A veritable river siphoned off somewhere between there and the Subura.*

XXXII

Valerius sent a message to Honorius requesting an urgent meeting at the commissioner's offices. He could imagine the reaction when the engineer discovered that his lawyer was still neglecting his court duties. He wasn't disappointed.

'You are a disgrace to your profession, young man,' Honorius spluttered. 'We agreed a two-week suspension, yet it has been almost two months since I last laid eyes upon you. The villain should have been long since whipped and his supply capped. Now you have the audacity to come to me seeking assistance in some foolishness.' But the old man's eyes brightened when Valerius explained what he needed. 'So you think these Christians are stealing my water?'

'It's possible. If they are, it will be in large amounts. The last time we spoke you talked of a veritable river?'

'That is true. From the supply controlled by the water castle on the Cespian Height. But the source is a mystery. My investigators have been unable to discover a leak or a deliberate breach.'

Valerius hid his disappointment. He had hoped the break would be obvious, but if Honorius and his men were mystified it must be well hidden. The water castle on the Cespian Height overlooked the ancient temple of Juno Lucina, which was an omen if you liked. It was one of many dozens ingeniously sited across Rome to control the supply of water from the city's aqueducts to the palaces, mansions, baths and public fountains, the ironworks and the tile factories and the state farms that thrived within the city boundaries. Each castle was sited on high ground and distributed water where it was needed through lead pipes and stone channels. As their name suggested, they were enormous structures, constructed in two or even three sections, and each contained a substantial reservoir in case of drought, or interruption of the supply from an aqueduct.

Honorius reached below his desk and produced a map of the water system, an enormous scroll formed of many different sections of parchment. He unrolled it and weighted it down with short sections of worn lead pipe.

'See here.' A plump finger indicated a point in the centre of the map. 'The castle is one of the thirty-five supplied by the Old Anio, which takes its waters from the Tiber above the twentieth milestone and enters the city close to the Viminal Gate.' Like every Roman, Valerius knew that the Old Anio, as opposed to the

New Anio, was notorious for the poor quality of its waters, known universally as rat's piss and of similar colour and taste, but Honorius insisted on elaborating. 'Only six per cent of the supply will ever reach an imperial building, and that for the latrines. Most is used for industry or irrigation. The rest ends up in the Subura, where they are less inclined to complain about a little cloudiness.'

Mention of Subura reminded Valerius that the warren of streets overlooked by the Quirinal, Esquiline and Viminal hills provided a perfect refuge for a secretive cult like the Christians. It was here Petrus had set up his herb shop and surgery, and close by that they had stumbled upon the young man preaching at the crossroads. He noticed Honorius frowning.

'Now that I consider it,' the water commissioner mused, 'this would be the perfect supply to tap if one needed any great quantity. We treat Old Anio with a little less respect than we give to the other aqueducts, precisely because of the quality of the water and whom it supplies.' He shook his shaggy head. 'Regrettable, but understandable. It may be that the engineer I sent to investigate this leak did not treat it quite as diligently as he would if he had been inspecting the Virgo or the Aqua Claudia.' He let out an unlikely chuckle and Valerius recognized the enthusiasm of a true professional. 'Perhaps it is worth taking a second look?'

Honorius summoned a work detail and they set off for the Cespian Height. Their route took them through the bustling heart of the Subura, but Honorius was a magistrate whose rank warranted the accompaniment of six lictors and their progress was swift as the crowds parted before the heavy ash rods of the bodyguard. As they walked, with the lictors at their head and the water gang behind, Valerius studied the narrow streets and wondered if he was wasting precious time. Was it really possible to find one man in all of this? Twenty minutes later they reached the base of the slope and it took another five to climb to the water castle. In scale, though not in splendour, the castle resembled its religious neighbour. This was clearly a working building, massive and brick-built, perhaps forty feet in height and forty paces long, supplied from the north by a main spur of the Anio.

The water commissioner came to a halt in the shade of the tower and instructed his men to check the exterior for leaks or signs of theft. 'By the by,' he turned to Valerius, 'you must pass on my congratulations to your father.' He waited for a reaction, but none was forthcoming. 'Bassus the geologist mentioned it only yesterday. Strictest confidence, of course. Surely he must have told you?'

Valerius nodded distractedly, wondering what the old man was talking about. Honorius shrugged and returned to the matter of the tower. 'You see,' he explained, 'how it supplies four main channels and numerous smaller ones.' He called for a ladder as Valerius studied the stone conduits and lead pipes. 'I do not normally do this these days, young man, but needs must and truth be told your little mystery quite invigorates me. I haven't had so much excitement since the Marcia collapsed during the consulship of Hosidius Geta.' He hauled his substantial bulk up the ladder, puffing noisily and resting every three steps, while Valerius hung on behind him with his good hand and tried not to look upwards. A gentle breeze ruffled the tree tops and from his perch Valerius noticed a hawk arc across the city seeking out some sleepy pigeon or sparrow. From this height they had an unsurpassed view across the shimmering rooftops to the marbled glory of the Forum and the columned temples of the Capitoline. The heart of Rome, laid out like some child's toy or commander's sand model. Valerius was reminded of the wooden table he had seen in Nero's palace and he wondered again at its purpose. Did the Emperor look upon the cityscape as Valerius did now and glory in its colour and diversity and magnificence? Or were its people only so many ants striving to supply his imperial coffers? Doubtless both, knowing Nero's capricious nature, plus a ruler's paranoia that below each roof lay a potential enemy. Honorius reached a narrow terrace running around the castle and clambered awkwardly on to it over the low wall. Valerius joined him in front of a wooden doorway set into the brick. The water commissioner searched in a leather pouch at his waist and came out with a large key. 'Good.' He frowned absently. 'It wouldn't be the first time I'd forgotten you.'

The key turned easily in the lock and the door

opened with only the barest squeak. Honorius ducked his head and ushered Valerius into the cool of the interior, where the rush of water echoing from the stone walls instantly assaulted his ears. Barred windows set high in the walls provided enough gloomy light to allow them to see each other, and as his eyes adjusted Valerius was able to make out the inside of the building. They stood on a walkway which encompassed three sides of a massive tank of dark, swirling water supplied by a foaming torrent at the far end. The constant movement and a sensation that something was about to emerge from the bottomless depths and swallow him made Valerius instinctively step back and make the sign against evil. Honorius saw his reaction and grinned.

'It affects people like that the first time,' he roared above the noise of the water. 'But don't worry, we don't lose many.'

Still shouting, Honorius pointed to the wall and Valerius caught the shine of metal. He made out a number of strange levers of different sizes. 'The smaller levers operate the opening and closing of separate pipes, the larger, the outlets for baths and factories and the imperial gardens. It is a simple system involving pulleys and axles. In theory, the leakage could come from any of these pipes; in practice it is most likely to come from the outlets with the biggest capacity.'

'So the leakage doesn't come from this castle?' Valerius found himself shouting even louder than Honorius.

'Not from the castle itself, but certainly from this system. We have measured the flow above and below the tower and the supply is down by as much as a tenth. I have the men checking each of the four major channels.'

'Four?'

'What?'

Valerius took the older man by the arm and led him through the door into sunlight and relative quiet. 'You said four channels?'

'No need to shout, young man. That is correct.'

Valerius walked around the terrace, leaning out to study the exterior of the castle and the channels running from it. 'I believe I count five large outlets.'

Honorius glared, annoyed at the attempt to contradict him. 'Yes, but the fifth is no longer in use. It is the conduit which once supplied the Glabrian baths. See,' he pointed through the door, 'the opening mechanism has been removed. The line has been dry for years.'

Valerius was Roman born and bred but he had never heard of the Thermae Glabrianae.

'They were built, I believe, in the consulate of Marcus Acilius Glabro, more than two hundred years ago,' Honorius explained in his dry voice. 'But they were demolished in the time of Augustus. The family hadn't had the money to maintain them for years. The land was handed to the state which naturally sold it to some unscrupulous property developer for housing.'

331

'What land?'

'The land where the baths had stood.'

'No, I meant where?'

Honorius thought for a few moments and then walked to the northern end of the castle. 'There,' he said. 'On the lower slope of the Quirinal Hill by the Vicus Longus.' Valerius's face lit up. Not the Subura proper, but close enough to make little difference. Honorius shook his head. 'I see where you are going, young man, but it is not possible, I assure you. The apparatus has been removed and the conduit sealed. Only the commissioner and his staff have access to these towers. Come, I will prove it to you.'

He led the way back inside and retrieved another piece of equipment from the leather pouch. This was a metal tube about a handspan in diameter, which he handed to Valerius. He then lowered himself on to his belly with all the elegance of a collapsing water buffalo before shuffling to the edge of the walkway at a point close to where the Glabrian mechanism had once been fixed.

'Pass me the ocular, young man,' Honorius grunted. 'And be careful with it. It is the only instrument of its kind.'

Valerius gave him the tube, noticing for the first time that one end was closed by a circle of remarkably clear glass. The water commissioner shuffled forward until he was able to place the closed end in the water and put his eye to the opening.

'The dogs!'

332

'What is it?' Valerius asked. 'What can you see?'

'The dogs,' Honorius repeated, this time in admiration. 'How did they do it?'

'Do what?'

'They have jammed the gate open and they're stealing my water by the lakeful. But the Glabrian baths were demolished more than half a century ago. Where is it going?'

Valerius stared at the dark waters. He didn't yet have the answer to Honorius's question, but he was going to find out.

Lucius looked down at the sleeping figure. Sleeping? No, not sleeping. Olivia was dying. The draughts of elixir he had smuggled into the house had given her strength and him hope, but now both were almost gone. Lucius closed his eyes and for the first time truly felt old. He had been a failure in so many ways.

Convention and tradition dictated that he should regard Olivia as a chattel over whom he had the power of life and death, but convention and tradition could never prevail over love. He had loved his daughter since the first day he had held her tiny body straight from the birthing room, porcupine-haired and squealing, the dark eyes sparkling even then with the intelligence and curiosity that would never leave them. He had loved her as child, girl and woman, and when the day came to give her away to another man he had wept in the privacy of his *tablinum*. How then could he have allowed his ambition to come before her happiness? The truth was that he had looked upon old Ahenobarbus and seen not a man, but an opportunity. Where the reality was foul-breathed, gap-toothed and pot-bellied, his mind had shown him a glittering reintroduction to the Emperor's court on the arm of a man he could call son. Even when the horror on Olivia's face opened his eyes to reality, his pride had not allowed him to acknowledge it. He was a Roman and he was her father; he had the right to command obedience.

Olivia gave a little whimper and he felt as if his heart had been chopped in two. He remembered a long night with Claudia at his side bathing their daughter's sweat-soaked brow when she had fought some childhood sickness as she fought now, and the tears of relief when the fever broke the next day. Surely there must be a way. He prayed then, for God's help, as he had prayed every night since she had become ill.

He still felt the pain, like some half-healed sword wound, of the day he had disowned her as his daughter. Yet she *was* his daughter and she had walked from the villa without another word, her chin held high and with an expression he had believed was contempt, but knew now had been pity. The true contempt had come from Valerius, and how could he blame his son when he himself had been in the wrong? Yet still his pompous patrician concept of dignity would not allow him to admit it. He had withdrawn to his villa and his hills and his olives, an empty husk of a man;

empty of feelings, of dreams, even of hope. There he had wandered aimlessly and become old.

He touched Olivia's head and recoiled at the clammy texture of her skin. Of course, she could never have come to him. He had no right to expect it, but he had dreamed of it every night. Every night he would go to the door of the villa and she would be there, smiling and asking his forgiveness. And in the dream, he gave it. And each morning when he woke he would despair, because he knew that even if she came, his true self would never allow him to do what was right.

When news came of the sickness, his first thought had been to go to her. Yet as his horse was being saddled all he could see were the long-nosed, disapproving patrician faces of men he had called his friends, and he heard a voice telling him that if he went he could never again call himself a Roman.

That was when the girl Ruth had been sent to him. She was only a slave, but her presence had opened a door and he had walked through it into the light of God, where Petrus had taught him that to forgive was a strength, not a weakness. He was still too proud to reveal his change of heart to Valerius, but from that day onward he had visited Olivia whenever it was possible. He had been planning to ask Petrus to help her when Valerius had tracked the healer down. Lucius had felt certain the Judaean would be able to cure her. Yet even that had not been enough. Now all hope was gone. What did they have left but despair?

He bowed his head, listening to the laboured rasp of her breathing. As his tears stained her coverlet a thin shaft of sunlight moved across the wooden floor to spotlight the deathly ivory of her features. It was only then that he understood God's message. When all else is lost a man will always have his faith.

He still had his faith.

And now he knew what he must do.

XXXIII

They arranged to meet back at the water castle early the next morning and Valerius hurried to look in on Olivia before he gave his orders to Marcus and his men. When he reached the house he was surprised to find a slave holding a scroll which invited him to call upon Fabia Faustina.

By the time he returned home the sun was coming up. For reasons he didn't understand the encounter had left him with the same feeling a blind man has on hearing the final piece slapped into place on a gaming board, not knowing whether he has won or lost. He had learned long ago in Britain not to ignore these instincts, but within minutes of reaching the house it was driven from his mind by a new crisis.

Olivia was gone.

He found Julia weeping on the bed and at first he feared the worst. The slave girl saw it in his face.

'No, master, not that. It is . . .' She shook her head,

almost overcome with emotion, but Valerius didn't have time to allow her tears. He took her by the shoulders and forced her to look into his eyes.

'Tell me, Julia. What has happened to Olivia?'

She sniffed and blinked her eyes clear. 'Your father . . . took her. He said she would die otherwise. I didn't know what to think. He said, "This way, we will both be saved and gain entry to the Kingdom of Heaven." What did he mean?'

Valerius felt his face harden. The old fool. But he had to be certain. 'Those were the exact words he used, Julia? *We will both be saved*? You are certain?'

She nodded. 'Certain, master.'

The exact words. The same expression Ruth had used to describe the rite of baptism. Lucius must have been driven mad by Olivia's plight if he believed that to dip her beneath a freezing waterfall would save her. Now he had even more reason to track down Honorius's water thief.

By the fifth hour he was back at the water castle with Honorius glowering like a man who had better things to do. Valerius had been tempted to go directly to the site of the former baths, but when he considered the matter further he couldn't see any reason why the water should not have been siphoned off *before* the Glabrian link ended, and several reasons why it should.

'The water flows down through that closed channel just below the parapet,' he told Marcus and Serpentius, whom he had asked to accompany him.

'You can see that it runs above ground for about two hundred paces down the hill before it disappears among the houses. I've had a look and there's no set pattern to its course. Sometimes it's buried beneath the street and runs under the buildings, sometimes it's a mini-aqueduct and passes over or even through them. It depends on the terrain. That's why we have to follow it. The only way we'll know if the water's still running is to check at one of the inspection hatches.' He showed them a key Honorius had given him to help lift the big capping stones. 'So we'll inspect at regular intervals when we get the opportunity. There has to be a fair chance that the channel has collapsed somewhere along the line, so it may be quite close. But if it isn't we'll follow it to the end.'

'What happens when we get there?' Serpentius asked. 'Maybe it's time to be Praetorians again?'

Valerius shook his head at the Spaniard's sudden enthusiasm for what he had once despised. 'We have no idea what we'll find. If it's what I think it is, it will be hidden in some kind of building, but probably not a public one. We may have to knock on doors or we may have to go through windows. You wouldn't want to do that in armour.'

Marcus grinned. 'I doubt he'd mind one way or the other. It's never stopped him before.'

'Honorius will have men here if, for any reason, we need the supply cut off. If we have time, we'll send someone back with word, but if not we use the old legionary signal system.' Valerius pulled a polished metal disc from the sleeve of his tunic and raised it in the air so that it caught the sun. 'Very simple. One flash for off, two flashes to restore the supply. The people here will give one flash to confirm. Understand?' They nodded. 'The tower is in direct line of sight from the south slope of the Viminal Hill, so that is where we'll make the signal. The two water men in the tower have been told to watch for it and they've rigged up a new mechanism to open and close the gate.'

With a bow to the commissioner they set off down the track that ran alongside the conduit. This was a mere side line of Old Anio, but it had been built to last, with arches of mortared stone ten feet tall carrying a single channel two and a half feet wide. It was also in remarkably good repair, with signs of recent masonry work that made Valerius ever more certain they were on the right track. They found it simple to follow the undeviating course down the slope of the hill, but then their problems started. Once among the houses the aqueduct maintained its line, but sometimes between the apartment blocks and sometimes directly through them, where the builders had made the water channel part of the structure itself. At last they came to a halt.

'It's gone,' the Spaniard said, looking at the building in front of them as if he expected the aqueduct to make a surprise appearance. 'It goes in the back, but it doesn't come out of the front. Maybe this is it?'

340

Valerius studied the *insula*. It was one of the smaller blocks in the area. 'I suppose it's possible, but it doesn't feel right.' He walked to the rear of the building, where the aqueduct undoubtedly entered at first floor level, and returned to the front where there was no sign it existed. They were about fifty paces from the Vicus Patricius and he followed what he thought was the channel's line out on to the street until he found what he was looking for. He took the key Honorius had given him and placed it in the hole in the stone block which covered the inspection shaft. It was heavy, but even one-handed he could lift it far enough to see the water flowing beneath.

For the next two hundred paces they moved from shaft to shaft, scrabbling on the ground among the stinking open sewers, random dog shit and rotting fruit for the next one, until, without warning, the Glabrian link took to the air again and marched in arched leaps to the lower slopes of the Viminal where it disappeared once more – directly into the hill.

'You think these people are moles?' Marcus asked.

Valerius didn't reply. He led them through the alleys at the base of the hill and round to where Honorius had told him the Thermae Glabrianae, once the pride of one of Rome's greatest families, had stood. They were on the far edge of the Subura now, on a slight rise where an infrequent, unlikely breeze ghosted its way among the houses to take the jagged edge off the intense heat. Here the apartment blocks were larger and an occasional sumptuous villa clung to the edge of the hill. Valerius turned to study them and his eye settled on one villa in particular.

'That's it,' he said. 'That's the one.'

'Watch out!' Marcus made the gladiator's secret sign that warned of danger to the rear. Valerius forced himself not to look round. 'The place is crawling with Praetorians and that bastard Rodan is nosing around looking for trouble.'

'Has he seen us?'

'I don't think so.'

'Then we go back the way we came. Be natural. Don't make a fuss.'

A few minutes later they sat together in the shadow of one of the aqueduct's arches on the opposite side of the hill. 'How were they waiting for us?' Serpentius demanded.

'They weren't waiting for us. They're looking for Petrus. Rodan knows what we know and he'll have every rathole in and out of this district sealed tighter than the stopper in a wineskin. We can't get in and the Christians can't get out. He'll scoop them up like fish in a net and then they'll go the same way as Sulla and Lucina.'

'Does it matter if Rodan gets to Petrus and a few of these Christians burn?' Marcus asked. 'The Emperor can't blame you just because the Blacks got there first.'

Valerius said bitterly, 'It matters to me.' He told them about his father and Olivia.

* * *

'Well, you were right,' Marcus said. 'We might get in but we'd never get back out with an old man and a sick woman. They have the house watched from every corner. Anyone who tries to leave will be picked up the minute they stick their nose out of the door.'

Valerius looked up the hill past where the channel disappeared into the rock. 'What if I could get in? Would it be possible to create enough of a diversion to allow me to get my father and Olivia away?'

'We could try,' the scarred gladiator said. 'But I don't see how you can get in unnoticed. The place is guarded as tight as a mouse's arsehole.'

'There must be another way.' Valerius began to climb the hill.

Minutes later they lay flat on the ground looking over the edge of the hill above the villa which had caught Valerius's attention. The Viminal was occupied mainly by a patchwork of apartments and small allotments, but here, where the hill was steepest and the soil thin and worthless, it had been left clear. The slope fell away sharply, almost a cliff, and the roof of the building was probably fifty feet below them.

'Well, that's that,' Marcus said. 'If you try to get down there, you'll be lucky if you only break your legs.'

Valerius had studied the face with equal care and he realized that Marcus was right. This was no conveniently fractured Dacian rock; it was weathered almost as smooth as glass. What was more, it was visible from the streets below where Rodan and his men waited. There had to be another route.

They searched the edge of the hill for an alternative and Valerius was beginning to despair when he noticed something unnatural in the dried yellow grass. It took a few moments before he recognized it. He was standing over yet another of the inspection shafts.

He walked back to the far side of the hill and did his best to work out the course of the aqueduct. When he was satisfied, he stood for a moment with his head bowed. He tried to visualize the interior of the channel below his feet. Could it be done? When he looked up, Marcus saw the same look in his friend's eyes as he had seen in gladiators making their final appearance in the arena: a confused mix of fear, resolve, certainty and confusion. Valerius handed Marcus the polished bronze disc and reached down to place the key in the capstone. 'Signal the water tower to cut the supply.'

The two gladiators looked at him in disbelief.

'You can't—'

'Just do it.' Valerius barely recognized his own voice. He knew that if he hesitated for even a second he would turn and walk away. With Rodan's Praetorians surrounding the villa there was only one way into the baptism chamber – through the subterranean passage ten feet below him. He was more frightened than he'd ever been in his life. More frightened even than in the final suffocating hours of the Temple of Claudius.

There, he had persuaded himself he was already dead. Here, he had to live. For Olivia and for Lucius.

Reluctantly, Marcus used the bronze mirror to send the single flash that warned the men in the water castle to stop the flow.

'Help me with this.' Serpentius hesitated and Valerius's fear made him snarl. 'Help me or by the gods I'll send you down there instead.'

The Spanish gladiator scurried to Valerius's side and together they heaved the stone aside. Serpentius took an involuntary step back as the shaft opened up at his feet.

Valerius stared into the dank black opening. The inspection holes they'd checked at ground level had been perhaps three feet deep, with the water clearly visible at the bottom. This disappeared into the darkness like a wormhole leading to the River Styx. It was two feet in diameter with rough steps cut into the rock to allow a man to descend safely.

'A lamp and a rope, at least,' Serpentius pleaded. 'I will fetch them quickly.'

'We don't have time. If the Christians finish their ceremony they'll walk out into a trap and my father and Olivia will be taken.'

Valerius stripped to his loincloth and handed his clothes to Marcus, but took the belt with his dagger and hung it from his neck. He sat on the lip and closed his eyes. His father had talked of faith in his God. Now Valerius called upon his own faith. Faith in himself. Faith in his courage. He was a Hero of

Rome, he wasn't frightened by a little dark passage. Messor had given him the idea. Messor, the skinny legionary his comrades had nicknamed Pipefish, who had shown more bravery than all the rest put together when he had slithered into the soot-blackened hell of the hypocaust below the Temple of Claudius. The attempt had been doomed, of course, and poor Pipefish had died nailed to the temple door as the flames of Boudicca's fire ate at his flesh. But he had got through the hypocaust and that was what gave Valerius hope.

Hope, but how much? Pipefish had been whip thin and greased with olive oil. Valerius was probably twice his breadth and his shoulders were heavily muscled from his daily training with sword and shield. How wide was the tunnel? How deep? He heard the water sound change below him from a violent rush to a musical gurgle. Soon. How wide? How deep? He wouldn't know until he got down there. At least if it was too narrow he would be able to turn back, with his honour and his conscience intact. His father and Olivia might die, but he would have done his best. He tried not to hear the voice in his head willing the shaft to be impassable.

The gurgling faded to a whisper. It was time. He turned and his foot searched for the first step.

'Wait!' It was Marcus. What now? 'The diversion. How will we know when you are ready to come out of the villa?'

Valerius cursed himself. Of course he should have

thought of that. One more mistake that could kill him. He cast his mind back to the front of the villa. It was a large building, surrounded by a walled garden, with a heavy door set back from the street. He remembered three windows at first floor level, all of them visible from the alleyway where he would have to make his escape.

'Give me my cloak and tunic.' Marcus handed over the clothes and Valerius bundled the heavy cloak into a ball with the tunic at its centre. 'I'll wave the cloak at the window above the doorway. Count to one hundred and then start the diversion. I don't care what you do, just get them away from the alley, but don't set the city on fire.'

Though the sun was high above them, he had never felt so cold; chilled to the very centre of his being. With a last glance towards his companions he climbed into the shaft.

XXXIV

The chamber stank of damp and the steps under his bare feet felt as slippery as if they were coated with ice. He had to grip tight with his single hand until his toes found and secured each foothold, whilst holding the bundled cloak in the crook of his right arm. At least he had the comfort of the circle of light above him and the anxious faces of Marcus and Serpentius that almost filled it. He reached the bottom of the channel, identified by thick, oily weed between his toes. The fear was more palpable now, as if someone was gripping his legs and pulling him downwards. He filled his head with Olivia's face and fought the feeling with all his strength. Carefully, he manoeuvred so that he was facing in the direction of the villa, before dropping to his knees. There was just enough space left to allow him to wriggle his legs backward into the opposite section of the tunnel. His nose was two inches from the brick face of the shaft and still he couldn't bring himself to break free from that life-giving circle of light. For a moment he felt a wave of claustrophobic terror and his bladder filled with ice water. Rope. Serpentius had been right, he should have waited. With rope he could have tied a line round himself and they would be able to pull him back if he became jammed. If he went without rope he might be trapped down here for ever. He could go back.

Coward. He heard the word Ruth had never spoken ringing in his head. He closed his eyes. 'I call on Messor and the spirits of Colonia to aid me.' The whispered words sounded hollow in his ears, but the very act of saying them had the effect of the herb-infused ale the Britons drank before a battle. He felt warmth again, and his courage returned. He lowered his head and inched his shoulders forward into the pitch black of the tunnel mouth.

It was tight. Very tight. He had to hunch his shoulders to avoid being wedged against the ragged masonry. But was it tight enough to give him a reason to turn back? He wriggled to make himself more comfortable. How far? Maybe seventy paces to the villa. And what then? But he knew there was no use thinking about what then, because that could drive a man mad. What then meant the channel narrowing to a tiny pipe, or diving deep underground where a man would die screaming with no hope of ever being heard. He felt for the hilt of the knife to make sure it was still attached. If . . . ? Don't think. Just go.

At first, he tried to use his hands to haul himself

along, but the walnut of his right could gain little purchase on the weed-covered stone and he made slow progress. Eventually he discovered that by pushing the bundle of his cloak forward, then digging his elbows into the walls and wriggling as if he were a snake, he was able to create a rhythm that gained him a few precious inches at a time. The tunnel roof was so low he felt it pressing down on his back and he suddenly realized that there truly was *no* going back. From nowhere the raw acid of panic filled his throat and poured like liquid fire into his chest. His head roared. He couldn't breathe. He couldn't move. His limbs thrashed helplessly in the confined space and he knew that if he didn't stop now he would truly go mad. Think. His mind screamed the word. *Think*. His brain frantically clawed for some memory that would save him. A face. No, faces meant people and people died. Faces meant Ruth and Maeve and Cornelius and Publius Sulla and the girl whose baby he had promised to save. Faces meant people he had failed. Suddenly he was in a battle line, his shield tight against the next man's, a sword firm in his hand. Death was all around him, but it meant nothing here, for this was the brotherhood of the warrior. The brotherhood of the shadow. And, in the shadow, he felt calm return. He was still trapped in a dark, airless tomb, but he was Valerius again, a Hero of Rome. He gritted his teeth, rammed his elbows into the walls and edged another six inches.

Time and space meant nothing in the dark. Even the

urgency to save his father and Olivia was diminished to a distant white spot at the entrance to a half-forgotten world, where light and air and life actually existed. All that mattered was effort and motion. Push the bundle, dig in the elbows, squirm, push. He was chilled to the bone, but the sweat coursed from his brow into his eyes. He imagined a galley slave hauling interminably at massive oars, the muscles of his arms fiery bars of glowing iron, knowing that his agony could only ever end in death. Push the bundle, dig in the elbows, squirm, push again. Something whirled and danced in the dust storm that was his brain and men came from the darkness to greet him. Legionaries who would tear a man's throat out with their teeth and then share a bloody wineskin with you. Men you could despise for their depravity and love for their loyalty. Lunaris, who had stood beside him to the very end at Colonia. Laughing Zama, who had taken a returned Roman *pilum* in the eye in Boudicca's last battle. Even Crespo, who had hated him more than any man before or since, yet had earned his respect for his fearless savagery in a fight. *Not so tough now, pretty boy.* Soldiers. And from each of them he took a soldier's strength and a soldier's ability to endure, an ability he had all but forgotten. Push, dig, squirm, push.

The air was thick now, almost solid in his throat, and he found it ever more difficult to breathe. He stopped for a moment to rest. He was glad, if gladness was an emotion permitted to a man buried alive, that he had declined Serpentius's offer of lamp and rope. The one would have killed him and the other made a coward of him. The flame of the lamp would have eaten the air; he had heard of it from slaves who had served in the deep mines. First the light dimmed, then vanished, then the men started to die. As he realized the significance of that thought a split second of panic returned like a lightning bolt through his brain. The air couldn't reach his mouth and nose from the shaft because his body was blocking the tunnel. But there should be air from ahead, because if there was not, it meant there was no way out. If he had had a rope around his waist at that moment, he would have tugged on it for dear life and screamed to be hauled back to the shaft. But he didn't have a rope. So he endured and pushed, dug and squirmed.

He tried to concentrate his waning mind on what he would do when he reached the outlet – kind Jupiter, let there be an outlet – but it was impossible to know what to expect. A simple drop from the level of the inlet channel? Something more elaborate and therefore more dangerous? What if there was a grille? They would be wondering by now what had happened to the water and he prayed that they wouldn't simply call off their meeting. No, they wouldn't do that. First they would investigate. Petrus would not gather his people at so great a risk only to abandon this most sacred of rites at the first sign of a problem. For the first time he realized there was a possibility they might kill him. He didn't think Petrus was that kind of man, but who knew about the others? Christus had led a band of rebels. There would still be men among his followers who had fought. Well, he would give them Rodan to fight; that was where the greater danger lay. That's what he would do, and while they were fighting the bastard he would escape with Lucius and Olivia. As long as there was an outlet.

Back on the surface Marcus and Serpentius had watched, horrified, as Valerius disappeared into the narrow shaft the way a man might make the first steps on his journey to Hades. Now they tried to work out what to do next.

'We can't just walk away and leave him in there. What if he's stuck?' Serpentius demanded.

Marcus studied the black hole in the earth. 'And what if he is? Are you going to go in after him? I'll face anything, man or beast, in the light of the sun, but I wouldn't go in there for all the gold in Mars Ultor.'

Serpentius had faced death many times in the arena and lived to spit in its face. He had known fear – although he would never admit it to anyone – but when he stared into the mouth of the shaft it was like looking into his own grave. 'We should never have let him go down.'

'How could we have stopped him? Did you see his eyes? Valerius is like a gladiator who has had one fight too many and goes out on to the sand seeking death. He would have gone down that shaft even if it was filled with fire.'

The Spaniard smiled sadly and shook his head. 'He isn't looking for death, old man, he's challenging it. Your friend Valerius will die some day, but he will die fighting for his last breath and screaming defiance in death's face.'

'It doesn't matter.' The veteran gave the inspection hole a final glance. 'He's beyond our help now. All we can do is come up with a diversion and pray that he lives long enough to need it.'

Serpentius nodded agreement. Thinking about the diversion would stop him thinking about the poor bastard stuck down in that black tomb. He pulled the dagger from his belt and held it up to check the edge. He didn't notice when it caught the sun.

A mile away, in the water tower on the Cespian Hill, a man noticed two flashes of light.

Valerius knew he must be close to the end of the channel. He didn't have any evidence for the assumption, only the knowledge that he was nearing the last of his strength and if he wasn't near the end he was going to die. No one who hadn't experienced it could comprehend the strength-sapping toll of being able only to move a few muscles at a time for what seemed like hours on end. In reality it could only have been minutes, but if his strength ran out now he knew he was finished.

He felt it before he heard it. A rumbling in his lower

belly and a compression in his ears that made him wonder if the tunnel was about to collapse. Then the noise, like muted thunder, and a pressure from behind like a gathering storm. Desperately he began to wriggle forward, real fear giving him new strength. He didn't know what was behind him, but he knew whatever it was meant danger and the only way to escape it was to go forward. The pressure built around his legs until it was something almost physical, and the thunder grew ever louder. A powerful wind whistled in the gaps left between his body and the tunnel walls. At last, he understood what was coming and the knowledge turned fear to outright, gut-wrenching terror. *This* was death. He scrabbled desperately at the tunnel walls, anything to advance him by a few more inches, but he knew it was pointless. There was no escape from the flood.

The shock as the freezing water smashed into his lower body paralysed him. In a heartbeat it was all around, surging in powerful jets past his shoulders and head with a force that would have knocked a cow off its feet. He screamed with the despair of defeat and closed his eyes and waited for the end. But although the water continued to pour past him above and below it didn't immediately cover him and he found he could continue to breathe. Slowly his mind informed him that his body blocked most of the pipe and was acting as a dam. The force was so great it even pushed him along a few inches. He began to haul his way forward, the water gushing past his face in frothing spurts, and he found he could move faster. All he had to do was stay alive and pray.

But disaster lay a few feet ahead.

When the water channel had been pushed into the hill more than two hundred years earlier, slaves had chipped their way through every foot of the unyielding rock from either side, and from the centre, where the inspection shaft had been sunk. The surveyors did their work so well that the diggers from each section met exactly where they had predicted – almost. When the tunnellers from the baths side met the tunnel from the centre, they found that they were slightly off line and compensated by making the final twenty feet slightly wider than had been specified. It was only a few inches, but when Valerius met the joining place he started to drown.

In a second the water was all around him. He became one with the flood and entirely at its command. His mouth and nose filled and he began to first choke, then suffocate. He held his breath until it felt as if his chest was about to explode before finally giving in to the inevitable. The darkness all around crept into his body and his bones, an inner darkness that he knew preceded death. Suddenly it didn't matter any more. He was free of responsibility, free of pain, free of life. The last time he had felt like this had been in the final moments of the temple. This time there would be no escape, and in a way he was glad.

He felt himself floating as the gods carried him off to whatever Otherworld the Fates had prepared for him. Then he wasn't floating, but falling, and a second later the euphoria was knocked out of him as he smashed into something solid and his eyes snapped open to see a bright light. He lay on his back spluttering as a cascade of water battered his chest. Gradually, he realized he was lying in some kind of pool.

He knew he should get up, but his head didn't seem to be connected to his body. And there was something else. Something he had to do. For a moment his mind continued to whirl, then everything came back in a burst of clarity. The cascade meant he was in the baptism chamber. He struggled to his knees and turned.

A ring of astonished faces stared back at him. He recognized a lawyer from the Basilica Julia and his plump little wife among the ten or so men, women and children his unorthodox arrival had scared into a frozen tableau of terrified eyes and gaping mouths. The room had been prepared for the ceremony, but they must still have been waiting for Petrus, the ultimate survivor. He saw with relief that there was no sign of his father or Olivia. An oil lamp flickered in one corner and the scent of some kind of burned spice hung heavy in the air. On a table in one corner a loaf of rough peasant bread lay beside a seven-branched candelabrum and an overturned flagon of wine which had stained the stone floor beneath blood red. The walls were windowless and bare, apart from a single device painted on the white plaster above the oil lamp. It was another of the pieces of symbolism the Christians were so fond of, a large X cut by a vertical stroke with a small half circle attached to the top:

☧

The symbol stirred a memory in him and he recalled seeing it once before. It was the same as the one that had been scratched on the chest where Petrus kept his healing powders. This must have been part of the old baths complex, possibly a holding tank before the water was distributed to the *caldarium* and *tepidarium*. When the villa had been built it had been kept as a storeroom. At some point the outlet had been stopped up, but the owner, no doubt one of Petrus's Christian converts, had re-opened it and somehow they had gained access to the water tower on the Cespian and restored the supply.

A moment of unnatural silence was followed by a clamour as they all started speaking at once. Valerius pushed himself to his feet and picked up the sodden bundle of his clothing, hauling the tunic over his head and wondering why he should be concerned about his nakedness when they were all likely to die in the next twenty minutes. Meanwhile, the flow from the inlet above him slowed to a trickle. Serpentius and Marcus must have heard the thunder of the water from the inspection shaft and signalled for it to be cut off again. By now they probably thought he was dead. But that wasn't important – all that mattered was to get these people out of here. 'Quiet.' He used the soldier's voice that had once cowed a legionary parade ground. 'You are all in danger, but I'm here to help you. I need everyone to stay calm.' The cries dropped to a subdued murmur. 'Whose house is this?'

A wiry, balding man raised a hand. At his side, a woman clutched a half-grown girl who stared at Valerius's wooden hand. His was another familiar face. Valerius searched his brain for a name. Probus? No, Pudens. That was it. Aulus Pudens, who had made a fortune supplying the arenas. A merchant notorious for cheating his suppliers and as unlikely a Christian as any man in Rome.

'I'm leaving you in charge. Which way to the house?'

Pudens hesitated. For a moment it looked as if he was about to protest, but his wife whispered something in his ear. He pointed to what looked like an alcove in the far wall and pushed his daughter forward. 'Praxedes will show you. Through there. It leads to a corridor.'

Valerius picked up his cloak and followed the girl. 'This way,' she said. She had long blonde hair and a sweet voice, made sweeter by the little whistle that punctuated her words through the gap in her front teeth. She explained what had happened. 'Someone said the soldiers were here. We were praying to our Lord Jesus for salvation when you popped out of the pipe like a giant water vole. Everyone screamed, even

Daddy. But I thought it was funny. Why is your hand made of wood?'

She led him to a door which took them through a storeroom into the villa. He left her playing with a doll and dashed upstairs where he could look across the square to where Marcus and Serpentius should be waiting for his signal. He dropped beside a window and opened the shutter just a crack.

And saw disaster.

Marcus had said the Praetorians had a guard on every corner. That had been an hour ago. Now the open area in front of the house was flooded with soldiers. A small army. It had never been a very good plan. Now it was exposed as a hopeless one. Rodan had the Christians in a sardine net. It was only a matter of time before he lost patience and sent his men to storm the villa.

Valerius slumped down by the window and closed his eyes. What had he got himself into? Think! There had to be a way out. He remembered the building as he had seen it from above. Could he climb the cliff? It was possible, but not with the fools he had left down in the baptism chamber. The idea burrowed into his brain like a tapeworm. Leave them then. What did they mean to him? He'd come for his father and Olivia. He wasn't responsible for a rabble of sheep who hadn't the wit to save themselves. Yes, he felt sorry for them, but that didn't make him their keeper.

He heard a shuffling noise and looked up to find Praxedes standing a few feet away holding the doll out so he could see it. 'This is my sister. Her name is Olivia.'

He shook his head at the madness of the world. When the gods called the tune there was really no option but to dance along. He reached out and took the little wooden figure with its black wool hair. 'Does your father have any rope?'

By the time he got back to the baptism room the men had recovered some of their nerve. Valerius studied the wall of belligerent faces. He knew he had to take control, but he waited long enough for Praxedes to whisper to her father. The bald man frowned, but with a puzzled glance at Valerius he followed the girl from the room.

When they were gone, the young Roman called for silence. There was no point in shirking the truth. 'This is an illegal gathering of a sect proscribed by the Emperor and if you do not do what I say you will all die.' He met each of their eyes in turn as he spoke. 'Have you any idea of the fate Nero has in store for you? There are a hundred Praetorian guards out there waiting. It would be better to throw yourselves on to their swords.'

'We are not frightened to die for our beliefs.' It was the lawyer. Of course it would be the lawyer.

'I watched Cornelius Sulla burn.' Valerius saw the man go pale. 'Are you prepared to watch your wives burn, or your daughters? No? Then follow my orders without question if you want them to live.'

361

All eyes turned to Aulus Pudens as he returned to the room carrying several coils of rope. Praxedes had shown Valerius the thousands of fathoms her father imported from Gaul for the Circus Maximus, where it was used to haul in the great sails deployed to keep the sun off the customers.

'I need as many sections of rope spliced together as it takes to make three hundred feet. Clear that table and bring it across here.' Valerius looked up at the black hole which had almost claimed his life. He'd discarded the idea of climbing the cliff and then using the rope to pull the others up, because the climb would have to be made in full view of the Praetorians, who would simply send a patrol to meet them at the top. That left only one option.

He pointed at the outlet. 'This is the way I came in and this is the way we will all leave.' He heard a man gasp and a woman's scream was stifled by her husband's hand across her mouth. 'All of us. I will lead, with the rope, and when I shout, each of you will follow me into the tunnel in turn, holding the rope. It is dark and it is frightening, but it is passable and you must call on your God to banish your fears.'

'No, I can't. I can't. I'll stick.' The whimper came from the lawyer's buxom wife. Valerius's decision had been made easier by the fact that, whether through abstinence or good fortune, most of the Christian adults seemed to be as thin as skinned rabbits. He went to stand beside the woman who, though a little plump, barely reached his shoulder. 'See how large I am compared to you, lady. If I can fit, you would go through twice.' He gave her a reassuring smile and patted her husband's shoulder. 'Help her. She will need your support. There is an exit midway through the hill. Just thirty paces away.' The distance was at least double that, but he told the lie boldly and nobody challenged it. 'Once I reach it, I will begin to pull you through. You will be able to push with your feet and your hands, and I will need all the help I can get, but do not lose your grip on the rope. With your God's help, you will only be in the tunnel for two or three minutes. Now.' This was the moment of truth, the moment that decided whether they lived or died. 'Who will be first behind me?'

No one would meet his eyes, and as the seconds passed he knew he'd failed.

'I will.' Praxedes broke the silence. 'As long as I can bring Olivia.'

Valerius could have kissed her. 'Thank you, lady. You are as brave as you are beautiful. We will wrap Olivia in your hand.' He looked towards her father. 'Tie a loop to her waist and set her in the tunnel after you have counted to fifty. When I've reached the exit shaft, I will pull her in a short way, so that you can follow.' He turned to the others. 'When Pudens shouts, I will haul them both along, so the next person can follow, then the next. The slippery weed in the tunnel will help me, but you must also use your strength.' He saw eyes drifting to the damp shaft, and sensed the reluctance growing. 'If you stay here you will certainly die. If you have courage – and faith – you will live.'

'Wait!' Valerius's heart sank at the call from Praxedes' father, but Pudens only raised his arms and called on their God to protect them. When he had finished they all looked towards the young man with the wooden hand. 'We are ready.'

Valerius went to where the table had been placed below the outlet. He stripped off his tunic and tied the rope around his midriff. Just for a second a voice screamed in his head not to go, but with a grunt he hauled himself into the stinking blackness. It was only when he was inside, with the damp stone pressing in around him like the walls of a tomb, that he wondered why none of them had asked what would happen if the flow resumed. He supposed it was because the answer was obvious.

This time he had the benefit of familiarity and he made good progress once he got back into the rhythm that had carried him to the chamber. He had one moment of minor panic when the walls closed in where the tunnel narrowed, but it passed quickly. True, every time he pushed himself along another few inches he thought he could hear the distant thunder of water coming to swamp him, but the rope barely hindered him and in a few minutes he saw the light of the exit shaft ahead. He felt a tug on the rope and realized Praxedes was telling him to pull her along. He hauled six feet of line into a coil and moved on, stopping to repeat the manoeuvre when he heard the shout from her father. The rest would have to wait until he reached the shaft. He only hoped he had the strength to pull them all. With a few feet to go, he froze at the sound of voices. Had Rodan sent a patrol to the hill after all? If he carried on they would arrest him. Worse, they might replace the stone cap and trap him in here with the others.

'Keep that bloody knife in your belt.' He recognized the gruff, welcome tones of Marcus and he could have wept.

'What difference does it make? He's drowned anyway, or he would have signalled,' Serpentius replied. 'We didn't stop the water quickly enough. Nobody could survive for that long.'

'You'll be dead if you don't help me out of here, you idle Spanish bastard,' Valerius shouted, his words magnified and made ghostly by the shaft.

The call was followed by the long silence of two men pondering a voice from the Otherworld.

'Hello?' Valerius had never heard Serpentius sound frightened. He clambered up, blinking, into the sunlight. Marcus stood back from the shaft eyeing him warily. Serpentius was a yard further away and looked ready to run for his life.

'Are you going to help me,' Valerius said, 'or must I wait until Rodan does?'

With a shout, the two men ran forward and pulled him out to lie gasping by the shaft entrance.

'We thought . . .'

He waved them away, untying the rope from his

waist. 'We've no time for happy reunions. Haul on this line, but gently now, and I promise you a catch the like of which you've never seen before.'

They stared at him and he knew how mad he appeared, but he didn't care.

'Pull,' he said. 'We have souls to save.'

Praxedes was first, her golden head appearing in the bottom of the shaft. Valerius descended a few steps to help her, but she refused to come out until he had rescued Olivia first. She was followed by her father and mother, and then, one after the other, the Christians emerged filthy and bewildered to fall on their knees and give thanks to their God. The lawyer's wife was second to last, her eyes tight shut, and finally her husband's face appeared.

Some thanked him, most just gave him wary glances before they set off towards their homes. Pudens was last to go. 'I have nothing now,' he said, running his hand through his daughter's hair. 'Except my life and my family. For them I thank you.' Valerius asked him if he had somewhere to stay and he said he did. Praxedes gave him a gap-toothed smile and the little family walked down the hill hand in hand.

'May your God protect you,' Valerius whispered. He turned to find Marcus and Serpentius looking at him as if he had just come back from the dead, which, in a way, he had.

'What now?' Marcus asked respectfully.

'First Serpentius can steal me some clothes, then we go back to work.'

An hour later they set off back towards the Forum. Valerius noticed a crowd lined up outside one of the government buildings behind the Senate House. 'What's going on?'

Marcus spoke to a vendor at a nearby fruit stall and returned with the information. 'It's some kind of census. Posters have gone up all over the city ordering the Judaeans and a few of the other provincial groups to register with the state or they'll lose their rights to stay in Rome.'

Valerius closed his eyes. Time was running through his fingers. How long had it been? Six days and he was still no closer to the Rock than he had been on that first morning. He looked at the long line of men, women and children. If he didn't succeed these people would all die. He had asked Pudens for information about Petrus, but the villa owner had sworn on his family's life that he didn't know where he could be found. Others organized the baptism ritual. Petrus came and carried out the ceremony, then he left. Today the location of the ritual had been betrayed. But by whom?

'Are you feeling all right?' Marcus looked at him as if he'd grown an extra eye.

Valerius shook his head wearily. How could he have taken so long to make the connection? 'Today I've been buried alive and almost drowned, but I've just realized that the worst is still to come.'

XXXV

The room looked and felt different. How could that be in so short a time? Murals he had always regarded as artistic and exotic now appeared merely vulgar and lewd. In the harsh light of day the wall hangings and the furniture seemed tired and worn. The scents which had once made his senses reel were no longer sweet, but cloying, and only just masked the unmistakable musky odour of the aroused men who queued here to couple with her. Fabia looked different too. She had lost the last bloom of youth in a few short weeks. The powder on her face was no longer to enhance her beauty, but to camouflage the lines in the corners of her eyes. Flesh that had been taut and firm had taken on the pasty texture that came with separation from the fine bone structure beneath. A new face. A middle-aged face. She sat on a couch opposite him, straight-backed and refusing to meet his gaze. 'You had no right to come here without an appointment.'

Her voice sounded like ice cracking in a frozen stream.

'You have never complained before.'

'You have never come here coated in filth and stinking like a sewer cleaner. You have never forced your way past my doorkeeper while I was entertaining a friend. Now I will have to have him whipped for failing in his duty.'

Valerius laughed, remembering the scene; the outraged underling and the semi-tumescent senator making his escape still dressed in the distinctive robes of a Vestal virgin. 'Your doorkeeper or the friend?'

She hissed like a snake. It was clear that everything they'd had was gone, but now he asked himself if it had only ever existed in his imagination.

'You called me here last night for a reason.'

She darted a glance in his direction, but looked away before he had the chance to read its meaning. 'To enjoy your company and exchange gossip. You were once an entertaining companion, although it is difficult to believe now.'

'I remember the verbal exchange as very one-sided.' Now his voice was as cold as hers. He should have felt hatred, or perhaps pity, but instead an empty space lay where his heart had been. 'You were keen to hear the latest news of my quest for Petrus, and interested in each and every detail about the theft from the water castle.'

'We were friends then. Friends are interested in each other's lives.'

'What we talked about was known only to Honorius

369

the water commissioner and two men I trust with my life.'

'Hired thugs, you mean.'

'Perhaps, but men I can trust – as I once trusted you.'

He saw her face go pink beneath the powder. But was it anger or fear? Then she smiled at him and he was almost disarmed as the beauty shone from her like the sun breaking from behind a cloud.

'Oh, Valerius, is that what this is about?' she said lightly. 'You would take a mercenary's word against mine? Who is to say that old Honorius, a man who has never been known to speak one word when ten will do, did not blurt out your plans as he devoured one of his legendary midday meals? Surely that is not enough to break up our friendship.'

Valerius rose from his couch. 'I suppose it is possible that Honorius might have talked to someone, but how did the Praetorians react so quickly? They were exactly where I thought I would find Petrus an hour before we were.' He was behind her now, caressing her neck as he had once done to give her pleasure.

'But of course they would be. Torquatus does not want you to get the credit for hunting down the Christian.'

'Yes,' he said, and she knew a thrill of fear as his voice hardened again and his left hand twisted in her hair and yanked her head round to face him. 'But that doesn't explain why Torquatus has been one step ahead of us ever since Nero gave me this task. It doesn't explain why Cornelius Sulla and Lucina were arrested when the only people who knew what was said were Gaius Valerius Verrens and the lady Fabia Faustina. That's right, Fabia. I didn't even tell Marcus and Serpentius what passed between Cornelius and me. Only you. You betrayed them.' His grip grew tighter and she cried out with pain. 'You condemned them to the stake and the cage. You condemned Ruth to death too, because Lucina told Torquatus where the next meeting was to be held.' She struggled, but he kept his grip. 'And you betrayed Olivia and my father, and for that I can never forgive you.'

'*I saved your father!*' Fabia's shout echoed from the walls. Valerius hesitated, reluctant to believe her, but he knew the truth when he heard it. He relaxed his grip and she collapsed sobbing on the stone floor.

'You saved him?'

She raised her head and her eyes were filled with an explosive mixture of pain and shame and righteous fury. 'Yes, I saved him. Saved him from Nero. Saved him from Torquatus. The doddering old fool would have been dead a month ago if I had told Torquatus everything I knew. I saved him today when I sent a slave to warn him not to go to the Christian ritual.'

'But . . .'

She fought to regain her composure. 'It's true that I told Torquatus about Cornelius and Lucina, just as I have told him most of what you tell me.'

Valerius shook his head. He'd known it since the moment he'd seen Rodan waiting for them, and perhaps for much longer, but part of him still didn't believe it.

'Why? Why would you betray me? We were . . .'

'Friends? I thought that once, Valerius, but would a friend have accepted my love without any intention of returning it? While I lay there thinking of you as my lover, you never thought of yourself as anything more than my client. A caring, affectionate client, perhaps, but a client all the same. Think. Does that make you better or worse than a degenerate like Posthumus in his pretty dress? He pays me and takes what he has paid for. You pretended you were my friend and used me just the same. Which of you made me more ashamed of what I am?'

'I'm sorry,' he said, and he truly was, but there were things he had to know. 'That still did not give you reason to betray me.'

'No. It did not. I have known shame since the day Seneca destroyed my father and forced him to send me to that place, but I buried my shame deep and I disguised it with a smile. I had manners and beauty and I learned quickly and that saved me from the worst of it: the low-born and the dangerous with their stinking breath and their dirty crawling hands and hungry mouths. They kept me for people like you – arrogant, perfumed patricians with power and money. I learned about power and I learned how to part you from your money and in time I was able to buy myself out and set up here. But the shame remained, Valerius. I knew I had lost my honour and that I would never marry, and I gave up hope . . . until I met you. When you came to me I understood that here was someone as broken as I. Britain had come close to destroying you, just as what I am had come close to destroying me. Your missing hand was as much a burden as my lost virtue. So I allowed myself hope, until I realized that hope was in vain.'

'I didn't know about Seneca. If I had it might have been different.'

Her face transformed into a bitter smile. 'No, Valerius, because you think of Seneca as your friend and Gaius Valerius Verrens stands by his friends. If you learn only one lesson from today, let it be never to trust your friends.'

'But Seneca didn't betray me, you did, and Seneca is not my enemy. So who is?'

She shook her head again. 'Still so loyal, Valerius. Who has most to gain if your father dies, and his son is implicated in his plotting? Ask Seneca about the marble. Ask him about the geological survey he has just had carried out on his estate. The estate which borders your father's.'

Valerius remembered the day Honorius had congratulated him on Lucius's good fortune and another building block fell into place.

Fabia nodded. 'Now you understand. But you are right, Seneca is not the man you must fear most. That man is Torquatus.'

The name was hardly a surprise, but it still didn't explain the lengths to which the Praetorian prefect had gone to sabotage a mission for which he was partially responsible. 'I can understand why Torquatus dislikes me, even hates me, but not why he would want to destroy me. I am no threat to him and never could be. Why would he want me to fail when he was instrumental in giving me the mission to hunt down Petrus and the Christians in the first place?'

'Because if you fail, Torquatus succeeds. He can't allow you to find this Petrus when he could not. That is why he has had Rodan dog your footsteps ready to pounce on Petrus. With the Christian in his grasp he would denounce you as a traitor who knew all along that your father was one of the people you sought. If your enemies have their way, you and Lucius will die on neighbouring pyres, Valerius, and the Emperor's greatest amusement will be in deciding who burns first.'

'That still does not explain why Torquatus should be so determined to have me killed, or what I have done to earn so much hatred.'

She laughed, short and sour. 'You mean apart from being you, so handsome and so strong and always so certain? He mentioned it once, quite casually, as if he was discussing a horse that needed disciplining. A family matter, he said, some cousin who had served with you in Britain. The man was a centurion in the Twentieth legion who sent Torquatus a letter claiming you had destroyed his career and demanding help to gain reinstatement. He died in the British rebellion, but our Praetorian prefect was left to salvage the family's honour. Such a trivial reason to die, don't you think?'

Valerius stared at her. It didn't seem possible. Crespo? Rapist, bully, murderer and thief, the man had been a senior centurion in Valerius's cohort. It had been Valerius's accusation which had forced Crespo into the service of Catus Decianus, Britain's procurator, who had made the decision to strip Boudicca of her lands and her people. Crespo had vowed revenge for that humiliation. Before he could fulfil his promise, the centurion, whose rape of Boudicca's daughters helped ignite the rebellion, had met a terrible end at the hands of the Iceni queen. Now Crespo had reached from beyond the grave to destroy Valerius. He could almost hear the gods laughing.

He shook his head. 'You could have come to me instead of betraying me.'

Some of the old spark returned and her eyes flashed. 'You can be such a fool sometimes, Valerius. If I had come to you, we would both be dead. While you are close to finding Petrus, Torquatus has to keep you alive so that he can take the credit. He tried to have you killed in Dacia because he already had Lucina and thought he no longer needed you. You must believe me, I have always tried to protect my friends, whatever Torquatus has asked of me and however he has asked it.' Her voice was close to breaking and Valerius realized how much anguish lay behind those words. A man like Torquatus had many ways of inflicting pain so that the wounds did not show.

She recognized the look on his face. 'Yes, pity me, Valerius, for there is no escape for me in this life. If you can find Petrus and present him to Nero you can still thwart Torquatus, but the only escape for Fabia Faustina is death.'

'No,' he said. 'Come with me and we will fight him together.'

'You mean die together? If I leave Rome without Torquatus's permission he will know that I have betrayed him; perhaps he knows it even now. If I stay it will give you the time to do what you must do.'

He hesitated, but he knew she was right. The only chance he had to find Petrus was to leave her. Another friend failed. He got up to go, all his anger forgotten.

'Wait, Valerius. There is more you need to know.'

She told him about Poppaea.

'In many ways she is very like me, trapped in a loveless world and forced to sell herself to stay alive. Perhaps that is why we became friends. You think you know Nero, but you do not. His subjects see a charming young man who wants to be loved for his talents. Yes, he can be irrational and even vicious if the mood takes him, but men look at his line, shake their heads and ask: how could it not be? But in the night, in the privacy of his palace, he is different, more beast than man, and willing to couple with either if Torquatus is able to provide it. Poppaea is not a wife to him; no woman could be. She is flesh, as we all are, and she survives by being willing flesh, but not too willing, for she must be seductive as well as available. Compliant, but a challenge for his talents in the bedchamber. And, of course, she must entertain, as we all must entertain who enter beyond the doors of his personal quarters. What sordid piece of theatre will Torquatus provide tonight? Will it please him? Will we be able to suffer it with a smile? Will we survive it?'

Fabia stared into the distance and Valerius knew that she was only telling him part of what went on in the palace. She wore the same look as a soldier who has stared death in the face, lost in the Otherworld that is at the centre of every human soul.

'Poor Poppaea, she confides in me, all unaware that I am part of the trap Torquatus has set for her. He knows that she hates him more than she hates Nero, and he fears her, because her access to Nero makes her powerful. To Torquatus that combination is a threat which cannot be ignored. He too is like a beast, and will lash out at anything which endangers him.'

'She confides in you and yet she has come to no harm?'

Her voice took on the fierceness of a mother leopard protecting her cubs. 'Believe me, Valerius, Fabia Faustina values her friends. Torquatus may have me by the throat, but there are things that I tell him and things that I do not.'

'Then with your protection she will survive. She does not need me.' He said it with finality and she shook her head at his failure to grasp what she was saying.

'You don't understand. Only by saving Poppaea can you save your father and Olivia, and only by saving Poppaea will you find Petrus.'

'How can that be?'

'It is very simple. Poppaea Augusta Sabina has become a Christian.'

The room seemed to suddenly go cold.

'Nero knows?'

She shook her head. 'Nero suspects.'

'Then Torquatus knows.'

'Torquatus believes he knows, but he has no evidence yet, and without evidence he cannot denounce Poppaea. If he does and Nero does not believe him, his own life will be forfeit.'

'How . . . ?'

'Cornelius Sulla first intrigued her, then seduced her. He opened her eyes to a world beyond the pain of this world. Somehow he arranged that she meet Petrus and from that day onwards she was a different Poppaea; a Poppaea prepared to challenge Nero's tyranny, to fight him from within his own palace.'

Still Valerius was not entirely convinced. 'You protect her, but you gave Cornelius to Torquatus? He could have exposed her with a single word.'

'If you had known Cornelius, you would know that he would never betray her. He sacrificed his brother to blind Torquatus to Poppaea, then went through the torments of hell to ensure she stayed hidden. That was the kind of man he was; if he gave his life for Poppaea he gave it gladly.'

Valerius remembered the burning red eyes in the blackened skull and wondered at the strength of will it had taken to stay silent. Nero was right not to underestimate the Christians. An enemy *without* fear is an enemy *to* fear.

'And you, Fabia?'

'Am I a Christian?' She laughed. 'Surely, Valerius, you understand by now that I am beyond saving. I have sent too many to their deaths for an unguarded word to believe I have any value. Yet I hope I still have some honour in your eyes. Each time I provided Torquatus with an opportunity to bring you down, I provided you with one to thwart him.'

He studied her, wondering if that was true and knowing that, in the end, it didn't really matter. He had to trust her.

'How do I find Petrus?'

'By finding Poppaea.'

'And where is Poppaea?'

'She sailed for Neapolis this morning. She will visit her people at the family villa while Nero makes his preparations for his great performance at the theatre in the city.'

He shook his head. 'You are talking in riddles. What does a trip to Neapolis have to do with Petrus?'

'You have spent days looking for a waterfall, Valerius, is that not true? Then perhaps it will not surprise you that the villa at Oplontis has the finest ornamental waterfall in the Empire.' She laughed at the sudden flare of comprehension. 'Poppaea has yet to be saved. To be saved, she must be baptized by Petrus, who has persuaded her that everyone who was to take part in today's ceremony should be sanctified along with her, including your father.'

'It's madness!'

'Yes, Valerius, but there is a joy in such madness, is there not? They are prepared to risk everything for what they believe. Do you believe in anything that much?'

He shook his head. Once, he had believed in the Empire and would have been happy to die for it, but not now. 'Only my family.'

'Then go to Neapolis and reach them before Torquatus. Perhaps by saving them you will save yourself.'

'Torquatus?'

'Do you think I am his only spy?'

XXXVI

'Pay off Sextus and Felix and thank them for their services, then take the seal and find a boat that will carry us to Neapolis.'

'What about you?' Marcus demanded.

'I'll join you at Ostia. I have some business to deal with before we leave.'

He rode north, taking the Via Salaria towards the estate at Fidenae, but on this occasion he rode past the gate and into the hills behind the neighbouring villa.

Seneca lay on a couch in the atrium, relaxed after his afternoon bath and close to falling into the shallow, mesmeric sleep he found conducive to deep and stimulating thought. This was his favourite time of day and the servants had orders not to disturb their master on pain of dismissal. When the arm closed like a band of iron round his throat he had just begun to reflect on the most interesting contradiction between friendship and trust, which in itself raised an interesting philosophical debate. In other circumstances he would have liked to continue the internal discussion, but the chill of a dagger against the voluminous folds of skin at his neck quite drove it from his mind. He had only a basic knowledge of anatomy, but enough to know that the point was less than an inch from the big vein pulsing in his throat. One thrust would bleed him dry in less time than it takes a person to swallow a cup of wine. He didn't understand why the analogy came to mind, but it was oddly comforting to know that a man could still think logically at the moment of his death.

'Give me one reason why I shouldn't kill you.' The harsh nasal voice cut through his musings. When he tried to reply all that emerged was a bullfrog's croak. The arm loosened, but only a fraction.

'Allow me enough time, friend,' he spluttered, 'and I will give you a thousand reasons why you should not kill me. I am Lucius Annaeus Seneca and therefore the act of dying and what lies beyond hold a certain fascination, but I have voluminous works to complete before I am ready to explore that particular avenue.'

'Whether you live or die is beyond your control, old man.' The arm tightened again and Seneca was embarrassed to hear himself give a little squawk of fear. He had often pondered the inevitability of death and he'd concluded that clinging to life must be mere folly when it only postponed the inescapable, but now, when death appeared on his own doorstep, he was unable to take his own advice. It seemed that no matter how brave the outer man, an inner man existed with a more fully formed sense of his own mortality.

'Whoever is paying you to kill me, I will triple the offer,' he choked.

'What makes you think I wouldn't gladly do it for nothing?'

Seneca sighed inwardly. It had been worth the attempt. But that voice? Despite the gruff disguise he believed he recognized the tone and inflection. With the little thrill of fear which accompanied the knowledge came also a tiny chink of hope. How fortunate to have a murderer who might be open to logical argument.

'Valerius? You would not harm an old man who taught you all you know. It would be a pity to extinguish so much learning, would it not?'

'But not to extinguish so much corruption. I could have forgiven you your avarice and your duplicity but not the way you used my father.' The tone offered no reprieve, but the words hinted at a possible avenue of escape.

'Your father is a very foolish man, Valerius.' Seneca risked the criticism knowing that it was only the truth.

'Foolish,' Valerius agreed. 'And vulnerable. He should have been able to rely on the support of his friends and family, but both failed him.'

'And for that I am sorry.'

'But his family did not betray him. Only his friends did that.'

The words were accompanied by a slight tightening of the arm muscle and a liquid squirt of fear shot through Seneca's bowels. Now he knew how the hangman's rope would feel. 'I would know nothing of that,' he blustered.

'No? But I would.' Seneca began to mumble a denial, but another increase of muscular pressure silenced it. He was close to choking. A hair's breadth from a crushed windpipe. Valerius continued: 'I know how my father was led towards a new and dangerous enthusiasm the way a blindfolded bull is led to the sacrifice. And I know that the Judaean girl Ruth was inserted into his household to ensure his conversion. I also know who was responsible for these things.'

'I—' This time Valerius used the knife to stifle the words. He knew Seneca too well to get into a semantic argument with him. If any man could talk his way from beneath the executioner's axe it was Nero's former mentor.

'What I couldn't understand at first was why. Was it possible my father's neighbour and friend was acting in his best interests? An argument could, after all, be made that a certain comfort was to be derived from the teachings of the man Christus, particularly for a lonely old widower who had lost his way. The girl Ruth's involvement was entirely innocent, driven by her faith and an inborn goodness.' Valerius's muscles tightened involuntarily when he mentioned Ruth and it was only when Seneca squirmed that he realized he was killing the philosopher. He forced himself to relax his grip. 'That innocence led to her death, but that would mean nothing to you. She was just another piece to be used then discarded in this greedy game you were playing.'

'Please . . .'

'Shh. There is more. Surely you are interested. It is a fine story, of a man who became too clever for his own good. My father was not the only fool. When you summoned me, I came, and when you charmed me I was convinced I was working for the interests of Rome, and not those of Lucius Annaeus Seneca. It was only after I walked in on your visit to my father that I began to realize the scale and subtlety of the web you had snared us in. Better to have kept Saul hidden: there is too much of Petrus in him and he shows too great a knowledge of the Christians not to be one himself. He is Petrus's rival for the Christian leadership, is he not?' He released his hold long enough for Seneca to nod. 'So, a perfect alliance. Seneca uses Saul's information to persuade his old pupil Valerius to bring him Petrus and thereby save his career, and his life. In the same instant Saul becomes the undisputed head of the Christians, a man more ably equipped to spread the word of Christus than a simple fisherman. The only flaw was Petrus, who was too clever for us all.'

He paused just long enough for Seneca to be certain that his time was up. Once Valerius had felt something like love for this man, but there could be no pity for an old fraud who would sacrifice every friend he had to recover his position.

'Even then, I might have forgiven. But that was not enough for you. You had to have more. Where is it?'

He felt Seneca freeze. 'I don't understand.' The hint of pleading in the philosopher's voice told Valerius that he understood very well. Seneca gave a little squeal as the knife point drew blood.

'How you must have rejoiced when the surveyor handed over the report about the marble deposits on the border of your estate. You would keep it close. You never were trusting, Seneca, and I doubt you have started to be now. Tell me where it is or I really will have to kill you and find it myself.'

A shaking arm pointed in the direction of a nearby cabinet. Valerius drew the other man to his feet, never relaxing his grip. Together they walked until Seneca was close enough to reach the polished wood. The cabinet had two doors, but Seneca ignored them. Instead, he reached below the top on the left-hand side and worked his fingers until Valerius heard a distinct click and some internal mechanism sprung the lid back to reveal a pair of scrolls.

'Pick them up.' The philosopher did as he was told and they worked their way together back to the couch. 'Unroll them.'

With his left hand Valerius took the papers. The first was the surveyor's report on the hills to the south. Valerius gave a low whistle as he read the sums involved. 'Congratulations, master Seneca. It appears you have substantial deposits of marble beneath your property, with a conservative value of tens of millions of sestertii and a possible value of hundreds of millions. But what is this? By some misfortune the bulk of the deposits, enough to make a man as rich as Crassus and Pompey combined, lie beneath your neighbour's land. Oh, what a temptation that must have been for a man who has never known the meaning of the word enough. That was when you saw the opportunity to ensnare your friend Lucius, and, when his trusting son naively followed him into the net, you had exactly what you wanted. As soon as Petrus was taken, the father and the son were to be denounced, the one as a Christian, the other for failing to report him.' He dropped the survey and picked up the second document. 'How fortunate, then, that trusting old Lucius has already mortgaged the estate to his old friend Seneca. See, he has even signed it, although the signature is a little blurred and shaky, but then he is an old man.' He threw the second scroll beside the first. 'You even made common cause with your worst enemy to ensure Nero did not snatch it away from you. Does Torquatus know how much it is worth? Of course he doesn't. If he did both estates would be confiscated by the state and Torquatus would already be sleeping in your bed. But did you really think you could trust him?' Let Seneca think the Praetorian prefect had betrayed him. The truth was that Torquatus liked to boast, even to a woman he believed he owned body and soul.

Seneca was too astute to deny the fraud. He knew the two papers screamed his guilt as clearly as a written confession. All that remained was the court's sentence. 'It would be a pleasure to kill you, old man. A little more pressure and you will lose consciousness; then it would be a simple act to drag your carcass through to the bath and slit your wrists and allow the Fates to choose whether you drown or bleed to death.'

The philosopher bridled. 'If I am going to die,' he spluttered, 'then at least do me the courtesy of making it look like murder. Thrust deep and let no man believe Lucius Annaeus Seneca took his own life in despair.'

'I have a friend who would beg me to take that advice, but I have another use for you.' He loosened his grip and Seneca collapsed forward, coughing. Valerius showed him the dagger to let him know the respite was purely temporary and produced another pair of scrolls from inside his tunic. He picked up a block of wax from a table at Seneca's right hand and allowed it to melt over an oil lamp so it would drip on the top scroll. 'Your seal. Quickly now.'

Seneca frowned, but complied. He tried to read what was written on the parchment, but Valerius whipped it away before repeating the process with the second.

'Two scrolls,' he explained. 'Both witnessed by you and two others, both recounting the tale of your deceit, including the parts played by Saul of Tarsus and Torquatus, commander of the Praetorian Guard. Enough to have all three of you executed. If anything happens to me or my father one scroll will go directly to the Emperor, the other to the Senate.'

Seneca flinched, but a surge of relief made him feel quite giddy. He was going to live.

Valerius picked up the geologist's report and the forged transfer paper and held them over the candle, only dropping them when the flames reached his fingers.

The philosopher watched with a puzzled frown. 'What will you do now, Valerius? You are a rich man, or at least a rich man's son. The money that lies beneath that hill would guarantee you a place in the Senate. With your intelligence, money and the right friends who knows what you could achieve? A consulship, given time, certainly.'

Valerius marvelled at the conceit of the man. 'I will do what Nero has commanded me to do. I will find Petrus and I will deliver him to the Emperor.' He saw the disbelief in Seneca's eyes. 'Not for you, or for him, but for the twenty thousand innocents who will die if I do not deliver him. Do you think he would count it a good bargain, your Christian? His life for twenty thousand others. Would that not place him even above his master, the Messiah?'

'Yes, he would count it a bargain.' The deep voice came from behind them. How long had Saul been listening? Had he been prepared to watch Seneca die without calling for help? Valerius decided he had never met anyone quite so ruthless.

The Cilician continued: 'Of course Petrus would welcome the opportunity to give his life for others. My brother in Christus has so much to atone for, after all. But Jesus died for all men, my young friend, not for a mere twenty thousand. If you can find him, Petrus will be a willing sacrifice. But first you must find him.'

XXXVII

The earth was angry today, snorting steam like breath from a hard-ridden horse.

Quintus Corbo often rode out to the little height two miles from Neapolis to gaze across the garlanded crescent of the Campi Flegrei. Perhaps great Homer had stood here looking out to Puteoli and beyond, over the glittering expanse of emerald and blue waters to the pretty little harbour town of Baiae and the naval base at Misenum. Certainly the poet had known of the Phlegraean Fields, because he had written of them in his *Odyssey*, where they had provided the inspiration for the forbidding lair of Polyphemos the Cyclops. More recently Puteoli had known fame as the harbour from which the Emperor Gaius Caligula had built his three-mile bridge of ships in a show of manic extravagance that had done as much as anything to bring him to his just and painful end.

Emperors and their peculiarities were on Corbo's

mind today, but that was not what brought him here. He regarded himself, perhaps unjustly, as little more than an enthusiastic amateur in the science of natural phenomena, but the gods had placed him in the best position in the entire Empire to witness it, here in the gigantic boiling pot of the ash fields. Epicurus of Samos had first expounded the theory that the explosive underground activity in and around the Mare Nostrum was a direct effect of air penetrating deep into the earth and taking on a new and ferocious energy which made it more dangerous than any other element. The only reason the entire world did not explode was because of the phenomenon he was witnessing at this very moment. When a certain amount of violently disturbed air had amassed in cavities below the surface, the earth allowed it to escape through fissures and boreholes, thus relieving the pressure. He had walked in the foul-scented hills behind Baiae and seen the hundreds of hot springs and sulphur pools where the escaping gases created great jets of super-heated steam that dotted the landscape, which the uneducated sometimes mistook for giants. Normally this manifested itself in a low fog, but today it appeared the entire peninsula was on fire.

A slight shudder made his horse skip beneath him. That was another sign that the trapped air was attempting to find a way out, but it was such a common occurrence that he barely noticed. The tremors had become more frequent in the past few days, but even Corbo's scientific mind had failed to register the fact.

That might have been because of his other concerns. Everything had to be perfect for the performance the following night. Corbo had recently been appointed one of four aediles in Neapolis and good fortune had given him responsibility for presiding over public entertainments rather than, the gods forbid, the workings of the sewers. The city boasted one of the finest theatres in the Empire and he took great pride in the events he sponsored there. Neapolitan audiences were notoriously difficult to please and regarded themselves as the most cultured of the Empire's citizens.

And the Emperor undoubtedly agreed. Because tomorrow night he would be performing in front of them. If anything went wrong, Corbo knew it would be the death of him.

He frowned and scoured his mind. They had been preparing for months, but was there anything else he could do? The theatre manager was an arrogant pedant, but he knew his job and was as aware as Corbo of the price of unforeseen disaster. He had made certain that every seat would be filled, and filled with men and women who had reason to love their Emperor. To doubly ensure the reception was nothing less than rapturous Corbo had recruited a thousand young men of artistic disposition who had been tutored in the various proper forms of applause; *bombi*, imitating the drone of bees; *imbrices*, the beating of a hollow vessel with a thin stick; and *testoe*, which was similar to *imbrices*, but with a more bass sound. These he would strategically position in groups of fifty around the theatre to sing the Emperor's praises at the appropriate moment. Members of the city guard would be on each of the gates to bar known malcontents. The programme itself was a carefully guarded secret, with each performer sworn to silence. They had been chosen for their aptitude rather than their brilliance. There could be only one star in this firmament.

He sighed and turned his horse back towards the city. No, there was nothing he could do but say a prayer and sacrifice a lamb to the goddess. If Minerva could not help him, no one could. The scent of juniper drifted to him on a light breeze from the great conical mountain on whose lower slopes he rode. He smiled. It was a comfort to live in the shadow of such a beautiful, benign and fertile giant.

Lucius dabbed at his daughter's brow with a cloth as the covered wagon lurched through the mountains. The sheet covering Olivia's body had become soaked with sweat and heat radiated from her flesh as if from an open fire. From time to time small moans of discomfort escaped her desiccated lips and he felt the guilt like a nail scraped across the inside of his skull.

For the hundredth time he repeated the prayer, calling on his lord God to give him the strength to endure. Of course he regretted her ordeal, but he couldn't regret the impulse that had made him bring her. It would have been much easier if the ceremony

394

had gone ahead in Rome, but the message he had received had been unequivocal. Olivia moaned again, almost a squeal, and he placed a jug of water against her cracked lips and poured a little into her mouth. He knew her suffering increased with every mile they travelled on this rutted track, but she must endure as he must endure. They were being tested, but if Olivia survived the test she would be saved, one way or the other. Neapolis was within a day's drive and the villa an hour beyond it. Another bump made him groan. His aged bones were not suited to this primitive form of travel. He thought of Petrus, and the Judaean's burning eyes immediately relieved the pain that racked every part of his body. Petrus would be waiting for them.

Lucius didn't fully understand why they were travelling to the villa, but Rome had become increasingly dangerous for a Christian. Would he have the strength to die for his faith? When he was in the presence of Petrus and worshipping with the other members of the sect he drew courage from them. Alone, he found it more difficult to be brave. Ruth had helped him to understand his weakness and to fight it. He didn't realize how much he had needed her until she was gone. Seneca had sent her to him; he was fortunate to have the philosopher as a friend. At first Ruth had been just another slave, but goodness and beauty shone from her like the light from the sun, the moon and the stars combined. He had become infatuated with her, but he would never have admitted it to anyone. Now he was alone again and death frightened him. He smiled sadly. Not quite alone. Valerius was a good son who cared for his father. If it were not for Valerius he would have died along with Ruth. At one point he had even believed his son might be brought into God's community, and saved. But the day of Ruth's death had revealed a Valerius he could never reach. A man estranged from every god, Roman or Christian.

His son would have prevented him from making this journey, if he could, and might even now be attempting to overtake him. That was why he had ordered the driver to avoid the main route from Rome. Tomorrow, God willing, they would reach the villa, Olivia would be saved and his own soul placed for ever in God's keeping.

Twenty-five miles to the west, Poppaea Augusta Sabina struggled to conceal her nerves. She had been sick twice already, but her illness had nothing to do with the motion of the enormous Liburnian galley. The ship was the fastest vessel afloat and could outrun any pirate who decided that the riches of an imperial convoy were worth the risk of taking on the heavy naval escort. No, the problem was what she had agreed to do. Was Nero really studying her with concern, or did the pale eyes hide a more sinister interest?

Fear made her mouth dry and she took another sip of wine. She lay on one of a pair of ornate cushioned couches in the shadow of a wide awning of gold cloth, cooled by the gentle salt breeze created by the ship's motion. All she could think of was Petrus. Was he becoming reckless? Bad enough that the most hunted man in Rome had somehow infiltrated her quarters in the guise of a dealer in fine jewellery, but to ask her to host this ceremony . . . She had pleaded with him, but his voice and his eyes were so persuasive. *Only by testing our faith and our courage can we truly come to God,* he had said. *Only by sacrifice will we gain the keys to the Kingdom of Heaven.* And she had agreed. It was as if he had hypnotized her with his talk of a new and better world, beyond the pain of this one.

She so wanted to be brave, but all she felt was trapped. Even if she went on her knees and confessed Nero would kill her along with the rest. He would do it quietly, out of the public eye, but she remembered the Christians, her Christians, being torn apart by the wild beasts. The girl trying in vain to save her child. At least that monster Torquatus wasn't accompanying them. He had stayed behind in Rome to deal with some crisis, but that didn't mean his spies would stop watching her.

'You are very pale, my dear. Perhaps you would like to sleep?'

Poppaea flinched at the voice, even though this was Nero at his most charming. She declined his offer to have the sides of the pavilion dropped to give her privacy. She preferred to see the sun sparkle on the waves like a million tiny diamonds, watch the yellow-eyed gulls squabble over scraps in the wake and feel the soft breeze on her skin. Suddenly each second of life seemed more precious than before. How had it come to this?

Nero studied his wife with the detached interest of a collector of fine statuary. Torquatus had hinted at a dark secret, but with Torquatus it never did to accept denunciation without proof, unless, of course, it suited your own ends. One had to admire the Praetorian prefect's commitment to the destruction of others. At another time he might have found the power struggle between them quite entertaining, but in his own way he had grown fond of Poppaea. Perhaps it was an effect of becoming older, but increasingly he found it difficult to maintain his enthusiasm for a life of constant excess. All he truly wanted was to sing upon a stage and receive the adulation he deserved. Instead, the gods had burdened him with responsibility for an Empire that encompassed more people than the census takers could count. Or perhaps not the gods. It was his mother who had set him on this path with her limitless ambition. The galley and the sea reminded him of Agrippina, and he felt that familiar twinge of regret that she was gone. Not guilt – the fault was her own – but, yes, regret that she was no longer here to guide him. If only she had supported him instead of trying to control him it would all have been so different.

Agrippina would have recognized the Christians for

the threat they were. Foul creatures spreading their filthy philosophy across the land like so much manure, each dropping encouraging a new crop of rabble-rousers. What was it that drew people to them? How could men risk their lives at the behest of an obscure criminal whose words should have died with him on the cross? He had personally questioned Cornelius Sulla in an attempt to understand them better, but instead of begging for his life the man had tried to *convert* him. It was a kind of madness for which there was only one cure. The soldier, Valerius, had been given his opportunity to find the leader of the sect, but he would fail. A strange choice of investigator, but Torquatus had been most persuasive in urging his appointment. These Christians lived among the Judaeans like diseased cattle hidden in a herd, so the Judaeans would die and the Christians would be wiped out with them. Without the leadership of the Judaean Christians the sect would undoubtedly wither and die, but he intended to make an example of the Roman converts. He would squash them one by one the way a beggar crushes lice between his fingernails.

Poppaea, lying back pale and beautiful on the padded couch, watched as he resumed his place in the bow and took up the first of the songs with which he would astonish the people of Neapolis. She preferred the screaming of the gulls.

XXXVIII

White smoke wreathed the rocky headland a mile to the east and for a few moments it looked as if the whole length of the peninsula was ablaze. The captain of the small cargo ship noticed Valerius's interest.

'The Fields of Fire,' he said morosely. 'A terrible place where people say giants walk at night. A good landmark for a sailor, though. Even when you can't see it for the mist you can smell the sulphur a mile away.'

Valerius thought the bay beyond the headland must be one of the most beautiful places he had ever seen. A sweeping crescent of rugged cliffs and sandy inlets stretched almost as far as the eye could see, dominated by an enormous, steep-sided cone of a mountain clad in a ragged cloak of greens and browns. At the foot of the mountain nestled the city of Neapolis, a glittering ribbon of cream and ochre surrounded by the scattered white dots that represented the grand villas of rich Romans escaping the furnace of a Roman summer. Beyond the mountain, rugged peaks stretched into the distance and formed an imposing backdrop that glittered in the heat of the morning. The sea around the ship was a restless blanket of blue and aquamarine, broken by the outline of three islands which dotted it like jewels laid out on a piece of shimmering silk.

To Valerius's surprise they sailed past the main port. 'Too many tax collectors,' the captain grunted. 'See that floating brothel?' He pointed to a golden ship larger than any other craft moored in the harbour. 'It means your master's in town and the place will be crawling with his guards. That's the place you want over there.' He pointed to a spot on the shoreline directly ahead where a river flowed into the sea, creating a natural harbour. 'Oplontis.'

They landed thirty minutes later and Serpentius and Heracles unloaded their gear while Valerius and Marcus walked from the harbour into the town to find horses. They were directed to a stable beyond the walls, where Valerius negotiated the hire of four reasonably sound mares and asked directions to the villa owned by Poppaea's family.

'A mile south on the Pompeii road overlooking the sea. Big place. You'd have to be blind to miss it.' The stableman laughed, eyeing Valerius's expensive tunic. 'They might even offer you a job, it being harvest time.'

Harvest time? Of course, why hadn't he considered

it earlier? All the way south Valerius had been trying to work out how Petrus would get his Christians into the villa unnoticed. Now he had his answer. Groups of itinerant farm workers would be travelling up and down the country from estate to estate supplementing the work of the local slaves. Petrus could turn up at Poppaea's gate and her overseer would allow them in, feed them and house them in the slave quarters. It was perfect. They could pass Olivia off as a wife who had been taken ill on the journey.

Fabia had said Poppaea would complete the journey overland, while Nero stayed in Neapolis to prepare for his performance the following night. She would travel with only her own personal retinue, stay at the villa for two nights, then return to celebrate his triumph with him. If Valerius's calculations were correct, that meant she was already at the house.

They walked back to the harbour through narrow streets that sloped down towards the sea, stopping for a drink at a public fountain close to a bakehouse. The water burbled and trilled as it fell from the pipe into a cistern and Valerius drank deeply from a cup scooped from the pool. His nose caught the scent of baking bread and he bought two loaves and handed one to Marcus.

As they emerged from the arcade into the sunshine he felt a slight tremor. 'What was that?'

Marcus felt it too, but he only shrugged. 'They must be milling the grain. Sometimes you can feel it in the next street when one of those big grinders is working.'

As they walked away they didn't notice that the flow from the pipe supplying the fountain had slowed to a trickle.

The steward stared suspiciously at the travel-stained, bearded figure in the thick robe. If his mistress wished to speak to the man alone there was little he could do about it, but what she had to say to an impoverished wandering labourer was entirely beyond him.

Petrus allowed himself a smile as the man bowed low and backed out of the room. 'Am I really so repellent?' he asked Poppaea.

'You said no one would be aware of your presence, yet the first thing you do is ask for an audience.' Poppaea tried to hide her anger. Her feelings for Petrus alternated between something close to worship and intense irritation at the casual way the Judaean played with other people's lives. 'That was hardly the act of someone who wished to keep his existence here a secret. Remember, you do not only place your own life in danger, but mine and many others.'

He bowed in acknowledgement of the rebuke. 'I merely wished to pass on my thanks for your hospitality.'

Poppaea frowned. She would never accuse Petrus of lying, but sometimes omission could be just as great a sin. What he didn't say was that his presence in this chamber increased his hold on her, and her reliance on him, in equal measure. She could never deny knowing him as long as the steward lived. Once, that complication might have been swiftly dealt with, but Petrus taught that all human life was sacred. 'When will you carry out the ceremony?'

'Your mother and father . . . ?'

'Are already on the way to Neapolis to greet the Emperor.'

'And the servants?'

'I have made arrangements. Only one or two remain and unless I call for them they will not dare to come near the pool.'

'Then the ceremony will take place once the moon has risen. You will be baptized and brought into the community of God and your soul will be taken into his keeping. God will live within you and you will live for ever with God's blessing.' Poppaea closed her eyes and a wave of relief washed over her. Never again would she need to fear Nero.

'And the others will know nothing of it?'

'They have never heard the name Poppaea,' he assured her. 'Nor do they know exactly where they are. Only that I have been given the use of the villa while the owners are elsewhere. They will be taken into God's keeping in a separate ceremony.'

She sniffed, blinking away a tear. 'I still do not understand why they needed to be here.'

'Because baptism carries with it duties and obligations.' His voice was gruff but gentle. 'By agreeing to share your salvation with others less fortunate, and allowing them to witness it, you have proved yourself worthy of inclusion in God's church.

By your willingness to place your life in peril, you have already become closer to God. We will be gone before sun-up and you may tell your steward that I vexed you in some way and you dismissed us all.'

Poppaea nodded. 'Tonight then.'

He smiled. 'Tonight.'

'They like their privacy,' Serpentius said.

'That usually means they have something to hide,' Marcus agreed.

Valerius studied the villa complex from the hillside. Serpentius was right. A high wall surrounded the buildings, but the owners had ensured they could not be overlooked from the hill by planting large trees at regular intervals around the inner perimeter of the wall. The combination looked daunting, but he knew it was an illusion. The twin barrier had been created to stop people from looking in, not breaking in. The three men were dressed in civilian clothing, with light summer cloaks to hide the fact that they were fully armed. Heracles joined them after leaving the horses, fed and watered, in the shade of a nearby olive grove.

'How long to get us over the wall, Serpentius?' Valerius asked.

'About twenty seconds.' The Spaniard grinned. 'The trees mean we can't see them, but also that they can't see us. I can get us inside just about anywhere.'

Valerius focused on the little he could see through the trees. He guessed that every olive tree, barley field and vineyard between here and the town was owned by the people who lived in the villa and that was where most of the slaves would be working. A twinkle of reflected sunlight alerted him to a potential threat. Not the sun glinting on a blade or spear point, but on water. A pool. Which meant . . . Now he saw it, camouflaged against the same grey stone that formed the hillside, an aqueduct that cut through the trees about five hundred paces away. An aqueduct that supplied the pool and its waterfall.

'We go over there.' Valerius pointed to where the aqueduct met the wall. He looked up at the sky, which was a clear blue dome. 'When the sun reaches its highest.'

As they rested in the shade, Valerius's eyes never left the villa complex below. Somewhere down there, behind the white wall and hidden by the trees, Lucius and Olivia waited. He had cursed his father as a fool for getting involved with the Christians, but could he really blame him for doing what he believed was right to save her life? Whatever happened, he had to get them out safely. He reached for the boar amulet at his neck, then remembered he had given it to Olivia. Would he live to regret it? If Fabia had been wrong and Poppaea had brought her imperial bodyguard, the whole thing had the potential to turn into a bloody disaster.

XXXIX

Deep beneath the mountain, in a process which had begun many millions of years earlier, the western tip of one of the fourteen major plates which make up the world's surface had reached a point where the pressure creating its momentum was insufficient to overcome the resistance of the crust through which the fifty-mile-deep slab usually travelled at a rate of one inch every year. Normally, the tip would have been pushed deep underground to be melted into fiery magma by the heat from the earth's core. In this case it would remain locked in place until the pressure behind it could build up a force powerful enough to shift it into motion again. Already, the pent-up energy was making the earth's crust creak with the strain. When the shift happened, the giant plate would cover in a single instant the distance it would normally take ten years to travel. That moment was fast approaching.

They made their way diagonally across the hillside. To Valerius's left the mountain, with its coat of vines and olive trees, rose steeply until the peak was lost in a shimmering haze. To his right, the slope became gentler as it fell away towards a turquoise sea that had never looked more welcoming. The intense heat was suffocating. Even Serpentius, who had been brought up among the sun-bleached hills north of Astorga, complained that if it became any hotter he would melt away. Rocks scorched by the sun reflected and magnified its power until it seemed every drop of moisture was being sucked from their bodies. Sweat soaked their clothing and ran into their eyes, creating salty deposits that quickly turned to grit and made them squint all the harder into the unyielding glare. After what seemed like an eternity, they gathered in the shadow beneath the final stone arch before the aqueduct crossed the wall into the villa gardens.

Valerius turned to the others. He had come to a decision. 'I'm going to do this alone,' he said. 'Wait here until I get back. If there's any sign of trouble give a single whistle and go back to the horses. I'll join you there if I can.'

'But—'

'This is my fight now, Marcus. You've risked your neck for me often enough already.'

Serpentius and Heracles made a cradle with their joined hands that allowed Valerius to boost himself to the top of the wall. He ran his fingers along the top course, half expecting to feel sharpened spikes or the jagged coral landowners sometimes used to protect their property. Satisfied it was clear, he used his elbows to lever himself up so he could peer through the trees. The elevation gave him a wonderful view across the villa complex to the sea beyond and the island of Capri, lying like a sleeping giant ready to wake and march off into the distant haze.

The villa made Seneca's house look like a modest family home. A sprawling two-storey masterpiece of pale stone, white marble pillars and terracotta tiles extended for at least four hundred paces down the slope. The centrepiece, flanked by two separate colonnaded walkways, was an enormous rectangular pool of sapphire blue, surrounded by white marble dotted with equestrian statues. At the near end, just below him, an ornamental waterfall fed the pool.

The fall had been created by diverting part of the supply from the aqueduct across a wide marble step to form a foaming cascade. To his left, exotic trees provided shaded refuges among the geometric pattern of pathways. The rush of water apart, the only noise was the hum of insects struggling through the over-heated air.

He slipped from the wall using the trees for cover and made his way down the slope. Now he was screened from the villa by the self-contained wings that flanked the pool. He stopped and listened again. He'd decided that his first priority must be to familiarize himself with the layout of the complex. Somewhere among the labyrinth of corridors, rooms and private gardens, Poppaea awaited her salvation at the hands of Petrus. He doubted the Judaean himself would be in the house. If he was right that the Christians had come in the guise of farmworkers, the area he sought was the slave quarters.

Ever since Fabia had revealed Poppaea's secret he had been wrestling with the question of what to do next. At first he'd approached it like a military problem, but quickly realized that the situation called for subtlety, not strength. He could not go charging up to the door. Poppaea's first instinct would be to protect Petrus. Even if he could get inside, she would deny everything and he'd be no closer to the Judaean, his father or Olivia. Somehow he had to reach them without her being aware. If the ceremony had taken place already, so much the better, but he doubted it. Journeying overland Petrus would only have reached Neapolis late the previous night or early this morning, giving Poppaea little opportunity to ensure the privacy they needed for the ceremony. No. It would be at night. Tonight.

He stopped in the cover of a group of laurel and oleander bushes. Still he wasn't far enough round to see beyond the angle of the massive building. As he waited, ready to move again, he remembered the pale, almost ghostly aura that had surrounded Olivia the last time he'd been with her. For some reason her features were indistinct, as if he was seeing her through a thick fog. He had once been told by a priest

410

that the memory faded as the loved one's soul faded. Was he too late? He shook his head to rid himself of despair, and as he did so he caught a whisper of leaves. He rose and turned in the same moment, his left hand automatically reaching for his sword. Too late. Something smashed into the side of his head and the world turned first grey, then black. His last thought was that he had failed them again.

Waking was too gentle a word for the endless struggle through the tormented darkness. When he finally opened his eyes he became aware of a darkened room with unpainted plaster walls and rough peasant furniture, and voices which faded as the owners realized he had recovered consciousness. He heard a door close and at first he thought he'd been left alone.

'You are very tenacious, my young friend, and very fortunate.' The soft voice came from close to his right ear.

'I don't feel fortunate,' Valerius could barely hear his own words, 'unless it's because I am in the hands of a healer. My head feels as if it has been crushed by a bear.'

'Your head I can cure.' Petrus smiled. 'A slit throat would have proved a much greater challenge.'

Valerius's left hand made an instinctive movement towards his neck before he realized how foolish the action was. 'My throat feels better than my head,' he assured the physician.

'True,' agreed the Judaean. 'But Isaac who acts as our guardian would have had it otherwise. He is a

411

former soldier,' he added, as if that was explanation enough.

Valerius raised his head, but Petrus placed a gentle hand on his shoulder. 'You should rest. I am sure you have many questions, but perhaps they can wait.'

A great weight seemed to be trying to drag the young Roman back down into the darkness. Then he remembered Olivia's features fading before his eyes. 'No,' he said urgently. 'There is no time.'

'There is always time,' Petrus said. 'We are all in God's hands. But perhaps . . . you came here for your father and your sister?'

Valerius shook his head. 'I came for you. You are the man they call Jesus's Rock?'

Petrus gave a sad smile. 'Of course. And you have soldiers?'

'No troops. Three . . . friends. You will come to no harm from me.'

'Not from you,' the Judaean sighed wearily. 'But the very fact that you are here means you are a threat . . . and not just to me.' Valerius heard the unspoken question. *Should I have you killed?*

'Your Christus taught humanity and mercy. I have read it.'

Petrus gently lifted Valerius's right arm, studying the walnut fist. 'He also said *If thy right hand offends thee, cut it off.* You, I suspect, sacrificed your right hand to save your life, or perhaps to save another. Sometimes a man must make sacrifices for peace. Sometimes he must be prepared to sacrifice something he loves for a cause he would be prepared to die for himself.'

There was a deep reluctance in his voice, but the words reminded Valerius of another man in another place.

'That is what Saul would have said.'

Petrus's head rose and for the first time Valerius saw emotion in his pale eyes. 'You have met Saul?'

'He says he is your brother in Christus, but I believe he means to betray you.'

Petrus drew himself up and for the first time Valerius saw the true stature of the man. In that second he understood why the Christus sect had survived its founder's death. Here was a leader other men would follow to the ends of the earth.

'There is but one God and one Jesus, his son,' the Judaean said solemnly. 'But each man views God in his own way, just as each of us has his own view of the path ahead. Three times I denied him, and still Jesus appointed me his Rock and his keeper of the truth. But the truth can be like poor wine, acid on the tongue and difficult to swallow. To understand the true Jesus and become closer to God, one must ignore the unreliable, accept the unbelievable and embrace the dangerous. Saul would take those parts of Jesus's teachings which are least palatable and consign them to the darkness, never to be spoken of again. He would sweeten the truth with honey so that it becomes acceptable to all men. In this way, he would ease the path into God's household for those

413

who find their minds troubled or their faith tested. But for me, Valerius, there can only be one truth, and that is the whole truth. Two men, two roads, but only one path can be chosen.'

'But Saul would have you dead.'

'Saul sees the road ahead in his own way,' Petrus said calmly. 'At heart he is a soldier, just as you are, and his methods are a soldier's methods. Whatever the future, it is God's will and I will be bound by it. There can only be one leader of the faith.'

They sat in silence for what seemed a long time.

'You talked of sacrifice,' Valerius said. 'There have already been so many sacrifices. Cornelius Sulla burned on a pyre for refusing to renounce his faith or betray his friends, your followers. His brother Publius, who died upon his own sword in the service of your God. And Lucina Graecina, a great lady humbled and humiliated, who once told me that she would gladly go to her death for the love of Jesus Christus. But they did not die for Christus, did they? They died for Petrus. Christus is gone. You have taken his place.' He looked up and saw a glint that might have been tears in the old man's eyes. Fear of the answer he would receive made him hesitate before asking what he had come to ask. 'They sacrificed themselves for you. Would you be prepared to sacrifice the lives of twenty thousand innocents for your faith?'

Petrus's face hardened as he heard for the first time of the Emperor's threat to the Judaeans. 'So many lives for one man?' He shook his head. 'It is no idle threat. To this Emperor human life means nothing. He will do exactly what he says. I must think on this.' He studied Valerius intently. 'How did you know to come here?'

Valerius explained about Fabia and the hold that Torquatus had over her.

'Then we must act quickly. I believe Torquatus underestimates Poppaea. She is already strong and she will be stronger still when she has been anointed by God. I believe she will prevail and Torquatus will fall. Faith can move mountains. Come, I will take you to your father and sister.'

'Wait.' Valerius struggled from the bed. 'I must know. Will you return to Rome with me?'

Petrus stared at him, but the certainty had returned to the grey eyes and Valerius knew the answer before he spoke.

'Yes, I will come, but first I must finish the work I have begun here.'

XL

They placed Olivia's bed on the marble walkway by the pool. When he saw his sister Valerius's heart dropped into the pit of his stomach. In the few days since he had left her, the thing that was killing Olivia had eaten away what little excess flesh there'd been. Hollow pits dented her cheeks and dark circles rimmed her eyes. Her lips, which even a week ago had been full and warm, were now pale lines covering teeth gritted in pain. If he had not known better he would have thought she was already dead.

Lucius stood by his daughter's side, whey-faced, exhausted in body and spirit, yet despite his condition Valerius noticed an unusual radiance behind his eyes, as if someone had lit a slow-burning fire inside. The old man sensed his son's presence and looked up wearily. 'Only Petrus can save her now.'

By now it was quite dark, but the clouds parted

above the pool and moonlight danced on the rippling waters like glittering shards of broken glass. A sing-song chanting announced the arrival of Petrus at the head of a small procession escorted by four torch-bearers. Valerius was astonished at the transformation in the Judaean. The careworn old man in the ragged, flea-bitten coat had been replaced by a commanding figure dressed in the golden robes of a high priest of a Judaean temple, his majesty exaggerated by a padded crown and his glory enhanced by a breastplate studded with precious stones. Behind him, in a simple white robe and accompanied by two handmaidens, Poppaea glided serenely across the marble, pale as a water nymph, her head high and her eyes fixed on the cascade at the end of the pool. Valerius stepped back into the shadow, but not before the dark eyes flicked towards him and widened in surprise.

The little procession arrived at the end of the pool where the ornamental fall turned the waters white. It was shallower here and steps had been built to allow the decorous access fitting to an Empress. Before Poppaea entered the water, Petrus proclaimed her ready to undergo the ceremony. As Valerius watched, a tall bearded man in a priest's robe emerged from the shadows and placed a hand upon her forehead. There was something familiar about the priest, but he couldn't be sure what it was. His father whispered that Poppaea was being asked the series of questions that must be answered before the sacrament could proceed. Eventually, the man nodded gravely and led her down the steps into the pool.

When they were knee-deep in the water he took her hand and walked with her to the gushing cataract. The moon had disappeared behind the clouds, but now a single shaft of light illuminated the two people by the waterfall. Valerius drew breath and he heard gasps all around him. It was as if he had known the man with Poppaea all his life, yet he knew he had never set eyes on him before tonight. Poppaea hesitated and a shocked hush fell over the watchers, but the hesitation only lasted for a second before she plunged into the foaming deluge with a cry of ecstasy. As she did so, the man raised his hands to the sky and in a voice charged with emotion called out an invocation.

'Lord our God, cleanse this unworthy woman of her sins and take her into your house, in keeping with your Covenant. Write your law upon her heart, place your almighty spirit within her and take her immortal soul into your keeping.'

When Poppaea emerged from beneath the fall her robe clung to her body revealing every curve and shadow, but Valerius only had eyes for the man who stood beside her. Was it a trick of the light? No, he had seen enough injury to be certain. In the centre of the priest's palm was the puckered scar of an old wound. He turned to his father, but Lucius's gaze had never left Poppaea. Valerius touched the old man on the shoulder. 'Did you see . . . ?' But when he turned back to the pool the figure in the white robe had vanished.

Poppaea's handmaidens quickly covered her in a white sheet and Petrus placed his palm upon her forehead, saying: 'You are reborn now. In the name of Jesus Christus, I name you Maria. God is within you, you are his temple, go in peace.'

When Poppaea walked from the pool, she seemed taller, and her eyes shone with the wonder of what she had just experienced. Even with her hair plastered against her skull she radiated an inner beauty that transcended anything she had possessed before. She walked within feet of Valerius, but gave no hint of recognition. Valerius studied the men and women around him, looking for the man in the white robe. They included the lawyer from the baptism chamber in Rome and his plump wife, who stared unwaveringly towards the waterfall. Valerius felt the ground shudder beneath his feet but none of them appeared to notice it.

Lucius tugged at his sleeve, his eyes bright with rapture. 'You saw it?' he demanded. 'She was reborn. God's spirit came in a shaft of light and entered her. Do you understand what it means? Olivia can be saved, but only if we place her soul in God's keeping.' The grip on his arm tightened. 'Will you join me, Valerius, and accompany her as she makes the journey towards salvation?'

'Did you see him?' Valerius demanded.

'Petrus?'

'No. The man with the wounds in his hands.'

His father opened his mouth, but before he could reply, a shout rang out from the hillside above.

'Riders! Riders from the north!'

XLI

The walls of the villa shone like a beacon in the moonlight as Decimus Torquatus urged his mount along the metalled road with Rodan at his side and twenty dust-stained Batavian cavalry at his back. It had been a long day and promised to be a longer night. The information had taken more time to extract than he would have believed, but his anger was somewhat assuaged by the outcome of the interrogation. If he had calculated correctly, Poppaea should still be here with her parasitic friends and he would sweep them up like songbirds in a net, her treason plain for all to see in her association with the bandits she had succoured. In a perfect world, he would be accompanied by more troops, but the century of Praetorian infantry marching behind wouldn't reach the villa until after dawn. He consoled himself that a force of twenty veteran cavalry was more than enough to cow a few religious fanatics. A man of little emotion, he was surprised by the flare of pleasure with which he anticipated their meeting. She would go on her knees to plead for his forgiveness. Perhaps she might even be persuaded to offer up a little more?

The thought brought a smile and he kicked the horse into a gallop. The only thing sweeter would be the moment when he presented her to Nero and forced her to confess her guilt.

'Quickly, get Olivia into the house,' Valerius shouted to his father, but Lucius stared back at him as if he was mad. The Christians waiting beside the pool milled around like chickens who have scented a fox but have nowhere to hide. Marcus, Serpentius and Heracles appeared at a run.

'The house!' Valerius snapped. He took one end of his sister's bed and signalled Marcus to pick up the other. At last, at Petrus's urging, the Christians began to move towards the villa. It was the only way. He couldn't get them out before the cavalrymen arrived, but he might be able to protect them in the great warren of intersecting rooms that made up Poppaea's villa. With luck, they would somehow find a way to escape.

He felt a hand pluck at his arm. 'Olivia,' Lucius cried. 'We must wait. She must be baptized.'

'Do you want to see her burn, Father?' Valerius shrugged off the clutching fingers. 'Because she will if we stay here. Don't you understand? Torquatus wants Poppaea, but the only way he can prove her guilt is to take you as well and make you denounce her in front of the Emperor.'

Lucius recoiled as if he had been struck. 'We would sooner die than betray our faith.'

Serpentius, running past them with a child in each arm, laughed. 'It's easy to be brave before you feel the heat of the fire, old man.'

By now they were at the far end of the pool, where a doorway led to a corridor connecting the pool complex to the main villa. Valerius led the way at the run. He found himself in a room with a large fishpond at its centre. Next door was the *lararium* where the family performed their daily homage to the household gods, and beyond it a room lined with the terracotta death masks of Poppaea's ancestors. Finally he reached a wide hall with stairs leading to the upper floor. Close by was a short passage to the villa's main entrance. He hesitated, tempted to take his chances in the open. But he couldn't leave without Poppaea and it might be too late in any case. He made his decision.

'Take Olivia upstairs.' He handed his end of the burden to Heracles. 'And get the rest of these sheep up there.' Petrus bridled at the insult, but Valerius ignored the old man.

'What about you?' Marcus demanded.

'I'll fetch the Empress. If I don't get back hold on as long as you can. I doubt they'll dare to burn the place, but if they do you'll have to get the Christians out any way you can.'

Marcus nodded. 'Depend on it.'

Valerius turned to go, but a strong hand gripped his shoulder. 'I will go with you,' Petrus said.

He brushed the Judaean aside. 'Your place is here with your flock. Get them to make themselves useful. Remember our bargain and stay alive.'

Petrus didn't argue and Serpentius herded the Judaean and the other Christians up the stairs. Marcus and Heracles followed with Olivia and carried her into a nearby room where her father took his place by her. Two of the Christians offered to help and Marcus set them to collecting beds and couches to barricade the stairway and anything heavy that could be used as a weapon. The others held their wives and children and stared dumbly at the walls, like cattle waiting for the slaughter.

Marcus studied the stairway. It was perhaps four paces wide and quite steep. Anyone who attacked up it was going to have to be quick and brave, but that suited the veteran gladiator well enough. The faster and braver they were, the quicker they'd die. But he understood that he couldn't defend the stairhead for ever. He called to Serpentius. 'I need to know what's up here. Check out every room and every potential way off this floor. Four of us can hold the stair as long as we can hold a sword, but only if they don't get behind us.'

'What if they have archers?' The Spaniard identified the flaw in Marcus's reasoning. A single bowman would pick the defenders off from the stairwell with all the ease of a child plucking peaches in an orchard.

Marcus spat against bad luck and pointed to the Christians. 'Tell those bastards to pray that they don't,' he growled. 'One way or the other we're going to find out tonight if their nailed god is any fucking use.'

Serpentius set off along the balcony. Marcus heard a soft cough and turned to find the two Christians carrying a padded couch about six feet long and of heavy construction. 'Good,' he rasped. 'Put it here,' he indicated the top of the stairway, 'with the feet outwards where they'll make life awkward for anybody trying to get close. But we need more. Couches, chairs, beds, cupboards. Get those other sheep to help you.' He grinned to give the men confidence. 'We'll make them fight for every inch of stairway and by the time they get up here they'll be begging us to kill them.' But not yet, he thought. He needed to leave the stair open until Valerius returned with Poppaea.

But where was he?

Valerius slipped silently along endless lamplit corridors. At every turn he expected to meet a slave or servant, but it was evident Poppaea had found some scheme to empty the house while Petrus and his Christians were here. He passed through the family shrine and the *lararium* back to the indoor pond and paused to get his bearings. Where were Poppaea's private apartments? Not near the pool, certainly, or he would have come across them already. So they had to be on the ocean side of the villa. He turned right towards an opening on the far side of the room. And stopped in his tracks.

The fish in the pond were dancing.

It was the only word for it. Hundreds of the tiny, rainbow-coloured creatures leapt and flipped, walking on their tails and somersaulting across the surface of the water. Below them hundreds more jerked erratically and swam elaborate patterns as if waiting their turn to escape. Natural curiosity made him hesitate, but he didn't have time to be distracted by the antics of a few fish. As he neared the rear of the villa the sound of a soft voice alerted him. In a luxuriously appointed room with broad windows overlooking the sea, Poppaea, Empress of Rome, knelt before a painting of the Christian symbol Valerius had seen on the wall of the baptism chamber.

Poppaea had changed from the simple white baptismal dress into a heavy robe of imperial purple and her long chestnut hair was tied neatly in place. She looked up in confusion. A week earlier she would have felt nothing but relief to have the reassuring figure of Valerius by her side, but now she had a more powerful protector.

'What do you mean by entering my private apartments?' she demanded. 'Why are you here?'

'I don't have time to explain. Torquatus is coming.'

She lifted her chin and the dark eyes flashed. 'Then let him come. I have no fear of Torquatus.'

Valerius couldn't believe what he was hearing.

'Why are you people so eager to die? Isn't it possible your God is giving you a chance to live? Come with me and I may be able to save you. Stay here and you give Torquatus everything he wants.'

She shot him a venomous glance and he started for the door. 'Wait,' she ordered. He bit back a comment as she gathered up the painting and placed it face down below a couch. Better that she should have burned the evidence of her new loyalty, but there was no time. At least she was prepared to follow him.

'Which is the quickest way to the stairs?'

He followed her as she made her way unerringly through one corridor after another, one room after another. As they walked she questioned Valerius. 'How did Torquatus know to come to the villa?'

Valerius guessed that Fabia had betrayed him, but he saw no profit in paying her back in the same coin. 'At the moment, lady, that is less important than the fact that he is here. Perhaps you can ask him when you meet, although I'm sure he has many more important questions for you.'

'Do not play games with me,' she snapped. 'Would he be content with me alone?'

Valerius shook his head. 'Even if he was satisfied with you today, he would come for the rest of us tomorrow or the day after. We would never be safe. And when he has you, he will use you to get to others. Nero will slaughter the Judaeans in Rome and your new religion will wither away.'

'The faith will go on,' she said with certainty. 'Jesus did not suffer and die on the cross for nothing.'

'Then let us hope it isn't put to the test.'

Serpentius returned from his reconnaissance. 'Nothing to worry about up here. There's a big room at the back with a balcony that looks out towards the sea. A couple of sitting rooms and a couple of small rooms for guests. The rest is servants' quarters.' He held up a thick gold chain. 'A man could get rich by mistake in a place like this.'

Marcus shook his head, but he didn't order the Spaniard to replace the jewellery. If you were about to go to war with the Praetorian Guard what was the point of worrying about a necklace? 'This balcony. How high is it? Can they climb to it?'

Serpentius pushed the chain inside his tunic. 'Not without a ladder.'

'Plenty of ladders on an estate, lad. You!' He pointed to the Roman lawyer who was sitting huddled beside his wife. 'Get out to the back and shout if you see any movement below the balcony.' The Christian hesitated. 'Now!' Marcus roared, and the man scurried off, leaving his wife whimpering. 'Mars' arse, what have we got ourselves into,' the gladiator muttered.

The two foragers returned with another couch, their fourth, this time laden with a pile of marble and bronze busts. Marcus picked up a head that was instantly recognizable as Nero: pouting lips and a weak chin that even the sculptor couldn't hide. 'Nice to know he's good for something. A few more wouldn't go amiss.'

The younger of the two men stepped forward. 'I am Isaac,' he said. 'I can fight.'

Marcus looked him up and down, taking in the athlete's physique, and nodded. 'Good.' He handed the man Nero's head. 'When they come, give them this with my compliments.'

They were interrupted by the sound of hooves clattering into the courtyard.

At last Valerius recognized the stairway. He gestured to Poppaea to go ahead, but in the same instant a crash shook the walls and the front door smashed in as the first Praetorians burst into the house.

'Get back,' he whispered, ushering her behind him. 'We need to find another way.'

'Where?' she demanded.

'First we need to get out of the house—'

'You!'

Valerius looked up to find Rodan standing next to a cavalryman in the doorway a dozen yards away with a triumphant grin on his burn-scarred face. He waited for the moment when the Praetorian would recognize Poppaea, but Rodan's expression didn't change and he realized the Empress must be hidden by the angle of the wall.

'Make for the sea,' he whispered. 'I will join you

there if I can. Go.' He felt her hesitate. 'Please go, lady.'

With relief, he heard a soft shuffle fading into the distance and he turned his attention back to his enemy.

XLII

Three more cavalrymen had joined Rodan, all wearing armour over their black tunics. Rodan carried the short legionary *gladius*, but the other men were armed with the big *spatha* cavalry swords Valerius had seen used to such good effect in Britain. The *spatha* could be fearsome when wielded from horseback and the weight of the sword cleaved helmet and skull, but it was cumbersome if the user was out of the saddle. Their armour and weapons made them slower, which was to his advantage, but more difficult to kill, which was definitely not. Valerius had no doubt he had to kill these men. The only way any of them were going to get out of this alive was if he defeated Rodan and Torquatus.

If Rodan had been alone he would have taken his chances and rushed the Praetorian. But five opponents called for a more cautious approach. He had to hold them long enough to give Poppaea time to escape.

431

He'd worry about what came next later, if there was a later.

'We don't need this one.' Rodan ushered the cavalrymen forward. 'Kill him.'

'Too frightened to fight me yourself?' Valerius's challenge made two of the men hesitate and look to their leader.

'There's no glory in killing a cripple,' the Praetorian sneered. 'Or a whore. I gave your pretty whore to my century after Torquatus finished questioning her. It was very instructive. I had her first, of course. She was a good fuck, your whore, at least then. I'm not sure if it was the forty-ninth or the fiftieth that killed her.'

The image of Fabia's obscene death lit a fire in Valerius's brain and he had to curb the instinct to hack the smile from Rodan's leering face. Poor Fabia, caught between Torquatus's threats and loyalty to her friends. When she had been forced to make a choice it had cost her her life. From somewhere deep inside he found control. Revenge would come in its own time. Now he knew without doubt he was going to kill Rodan, and Torquatus too, or die in the attempt. He kept his voice steady so that the Praetorian wouldn't know he had reached him.

'I'm no whore, Rodan,' he taunted the other man. 'And I only need one arm to beat you. Old women and children are more your style. That's why you're afraid to face me.'

Valerius retreated half a step as he spoke. The

corridor was only wide enough to allow two men to approach simultaneously and even then they would hamper each other. But no matter how well he fought he couldn't stay in this position for long, because Rodan would soon find a way to outflank or get behind him. He was close to the corner now. One step from his escape route. He tried to recall the layout of the ground floor. Where could he make his next stand, and the one after that? If he could disable one or even two of them, it would take some of the fight out of the others. But first they had to come to him.

'Are you women?' he goaded the two cavalrymen. He spat in the direction of Rodan. 'If this coward won't fight me you will have to. I am Gaius Valerius Verrens, Hero of Rome, and I hold your deaths in my hand.'

He recognized the moment of decision. The trooper was lanky and spare and the mail of his auxiliary armour hung on him like an oversized tunic. Valerius guessed that he would have quick hands, but that the mail would slow him. If he had attacked alone he would have had a chance. He could have pinned Valerius in place and worked an angle to allow the second man to reach his undefended right side. But the soldier sensed the danger in this one-armed civilian and he urged his comrade with him.

Valerius saw them come and it was as if he could predict their every movement. He slid to his left and took two steps forward so that the tall man half shielded him from the second attacker. His enemy had expected him to run, or at best try to hold them, and the advance surprised him. The cavalryman was a veteran of the German frontier wars, but his most violent duty in the last five years had been putting down civilian bread riots. Though he wasn't aware of it, he had lost the edge that means the difference between life and death on the battlefield. He was wary of the confident young man in front of him, but not frightened. Valerius saw the calculations going through his mind. Two against a cripple? It would be over in seconds. But he had never faced a left-handed swordsman, or a man who had been trained by gladiators. Speed was as great a weapon as the *gladius* in Valerius's hand. In the split second it took the cavalryman's mind to work out how to deal with the unfamiliar threat, Valerius was already inside the point of the long *spatha*. Roaring with the fierce joy of mortal combat he brought the *gladius* in a raking cut across the cavalryman's eyes that left him blinded and shrieking in disbelief. As the man clutched at his ruined face Valerius smashed a shoulder into his chest, throwing him back into the second soldier. Ignoring the second man had been a gamble. Already he was swinging the big cavalry sword in a wide arc that would bring the edge down on Valerius's exposed neck. His comrade's reeling body had slowed him a fraction, but still the blow should have been deadly. All the long hours of repetition on the hot sands of the *ludus* had conditioned Valerius to meet any threat from the right with his shield. Today he had none, but the reaction of his right arm was automatic. He brought his forearm up to meet the attack and the edge of the sword bit deep into the seasoned walnut of his artificial hand, carving off a long splinter and slicing its way across the leather socket. Valerius screamed as his arm dissolved in a fiery bolt of pain that seared all the way to the centre of his brain. His mind told him to deal with the insult that had been done to his body, but he knew that to hesitate was to die. He had one chance. The block had opened up the cavalryman's guard. Valerius speared the point of the *gladius* upwards into the pale flesh of his exposed throat, spraying a dark rainbow of blood across the white walls of the corridor.

As the man fell a shout of dismay rang out from Rodan, but Valerius didn't have time to savour his triumph.

He ran.

XLIII

Torquatus marched into the villa and studied the unaffected opulence around him. Perhaps, when he placed Poppaea's treason before the Emperor, he would be rewarded with something similar. Nero could be very generous to his friends.

'Where is she?' he demanded.

'We're searching the house, but we think she's on the upper floor.' The decurion in charge of the cavalry detachment's tone was respectful, but not deferential, which Torquatus found slightly irritating. 'They've barricaded the stairway.'

'Slaves and servants,' the Praetorian commander said dismissively. 'It will be the work of a few moments to sweep them aside.'

The decurion bit back an unwise comment. He'd seen the barricade and didn't like the look of it at all. One thing was certain, Torquatus would not be the first to the top of the stair testing the defences.

Privately, he considered his commander a fool for not waiting for the infantry, but he knew there was no point in arguing. He nodded and drew his sword.

Torquatus accompanied him to the bottom of the polished wooden stairway. He smiled coldly as he saw the pathetic jumble of couches with two or three frightened faces visible behind them. At his back, the decurion formed up his men for the assault.

'In the name of the Emperor, hand over your mistress and I will spare your lives,' the prefect shouted.

Above him Marcus, hidden by the Christians he had told to show themselves at the barricade, exchanged glances with Serpentius. If the Praetorians believed Poppaea was with them, he wasn't going to tell them differently. At least it meant Valerius was still free. 'Why don't you come and get her?' he shouted.

Torquatus recoiled at the challenge. 'Then in the name of the Emperor I sentence you to death.' The words brought another disapproving glance from the decurion. He had experience of fighting men who had been given no hope, and therefore had no fear. Better to make them think surrender was possible. Even if it wasn't.

'Get on with it!' the Praetorian commander ordered.

The decurion drew his sword and turned to his men. Fourteen. The others were searching the rest of the house. He pointed to the barricade. 'It's nothing but a few pieces of furniture with unarmed slaves behind it. They'll shit themselves when they hear you

437

coming, so let's hear you roar when we hit the stairs. Now!'

They ran at the stairway in two columns with the young officer in the lead. He took the steps two at a time, screaming at the top of his voice, but the scream died in his throat when he saw the heavy wooden cabinet being manhandled over the top of the barrier. 'No!' he shouted. Too late. Five feet of lacquered oak caught him in the chest on its first bounce and crushed his breastplate. He felt his ribs splinter as he was hurled backwards along with two of the men in the right-hand file. A moment later the cabinet was followed by a bed that smashed the first soldier in the left column over the banister to plummet head first on to the stone floor below. The man just had time for relief that his helmet had taken the impact that would have crushed his skull before his neck snapped like a rotten twig.

The setback won Marcus and Serpentius a moment's respite, but the cavalrymen were experienced enough to know that the key to victory was ignoring their losses and maintaining momentum. There were still plenty of them to do the job and they'd make these slaves pay in blood when they got to the top. The first man to reach the barrier grabbed at the legs of the nearest couch and tried to haul it clear.

Marcus had watched with satisfaction as the missiles thrown by Heracles and Isaac the Christian smashed into the attacking ranks. Four down. Eleven to go. When the Praetorian started tugging at the couch he rose to his feet, reached over the barricade and swept his sword downwards.

The soldier screamed and stared at the blood arcing from the stump of his wrist. He looked up into the scarred face snarling down at him and threw himself backwards away from the glistening blade. To Marcus's left another Praetorian hacked at the barricade, throwing lumps of horsehair stuffing into the air until Serpentius stabbed him in the eye and he fell back spouting gore over the stairs. Something round sailed out over the barricade and hit the helmet of a third a glancing blow that sent him staggering to the rear. The old gladiator turned and found Valerius's father ready to throw a second marble bust from the pile behind them.

'Fall back.' The hoarse shout brought the first attack to a halt and the remaining Praetorian cavalrymen retreated, carrying their wounded and dead with them.

'Are your men cowards or just fools?' Torquatus demanded as the decurion hauled himself to his feet, gasping as the ends of his broken ribs ground together. The young soldier ignored the insult. He knew he'd been guilty of underestimating the men holding the barrier, but Torquatus had been at fault for insisting on an immediate assault. Now he looked up at the barricade and saw it as a military problem instead of an inconvenience. The answer came to him quickly.

'Grappling hooks.' He gave the order through gritted teeth, pointing to one of the men recovering from being hit by the cabinet. 'Get rope and anything we can use to haul this clear, and call up as many of the others as you can find.'

Torquatus looked on impatiently as the decurion groaned while one of his men strapped his broken ribs with cloth torn from a bed. The injured cavalryman returned with another four men, each carrying a length of rope to which was tied the snapped-off top of a pitchfork with the tines bent at an angle that turned the implement into an improvised hook.

The decurion tested one of the forks for strength. Not perfect, but it would only take one of them to hold and the men defending the top of the stairway were finished.

On the landing above, the tense silence worried Marcus more than the earlier assault. 'They're up to something, and it's not going to be pleasant.'

'Fire?' Serpentius suggested.

'Not much we can do about it if they do. Heracles, get the Christians to find sheets and start twisting them together and tell them to be ready to retreat to the balcony at the back of the house.'

'What about the girl?'

Marcus looked behind him through the open doorway where Lucius now crouched holding his daughter's hand as Petrus led the Christians in prayer. 'She'll just have to take her chances like the rest of us.' Valerius was a soldier; he would understand.

The giant Sarmatian went to pass on his instructions. Petrus looked up at him expectantly. Heracles shook his head. No point in giving false hope. He crouched beside Lucius as he sat holding his daughter's hand. What a waste. She was beautiful as an alabaster statue and her helpless innocence moved something inside him, but Heracles had seen enough death to make him a practical young man. Marcus was right, there was nothing to be done. He handed his dagger to the father.

'If it comes to it,' he said, 'it would be a kindness. Things will not go well for us if they succeed.'

The look on the old man's face reminded him of one of the tragic masks they used in the theatre. Heracles left them together and returned to Marcus and Serpentius.

'Now!'

All three reacted to the shout, but Marcus was momentarily distracted by the lack of action that followed it. When something fell beside him with a metallic clatter he instinctively jumped away as it was pulled back to hook on to the couch in front of him. In quick succession four more hooks landed and two of them caught their targets. Too late Marcus realized what they were and reached to free the hooked claws. The barricade began to disintegrate in front of him.

Heracles was the only one of the defenders to get a hand to one of the grapples and immediately used his enormous strength to fight the power of the men on the other end of the rope. If he won the deadly tug of war at least part of the barricade would survive and give the defenders something to fight for. Lose, and the way would be open for the attackers. Serpentius ran to his friend's side, but it was impossible to get his hands on the rope or the metal hook without obstructing Heracles. The Praetorians too understood the significance of the rope and three men sprinted to add their weight. Heracles' face reddened and the muscles of his enormous shoulders bulged as he put every ounce into the struggle. At first it appeared he was holding his own, but slowly, inch by painful inch, the giant Sarmatian was forced to give ground. The feral snarl that twisted his face never altered as the incredible pressure on the rope first pulled him upright and then toppled him down the stairs along with what was left of the barricade.

Now the cavalrymen attacked, with the bandaged decurion at their head, dodging the furniture that tumbled around them. Heracles was stunned by the impact of his fall and he struggled dazedly to his feet as the soldiers reached him. The first man stabbed the young giant through the body and wrenched his *spatha* free in a savage gut-spilling twist. The blood drained from Heracles' face, but still he stayed upright, his hands vainly trying to contain the coil of blue intestines bulging from his torn stomach. As he swayed on the blood-soaked stair a second cavalryman swung a cut at his neck which almost severed his head. At last the big man fell, and, as they passed him, each of the enraged attackers hacked at his defenceless body until it looked as if he had been mauled by a pack of wild beasts.

'Prisoners,' the decurion roared. 'We need prisoners.'

Marcus and Serpentius had watched Heracles die. Now they fought for their lives as the Praetorians reached the top of the stair. The attackers outnumbered them six to one, but Marcus had won his freedom with the speed of his sword. The men who faced him were astonished by the whirlwind of glistening iron that met them and two wounded in the first few seconds taught them to respect the lightning blade.

Serpentius fought with a cold smile and matched his opponents cut for cut. The swiftness of his strike had earned him his name and now he lived up to it, keeping the Praetorians at bay as they vied for the opportunity to kill him. With a twist of his wrist he sent one of the long *spatha* swords spinning from its owner's hand. The blade dropped by the door of the bedroom where the terrified Christians watched the fight with wide-eyed horror. Serpentius heard a shout and when he looked up Isaac had picked up the sword and was running at the Praetorians surrounding him.

Two of the Spaniard's opponents turned away to meet the new threat and now he was able to take the fight to the startled cavalrymen. He laughed as one of the men reeled backwards holding his arm, but a quick glance towards Marcus told him the older man was tiring at last. The veteran gladiator was forced back to the door of the bedroom along with Isaac. Serpentius allowed himself to be pushed back alongside them.

A high-pitched scream told them that Isaac's brave fight had run its course. In a daze, Lucius walked forward to take his place and his hand closed over the wooden hilt of the fallen sword.

XLIV

Valerius ran through the corridors with his right arm a throbbing mass of pain. Blood wept from beneath the leather socket, but he couldn't be certain how serious the wound was. If he had the opportunity he would stop and tighten the laces and hopefully slow the flow, but that didn't seem likely. The curtained doorways of the house passed in a blur and he heard shouting and the sounds of running feet as Rodan and the two unwounded Praetorians pursued him. He knew he wouldn't be able to fool the cavalrymen twice. This time they'd take their time and work him into a position where Rodan could kill him at his leisure. Rodan would enjoy that. His only hope was to lead them as far from Poppaea as he could. He thought of his father and Olivia but there was nothing he could do for them now except put his trust in Marcus, Serpentius and Heracles.

He found himself back beside the indoor pond and

noticed indifferently that the dancing fish were now belly up on the surface, their vibrant colours dulled by death. His racing mind told him this was some kind of omen; if he didn't lose his pursuers in the next few minutes his future was just as bleak. He turned left into a walled garden surrounded by marble pillars. Among the flowers and herbs stood a polished bronze statuette of a wild boar cornered by dogs that gave him a queasy feeling of fellowship. For a fleeting moment he considered hiding among the flower beds, but the cover was too thin and he would rather go down fighting than be dragged skulking from behind an oleander bush and butchered among the roses.

The next turn found him back at the swimming pool.

He ran along the marble tiles past the sitting rooms for Poppaea's guests. The waterfall was in sight and he knew precisely where he would cross the wall when he climbed the slope. The only question was whether he could reach the trees before Rodan and his men arrived. Two more cavalrymen appeared from nowhere in front of him. No time for hesitation. Swerving to the right between two marble pillars he hit the water in a shallow dive that took him halfway across the pool and launched into the overarm stroke he had been taught as a child. The sword hindered his technique and his tunic slowed him further, but he knew that the Praetorians in their chain armour were unlikely to chance the water.

He hauled himself out on the far side and turned for

the slope. Only then did he realize how close to exhaustion he was. As he hit the incline his pace slowed and each step became agony. He would never reach the trees in time.

Desperately, he turned to face his pursuers. There were four of them now, with Rodan just coming into view from the main villa. He searched for some weakness or alternative escape route, but there was none. Out here in the open any one of the *spathas* outreached the *gladius*. They would surround him, one or two of them would attack, and while he was occupied the others would chop him to pieces.

But he was Gaius Valerius Verrens, Hero of Rome, and he would not die like some tethered lamb. He thought of Ruth and Fabia, and with a roar of defiance he charged the five men, pre-empting their attack and praying for the chance to take Rodan with him. The first Praetorian caught his attack on the long blade of his sword, but with a twist of his *gladius* Valerius raked the man's wrist and he let out a howl of pain. As he turned, he knew the other swords were coming for him, but the battle madness was upon him and nothing mattered but to kill. Blood for blood. Let the god of battle decide. He spun, sweeping another sword aside, but the flat of a blade caught him on the side of the head and he went down hard.

With the strength of despair he twisted and tried to get to his feet, lashing with his sword until a boot stamped on his back and he felt iron at his throat. 'Don't kill him yet!' The shout came from Rodan, but Valerius took no hope from it. Three cavalry-men dragged him back to where the Praetorian stood among the marble columns. Smiling, Rodan pulled a dagger from his belt.

'Maybe I'll let you live after all. It will be a pleasure to watch you and the old man burn, and the girl of course. But first,' he raised the dagger so Valerius could see the gleaming point, 'I'm going to take your eyes.'

The earthquake had its origins in the convergence of the African and Eurasian tectonic plates. As the two giants met, the larger forced the smaller towards the earth's core where it had recently become stuck many miles below the surface of the planet's crust in the area just south of Neapolis. For weeks, elemental forces had been at work as the power of billions of tons of remorselessly shifting rock – the motion of an entire continent – built up behind the stoppage. Now, a single sudden movement broke the deadlock. This massive bolt of energy pulsed outwards in a series of enormous shockwaves. Much of the force would be dissipated in the mass of the planet, but for those inhabiting the crust above the epicentre of the quake, it would seem like the end of the world.

Rodan froze like a rabbit confronted by a foraging stoat. The initial shock broke with a roar as if all the gods cried out in pain together and the earth began to lurch like a bucking horse. The men holding Valerius instinctively tightened their grip as the marble pillars around them first shook and then swayed alarmingly, bringing roof tiles and pieces of the portico down on them. They looked questioningly at Rodan, but the centurion snarled at them to keep Valerius pinned and advanced over the rocking ground with the blade glittering in his hand.

'The last thing you'll ever see is the point of this knife.' Another shock made the ground flow in waves under Valerius's body and he used the moment to try to break free. His captors cried out in terror, but they maintained their hold and for a moment he feared the movement of the earth would break his back. Rodan stumbled as the marble mosaic beneath his feet began to disintegrate, but he managed to stay upright and now he was only feet away. Valerius felt his bowels loosen at the thought of the knife biting into his unprotected eyes. He would never see again. Never look on the ocean or a cornfield being dusted by the wind. Never look upon a woman's face. He struggled desperately against the force pinning him down, and called on the gods to come to his aid.

Rodan screamed as the ground vanished beneath him and for a fleeting moment Valerius thought his prayers had been answered. But the hole was a mere four feet deep and the Praetorian waved the knife mockingly as he prepared to climb out. He had barely moved when another thunderous roar seemed to twist the world on its axis. The two ragged lips of the gap slipped obliquely across each other with Rodan pinned between. The Praetorian let out an inhuman cry as his lower body from the hips down was caught between two unrelenting surfaces, his flesh torn and his bones pulverized by the primeval power of the earth's fury. From six feet away Valerius heard the sickening sounds of snapping and grinding. The cry turned to an animal shriek as Rodan realized exactly what was happening to him. His eyes bulged from his head, the blood drained from his face and his upper body began to shiver and flop like a newly landed fish.

Another shockwave rippled through the ground, adding to the doomed Praetorian's involuntary gyrations. The three men holding Valerius exchanged wide-eyed glances and fled in the direction of the villa. As the tremor reached its climax the fluted columns holding the portico collapsed one by one. Valerius knew the whole structure was about to come down on him, but he was paralysed by fear and exhaustion. Only when Rodan's body gave one last convulsive shudder was the spell broken and he found the will to crawl towards the open ground of the garden.

Inside the villa, Marcus and Serpentius fought back to back in the doorway of the room where the Christians cowered, their swords creating a whirling arc of iron that was the only thing keeping them alive. Marcus felt his strength draining and the veteran gladiator had already resigned himself to death. He was only being kept alive by Serpentius's speed, but even that could not last much longer.

The earthquake saved them.

When the first tremor shook the villa like a rat in a terrier's mouth the Praetorians around them froze. Serpentius took advantage of the moment's indecision with a savage lunge that sliced into his assailant's windpipe. As the man fell backwards, the wooden stairway began to fall apart and his comrades retreated past his body the way they'd come. The injured decurion was the last to go, shaking his head at the folly that had brought him here.

At the base of the stairs Torquatus roared in frustration, but the ground beneath his feet tossed like a choppy sea and he felt the whole building creaking around him. As the stairway collapsed he took to his heels with the rest and rushed for the safety of the open air.

XLV

A woman's scream split the doom-laden silence between a pair of shockwaves.

Poppaea!

Valerius struggled to his feet, picked up his sword and stumbled towards the death trap of the house. Flames poured from the ground floor, evidence that at least one oil lamp had been upended to set the villa on fire. Tumbled pillars and broken statues added to the Stygian confusion in the corridors.

He ran blindly through the choking, smoke-filled darkness until he reached the room where he'd found her praying. It was empty, but a second scream drew him to the open window and out into a blizzard of falling tiles. One of the clay missiles hit his shoulder a glancing blow, but his mind was too focused to register the pain. He followed a path that took him downwards, towards the ocean. He guessed that there would be access from the villa to the sea. An estate of this size must have a harbour where fishermen delivered the day's catch or favoured guests could be landed by boat. There would be a road and it was the road Valerius was looking for.

When the earthquake struck, Poppaea would have been terrified. He had sensed an immense well of courage within her, but the tortured writhing of the earth created a spastic panic that even the strength of her faith would not have been able to overcome. She would instinctively have sought refuge outside the walls. Yet the safety of the open air was an illusion. This was where Torquatus's men would come, driven by those very same fears.

He found a gateway, the door standing wide, and ran through it into the open. The narrow road ran parallel to the cliffs and he almost didn't see the glint of reflected moonlight. It caught the corner of his eye and he turned without thinking, abandoning the cobbled pathway for the ankle-breaking tussock grass of the cliff top. The glint he had seen was silver – the silver of a Praetorian officer's sculpted breastplate. A hundred yards ahead, close to the cliff edge, he could just make out the purple sheen of Poppaea's dress as she struggled with a dark-clad figure. Torquatus.

The Praetorian had Poppaea by the shoulder and was attempting to drag her back towards the roadway as she spat and scratched, her dark hair flailing around her head. Valerius saw Torquatus draw back his hand and whip it across Poppaea's face. As she sank to her knees, stunned by the blow, he felt the rage rising inside him like a storm ready to break. He remembered Fabia's sapphire eyes and saw them go dull. Lucina, her nobility crushed and driven beyond the edge of madness. The dying flutter of Ruth's final heartbeat. His anger gave him new strength and he charged through the grass and bushes.

Torquatus's head came up at the sound of a nailed sandal on stone and his lips drew back in a snarl as he recognized his attacker. He lifted his sword to meet the assault.

Valerius crabbed to his left, forcing Torquatus to turn with him, his sword in his right hand and his left still gripping Poppaea's dress. The refusal to release his prisoner left the Praetorian's flank open and Valerius was confident he could take advantage of the mistake. But Torquatus was no innocent. He had served in the legions, and five years at the centre of Nero's court had taught him how to use power. He brought the edge of his blade within a hair's breadth of the pale skin at Poppaea's throat. 'Make one more move and she dies here and now.'

Valerius froze.

'I am the Emperor's representative here,' the Praetorian rasped. 'Tonight I will present the traitor Poppaea Sabina to my lord along with the evidence of her guilt. When she watches the man Petrus and his ragged crowd of renegades put to the question I have no doubt she will exhibit that pleasing Christian trait of sacrificing herself to ease their pain. It will be most instructive, for her, and for you. Because

I intend you to be the first to feel the kiss of the glowing iron.'

The words were confident enough, but Torquatus's eyes kept flicking towards the house and Valerius knew the Praetorian commander was only bolstering his own courage. He was also bluffing.

'You won't find any help there, Torquatus. Your friends will be halfway to Rome by now.' Valerius took a step forward just as another shockwave rumbled through the earth. It threw him off balance and the movement was exaggerated by his weakness. In the same instant Torquatus noticed the blood dripping from his opponent's right arm and saw his opportunity.

The point of the *gladius* snapped out in a perfectly executed lunge that should have pierced Valerius through the body. In his mind, Torquatus was already withdrawing the blade in the twisting gutting stroke that would leave a man screaming for a merciful end. He was quick but not quick enough. The years of training on the hot sands of the *ludus* had given Valerius a gladiator's instinct for survival. At the last second he pivoted and allowed the sword to slide across his body, so close that the razor edge sliced through the cloth of his tunic. A right-handed fighter would have been forced on the defensive, but the movement positioned Valerius to counter-attack with a rising backhand cut designed to take Torquatus's head from his shoulders. The Praetorian cried out as the sword sliced towards his exposed throat, but loss of blood had slowed Valerius's reactions and that gave Torquatus the heartbeat he needed to step back out of the arc of the younger man's sword.

Valerius knew he had to finish the fight quickly. Every second left him weaker; each moment of delay made the outcome more certain. His legs felt as if they were moving through deep sand. Torquatus shimmered in his vision as if he was seeing him through a haze, now a giant, now a midget, but never clear enough or close enough to find with the point.

Poppaea stirred in the grass at the Praetorian's feet and Torquatus laughed as he sidestepped another pathetic lunge of Valerius's sword. 'Not so heroic now, my friend.' He circled away so that Valerius had his back to the crumbling cliff edge. 'Just a wounded beast with nowhere to run.'

Without warning, he darted forward and forced Valerius to meet blade with blade, the clash of iron singing in the night. Torquatus was the stronger and faster now, and the younger man was forced to take another step back as the Praetorian hacked at his weakening guard. He felt the ground falling away beneath his feet and knew the cliff could only be paces away. A smashing blow numbed his fingers and the *gladius* dropped from his hand. Torquatus's face twisted into that familiar mocking smile. One more attack and it was finished. Valerius might have succumbed to despair, but instead cold fury sharpened his mind. Death had no fears for him, but victory for Torquatus would mean death for those he loved.

He would not allow that. He saw Torquatus's eyes narrow the way a hunting lion's do the instant before the charge. When he came, it was with a savage swing at his victim's defenceless head, but in his eagerness the Praetorian had overlooked the young Roman's artificial fist. The block was too feeble to stop the blade entirely and Valerius felt a line of fire slice across his cheekbone. But it gave him the opportunity he needed. He grabbed Torquatus's tunic with the fingers of his left hand, and threw himself backwards. The Praetorian commander flailed desperately as their combined momentum vaulted him over Valerius's falling body and the weight of his armour carried him beyond the cliff edge. Valerius watched the shrieking figure disappear into the darkness. His cry of triumph was as short-lived as it was pointless. For in killing his enemy he had also killed himself. The impetus he'd used to throw Torquatus was unstoppable, and now it combined with gravity to somersault him too towards the void. He felt the instant the world vanished beneath him and a moment of weightlessness which was the prelude to death. But his fall was short, sharp and ended with an agonizing tug that ripped through his wounded arm and tore the tendons of his right shoulder. He opened his eyes, surprised to be alive. The dusty earth of the crumbling cliff face stared back at him from a foot away. He twisted his head and looked upwards. The bindings for the leather socket had tangled among the roots of a small bush to halt his plunge. But for how long? His saviour was a

457

very insignificant clump of leafless twigs and a single unwise movement or another shockwave would pull it free. Blood dribbled down his arm in a warm stream from beneath the cowhide socket. He could feel the life draining from him.

He allowed his head to drop and closed his eyes. The passage of time had no meaning, only the dreadful fire in his arm and shoulder. He couldn't be sure how long he had been hanging when he felt the light brush of a hand clutching at his arm. He looked up into a pale face with wide, frightened eyes, half hidden by the dark hair that cascaded over them.

'Leave me,' he whispered. 'Save yourself.'

'No.' The word was fierce, almost a snarl. Poppaea squirmed further over the edge, determined to get a better hold. 'If I sacrifice you to save myself what does that make me in the eyes of my God?'

Valerius let out a groan. 'Alive,' he said. 'And alive you can save the others.'

'Petrus?'

He hesitated, but he couldn't lie. 'Not Petrus. Petrus must die to save the Judaeans, but you must live to save my father and Olivia.' He felt the bush shift. 'Please. All you will do is kill us both and you will die for nothing. Listen. There was a plot against you. Rodan led it. He came to the villa and threatened you. Tell the Emperor . . . tell him Torquatus heard of the plot and died a hero protecting you. Do you understand?'

'But the soldiers will know the truth.'

He shook his head and another bolt of pain shot up his arm. 'No. Rodan will have given them their orders. They were duped. They are leaderless now. Act like an Empress and they will say anything that will save their necks.'

Warm, salt tears dropped on to his face and he knew he had convinced her. The fluttering hands left his arm and he waited to die. When the new hand closed on his arm like an eagle's talons he was already halfway to Elysium. He had a vision of Apollo reaching down from his chariot to pull him into the heavens, but when he looked up the savage, weathered face staring back at him was far from godlike.

'You didn't think you'd get away that easily,' Serpentius growled as he hauled Valerius effortlessly to safety. 'There's still the matter of my outstanding wages.'

The last rumblings of the earthquake had subsided. Marcus and Serpentius used twisted sheets to lower their charges from the wreckage of the upper floor. The living and the dead.

'Why?'

'He died fighting to save your sister.'

Valerius stared down at the shrunken figure and felt a curious mixture of guilt and disbelief. Grief would come later, he knew, but for now an empty void occupied the space his soul normally inhabited. He pulled back the sheet that covered his father's body. The old man's face was set in an expression that mirrored the moment of his death: a frown of indignation, a grimace of pain. A single stroke directly to the heart, Serpentius said, from a soldier who knew his business, and had himself been cut down a moment later. The other casualties, including Heracles, Isaac and the dead Praetorians, were lined up alongside Lucius. Outside, Valerius could hear Poppaea coldly informing the surviving Praetorian cavalrymen that her word was the only thing that stood between them and a painful death at the hands of the Emperor's torturers.

'We couldn't stop him. One minute he was as meek as a lamb and praying with the rest of them, the next he had a sword in his hand,' Marcus explained. 'He was a hero. You should be proud of him.'

'He was just a harmless old man.'

'Your father sacrificed his life for those he loved. What greater gift can a man give?'

Valerius stared at Petrus. At that moment he hated the Christian leader more than he had hated Torquatus.

'My father died because he was foolish enough to follow you.'

Petrus studied him. The day had taken a toll on Valerius that even his father's death didn't explain. Did he realize how fearsome he appeared, this young fighter with the mark of his suffering stamped on the sharp planes of his face and the fresh scar still bloody on his cheek?

'He came here for a reason,' the Judaean pointed

out gently. 'He wanted to save your sister. Would you deny him in death something he risked everything for in life?'

Olivia lay deathly pale on the bed Marcus and Serpentius had placed by an open window. For answer, Valerius gently picked up his sister's body and, despite the lancing pain of his injured arm, carried her towards the garden pool.

'Who will be her sponsor?' Petrus looked to the Christians, but a voice from the doorway answered him.

'I will.'

Valerius turned to meet Poppaea's steady gaze and Petrus smiled at her. 'You understand what this means, my child?'

She nodded and took her place by Valerius's side. As they walked, she said quietly, 'Do you understand what this means, Valerius?'

He nodded. 'I think so.'

'We are linked, in life and in death, by faith.'

'I am not a Christian.'

'But you will always support Olivia?'

'As long as she lives.'

'Then that is enough.'

The water had drained away through a wide crack in the pool bottom, but the aqueduct had survived and a steady stream still poured over the artificial waterfall. Petrus went first and Valerius waited while Poppaea whispered the sacred words in his sister's ear. When she pronounced Olivia ready, he took his place beside the Judaean. Belatedly, he remembered the questions Poppaea had faced.

'She cannot answer for herself,' he muttered. 'And I cannot answer for her.'

Petrus the healer smiled his gentle smile. 'Your father has already answered for her.' He placed his hands on Olivia's brow and Valerius felt his sister twitch in his arms as if some force had surged through her. He looked into Petrus's face and saw fierce concentration there; the face of a man fighting with some troubled spirit, or perhaps with himself.

Eventually the Judaean was satisfied and Valerius carried his sister into the foaming cascade where the waters surged over them, sharp and cold from the mountain above. He heard Petrus repeat the words that had been spoken earlier for Poppaea. This time there was a subtle difference.

'In the name of Jesus Christus cleanse these unworthy souls of their sins and take them into your house, in keeping with your Covenant. Write your law upon their hearts, place your almighty spirit within them and take their immortal souls into your keeping.'

His life had changed for ever.

XLVI

Nero frowned as he studied the dark-haired figure kneeling before him in the throne room of his commandeered Neapolitan palace. Poppaea had sent word by messenger of the troubling news and now she was here to provide him with details of Rodan's treachery and Torquatus's late-flowering and ultimately fatal heroism. It was perplexing, but he would not let it spoil his mood.

'The Praetorian centurion planned to abduct you and sell you to the pirates of Sandalion?'

'Just so, Caesar,' she said quietly. 'He admitted as much before good Torquatus killed him.' Her voice choked as she spoke the Praetorian prefect's name and Nero could see it distressed her.

'Rise, my dear. You must not kneel before your Caesar. A chair for the Empress,' he ordered.

Strange that Torquatus had shown such concern for Poppaea after so many years of enmity. Then again, perhaps not. He had hinted at some great coup in the offing. This was undoubtedly it.

He waited until she was seated before he resumed his questioning. 'And the traitor's accomplices?'

'All dead, Caesar. The Praetorians who rode with Torquatus were most thorough.'

'Of course,' he mused. 'They must be rewarded for their diligence. A pity, though, that none was spared to be put to the question.'

A second figure had been waiting in the shadows. Now Nero waved him forward. Valerius marched across the marble floor and knelt before his Emperor.

Nero's tone changed. Imperious and harsh. Each word a challenge. 'You accompanied Torquatus here in search of the traitor Rodan? Why, when I had given you such an important mission to complete? You understand it is death to disobey your Emperor?'

Poppaea drew in a sharp breath. Valerius raised his head and Nero felt a shiver of unease as he saw the angry reddened eyes and the raw scar that disfigured the drawn features. Here, for the first time, he was seeing the Gaius Valerius Verrens who had stood before Colonia and defied the hordes of the rebel queen.

'My Emperor honoured me with the title of Defender of Rome.' The voice was as hard as the face from which it emerged. 'What is Rome if she is not the man who rules her? A threat to Caesar's wife is a threat to Caesar himself. When I discovered that threat I did what any soldier would do and moved against it with all the forces at my disposal. If that means death, so be it.'

Nero scowled at the provocation and wriggled in his golden chair. He was already becoming bored with this conversation. All he truly wanted was to let his mind return to the triumph of the previous night. He had defied the earthquake to entertain the people of Neapolis even as they fled in terror from the crumbling theatre. As the rest of the world panicked, he alone had stood firm and his sweet voice had never faltered. It had been the finest performance of his life. For the first time, he knew that he no longer needed to stand in the shadow of the gods. That knowledge allowed him to view the events Poppaea had just related, and Valerius had confirmed, with more equanimity than might otherwise have been the case. In Torquatus he had sensed a growing problem; a boil which might, at some point, require to be lanced. There were questions, of course, but they could be kept for another time. However, there was one more matter to be resolved.

'You were tasked with finding this . . . Rock . . . and the time you were allocated ends at sundown. You are aware of the consequences of failure?'

Valerius nodded slowly. This was the true reason for his presence and now the moment was here his throat felt as if it was filled with sand. Twenty thousand lives depended on his next words. 'I plead for Caesar's indulgence.' He saw Nero's eyes harden but he kept his voice steady. 'The man called Petrus, known as the Rock of Christus, is in my custody in Rome, to be presented in chains at the Emperor's convenience.'

This was the great gamble. If he delivered Petrus to Nero at the same moment Poppaea announced that Rodan had turned traitor and Torquatus had died, the Emperor would undoubtedly link the events. Yet, by not doing so, he risked Nero's insisting that his deadline had not been met and ordering the massacre of the Judaeans in any case.

Nero's cold eyes studied him intently and Valerius felt sweat break out on his brow as he saw the calculations going through the other man's mind. He would never realize his good fortune. From the moment the Emperor had announced his decision to a trusted group of officials he had been bombarded by concerns about the inconvenience and the expense of the massacre. Rome's Judaeans formed a small but crucial element of the city's economy, and their loss would have a significant negative effect on imperial finances at a time when the financial forecasts were already poor. Twenty thousand executions would necessarily require to be carried out by a full legion, so the victims must be gathered and marched to the circus, with all the organizational and security implications that entailed. And did he understand the effort required to dispose of twenty thousand bodies?

'I am inclined to be merciful.' Valerius felt the room spin. 'The Judaeans will be spared. You will deliver this man to me on the nones of June . . .' It was only when the Emperor's voice rose that Valerius realized he hadn't heard a word of the rest of the speech. He looked from Poppaea to the man on the throne.

'I said Gaius Valerius Verrens, Hero of Rome, has the Emperor's thanks and is free to return to Rome.' Valerius rose shakily to his feet and bowed. He walked towards the sunshine and freedom and a day he had thought would never come. 'And Verrens?' He froze. 'Perhaps it would be wise if you took up the offer from my friend Vitellius. A spell in the provinces might be beneficial to your health.'

Nero turned away, and Valerius found he could breathe again.

'Come, my dear.' The Emperor led his wife towards the scale model of Rome which had accompanied them to Neapolis. 'I will show you my plans for our new home.'

Poppaea smiled sweetly. She immediately noticed a change in the landscape between the two hills of the Palatine and the Esquiline. In the valley, the land currently occupied by ten thousand Romans was buried beneath the largest palace the world had ever seen.

Nero saw her startled look. 'Do not worry, my love,' he said cheerfully. 'The gods will provide.'

XLVII

Fourteen months later, on a hot August morning with the scent of old smoke still heavy in the air, Valerius stood beside a sombre, dark-haired woman, close to the place where Cornelius Sulla had died. They were on the far edge of a large crowd who had gathered to witness another execution.

He had last seen Petrus on the day he delivered him up to Nero. Now he watched as a team of executioners erected an inverted cross in the soil of the Vatican fields and placed the elderly Christian against the rough wood. Valerius flinched when he heard the old man's shrill cry as the first of the iron nails pierced the flesh and fragile bones of his feet. There was a moment of consternation as the executioner realized a single nail would never hold his victim in this unheard-of position. The crowd hooted as further nails were added, before Petrus's hands were fixed likewise to the arm of the cross so that he hung upside down with the blood running down his bony white legs.

'It is cruel,' Olivia whispered. 'He was a good man. He does not deserve this.'

Valerius looked at his sister. She was still pale, still thin, but she had insisted on riding from the estate to Rome and showed no sign of fatigue. The house on the Clivus Scauri had been burned along with thousands of others in the great blaze in July which had consumed seven whole districts of the city and incinerated thousands of men, women and children. Fires were a common enough occurrence in Rome, but Nero and his officials quickly found evidence that the Christians had been to blame for this one. Petrus's execution was only the beginning.

'He asked for it to be this way.' Valerius placed an arm round her. 'He said he was not worthy of dying in the same manner as his Lord. He is an old man. It won't take long.' He knew that the head-down position in which Petrus was hanging meant his inner organs would slump down and crush his lungs and heart. No man of his age could live for more than a few minutes in such agony. But he had underestimated Petrus's resilience. It was forty minutes before the fisherman who had watched his Lord walk on water died with the name of Christus on his lips.

Valerius thought he heard a whisper in the air, and for a moment he had a vision of the tall man beside Poppaea's waterfall. He realized that if he did not have faith, at least he had hope.

Historical Note

The story of the early Christian church is a very murky one indeed. If history is written by the victors, the earliest history of Christianity has almost certainly been moulded and sanitized by those with a vested interest. The church was torn by disputes over its future direction and a number of different sects developed which were only reconciled at the First Council of Nicaea in AD 325. One of the earliest arguments was over the conversion of Gentiles and was between St Paul (Saul) and St Peter (Petrus). Both are said to have been in Rome in the early 60s and Saul is recorded as meeting the philosopher Seneca's brother. They undoubtedly lived an underground existence in a time of fear, persecution and betrayal. Single-minded individuals with hugely different characters, Paul, a Roman citizen and former soldier, was a pragmatist who had initially persecuted the Christians before joining them, while Peter, a simple fisherman, was driven by his absolute faith in the teachings of Jesus Christ. Could Paul have betrayed Peter? *Defender of Rome* is a work of fiction and it is a novelist's privilege to bring out the worst in his characters, but there is some evidence, admittedly circumstantial, to suggest the possibility. Apart from their dispute, in AD 80 Bishop Clemens (later St Clement) wrote: *Through envy and jealousy, the greatest and most righteous pillars [of the church] have been persecuted and put to death . . . Peter through unjust envy.* Envy and jealousy are emotions which develop within a structure, not without. It would not be the first time one leadership rival took advantage of an opportunity to get rid of another.

Galilean, Judaean or Jew? Jesus and Petrus had their origins in Galilee, and would have been brought up in the Judaic or Jewish religion, so all three are applicable. But in Rome, Petrus would have been bracketed with the city's Judaeans, so I have used Judaean as the generic term to avoid confusion.

Nero was the first Roman Emperor to take the threat of Christianity seriously and his response was typically brutal and imaginative, even before the Great Fire of Rome. There is no historical evidence that his wife Poppaea, who died either in childbirth or from Nero's abuse while she was pregnant, depending on which source you choose to believe, was linked to the Christians, but the true story of Lucina Pomponia Graecina suggests that Christian influence did reach the highest levels of Roman society even at that early stage in its development.

Valerius meets many interesting historical characters on his travels. Seneca was the most influential man of his time before he fell out of favour and was eventually forced to commit suicide. Aulus Vitellius, who may or may not have been commander of the Seventh legion, was flattered into accepting the imperial purple during the Year of the Four Emperors and paid the inevitable price. Nero's Praetorian prefect, Offonius Tigellinus, survived his reign so I have taken the liberty of replacing him with a fictional character, Torquatus, so that he could meet a suitably satisfying end.

The cities of the Bay of Naples were struck by earthquakes several times before they were buried in the Vesuvian eruption of AD 79, including one during Nero's visit to Neapolis. You can still see the effects today in the shops and bars of Herculaneum, and at the Villa Oplontis, which is well worth a visit for a glimpse of true Roman luxury.

Acknowledgements

Thanks once again to my editor Simon Thorogood and his wonderful team at Transworld, my agent Stan at the Jenny Brown Agency, and most of all to my wife Alison and my children, Kara, Nikki and Gregor, for the unfailing support which sees me through the toughest times. Special thanks to Lorna Sherman and Ross Leitch for giving me an insight into how an earthquake happens. Philip Parker's brilliant *The Empire Stops Here* was an impeccable source for Valerius's venture into Dalmatia, Moesia and Dacia, and Martin Goodman's *Rome & Jerusalem* was one of many excellent books which helped me navigate the choppy waters of early Christian Rome.

CALIGULA
By Douglas Jackson

Can a slave decide the fate of an Emperor?

Rufus, a young slave, grows up far from the corruption of the imperial court. He is a trainer of animals for the gladiatorial arena. But when Caligula wants a keeper for the emperor's elephant, Rufus is bought from his master and taken to the palace.

Life at court is dictated by Caligula's ever shifting moods. He is as generous as he is cruel – a megalomaniac who declares himself a living god and simultaneously lives in constant fear of the plots against his life. His paranoia is not misplaced however: intrigue permeates his court, and Rufus will find himself unwittingly placed at the centre of a conspiracy to assassinate the Emperor.

'Jackson brings a visceral realism to Rome in the days of the mad Caligula'
Daily Mail

'Light and dark in equal measure, colourful, thoughtful and bracing'
Manda Scott, bestselling author of the
Boudicca series

'A gripping Roman thriller'
Scotland on Sunday

CLAUDIUS
By Douglas Jackson

'What stands out are Jackson's superb battle
scenes . . . I was gripped from start to finish'
Ben Kane, author of *The Forgotten Legion*

Rome AD 43. Emperor Claudius has unleashed his
legions against the rebellious island of Britannia.

In Southern England, Caratacus, war chief
of the Britons, watches from a hilltop as the
scarlet cloaks of the Roman legions spread
across his land like blood. He must unite
the tribes for a desperate last stand.

Among the legions marches Rufus, keeper of the
Emperor's elephant. Claudius has a special role for
him, and his elephant, in the coming war.

Claudius is a masterful retelling of one of the
greatest stories from Roman history, the conquest
of Britain. It is an epic story of ambition, courage,
conspiracy, battle and bloodshed.

'Rightly hailed as one of the best
historical novelists writing today'
Daily Express

HERO OF ROME
By Douglas Jackson

**The warrior queen Boudicca is ready to
lead the tribes to war.**

The Roman grip on Britain is weakening. Emperor
Nero has turned his face away from this far-flung
outpost. Roman cruelty and exploitation has angered
their British subjects. Now the Druids are on the
rise, stoking the fires of this anger and spreading the
spark of rebellion among the British tribes.

Standing against the rising tide of Boudicca's
rebellion is Roman tribune, Gaius Valerius Verrens,
Commander of the veteran legionaries of Colonia.
One act of violence ignites the smouldering British
hatred into the roaring furnace of war.

Colonia will be the first city to feel the flames of
Boudicca's revenge, and Valerius must gather
his veterans for a desperate defence.

**'A splendid piece of story-telling and a
vivid recreation of a long-dead world . . . The
final battle against Boudicca's forces is as
vivid and bloody as anyone might wish'
Allan Massie**

ROME: THE EMPEROR'S SPY
By M.C. Scott

'Stop this fire, whatever it takes. I,
your Emperor, order it.'

The Emperor
Nero, Emperor of Rome and all her provinces,
feared by his subjects for his temper and cruelty, is in
possession of an ancient document predicting
that Rome will burn.

The Spy
Sebastos Pantera, assassin and spy for the Roman
Legions, is ordered to stop the impending cataclysm.
He knows that if he does not, his life – and those of
thousands of others – are in terrible danger.

The Chariot Boy
Math, a young charioteer, is a pawn drawn
into the deadly game between the Emperor
and the Spy, where death stalks the drivers – on
the track and off it.

From the author of the bestselling *Boudica*
series, *The Emperor's Spy* begins a compelling
series of novels featuring Sebastos Pantera. Rich
characterisation and spine-tingling adventure
combine in a vividly realized novel set amid
the bloodshed and the chaos, the heroism and
murderous betrayal of ancient Rome.

THE LAST CAESAR
By Henry Venmore-Rowland

AD 68. The tyrant Emperor Nero
has no son and no heir.

Suddenly there's a very real possibility that Rome
might become a Republic once more. But the
ambitions of a few are about to bring corruption,
chaos and untold bloodshed to the many.

Among them is a hero of the campaign against
Boudicca, Aulus Caecina Severus. Caught up in
a conspiracy to overthrow Caesar's dynasty, he
commits treason, raises a rebellion, faces torture
and intrigue – all supposedly for the good of Rome.
However, the boundary between such selflessness
and self-preservation is far from clear, and keeping
to the dangerous path he's chosen requires all
Severus's skills as a cunning soldier and
increasingly deft politician.

And so Severus looks back on the dark and
dangerous time that history remembers as
'The Year of the Four Emperors', and recalls the
part he, and those around him, played – for good
or ill – in plunging the mighty Roman Empire
into anarchy and civil war . . .

**Telling the thrilling story of a brief but pivotal
moment in Roman history, *The Last Caesar* marks
the debut of a remarkable new literary talent.**